MARTHA FINDS REST

BETHANY'S PEOPLE - AN EASTER STORY

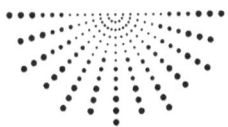

BILL KEMP

NOT PERFECT YET Publishing

While scripture is never directly quoted in **Martha Finds Rest**, there are many paraphrases and mash-ups. The word choice and phrasing used by the author usually reflects the **New International Bible** (NIV®) translation, copyright held by **Biblica** – The International Bible Society, obtained under the fair use agreement displayed on their website: www.biblica.com.

For other inquiries please write: contact@billkemp.info

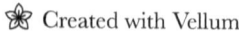 Created with Vellum

Dedication:

For my mother. A gentle mix of Martha and Mary. A middle child who never said an unkind thing about anyone.

Please Note:

Bethany's People is a fictional account of real people caught up in some of history's most significant events. Unfortunately, we only have a few verses about the sisters Mary and Martha and their troubled relationship. Their brother Lazarus is silent in the Bible and best known for dying at an inconvenient time. A novelist has to spin a good deal out of whole cloth.

I can, however, attest to this:

1) The history and culture of ancient Bethany has been thoroughly researched and I do not knowingly write anything false about the settings for my stories.

2) The events which are foundational to the Christian faith are told in a way that honors Jesus Christ and the ongoing mission of his church.

3) I have not met any of Bethany's people. My over-active imagination surely misrepresents them. When I get to heaven and Martha sets me straight, I am prepared to accept that what really happened was even more remarkable than my meager fictions.

— *Bill Kemp*

"That which is missing cannot be counted."
- Solomon the Wise King

You have lost count
Missing is the meaning of your life
Come
Let me share your bag of troubles
I am gentle
My pace is easy
We will count the steps
Down into a well,
And then up
We will count the days
One day
And then another one
Six in a row and then a rest
Three in a tomb,
And then what?
I am gentle
Come

- Jesus *

* Note Martha cannot read what we call scripture. This epigraph is as she would remember things.

PROLOGUE

"Martha, Martha, go back to bed."

Those were the last words my mother spoke to me. People double my name when they want to mock me. When they want to point out that I am large or plain or slow to catch on to a joke. Other people. Never my mother. Until that night. There it was, mocking. From the woman whose patience I drank in like water.

What was she saying? *Martha, Martha, why are you always busy? Look at me. I'm resting. Even as I prepare to labor and bring your sister into this world, I rest. You are barely twelve. You still have time to simply be Martha. To be open. To be waiting. To be being instead of doing.*

Was my mother really that wise? The farther I get from Bethany, the clearer it is to me. All wise people are wise in the same way. They understand resting. Years later, when Jesus took that same mocking tone with me, I hated him for it. Those who cannot leave their work, who are shackled to their past, resent those who are free.

The farther I walk, the clearer I see it—the day that I became only a worker. The day I stopped being myself.

I had a painful entry into womanhood. Mad Archelaus

was on the throne, life was difficult, and births were rare. Is insomnia a path one can choose that early in life? Or is it a role that is thrust upon you by birth order, communal duty, and unfulfilled dreams? No. It is a curse, a demon as strong as any of those that have bound my little sister, Mary. As she embraces her madness, I do mine.

"It will be a girl," my mother had said shortly after she began to show. From then on, I did not sleep more than three or four hours a night. Instead, I walked the narrow circle around the well in the middle of our village. My mother was taking time out of each day to show me what I should do for her. At night, I repeated her instructions, my bare feet hardly disturbing the fine dust of that circle. She taught me, word by word, the songs we sing when women labor. In our village, each change of season, each phase of life and death, each remembrance day celebrating a hero or a battle has its own tumble of words. My mind wasn't built to hold such airy stuff.

The song I was to sing as her oldest daughter was one of the most difficult songs in the birth cycle. It consisted of a chain of names and deeds—so-and-so begat so-and-so—all the way back to Sara the wife of Abram. That woman, whose name begins every birth song, had left Ur. Who names a city Ur? Sara left Ur of the Chaldeans when she was near eighty —left all she knew and came south, never again to be comfortable with the language she had to speak. Never again to smell familiar plants or know the birds by their songs or visit the grave of her ancestors. Why?

The Voice to Abram came,
Not Sara.
Not from the god she knew
But with a rest to relinquish,
A wasteland to tread,
A new poverty to know.
Sara's no was left unsaid.

No complaint.
Because of this,
She will be
Our mother.

Does every woman step into a similar unknown when she becomes pregnant? My young mind could not sleep with such concerns weighing on my chest.

"Martha, Martha, go back to bed."

"No," I responded softly, but defiantly.

In the dimness, I crept into the front room. I took the empty water jugs out to the village well. It was too dark to see the steps I had to take, round and round, into that hole, to reach the water. So I left the empty jars there and began my journey of remembrance. I repeated the birthing songs before the little sliver of the moon, tipped as newly born ones are in the summer, such that it could not hold water. Then I saw it. The crescent of my mother's belly would spill its water.

Hurry up, little sister, I sang to the night.

My mind was clear. I could name every herb and what it remedied. I could sing, if I chose, all the songs of the women without missing a word. Going back to bed was out of the question. Nor could I sit still in the darkness and wait. I went back to find my project.

It was a wretched piece of hide. No one understood why I wanted it. A week before Mary's birth, a lion had cut down a young calf, three days old. There was a boy tending the herd. He ran past me in the dark. I was sitting by the well. I startled him. He had only meant to grab something from a house and then be off. He swore, then ran away empty-handed. My father found the carcass in the morning and carried it to a gathering of the men. They had a long, grave discussion, for the cattle were not owned by our people, but by a wealthy man in Jerusalem. Some argued that they should tell the absentee owner that his calf was born asleep and did not live long enough to find a teat. These things happen. The village should not suffer for it. No one thought the owner would ask for the body. All agreed that any talk of a lion would cost Bethany the grazing rental money it depended upon.

I stepped forward. "I'll take it."

I wanted to make a travel bag from it.

"You'll never get it stitched together," my father said. "Even if you do, it will be too soft. The skin's too thin. It will not last long."

He was wrong. Thirty years later, I still have it. The wounds the lion made have disappeared within the fine needle work. Its embroidery tells my life's story. It tells of Mary's marriage to a Pharisee and the divorce that ended her childhood, just as a death ended mine. She was fourteen and too sensitive to receive rejection. She ran from us. I would have made Father take her back.

"Martha, Martha, I don't need your tears." And she was gone.

I felt like the center of my life had vanished. Fifteen years, I worked alone, pushing back my grief for her. Then Thomas the stonemason, who had expanded the grave in the grotto for so many in our village who were dying from the spring fever, told me the rumor that she was living as a sorceress in Magdala.

Then suddenly, she returned. Same Mary. She had learned things on her journey. I asked her how to write the word *Magdala*. She took my hand and moved it through the dust on my work table. Then I stitched it on the bottom of my bag. She asked if I wanted to put the name Jesus there, since he had sent her home to me. I said no. My bag is for family.

The bag also tells of my brother, Lazarus. It shows him joining the rebellious Zealot fighters and then coming home changed. For him, I stitched the broken chain. When I have time, I will find an image to describe his recent journey through *Sheol*. He told me that I should picture the afterlife as a pit—a bottomless hole. How does one embroider that?

I decided that Jesus deserved to be family when he called my brother back to us from *Sheol*. Jesus now has a single long stitch, with twelve little dashes following it for his disciples. The one called James has a bag as large as mine. I fill it with food each time they visit. Now, others will have to do that.

My bag holds threads and thongs and things yet to be made. It is as much a tool of my trade as my scrapping flint or the thin bone awl I sew with. It's never far from me. If I sit at my merchant's table in Jerusalem, it is there. If I attend a childbirth, it holds my medicinal herbs and the knife I place under the woman's bed to cut the pain. If I go with the other women to prepare a body, my bag holds sacred items, including a small parchment scroll, which I am told reads:

Hear, O Israel: The Lord is our God. The Lord is one.

When we place the body upon the resting stone in the grotto, it is my duty to put this scroll by the right ear of the deceased and say, "Hear, O son of Adam, the Lord is your God," or "Hear, O daughter of Eve, the Lord is your God." Then the whole village circles the resting stone forty times. Why forty? It is the wilderness number. From slavery in Egypt through forty years of wilderness to the promised land, our ancestors walked in faith. From slavery to this life, through death to what lies beyond, we all must walk. But we don't need to walk it alone. Forty revolutions show that all of Bethany walks in faith with the one passing.

When Jesus died, I reached in my bag. I could not find the scroll. The men came quickly for him. He fell off the cross and into a stranger's arms. I barely remember what happened next. There was a meal in Nicodemus's house. The men cursed themselves for having failed him. The women from Galilee drank and wept. No one said a proper goodbye to this gentle rabbi. I wanted to say goodbye. Instead, I shouted, "Jesus, Jesus, why didn't you run from here?"

I drank too. I stumbled to the floor mere feet from the table in Nicodemus's banquet room. I awoke the next day angry. I stumbled, wanting to do something for Jesus, but he was in the pit.

Why was I angry? I never expected Jesus to be Messiah, to take the throne. My sister looked sane, though quiet. My brother was still alive. I didn't have any further miracles to ask Jesus for. And I didn't need him criticizing me for rising before dawn to get my work done. No, I had no reason to be angry, except for my own life—forty years and nothing to show for it. Soon, I, too, will be laid on the resting stone, for I am a child of Eve, born to sorrow, born to toil.

The last carefree memory I have from childhood is this: I am working the hide of that calf killed by a lion. I am pounding it smooth. Working by feel beneath the mere sliver of a falling moon. Working beside the dark pit of Bethany's well. My father comes to me. He has my five-year-old brother in tow. Lazarus leans against our father's leg.

"Your mother is in labor."

With the dawn, they went off to the city. I stayed with my mother. She began her screams with the rising of the sun, for Mary was born awkwardly. By afternoon, she was gone. Goodbye, Mother.

My work began. I raised Mary. She was more a daughter than sister to me. Yes, the other women helped. Aunt Rachel was my rock until the child turned ten and became rebellious. Rachel gave up on her then, but I never did.

We have a saying in Bethany: *Our day begins with saying good night.*

Father tried to explain this to me. I didn't have time to listen. Then he died. Jesus also tried to teach me. I didn't have time to listen to him either. I only remember what Lazarus said. When Jesus called him out of his grave, his first words to me were, "*A new day begins with saying good night.*"

"What do you mean, brother?" I asked.

"It's how we do things."

It was evening then. The disciples were hungry. But Lazarus, Jesus, and Thomas wanted to stay a while longer in the grotto.

"I have to go cook. People are hungry."

"Stay," Jesus said.

But I could not. I had work to do.

Then Lazarus said, "Martha, our day begins with saying good night because the Lord-God created the world, and all that is, in six days. There was evening, then morning—a new day. First, the Lord-God said good night to darkness, and there was light. Then he said good night to the emptiness, and there was creation. He said good night to the chaos of the waters, and he made dry land. Before we begin our Sabbath day, we say good night to all those who have gone before us. Before we begin our work, we say good night to our own self-importance. For in six days, God made the heavens and the earth. Then God rested. We should too. Before we begin each week and all that we have to do, we should rest."

This, then, is how I count my days, that I might have a heart of wisdom. Jesus died on a Friday. One day. And when it was evening, we said good night and entered the home of Nicodemus. There, we spent the second day, for it was the Sabbath. And then it was evening and morning, a third day. A simple thing, once you see the pattern.

Sometimes, the wind will come up, and a storm lays siege against Bethany for three days. We will have wind and rain. It will seem endless. Then, on the evening that begins the third day, we stand together as a village and face the west. We say goodbye to it. The next day breaks calm and bright.

Why? There is no rational reason for such foolishness to work. But it always does. I have stood on with others and said goodbye to storms dozens of times. How does one incorporate a lesson like this into life? How do we accept trauma for what it is—a passing storm? How do we say goodbye to our disappointments? How do we stop struggling, like a child who refuses to go to bed? Perhaps it begins with numbering our days and taking a Sabbath rest every seven.

No. I don't think Jesus even wants this. I have listened. I have heard what Jesus says to his disciples in private.

"Work, for the night is coming when no one can work."

And my father said something similar: "Rest when you are dead."

PART I
THE LOWEST SATURDAY

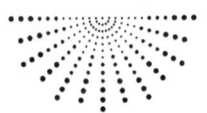

Jerusalem around 30 AD
The Sabbath Day that ends the Passover Festival

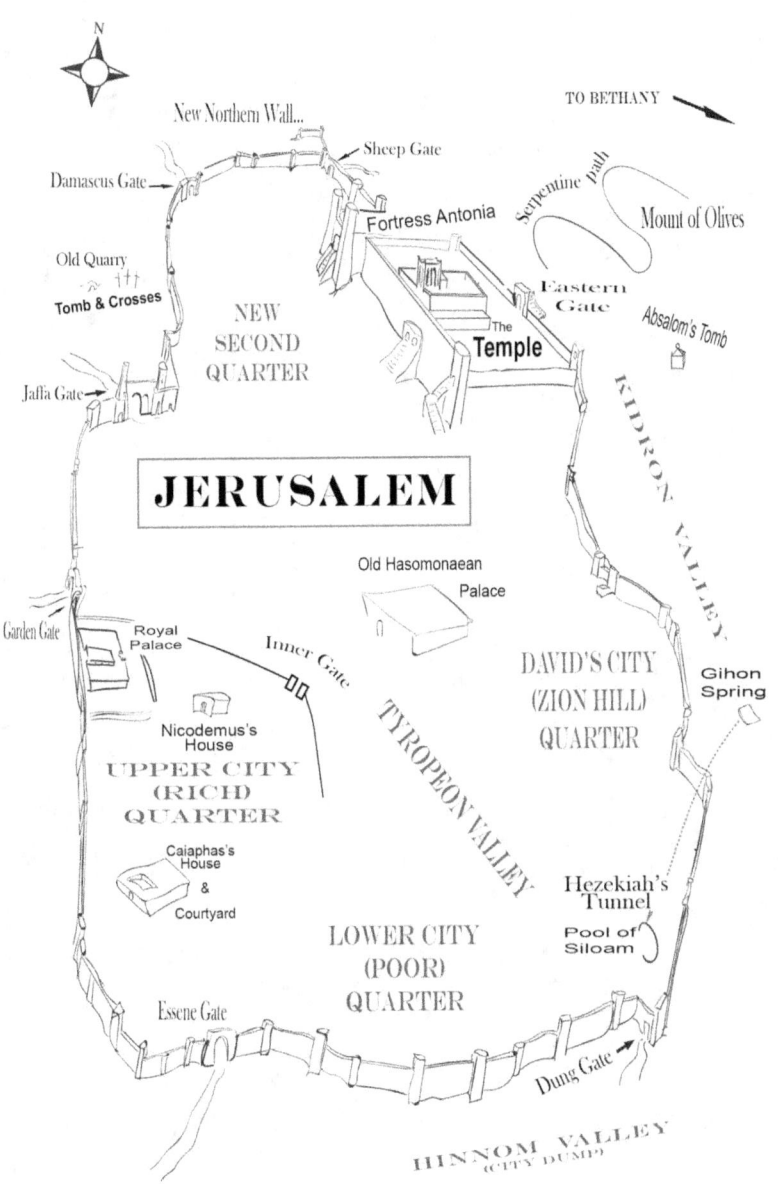

1

SUNRISE

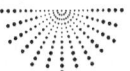

MARY

In a moment, the sun will rise. I wait for it. Such an odd house. It has this landing in the stairway to the great banquet room. Above me, Martha sleeps. Below, the mansion. Here, though, a porch has been created, from which I can see all of Jerusalem spread out like a labyrinth. This house sits at a dead end. Other cul-de-sacs have bathhouses, carpenter's shops, wool-spinners, cheese-makers, butchers, and public latrines. This place is more than just a rich man's home; it is a cloister for learning. Nicodemus curates its library of varied scrolls—only some of which are accepted as canon by his Pharisaic brothers. In his garden courtyard, there is a fountain that competes with the oral learning but, along with the scent of the oleander, refreshes the spirit. From my landing, I look east and see that what is coming will not be a normal day. No. As ultramarine turns to pink, I see apocalypse. Christ is dead.

Clustered at the bottom of the steps are jars—large ones, waist high, for the water used in purification rituals, and assorted smaller ones to hold figs, dates, and wine. Down the hall and to the left is the kitchen with its great oak table. I recently left the men there, gently closing the door to contain their words, climbing the stairs, not so much to see the sun, but to partition the varied forms of inactivity that infects this house, the hope-lost ennui that sleeps above from the dour academic argue-it-to-death utterances below. Anxiety can take many forms, most of which multiply as they blend. It is best to keep your worries separated.

Dawn. An ant-like red glow above the buildings.

Yes! I bow my head. I lift my arms. Longer, longer, even though they ache. I hold them up until every bit of the sun has cleared the city wall. I hold them even though I know I am being watched. *Go away!* Perhaps he expects me to sing. I am mute. He wants to see if it's an act. That is why he watches. In my mind, I shout, not my usual morning prayer, but this appeal for Martha:

> *Sister, sister.*
> *Steady as an ox.*
> *In times of illness,*
> *You heal.*
> *In times of famine,*
> *You fast for each malnourished child.*
> *You have buried mother, father, and brother.*
> *This, though, has defeated you.*
> *May all that is holy*
> *Redeem you.*

Dawn at last. I turn now and nod to Simon the Zealot. He is one of the twelve that followed Jesus. I go down the stairs. He stays above. Always watching, that is Simon. I return to the kitchen. I put my hand to the door, but pause. Nicodemus has just said my name with a disparaging tone. Now my brother speaks.

"You say she shoved Martha's hand into his side?"

"Yes. We were busy, preparing Jesus for burial. Tell me now . . ."

I enter, and they go quiet. Nicodemus doesn't look up. But Lazarus smiles and asks, "Are they all still sleeping?"

I nod yes.

"Everyone? Martha too?"

All I can do is nod. I haven't spoken since coming to this house. Yet they still ask me questions. *Go back to your talking. You'll feel better.* Last night, everyone took their turn. The disciples explained how they scattered, the Galilean women how they wept. Martha blamed the city. She swore down curses on the ground, the children, the mites, the priests, and the burnt-meat sooty smoke that drifted toward her from temple three times each day. Lazarus spent the night calming her, shifting her wrath away from targets in that upper room. More than once, the table's small knife ended up in her hand, and he had to pry it from her fingers. *Yes, I saw that. Who was she going to stab? Not Nicodemus, he invited us here. Not Judas, he didn't make it.*

Bending so that only my brother can see my lips, I mouth, *Martha's broken.*

"She says Martha is sleeping," Lazarus interprets.

"Good. I don't want to have to deal with her."

"If it weren't for the Sabbath, she would be gone from the city. This is her hour for household chores." His ear tilts to the door as if listening for her broom and morning song. "On normal days."

"The woman is hysterical."

"I never thought I'd see her break."

"You didn't see her break. We did."

I see it now. What lies below the surface of Nicodemus. It's not just a lack of sleep. It is fear—unexpressed, but real.

"As I was telling you before, your sisters made things worse for everyone. I had my hands full. I had to get a ladder. I had to stop the Romans from throwing Jesus's body out on Gehenna's dump where the dogs would eat it. I had to get Pilate's permission. So I spoke to my friend Joseph of Arimathea. He had a new tomb near the cross."

"I would like . . ."

Nicodemus waves the interruption away.

"Together, he and I went to the cross. Just in time. They'd declared Jesus dead. So I went to work, set up the ladder. Now, Jesus was such a thin man—he looked weightless as he hung above me. Then I pulled his hands free from the nails, and suddenly I couldn't hold on to him. My friend Joseph staggered trying to catch him. He would have dropped the body. But there was a young man, one of the disciples."

"John?"

"Oh yes. John. I knew him from before. Another story. Another problem for us. That's if he stays around. You know how John was . . ." Nicodemus glances at Mary, uncertain how much to say.

"Caiaphas's orphan child. Mary and I know more of the story than you do," Lazarus says. "But about the grave. Tell me . . ."

"I'm getting there. Together, John and Joseph struggled to hold Jesus. I hurried down the ladder. And all the while, Martha was screaming, ranting, 'Don't let him touch the ground!' Over and over. She grabbed Jesus's legs, weeping. She pulled to the left. But my friend's grave was the other way. He struggled, but Martha renewed her grip farther up. Her face was in the dead man's side. We were pleading with her. We had planned for a burial, but not for this."

Her hair brushed his wounds. That is what I saw in the lamplight last night. Black clumps of blood in Martha's gray hair.

"The plan was that Jesus would first be laid in his mother's lap. The soldiers weren't eager to give us this final courtesy. I had to pay in advance. So I peeled Martha away. Joseph and John carefully arranged the body. You would be weeping, Lazarus, to see it. I almost was. Jesus lay like a child, his mother speaking softly, tenderly. Perhaps it was her lullaby. And John, he had his arm on her shoulder. He said, 'I'll be your son now.'"

Nicodemus pauses, pinches his nose. "When I was away, studying in Alexandria, I did what young men do. I went to the theater. I saw tragedies acted so well that there wasn't a dry eye. The end of Jesus was like that. At least it would have been without Martha. I was doing all that I could to contain her, to put a boundary around this precious moment—a mother saying goodbye to her son. Never in all my trips to the theater did I see a man behind a mask play a part so well."

This is real! Suddenly, I am angry. Lazarus holds me down.

Nicodemus mutters on, "If you had been to a play by the Greek Aeschylus, you would understand what I am about to say. In the tragedy of Jesus, which I saw acted out on Friday, each person had a role to play. For example, earlier in the day, the trial before Pilate. That, too, was like theater. The governor had a line to speak and he spoke it. Then the crowd sang out like they were the scene's chorus. Then Pilate strutted downstage and shouted, 'Behold the man.' Then the crowd, 'Crucify him.' Everyone had their parts. They put on masks. In the theater, a man can play a woman or even a wild beast. A sober actor can embody the rage of Achilles. Yesterday, Martha played a role that was godlike. Zeus. The Leviathan. A storm. No . . . the apocalypse of Sodom and Gomorrah."

He looks at me. He mumbles an apology, but it merges into something else he wants to say to Lazarus. "I am only trying to speak honestly. Theater digs into the deep well of the human psyche. Aeschylus has these winged women. He calls them Furies. They are all consuming, vengeful, and unrelenting."

"Martha has a demon?"

"No. She's not possessed. At least I hope not. I'm saying that she is not herself. She has this mask on. Maybe she'll wake out of it. Take the mask off. Stop playing the role. Yesterday, she was a Fury. Furies are goddesses of justice. They bring grief to inhospitable hosts—something very much on my mind today. They bring revenge on pompous officials.

Let's say a city council sides with the wicked and oppresses a widow. In a Greek tragedy, these Furies would appear on stage to right the wrong. They also track down those who fail to keep a vow. Maybe that is what enrages Martha. Jesus made many promises. Now, he's dead. I know it sounds irrational, but maybe she's angry because he left so much undone."

"There are three Furies in those plays. Three women at the cross?"

Nicodemus raises an eyebrow. He doesn't expect a simple leather merchant to know this.

"Where did you see Greek plays?"

"In hell. Go on. How is Martha a Fury?"

"Don't overthink this, Lazarus. The analogy breaks, and the lesson that I am trying to teach falls apart. On an abstract level, the women represent a theme: the great wheel of Justice. Martha, Mary, and even Jesus's mother—did I mention that sometimes a Fury can be beneficial? We must watch things unfold, so to speak. Above all, watch the women. We have come, I fear, to fragile times. Vigilance is called for. Note how each actor moves across the stage and how action leads to reaction. Limits get crossed. Things fall apart."

"That's why I want to go to Jesus's tomb," Lazarus says.

"No. It's out of the question. You must stay here. Your sisters need you. Things are unstable enough. Martha is beside herself. Mary and Jesus's mother are close to that edge. Women have a way of feeding off each other in an escalating cycle of grief. Hysteria spreads, like panic on a battlefield or the plague after a famine. Look. It was all I could do to drag Martha into my house. She would have stayed at the tomb cursing the soldiers until sunset. She was loud enough to wake the dead."

"When Martha's angry, there's always a reason," Lazarus says carefully, like a lawyer laying out a case for leniency.

"This is Jerusalem!" Nicodemus thumps the table. "Crucifixions are educational events. We watch them respectfully.

The wind might shift tomorrow. Any one of us could find ourselves out of favor and carrying our own cross through the streets. Treat those in authority with respect. Treat the Romans as our guests, and in the hour of your disgrace, they might grant you some measure of decency. Pilate was good to let us have the body."

And yet he sent Jesus to die.

"You and Joseph did your best for Jesus's body," Lazarus concedes. "Still, I would like to go to the tomb and see it as soon as it is light enough."

"No. No. Didn't I tell you about the soldiers? Caiaphas warned Pilate that his disciples might do something. And you must lie low. They know about you. Caiaphas called you out by name. He asked his guards, 'Why haven't you arrested Lazarus—the one the crowds call Jesus's greatest miracle?' You'll find yourself in his pit in no time. The thought of it scares me, and I have some protection being on the Sanhedrin. Believe me, it wasn't my intention to host Jesus's disciples upstairs. One of my students, Mark is his name— bright boy, but . . ." It may just be the lack of sleep, but Nicodemus again searches for the right word.

Deceptive, I mouth at him. He shrugs, then accepts the word as his own.

"Deceptive. Yes. This student of mine lets Jesus and his men into my house, gets my kitchen staff to leave out a lamb so they can have their Passover meal. They were here just before Jesus got arrested. Meanwhile, I've been called away."

"Where?"

"You shouldn't be surprised at this. I was eating with the high priest that night. He has been discussing ways to get the Sadducees and Pharisees to work together on the council. Out of the seventy, the seats are divided . . . Oh, you don't care about that. Just know I was invited and the meal was pleasant —nothing important discussed—but I had no idea Caiaphas was preparing to arrest Jesus. And I didn't know about Mark giving my banquet hall to him until I returned home to hear my servants complain of the mess the disciples had left. Didn't Thomas tell you this?"

Lazarus shakes his head.

"You were with Thomas in Hezekiah's tunnel all that time. What did you talk about?"

"Getting out."

"And?"

"The threat of earthquakes."

2

HIS MOTHER'S SON

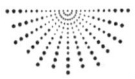

MARK

A young man stands outside Nicodemus's door. The door is closed, and it would be improper for him to knock. Holding his breath, he pushes the door. It creaks forward a half inch before stopping with a dull thud. He remembers the great oak beam that leans against the wall beside the door on the courtyard side. He has always wondered about its purpose and now he knows. It secures the door. Here in a wealthy, gated neighborhood, the leading Pharisee of Jerusalem feels the need to prepare his home to be a locked keep. *Strange.*

"There isn't any reason for the house to be open . . ." he says to assure himself. He looks at the long shadow cast by the adjacent Herodian palace and guesses it to be six-thirty in the morning. *The others won't come for another two hours.*

He moves nervously into the palace shadow and watches. He rocks side to side on the balls of feet, his hands drawn high. Birdlike, yet silent. Small. Dark. Easy to miss. John Mark always comes early. He enters the streets at dawn. He grabs what he can eat while walking from his mother's table. Sometimes, breakfast has to be stolen from the market square. He passes unnoticed behind the stalls, as the merchants set up. Today is Sabbath, and the markets are closed. Even

Jerusalem's dogs are hungry. He shares their fate, because his mother left nothing out for him, or to be more accurate, their houseguests ate it all. To make matters worse, last night she feared him sick and gave him only broth.

"Should starve a fever," Miriam had said, even though Mark had not allowed her to touch his brow. The broth contained medicinal herbs, giving it an unappealing smell. It had the unwelcome aftertaste of anise.

He is a man, just barely. Hair grows unevenly and imperceptibly on his dark chin. He has no work other than studying, running the occasional errand for his rabbi, and fetching the odd coin for information given to the temple guards. His mother is widowed. Custom dictates that he should find real employment and care for her. Instead, he has left this task to the uncles who live with them and Barnabas—lucky man— who doesn't.

Uncle Barnabas came to this country decades ago and now owns land. He provides work for the multitude of John Mark's extended family. Twenty-eight people normally sleep crowded cheek to jowl in Miriam's house. At festival time, that number triples. At night, the teen never knows who he is tripping over as he searches for a small square to call his own. His mother is incapable of turning anyone away.

"You can always sleep on our roof," she said on Monday to a large family of pilgrims who required fifteen minutes to explain how they were related. "Markie, go fetch your cousins some water."

That was the other thing that annoyed him. She used his Roman name, Mark, recalling happier times in the port of Alexandria. But here in landlocked Jerusalem, Hebrew names are preferred. His father, as those in the diaspora often do, gave him a second name. John. This name is too common in Judaea and must be lengthened to prevent confusion. Since his father died before they immigrated, Mark isn't called John bar Aristobulus. At his *bar mitzvah*, he stated his desire to be called

John of Alexandria. No one seconded this. Now, he calls himself *Gershon*, which means stranger. This recalls Moses's life in the exile from Egypt when he said, "I have been a stranger in a strange land."

The weather has been warm all week, and the festival crowds larger than expected. Mark has carried this and that up the three flights of stairs for the houseguests on the roof. They are cheerful, when he isn't. They hint that he should take interest in their daughters, when he doesn't. They had anticipated Thursday's Passover meal with baited breath. Mark had dreaded the additional work. Then Nicodemus unexpectedly invited Mark's extended family to feast in his banquet room. *Why?*

It took two days for Mark to unearth the truth. His mother had sent Uncle Barnabas to beg for the room.

"You always enjoy serving people on our roof. The weather should be good. Why is this year different?"

"It just is," she said. "I've invited a rabbi from Nazareth. We'll serve just thirteen men on our roof. But the family will dine with Nicodemus. Understand? That's less work for you."

But plans quickly changed when Nicodemus was invited to dine with the high priest.

"Your mother may be in danger," Nicodemus said ominously. "Tell her not to host the Galileans."

That was Wednesday evening. Mark had to move quickly. He knew his mother would ignore the Pharisee's advice. She would not shut the strangers out.

"Is your upper room still available to us?" he asked his teacher.

"Yes. But my servants will come with me to Lord Caiaphas's complex."

Later, Nicodemus's cook explained this to Mark, "The Monkey is *allowing* us to cook separate dishes for the Pharisees he has invited. For purity, you see."

"Nobody wants to be poisoned."

Everyone in the lower class refers to the high priest as the Monkey. This began as a mistranslation of Caiaphas's family name, but stuck when people noted the man's long arms. He has a way of pulling people close and breathing in their face as he persuades them to support his political ambitions. He has a way of being apelike and just shy of expressing real humanity.

"Can you leave behind one Passover lamb? We have a dozen extra guests this year."

The man liked Mark and knew that Nicodemus would want it. "The Monkey invited us. He'll at least have to provide our meat."

The cook showed him where the produce was kept, so all that was needed for the Passover could be made. Mark set his plan in motion. The soon-to-be-arrested Jesus would be served at the rich man's house. The immigrants' Passover was moved back to Miriam's.

"Safer this way," he explained to his mother. What he hadn't told her was that he, personally, wasn't planning on celebrating the Passover meal. *What makes this night different from all the others? I get to spend it alone.*

"You'll eat with them. And make sure everything is okay?"

"I will host them just as Nicodemus would."

Perhaps this was teenage rebellion. For John Mark, the whole exodus of his family from Egypt was ill-conceived. In Alexandria, he was taught by rabbis every bit as competent as the teachers Nicodemus hired. The city had a bustling seaport that launched a dozen Roman grain ships every day. In Egypt, the food was better and his life made sense. In Egypt, his father was still alive.

The seder ritual, with its emphasis upon crossing the Red Sea and finding freedom in a promised land, is bitter for Mark. So that evening, he hid and ate only what he found in Nicodemus's great kitchen. Late in the evening, he crept up the stairs and watched while hiding as Jesus lifted the bread, said, "This is my body," and broke it. Then the Galilean shared Elijah's cup and called it his blood. *Strange.*

When the meal was over, they went out to the Mount of Olives. Fascinated, Mark followed them. Like the disciples, he fell asleep in the warm spring night under the full moon. Suddenly, he was awakened by the sound of a giant thudding past his head. There were men with torches and swords thrashing through the underbrush. He stood to run, and someone grabbed his cloak from behind. Down he went, tumbling.

Adrenaline turns every teen into an escape artist. Naked, Mark made his way back into the city. His breathing barely back to normal, he crept into his mother's house. There, he felt for the ill-conceived doorways that connected the tenement's rooms. From memory, he navigated the irregular rear stairway, tripping only once and cursing faintly.

"What happened to you?" his mother asked.

"Bandits," John Mark had lied. The word accurately expressed his feeling about Jesus's disciples. Yet the man who had stripped him of his garment had been a temple guard.

So turning from his mother and her investigating lamp, he scrambled over sleeping bodies that filled the entry room, lunged through a doorway, and tripped again on a step that maliciously tipped both down and to the left. Somehow, he found his spare tunic and a space behind the fattest of his aunts. Then he heard the soft sound of rain. Some of the homes on this steep hill have been in continuous use since the time of Alexander the Great. None of them can resist the hydrology of the place. Water runs through the lower rooms each time it rains.

On Friday, Mark found a secluded space under the stairs to sleep. He had already decided to skip his classes. Midway through the afternoon, they found him. These unwanted houseguests descended from the roof like a plague of locusts. They jabbered in their distant language. Mark understood every word, but he pretended not to. He answered them in the common Greek that the traders used.

"The sky is black," one said.

"There's rumbling," others said.

"Thunder?" Mark asked incredulously. It was only three in the afternoon. Up until then it had been a calm spring day.

"No. Longer. Deeper. You can feel it in your feet."

"We get earthquakes here," Mark's mother said with concern.

"I'll take a look." Mark didn't stay on the roof long. "It's hailing."

Then the ground shook.

"Apocalypse!" one of the guests shouted.

But their fears were short-lived. Later, Mark went up to inspect the roof and found a menacing crack.

"That wasn't there before."

When his uncles returned from the fields, they confirmed this. They differed, though, on whether this crack hinted at more serious earthquake damage hiding below.

"No. It's simply the way these houses are. Subsidence is normal."

"Even after centuries?"

This discussion required much movement from room to room, for the flat roof joined like a crowded umbrella three buildings that were never intended to be yoked. Prior to the city's population boom, the scattered houses in the Hill District, or *Ophel*, were distinct, individually owned, and carefully maintained. An economic boom occurred under the rule of Herod the Great. Neighborhoods changed. Rentals became common, the population more diverse. Deeds were subdivided, and the better families of Jerusalem moved to the flatter and more accommodating northern district of the city. The vacancy allowed a colony of African day laborers to dwell together on the hill.

"I feel like the Queen of Sheba living here," Miriam often said.

It was true that a thousand years ago, young David, still an inexperienced king, had chosen this hill for his capital. David was a shepherd boy, a soldier, and a man who knew how to build alliances. He knew nothing about building a city. He simply took the ancient Jebusite city as he found it. He added some height to its protective walls and reinforced its gates. He left his capital small. A few hundred dwellings was all the city he could imagine. Even during his lifetime, Jerusalem overflowed the plans he had for it.

It was Solomon, not David, who brought a Queen of Sheba out of Africa. Solomon hated the *Ophel*. He surveyed the broader hill just north of it and built his temple there. Then he built his palace north of the temple where he could overlook it. He designed avenues with grand stairways and palm trees. New walls were laid out in ever-broadening concentric circles and a bustling marketplace planted in the middle of the city. Like spokes on a wheel, Solomon's roads passed through Jerusalem's seven gates and its trade routes reached to the ends of the earth.

Over the centuries, Jerusalem had sporadically been broken down and rebuilt. Each war, exile, and revolution brought new complexity to the city's ancient plan. Only in the reign of Herod the Great did the city find an architect with the vision and genius to match that of Solomon the Wise. Like everyone else since David, the Romans and Herodians ignore the *Ophel*. Further, *there is nothing noble*, the young man thinks, *about living with your mother*.

3

SOMEONE TO BLAME

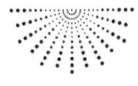

MARTHA

I t's late.

What's happening? I was dreaming . . . I never dream. I'll have to tell this one to Mary.

The light! Can't look at it. *Where am I?*

Orange squares of afterglow inside my eyelids. Five squares. Windows. *That many? That high?* Yes, and five more on the other side. Too much light.

First things first, I'm on the floor. Wide cedar planks. Imported wood that's been smoothed with a stone and then oiled. Who could afford such a thing?

Nicodemus.

Where's my bag? Here. How did I let it get so far away? Someone could have stolen from it.

It's wet. And my chin's wet. I've been drooling.

Now I remember. I ate at his table. It was night. I didn't leave the city.

Why? I always go to my own home. To Bethany. There, I light the candle that begins the Sabbath. I serve the meal. I go to sleep after the kitchen has been put to rights. Then I sleep maybe half the night. Never past dawn.

I must have been drugged. What was in the wine? One cup. No, two. Three at most.

Above me, I can see blue sky.

It's Saturday morning . . .

"Damn!" I say out loud, and my voice croaks. I ball the blanket up and throw it away from me. "Damn! Damn it all!"

My voice echoes clearer now, but I am thirsty.

I know how to sneak out of town during the night. But if it is Saturday morning, I'm trapped. I must stay here until the city gates open at the end of the Sabbath. What did he say to get me to come to his house? The spider has me now for a full day.

He invited Mary and me to eat at his table. Yes. And he told me that Lazarus was at his house. And he was. My brother ate beside me. See? There is the table. We ate. It's still a mess. No one has cleaned it up. Why? Because it's Sabbath!

There were others with us. The long table was full. Disciples of Jesus. Women from Galilee.

Look, a body!

One of them on the floor. Another one.

Are they dead?

No. James is there, snoring like a goat in heat.

How did they get here? Who is Nicodemus to them? Did the spider sting us all? Did he drug our food? My brother trusts him. He kept saying we could trust Nicodemus. Mary said nothing. Odd. It's time to see who's left.

I get up to my knees. Then I fall back down.

The room is turning.

Again. This time, I stand. I shuffle to the body next to James.

"John!"

John doesn't snore. Opens one eye, blinks, then returns to sleep, quiet and calm. He is an innocent youth, not yet thirty. He is not *am ha'aretz*. I can't take him back to Bethany, even though he has a thing for Mary.

Where is Jesus?

Oh, yes. Jesus is dead.

I sit at the table and try to remember. There is a cup before me.

There is broken bread scattered on the table.

Remember . . .

It was almost evening, and Jesus was dead. Nicodemus came with a ladder. He had another Pharisee with him. Another rich man. This one had a spare tomb. Imagine that —to be that rich.

Then Mary did something to offend me. What else is new?

Something with my hands. I became upset. Nicodemus was surprised that I yelled at her. She's my sister. I'm allowed to yell at her when she's being stupid. We left the tomb, and I wanted to go home. But they pushed me through the Jaffa Gate and into the city. They made sure I couldn't go home to Bethany. People know I sell leather. Being out on the Sabbath would be bad.

"Nicodemus will hide you," someone says.

Why hide in the city? Fools.

Don't they know the Monkey has a spy on every corner?

Jesus's disciples should just have kept running. They were outside the walls when their rabbi was taken. When the high priest starts making arrests, you scatter. His power ends with the wall.

This room looks so different in the daylight.

Bethany is safe. Jesus told us to stay at home. But Nicodemus put us in this room. He made me drink. He kept pouring. Why didn't I stop him?

Look, the cup before me is half full—the dark liquid like blood.

Suddenly, I remember.

Jesus was on the cross, dying. I lifted a sponge to his lips.

Vinegar and . . .

He refused to drink. I had added an herb to the wine—the

one my mother had shown me would ease pain and make his death gentle. He still refused to drink. I begged and begged him.

Suddenly, I'm sick. I retch.

"Martha," a voice hisses.

Over in a dark corner is Simon the Zealot. He stands, and something else glints. It's his knife—the Zealot's short blade—hidden beneath the folds of his cloak, except when the fabric gaps. He moves toward me, something in his hand.

"Water," he says, holding out a bowl.

"Thank you." I drink.

"Nice bag," he says. He's seen it before, but the light is brighter here than in my dim house. I show him the embossing. There is a broken chain pattern running around the top flap. There are palm branches on the sides.

"I did that to make Lazarus happy."

Simon nods. He has that in common with my brother. Boys running in the dark. Lying in ambush for the Romans. Catching humble merchants instead. Beating them. Or coming at night to Bethany. Stealing the odd farm tool. Begging for supplies. Searching for a Messiah. Foolishness, and yet the stitches remain. Thankfully, the bag has darkened, and it is less obvious now.

"I was surprised to see you here," I say to him.

"There was nothing more I could do," Simon says. "I told you that last night."

"Excuses," I say, even though I don't remember last night.

He is small, thin, scarred from a life in the wilderness. His face is lined like an old man, though he's barely forty. So different from the other Simon, the one we call the Leper, though he isn't. Then again, this little Simon isn't a Zealot anymore.

"You think I'm to blame? That I failed Jesus? That I failed to gather my old Zealot friends into an army? That I didn't try to save Jesus?"

"You weren't at his trial." This much I remember. It was earlier on Friday. Before the drinking. "I'm not accusing. Just stating a fact. None of you, except James. Him, I dragged. And Nicodemus was at the trial. None of these other bodies you see asleep around us were there. And when Pilate asked what should be done with Jesus, I shouted, 'Exile him.' I was alone. No one added their voice to mine. A few dozen men might have tipped the scale."

"Should I have brought my friends who are known to be Zealots into Pilate's court? A good plan requires time." Simon is being defensive. I don't like his tone. "They were watching for us at the gates. And I don't have any normal friends."

"I found a way in. So did Mary and Lazarus."

"Mary? Did she lose her voice from shouting? Did she bring a hundred women to sway Pilate's opinion?"

"But you were the one who made a promise to me. You said you would gather an army and save Jesus. That the Zealots had weapons. That you knew secret ways beneath the walls."

"Oh." He nods. "I see it now. I should have taken my army in through Hezekiah's tunnel. Like your brother and Thomas. How did that work for them?"

I look around.

"Where is Thomas?" I ask.

"Thomas is lost. Don't you remember the earthquake?"

"But you are here. And them?"

He shrugs. "When you lose a battle, you scatter. Sometimes, the best place to rendezvous is where you ate your last meal, assuming the enemy doesn't know that place. Each man took a different path. Thomas chose badly. Tunnels are not kind to giants."

"What do you know? Useless."

"I did what I could. Made some contacts. Then came back to the city. By then, it was too late."

"You could have at least helped us bury Jesus."

"I had another body to tend to," he says cryptically. "Someone Jesus trusted."

"Who?"

"I saw you counting," he says. "How many do we have left?"

"His mother. Two women from Galilee. Ten disciples."

He tilts his head, as if I can guess what he's thinking.

"Thomas," I say.

"Guess again."

"Judas."

He nods.

"Dead?"

"Hanged himself."

"Good."

He raises an eyebrow.

Something of Friday night is coming back to me. Simon and James were talking about Judas. And Mary was beside me. *Where is she now?* I count the room again. Simon pours me more water. I am thirsty, but the act of drinking makes my head hurt again. Last night, she was here. We drank the rich man's wine. Lazarus was to my left, and Mary leaned upon my right breast.

Sister, she mouthed.

"Mary, Mary," I said, stroking her short stubble. *Why did she cut her hair?* It had been so beautiful—long, red, a white streak running past her left ear. Unique. Mary with green eyes. Where others saw mischief, I saw beauty. I am dull and steady; she brought color to gray Bethany. Last night, she was warm and damp. I feared the fever that once took our brother. I felt her head—front and back, as we do in Bethany. There was a lump the size of a goose egg. It was solid and high. Red in the lamplight.

"What's this?"

She looked around for something. She found pen and ink.

Mary can write? Did Jesus teach her this? She wrote five letters, one word. Black ink on an empty terra-cotta dish.

"Judas," John read for me.

"He hit you?" I asked her.

She nodded. And this, she seemed to want me to know, was why she is unable to talk. I think not. I think she gave her voice to Jesus. The songs she sang. The stories she told about him since he sent her back to Bethany. Last week, when she gave her precious perfume as an anointing on him and he rejected it, her voice began to fade. Then he died. Judas. The blow to the head. Physical injury doesn't take a voice this way. I think when she is ready to talk again, she will.

Still, the man from Kerioth hit my Mary. So now I say to Simon the Zealot that Judas's body should have been dragged to Gehenna and his bones left for the dogs.

He looks offended. So I say it loudly, "You all loved Judas. See where it got you?"

"No," John says. He's awake now. "We envied Judas; we didn't love him."

"Well. Well. Still a little testy?" Simon makes a *tsk-tsk* motion. "You don't have to be jealous of Judas anymore. I buried him."

But they had loved Judas. Even Jesus did. Don't they know that appearances can be deceptive? Like my aunt Rachel's departed husband, Judas, is from Kerioth. I should say *was*. He rarely admitted it, though. Kerioth is little hick village on the edge of the Negev. Judas wanted people to think he was from Jerusalem, that he had connections. He didn't dress like an *am ha'aretz*. His clothing was neither simple nor cheap. He was striking to look at, with long, wavy, jet-black hair. He never covered his head. I once saw Mary running her hand through it. That's why John was jealous.

"Each of the guys are my brothers," Mary said when I asked her about it. "I would never be interested in any of them. It would get in the way of my following Jesus."

But John was more of a brother to her than any of the other disciples. They are the same age and knew each other before Mary went off to Magdala.

John makes a face and turns away, leaving us to wake Peter.

"You can be cruel," I say to Simon. The Zealot shrugs and goes back into the shadows.

"None of you are safe here," I say to the room.

"Give it a rest," a voice behind me groans. It is James. He is flat on his back and has his arm over his eyes.

"Rest? I've done enough of that already."

4

BURIAL PRAYERS

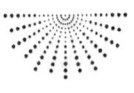

MARY

Thinking of earthquakes and unintended burials, I go to the landing. Here, the stairs bend the corner of the house and exit briefly onto a walled space on the neighbor's roof. A temporary booth shields the stair climber from the spring rains but allows me to scan the eastern sky and the rooftops of the single-story dwellings below. People in the city make full use of their flat roofs. Even though it is Sabbath, I can see work being done on more than one.

It seems an odd space until I figure out why. From here, Nicodemus can confirm that the smoke from temple sacrifices still ascends on schedule. Like that of Adam's son Abel, the city's worship still seeks to be accepted by the Holy One. Today, a lone dark cloud hovers there. The smoke will not rise.

Other sacrifices are more important now. I lift my arms in prayer.

Jesus,
We buried you well.
Sweet, soft you lie,
In a garden tomb,

Your work done.

Lazarus,
We buried you well.
In the company of our ancestors,
You did Sheol's rounds,
Until Jesus said, "Enough."

But Thomas,
Trapped in stone,
Forsaken, not buried.
Let him not die with doubt alone.
Amen.

HAVING PRAYED, I WAS GOING TO GO CHECK ON MARTHA. I hear a noise. Someone is at the front door. Has the high priest sent his men to bother us on this somber day?

5

THE BURIED ONE

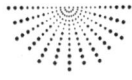

THOMAS

Meanwhile, Thomas awakes in the dark. Reaching out, he feels the stone walls of his prison. The slimy sandstone below him gently curves, having been channeled by centuries of water. Farther up the tunnel wall, there is limestone with rounded aggregate. Rows of these harder quartz pebbles have popped off, leaving round dimples. Feeling down his body, Thomas finds his clothes are wet with water and piss.

"I'm alive. Damn it," he croaks.

Then he has a comforting realization. The pain is not like it was before. In fact, his entire left side is numb. He can move one arm. It waves in the darkness, unseen. Farther down, his hand strikes the stone that pins his left knee. The stone feels round . . . He calculates the volume. Three hundred pounds. Limestone. The grainy kind found under Jerusalem's *Ophel*. Stone no sensible mason would carve anything from. No sensible builder would place his house on this rock. This isn't what comforts Thomas. It is the fact that he will die soon.

"Lazarus," Thomas calls. There isn't an echo, only deadness, the trickle of water. He says his friend's name three more times.

Lazarus is lucky, Thomas thinks. With his free hand,

Thomas counts the reasons for believing this. First, the man had a stable and hard-working older sister named Martha, who more than made up for the early death of Lazarus's mother and the grief-fueled senility that drained his father's later years. Thomas himself had a more complicated family, which he fled at age fourteen. Second, Lazarus survived six years as a wilderness-dwelling Zealot, even though his weak eyes made him a terrible fighter. The average recruit lasted six weeks. Third, and perhaps Thomas would have led with this if he were making this list for the benefit of others, Lazarus had come back from the dead.

Forming his hand back into a fist, Thomas says, "Lazarus. You lucky dog. You found a way out of this tunnel. You survived the earthquake."

Thomas laughs. Then the darkness makes him rethink his list. Lazarus could also be a luckier man having died instantly when the tunnel roof collapsed.

"Oh, to be working. Pounding even crap rock like this." Thomas says to brush this thought out of his mind. He calls again, "Lazarus! Wake up. Come out of hiding. Lazarus, light a torch so I can see you. Lazarus, come forth."

Lazarus doesn't answer. The quiet brings memories to Thomas. He remembers the night after Jesus called Lazarus out of the grave in Bethany's grotto. It was nearly night, and people were hungry. Martha invited everyone to her house. She cooked. But Lazarus wasn't hungry, and he wasn't ready to leave the grotto. So Jesus and Thomas had stayed with him. John was there, and a strange man from Jerusalem came to join them. He was a Pharisee. *What was his name? Nicodemus.*

"Lazarus, have you cheated death again? Or are you waiting for me at *Sheol's* gate? Will you be my guide?"

Thomas knew the truth now. Lazarus hadn't run toward Jerusalem to save Mary. He followed Mary because they both knew Jesus was about to die. Even though Thomas had fled to Bethany when Jesus was arrested, he followed Lazarus and

Mary. Why? Because Martha had asked him. And when they had split up, when Mary chose to sit and weep in Gehenna, Thomas had followed Lazarus as the lesser of two evils. That wisdom seemed questionable now.

Lazarus had explained his plan. He knew Jesus would die, but he hoped the rabbi would be stoned or beaten. It would make their work a whole lot easier. The bodies of the crucified usually hung on the cross for days and then got thrown in Gehenna, the smoldering dump where dogs ate their remains. But if Jesus had only the high priest to deal with—*yes, it was temple guards that arrested him*—then Jesus's body would end up lying under a heap of rubble. Alternatively, they could choose to simply throw Jesus off the temple's high pinnacle. Either way, Lazarus would be lucky. He would have Thomas to carry the body back to Bethany's grotto. They would place Jesus in the grave Lazarus just vacated.

"Give me a ball of yarn," Lazarus had said. "Have Martha or Mary hold one end. Then roll the stone back on us."

Lazarus would guide Jesus in and out of the underworld. Wonderful plan. Except when there's an earthquake.

The quiet of the tunnel lent itself to unraveling conversations. Trivial things that were said and taken at face value before, now take on a symbolic richness. Being forced to do nothing is a sacrament. Awaiting death provides useful and sacred time. The past two weeks had been hectic for Thomas. Now, there was time to reflect upon the actions and the words of Jesus and his friends.

So, before this madness, calm. Lazarus resting in the grotto. Jesus had called him out of the grave. That must have been work, because Jesus looked tired. One of the lessons Thomas had learned when he followed Jesus was to rest whenever the rabbi rested. Jesus could display incredible energy when he was healing people and walking from town to town. The rabbi shouted his messages, standing on his tiptoes so the crowds could hear him. But he could sleep anywhere—even in a boat while there was a storm.

They all just wanted to rest. It was a miracle, but Jesus had brought the dead back to life before. Thomas was as jaded as any of the disciples. He was ready to call it a night, but this Nicodemus had questions. Thomas liked people who asked questions. The Pharisee pressed Lazarus to speak about the people he had met during his four days in the underworld.

"Did you meet anyone famous?"

"I saw my mother," Lazarus had said.

"No. I mean . . ."

"The dead aren't quite as interesting as you would think." Jesus laughed.

Nicodemus persisted. "What about Odysseus? Moses? Socrates?"

Lazarus shook his head and spoke instead of an uncle from the village, whom Nicodemus didn't know. The man had loved music, but since the world below doesn't allow notes to follow in sequence, he couldn't sing. 'Timing is everything,' Lazarus had heard his uncle say.

The Pharisee stood to leave, but Jesus motioned him to sit. Only now, reflecting back on the conversation, did Thomas realize what Jesus was doing. Jesus wanted to speak to Nicodemus about spiritual rebirth. Difficult subjects have their prerequisites, though. Jesus provided room, first, for Lazarus to speak of natural human death and rebirth.

Jesus asked, "What about the man who planted that palm tree?"

Lazarus had stared blankly into the darkness, as if the recently dead man needed time to remember the features of the village he had called home for almost forty years. The palm tree was famous. It had stood for seven generations as the lone vestige of Bethany's connection to the royal Hasmonean dynasty. Nobody famous ever lived in Bethany, but when Judas 'the Hammer' Maccabaeus retook the royal city from the Seleucids, he planted that tree.

The reason palm branches were strewn before Jesus when he rode a donkey through the Eastern Gate of Jerusalem was because the people had waved palms before their liberators the last time Israel had freed itself from foreign oppression. The priests and the Herodian nobles who lined the wall and watched Jesus ride the donkey, and Thomas hold the animal's nose, had reason to be outraged. They had little claim on the Hasmonean house that once ruled in the city and struck coins with palm trees on them as a symbol of newfound freedom.

But Lazarus couldn't have seen the tree that Judas Maccabaeus had planted, even if it had been light and his eyesight better. The landmark is now a mere barren stalk. When the rich man Simon had been exiled from Jerusalem because of his leprosy, he had taken his wealth to Bethany because he had Hasmonean ancestors. He took possession of the land near the palm tree, adjacent to Martha's house. Even though the villagers begged him not to disturb this living monument, Simon built his house with the tree enclosed within his courtyard walls. Since then, the tree has been dying. Martha considers this a bad omen.

"Our village will soon be no more," she had once complained to Thomas.

"Sometimes a tree is just a tree," he answered.

"No!" Martha was often angry. "Our freedom will end when we forget the names of our patriots."

"Like Judas Maccabaeus?"

"Yes. The young don't care that Simon is killing our memory tree."

But Martha had been gone, fixing food for the other disciples when Jesus asked Lazarus about the man who planted the palm tree. Now, in Hezekiah's tunnel, Thomas struggles to remember the whole conversation.

"Did you meet any freedom fighters in Sheol?" Jesus had asked Lazarus.

"Yes," Lazarus responded. "I met Judas Maccabaeus."

Nicodemus perked up and asked, "What was he like?"

"There are balconies in the underworld. People see scenes from their lives. Little dramas replayed without context or meaning. Judas the Hammer was watching the crowds cheer. The scene was one of a victory parade. And he was weeping."

"Weeping?"

"Pitifully. Like a lost child."

"What did you do?"

"I told him that, even now, the nation remembers what he and his brothers did—how he was a great military general, not only defeating the Seleucids, but adding territory to Israel. He said, 'I would rather be herding sheep in obscurity. I'd rather have one more day in my village of Modiin than all the eternal glory of this place.'"

Thomas groans remembering this.

Nicodemus had taken offense. He accused Lazarus of plagiarizing Homer—that Achilles had said a similar thing when Odysseus found him in the underworld.

Lazarus said, "You asked. I told you."

Jesus stepped in. He offered that those who sing great songs capture something true from the eternal realm and speak it into our world of time and space. Wisdom is wisdom. Homer and Lazarus were both visitors in Sheol. We shouldn't find it surprising that they tell similar stories.

"I'm in no hurry to die," Thomas says, in spite of the pain.

6

GOOD QUESTION

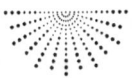

MARK

On Sabbath days, the men of the city worship wherever great rabbis can be found. Pilgrims and the uninitiated expect this to be the temple courts. Mark shakes his head at them. *They might as well be women.* Apart from Philo of Alexandria, the greatest living rabbi is Nicodemus, and his courtyard is always full on Sabbath. Mark goes early. In this city, it is good to be first. First to choose your seat. First to ask the rabbi a good question. First to discover what's really going on. Today, he has many questions. Throughout the week, the classes that meet at Nicodemus's house are usually led by lesser scribes and rabbis. When the master pops his head in, there is usually no chance to distinguish himself from the others. Mark has learned a secret. On Saturdays, Nicodemus takes his seat across from the courtyard's fountain a full hour before worship. Mark's habit is to silently wait for him.

"John Mark, do you have a question?" the master asked last week.

"When the dead come back to life at the resurrection, what kind of body will they have?"

It was a good question—one that Nicodemus could not

dismiss by telling him to search a particular volume in the library.

"Do you ask this because of recent events?"

Like everyone in Jerusalem, Mark had heard the rumor of a man who had been brought back to life in the nearby village of Bethany. This was not the reason he asked this question. Nor did he ask it because one of the house servants had told him that Nicodemus was familiar with the family and had met the miracle worker, Jesus, who pulled off the trick.

Instead, Mark asked about resurrected bodies because of an African legend that he had been told as a child. The legend claimed that some people become butterflies when they die. Mark has outgrown this folk tale. Yet he has observed how caterpillars spin cocoons and how butterflies emerge from these tomb-like structures.

"No, I do not ask because of the miracles attributed to Rabbi Jesus," Mark said. "I ask because I have heard my uncles singing funeral songs as they plant seeds in the fields."

"You have learned the song that comes out of our time of exile? The one that says, 'That those who go out into the fields weeping as they bear their seed shall in time return with gladness. Rejoicing as they bring in the sheaves.'"

"Yes."

"Then realize that all of life is in transition. Seeds die and become plants. Plants grow and become stalks of wheat. Wheat is made into bread. The loaf is broken and becomes nourishment for the farmer who plants the seed. We should not mourn as others do who have no hope. We have hope in a Lord-God who has designed all things to change. Death is just one step in a very natural process."

Nicodemus lapsed into silence. Mark did not speak again but spent the week since thinking of his next question. Now, he comes early on Sabbath to sit with the master once more.

Only the door is locked. It is now well past sunrise. He timidly knocks.

7
NICODEMUS MAPS THE CITY

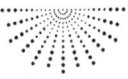

MARY

I know that Nicodemus is afraid. He has barred the main door but left the servant door open. Why? He must expect his enemies to be forthright and announce themselves properly. How did he survive this long in Jerusalem?

I near the kitchen and can tell that Nicodemus is again complaining about how complicated Jesus has made his life. There is a knock at the main door. Lazarus sticks his head out, looks at me, and nods in that direction. I shrug.

He and my sister expect me to see things all the time. I have limits. It's not a matter of distance, though last week Jesus drew a circle around Bethany and prevented me from watching him in Jerusalem. I didn't see him get arrested. I had to run to town to see him go to the cross. I had to get knocked out by Judas to really see what the cross was all about.

Most of the house is between us and the front door. I close my mind and walk my vision into the courtyard where a fountain bubbles. This isn't natural. Nicodemus must have his servants carry water to a rooftop cistern. A small dribble falls the eight or so feet onto the statue of a fish in the fountain. I bet the Greeks taught him how to do that.

I'm still walking my mind through the courtyard with its plants when my brother says, "What are they waiting for?"

He doesn't understand the concept of a locked door. He has traveled far and stayed in the homes of a hundred strangers, but this is his first night behind a locked door, unless you count *Sheol*.

"Caiaphas may have the manpower to arrest a wandering rabbi in a garden at night," Nicodemus explains, "but he can't come into the home of a fellow member of the Sanhedrin without an invitation. I'm not inviting. Neither am I turning my place into a sanctuary for Zealot sympathizers. The Romans don't knock. It's probably just John Mark."

"Jesus wasn't a Zealot."

"Caiaphas knows that. The Romans don't. None of us are safe until the Romans leave. You remember what Pilate did to the Galileans who wanted to make a sacrifice in memory of those who resisted at Magdala? He sent his men right onto the temple grounds and slaughtered them as they stood in line with their offering. Our fate may be similar. I can provide a single Sabbath day of safety to Jesus's followers. No more. As for the two of you, didn't I warn you to stay in Bethany?"

"My father thanks you from his grave," Lazarus lies. "I'm here, though. I want to see Jesus's grave before I go home."

"You can't. It's too dangerous."

I mouth to him, *Just sneak out.* He nods at this. We can both see that our host hasn't slept. Perhaps he will nod off if we keep him talking. My brother is on a fool's errand, but I am willing to help. He says that *Sheol* is a maze. Endless corridors. Gray upon gray. He knows that Jesus is lost in death's domain. Lazarus hopes to call for him. Guide Jesus by his voice back to life. But to do this, Lazarus must go to the same portal that Jesus used to enter *Sheol*.

"I guess I would understand it better if you explained to me how it all went wrong for Jesus," Lazarus says. "I was stuck in the cave, you see. I missed everything."

Nicodemus pauses. He looks toward the door that leads to the courtyard. In another hour, men will be gathering there to hear him teach. He is already in teacher mode. He spreads his hands out over the table, as if unrolling a scroll or a map.

"A tragedy in four scenes. Four principle actors. Four locations."

Nicodemus stabs his finger in the middle of the table. He speaks slowly, as if we aren't as familiar with Jerusalem's geography as he is. "Here is where we are."

Then he moves his finger south, near to where Lazarus is sitting. "Friday morning, the council met in private in its chambers."

"The round room at the high priest's complex?"

"Yes. I was only home for an hour or two when I got the summons. I had to return to Caiaphas's house. The messenger was urgent. Said that my vote was needed to advert a crisis. All seventy of us were required to be there by dawn."

It's easy to imagine Nicodemus grumbling, stepping out his front door, and turning left down the broad street. The smoothly set stones beneath his feet would gently slope down and to the southwest, past the noble homes of the city. Then suddenly, the wealthy upper quarter ends. There is a wall—a low gateway that used to have an iron grate.

"Jesus had already been arrested?"

"Yes. Caiaphas took him from his pit—you know, the cracked cistern below his courtyard."

I take Lazarus's hand. I let him feel the lump on the back of my head. It means nothing to Nicodemus. Last night, I explained with signs to my brother that I had spent much of Friday in that same pit. Not at the same time as Jesus. Maybe minutes later. Judas struck me. I was placed in the black hole like a salted fish.

"So I went to the council chamber in the complex of the high priest."

I see it as Nicodemus says it. I see the man taking his little gold lamp. Walking the empty streets. Going down those two irregular steps beneath the partition between quarters of the city. These steps have been worn shallow in the middle by a century of foot traffic. Beyond them, the cobblestones become irregular, not just because the workmanship has diminished, but because Caiaphas altered the city's plan. He wanted an open space in front of his walled complex. He had several houses torn down and an irregular pavement laid. In Judaean cities, open spaces like this usually have a well. This emptiness simply serves to hold the queues of vendors requesting permits and lost pilgrims seeking aide. The gray masses gather each morning at dawn to meet with the city's scribes. But this meeting was too early for that.

"You know, Lazarus, I don't know why I allowed myself to be voted onto the Sanhedrin. Me, one of Jerusalem's seventy? I guess it's an honor. But I would have just as gladly gone on simply being a scholar. I should never have set foot in those ugly buildings. Politics. Someone has to do it, or so I've been told."

"So you saw Jesus?"

"Right there." Again, he stabs the table in front of Lazarus. "Your father would have called it the house of Annas, but no one remembers that today."

Caiaphas's father-in-law, Annas, built a small complex there. Geographically, it is the center of Jerusalem. From it, the priesthood maintains a finger in every pot. Gentle, old Annas still walks the corridors of the complex. He was a better realtor than a high priest. He made a fortune during King Archelaus's chaotic reign. He bought up the property vacated by the dozens of noble families who fled the city. His shrewdest move, though, was to give the ambitious man who married his daughter the house next to the priesthood's complex. That house has a cracked cistern that holds no water. Not a problem for a man who has maids to fetch his drink.

I tremble. I went to the Monkey house to find Jesus. I opened the wrong door and found Judas Iscariot. He smiled, and before I grasped the significance of him being there, he struck me.

Jesus and I. Same pit.

"Jesus stood trial before the seventy," Nicodemus continues. "Witnesses were brought in. He was mute until the end of the proceedings."

I pantomime Jesus being slapped.

Nicodemus sees this and hisses at me, "Were you there?"

There is anger in his eyes. Guilt will do that. I don't answer.

Nicodemus resumes, "Instead of answering his accusers, your Jesus said not a word until it was over. Then he said something blasphemous that I won't repeat. It was then that the high priest had him struck. Satisfied?"

I nod. I can see it in my mind now. This is the way my vision works. Sometimes things are hidden. Then a person connected to them reveals their emotional experience of that place and for the merest of moments I can see it through their eyes.

The council chamber for the seventy elders is round. The ceiling is domed—the only place in Jerusalem that employs this trick—an expensive gift from the Romans, given by Pilate to win forgiveness for the heavy hand he used when he first came to town. The Monkey was new to his position as well. They both overplayed their hand in the beginning but came, as enemies often do, to understand each other. The Sanhedrin's round chamber room—you would think it simple until you look up. There, in the center of the dome, right where a cornerstone should go, is an opening. Sky above. As Jesus stood trial, it was just turning pink. From it, a circle of light falls. It illuminates the raised dais and the red chair where the high priest sits. This spotlight also includes Jesus. Nicodemus, having earned a seat in the front row, sits just beyond the light. He could reach out and touch him if he wanted. They are separated only by air and a commitment to silence.

"Then Caiaphas had him bound and sent to Herod Antipas, because your Jesus is a Galilean and his ruler is here for the festival." Nicodemus points west, toward the courtyard and his front door. "Jesus stood a second trial there."

Here, our host has things confused. Herod had been displaced.

"Last night, Martha said that the guards took Jesus to the old Hasmonean palace."

"Martha's crazy. Herod's palace is right there. He's my neighbor, when he's in town."

No. Nicodemus and Martha were both misled. This year, the Romans had other plans for the Galilean ruler. They put their friends in the palace next door, and Herod had to make do with the old Hasmonean one. The shift in venue meant that my sister missed this trial of Jesus. She blames herself for being two steps behind and three beats too slow all day Friday. Try as she could, she couldn't save Jesus.

"But it couldn't have mattered what Herod thought," Lazarus says.

"Never does," Nicodemus concedes. "Caiaphas was just building his case against Jesus. Making it level on all three legs of the stool, so to speak. The Romans have broken the Jewish kingdom in two. Jesus has to appear to be a contender for Herod Antipas's throne, as well as the land that Pilate governs in Judaea. Two secular trials and a sacred one. In all three, it wasn't about what Jesus did. It was about what he could do. The Zealots talk about a Messiah that rules it all, as King David did. Some say that the whole world will bow before him."

"Anyone who says that doesn't know Jesus." Lazarus shakes his head. "The rabbi was across the Jordan—not gathering an army, mind you—helping the people there."

"Was he a rabbi or a Zealot? If all he wanted to do was to teach and heal, he should have kept going. Leave the region entirely. There are communities of Jews in all the major cities of the empire. Or if he didn't want to contend with Roman power, go to Babylon, Persepolis, or even the land beyond the Indus River. No one would have stopped him from teaching the things he taught. This is a unique time in history. The roads go everywhere and the borders are porous. Wisdom is honored in every court, except that of Herod Antipas."

"And the round room of the Sanhedrin."

"Yes. I hear that Jesus has been coming to Jerusalem for years, and every time people recognize him, he disappears. It's as if he wants people to think he's . . ."

"Divine?"

"I was going to say subversive."

There is a pause, and I am thinking it is time to go upstairs again and check on Martha. The look on Lazarus's face, though, keeps me here.

"I don't know why he came this year." Nicodemus waves to the east, as if to shoo Jesus to safety.

"I do. He came back because of me," Lazarus says.

"You can't blame yourself for dying."

Or your sisters for begging Jesus to return.

Lazarus is silent, his face a mask. Nicodemus, in a rare gesture of kindness, puts his hand on Lazarus's shoulder. The moment passes quickly, and the Pharisee returns to his task of making the table a map of the city, and yesterday's events easier to understand. He points over his shoulder, to the north —toward the temple, the fortress Antonia with its Roman garrison, and the walled courtyard that acts as an auxiliary space for both complexes.

"So it was almost noon before the final trial could take place. Pilate questioned Jesus privately. Then he brought him out before the crowd gathered in the square. That is where I found Martha. She asked if I had seen you or Mary. Then she pulls out a dozen coins from her bag. She had a bribe in her hand. She shouted that I should do something. Even then, she wasn't herself."

"Was the bribe for Mary or for me?"

"No. Aren't you listening? Martha and that glutton."

"James?"

"Yes, he was there with her. He was pretending to be an idiot. Martha had a plan. She thought we could trick the Romans into releasing Jesus. Totally irrational. She begged me to help her. So we went into the fortress, looking for Jesus. I came prepared. I produced a document saying that I was to receive the man Pilate pardoned for Passover. It was . . ."

"Forged?"

"No. No. Someone has to care for the prisoner that Pilate releases each spring. He gives the elders a misfit every year. It's a challenge. 'Let me see if your religion can turn this bad apple good.' This year wasn't my turn, though. Jesus's name wasn't on the document. But you wave an official-looking scroll and hope for the best."

"You took my sister into the Fortress Antonia?"

"It's not as bad as you might think. The Romans keep the place spotless. It's how they are. And we had that man, James, with us too. Why should the guards care which bandit I took responsibility for?"

"And?"

Nicodemus sighs. "I failed. I ended up with Barabbas instead."

For the first time this morning, we all look at Barabbas. He doesn't flinch at the sound of his name. The Zealot parolee sits in the farthest corner from the door. His knees are drawn up. He stares straight ahead, as if the woodpile opposite him holds his fate.

Suddenly, I can see it. This kitchen with the four of us, represents all of humanity. My brother, those who have died. Nicodemus, those who live only in their minds. Me? I represent the sisterhood of those who are fully aware. The women who give birth to sons knowing that they will go off to war and die. The women who give birth to daughters knowing that they will speak, but never be listened to. I know the future, but I can't act to change it. But Barabbas, he is the opposite of each of us. He is broken now, but before yesterday, he represented all those who actually act upon what they believe to be true.

Yesterday, the whole world was here in Jerusalem. And this very table its center, an axis around which the events of Friday circled. A thousand yards to the south, the Monkey convened the high council. A thousand yards to the west, Jesus was crucified. A thousand to the east is the Mount of Olives where Jesus began his fateful ride into Jerusalem. And a thousand to the north, a cobblestone square, a place where pilgrims often queue before entering the temple. At a whim, though, Pilate can demand the space. Twice this week, he has used it for equestrian practice. But on Friday, Pilate brought his chair to the porch of this square, and the stage was set for a final decision regarding the matter of Jesus of Nazareth. The sun was high overhead, and the place smelled of manure. If I had been there, I would have repeated to Pilate the secret words his wife had said in their bedchamber that morning. I would have convinced him to do what was already in his heart: let Jesus go.

I would have failed. Not because the governor isn't persuadable. But because Jesus had decided to take the place of this Zealot named Barabbas. A daughter of Eve can never win against a son of Adam that has his mind made up. Seeing the future and not being able to change it is the most terrible of curses.

"So Jesus went to get crucified, and I went to get my ladder. It was there." He now stabs the table to the west. He does it hard enough that the salt bowl in front of me bounces. "Your sisters were there, and they followed us to the grave."

"Can I go to it now?"

"No. You are as bad as her." He points at me.

What?

"It's what I told you about earlier. Her witchcraft pushed Martha over the edge."

He knows nothing!

"I'm sure she only did what women always do before a burial," Lazarus says.

"With women, things are never simple."

I act. I push the salt bowl off the table. The bowl shatters. It's not supposed to do that. Too much brokenness.

"What is broken above is multiplied below," Lazarus says. This is an *Essene* proverb. They have many apocalyptic sayings. They see the future. The Messiah comes; the world ends. There is a mysterious bond between heaven and earth. If our spiritual future is forsaken, then our present-day decisions will be disastrous. If our relationship with the holy one is compromised, the fellowship we have with our earthly friends will be shattered. In the Essene's understanding of the afterlife, there is plenty of time for regret. In *Sheol*, that pit of death, the lessons we fail to learn here are studied again and again until perfected. As above, so below.

"Huh?" Nicodemus is not an Essene.

Nor is Lazarus, though he has spent time with the Essenes.

"As above, so below," he repeats. "Just something I picked up."

Barabbas has quietly moved to my feet. He picks up the broken pottery of the salt bowl. He tries to grasp the salt between his thick fingers. As the dish fell, so did he. In this simple act, he shows his earnest repentance.

You are redeemed, I mouth. *As above, so below.*

8

THE GIFT OF FLIGHT

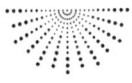

MARTHA

This room is amazing—bigger than the banquet hall at Simon the Leper's. Look at those windows! Each one has a wooden lattice to keep the birds out. Now, I can see. It was only darkness last night. Must be a hole up there in one of those windows. No, in two.

Bird in, bird out. Two holes. Lazarus was to my left. I remember that much. He kept talking. It made me glad to see him being his old self. He talked of Thomas being in the cave with him, said it was darker than *Sheol* when the earthquake happened because his torch fell into the water. He kept calling for Thomas, and his voice bounced back because there were rocks filling the tunnel between him and the giant. He's telling this story when the bird comes in.

My brother points to it. We watch this bird come in that window. Just appears out of the darkness. It flies the length of the hall, goes out the other side through that window. Must have known where the hole was.

My brother stands and lifts his cup like he means to give us all a blessing. He says, "We've just seen a swallow come in from the darkness, fly for a while in the light of this place, then go out into the darkness beyond. So is our fate. We come into this world from who knows where. Who or what we were before our birth is only darkness. We live a short time in the light. Then we disappear out into another darkness."

"You've been there." John points toward the western window. "Tell us about it."

Lazarus puts his finger to his lips and shakes his head.

Nicodemus says, "I had hoped that Jesus would have been more . . ." Then I see him searching for a word that everyone would understand.

Lazarus supplies it. "Illuminating."

"I had hopes for your rabbi. I thought he'd be more helpful than Jerusalem's teachers. That bird has been a better teacher than all the wise men of Jerusalem. That bird is a better teacher than Jesus. Why? Because the bird is alive and Jesus is dead. Learn a lesson from the bird. Stay here tonight and tomorrow, but when the Sabbath is over, take leave and scatter."

To this, everyone says, "Amen."

WHERE ARE PETER AND JOHN?

I'm watching people wake up, telling them we need to leave as soon as the Sabbath ends. At the west end of the room, I find a door. I step out onto the rooftop terrace, the cool morning breeze in my face. It is perfect weather for walking. I find my missing men.

"When a wolf kills a shepherd, the sheep know to scatter," I say. It is an *am ha'aretz* proverb. I've startled them.

"How are you feeling?" They feign concern.

"Like a fish in a basket," I say.

"You must have a headache," Peter says. "To drink so . . ."

"Jesus is dead. Why are you two here? You could have been halfway back to Galilee by now."

"We want to stay nearby," John says. "Can we come with you to Bethany?"

"No. My village is too close. You should be ready to go. They'll open the gates briefly at sunset. With luck, you can mix in with the departing pilgrims, but you'll have to get in line. Not everyone will get out that wants to. It might be better to go to the Sheep Gate and . . ."

"Jesus's mother wants to stay," John says.

"My wife is also here. Perhaps next week——"

"No. Women can blend in. Jesus's mother seems to be able to take care of herself. But not you two. John, you defied your father and stood near Jesus, even when he hung on the cross. And Peter, your Galilean accent will give you away once the pilgrims leave."

They nod, but I can see them choosing to ignore me. They are at the window that overlooks both Nicodemus's courtyard and the street that passes between his mansion and Herod's palace.

"What is it?"

"There's someone in the shadows," John whispers. "He's watching the main door."

Indeed, I see a nose, then an eye. A dark face swaying in and out of the shadow. Suddenly, it's gone, and there's the sound of the oak bar being dropped from the courtyard door.

Voices.

"I think one was Lazarus," Peter says. "Perhaps the other, Nicodemus."

"Fools!"

9

THE CLEOPAS DECEPTION

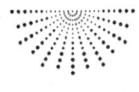

MARK

There is a noise behind the door. A grunt. A curse. The heavy oak beam can be heard sliding, then a thud. It's fallen to the floor. Someone unfamiliar with it, someone weaker than Nicodemus's head servant has unbolted the door. Mark hurries back into the shadows, around the stone wall corner that separates the Herodian palace from the servants' alley.

A bald head pops out. He has never seen this man. A pudgy figure appears, poorly dressed, moving gingerly, gently keeping the door from making a sound as it closes. *Is the man injured or recently ill?* In these tentative steps, there is nothing physically amiss. Mark suspects a psychological trauma or a congenital deformity of mind.

"Idiot!" Nicodemus is in the doorway. "You are a fool. Come back. You can't go out the Jaffa Gate looking like that."

The man seems to notice what he is wearing for the first time.

"I'll go with you," Nicodemus offers.

"You've done enough, my friend. Tell Martha . . ."

"No. Dressed like a rag merchant, on the Sabbath.

Lazarus, you'll be arrested. Come on. I'll dress you like a Pharisee and vouch for you."

The man nods his head and withdraws. "And show me the grave?"

"Yes."

Mark considers this. Behind is a dead-end alley leading to the inner wall that divides the upper quarter from the rest of the city. Servants needing to save steps and avoid unnecessary searches will come this way, step into the Herodian palace's kitchen area, say hello to the workers there, go to the far end of the room, and step out beyond the security barrier into Jerusalem's northern quarter. From there, the Jaffa Gate is but a short way. He can wait there. See if his teacher really does go with this man.

Meanwhile, Mark mulls over Lazarus's use of the words *my friend* with Nicodemus. On Friday morning, when Jesus had been arrested in the garden, Mark assumed that his rabbi aided the high priest, if not in providing information about the Galilean's movements, at least in being a witness for the prosecution. Now, it appears that Nicodemus has been a secret admirer of Jesus.

Mark enters the kitchen of the Herodian palace and finds it empty. The room is twice the size of the one at Nicodemus's mansion. A line has been drawn down its center. The cabinets and utensils on either side look identical, but they serve different worlds. The kosher food required by Jews is prepared in the eastern half. Everything prepared for the palace's other guests is cooked separately and brought to the hall in dishes that never cross the line. Further, he has observed the Herodian staff managing a calendar of unimaginable complexity. Not only must they separate pork from lamb, they must make sure that the Nabatean relatives of the king and the diplomatic guests from Parthia are never seen by the high priest or the other men who answer to Pontius Pilate.

Duplicity, diplomacy, and discretion—these things keep both the

Sadducees and the Herodians in power, Mark thinks. *I won't learn these skills from Nicodemus. He is a child in this city. He may have everything taken from him at any moment.*

This troubles him, for his extended family depends upon the man's charity to supplement what they earn working on Uncle Barnabas's farm. They have put all their eggs in what today appears to be a very insecure basket.

"John Mark," a voice says from the dimness behind him.

He isn't startled. He recognizes the Idumean accent of a fellow immigrant, Tamar. She is dark, like he is, but has Arabian features.

"What are you doing here?" he asks.

"The Monkey sent me with a gift for his friends that . . ." She produces a large sack of fine dates, a fruit that can cross the line. Caiaphas has spies among both groups of servants in this palace.

She offers Mark a handful, which he accepts greedily. Then, having retied the sack and placed it in the middle of the room, she disappears. She has many chores on this Sabbath.

Now in the northern quarter of the city, he meanders toward the Jaffa Gate. The grandest of Jerusalem's gates, it faces west. Fifty feet from it, though, he encounters a line of pilgrims.

"The gate is closed," a man repeats as he walks back the line. Some believe him and drop out of the queue. Most become angry. *What right do they have?*

He isn't surprised to see the gate closed. The Sadducees on the city council insist upon a strict observance of the Sabbath, especially during religious holidays. All of Jerusalem's rabbis are in agreement that a faithful man should walk no more than two-thirds of a mile on the Sabbath. The dividing detail, however, is whether civil ordinances should mandate these matters of conscience on everyone. The Pharisees would permit these pilgrims to exit the city and then find a place to rest in the surrounding fields. Most of them can't afford one more day paying Jerusalem's exorbitant prices.

"How can we be sure they won't keep walking?" the Sadducees ask. "If a pilgrim ignores their higher nature and goes over the Mount of Olives to Bethphage and then, finding their sinful way inviting, descends even to Jericho, won't they have spoiled any holiness our rituals have given them? Worse yet, what if a man traveling west makes it the seven miles to Emmaus, won't they find themselves no better than a pagan?"

We would permit this, John Mark thinks. He is glad to be studying to join the more generous Pharisee party. But in Jerusalem, *they* don't make the rules.

This simple truth seems incredible to the young man's idealistic mind. Most people respect the Pharisees. In terms of sheer numbers, there are more Pharisees than any other party among the Jewish people. It wasn't until his family came as refugees to Jerusalem that they even heard of the Sadducees. Why should innkeepers, priests, and petty government officials have their own party? And why should they be in charge? And why must the Romans always choose the next high priest from among the Sadducees?

"John Mark."

He has been lost in thought. He turns and sees Nicodemus. The strange bald man is with him. Only now, Lazarus wears a blue robe. It is too tall and wide for him. He has the hood up, even though the day doesn't require it.

"I was hoping you would come early. I have a task for you."

"Sir, I was by earlier, but the door was . . ."

"Yes, yes. There isn't time to explain. My friend here is in need. His wife has died, and only I know the way to the grave . . . You see, he is a relative of . . ." Nicodemus is a poor liar. He lacks the needed simplicity. Liars learn to say only what is obvious. Great liars lay down a bread crumb trail, allowing the listener to make up their own story as they follow it away from what must be hidden. No one would believe that a wealthy man doesn't know where his family's grave is. The story is beyond repair, but Lazarus steps in to help.

"My name is Cleopas. We have come for the festival, and my wife has sickened. Suddenly."

Mark is impressed by how the merchant has adopted both the word choice of a rich man and an accent that is vaguely foreign. The pseudonym is well chosen too. Cleopas of Antioch is a respected name among the Pharisees. His letters and teachings have been debated in John Mark's hearing. He also lives far, far away.

"Yes. Yes. We are on a mission, so to speak. For an empty grave. There's a new grave . . ." Nicodemus makes another stab.

"The one for Rabbi Joseph of Arimathea?" Mark asks.

"Yes . . . No," Nicodemus says. "That's not important now."

"Joseph is my brother-in-law," the other lies again. His accent has been adeptly shifted to match the way Judaeans from Arimathea extend their sibilants.

"So you won't be leading the Sabbath gathering at your house," John Mark asks Nicodemus.

"No. I've asked Rabbi Joseph to fill in for me."

"Oh?" Mark looks incredulous.

The man claiming to be married to Joseph's dead or dying sister winces. "Your teacher and I have two griefs on our hearts that pull us in opposite directions. You can help us greatly. But please don't ask so many questions."

"A mutual friend of ours was lost in yesterday's earthquake," Nicodemus says.

"Where?"

"Somewhere in the city." The Pharisee motions vaguely over his shoulder. "But it's urgent that we go out the Jaffa Gate. Right now. To see about this grave."

"This friend and I were exploring Hezekiah's tunnel."

Why? John Mark thinks but doesn't dare ask. That grown men would be exploring a tunnel is unbelievable, unless, of course, you are a Zealot seeking to enter the city undetected.

"My friend is a tall man. His name is Thomas, and he may be hurt."

"The giant who follows Jesus?" Mark asks.

"Yes. The man may be hurt or captured." Nicodemus sounds annoyed.

"Thomas is a stonemason. He was showing me the city's foundations. You see, I can't swim. When the ground shook, I found myself in the water." Lazarus speaks patiently, with confidence. An ordered account rings true, even when it is not. He pauses and tips his head to the south, where the rain goes as it drains. "I emerged in the Pool of Siloam . . ."

"Yes, yes," Nicodemus says. "And unlike my friend, the giant is strong enough to go another way. There are other exits. For instance, a shaft near the temple courtyard's grand stairway."

"I know it. It has smooth walls. Fathers throw copper coins down it when they pray for their daughters to find men to marry. No one could climb . . ."

"Call for him at noon, when the sun shines down the shaft. Then get a rope if he answers." Obviously, the stranger has thought this through. He waits for Mark to nod, then continues, "It is rumored that a pit exists below a potter's workshop in the Essene quarter. They have dug it for the clay. White. Fine. No pebbles."

And untaxed, Mark thinks. This pseudo-Cleopas has dropped all pretext of being from far away.

"But it connects, you see? Ask around."

"For a giant?" Mark shakes his head but turns, accepting his mission.

He has gone a few steps when the stranger calls, "One more thing. When you can, go out the Water Gate. Ask the woman at the Gihon Spring if she has seen him."

"There won't be any women there. With the Sabbath . . ."

"One maid named Tamar works on the Sabbath. She has the pool to herself as she does the high priest's laundry. She also can be bribed for information."

Nicodemus nods, as if this is common knowledge, and hands Mark a coin. The irony is not lost on the teen. He smiles and asks, "Where should I take this Thomas if I find him alive?"

"There is a Pharisee living in exile in Bethany named Simon," Nicodemus says.

"The leper?" John Mark asks incredulously.

"The high priest *says* Simon has leprosy. Those who were hired to examine Simon's back . . . They have shared an interpretation, you see. Maybe they actually did see white spots on Simon's back." Nicodemus shrugs. "How can a man that the high priest wants exiled know for sure?"

"And if I find that the giant is dead?"

"There is a grave with room for him in Bethany," Lazarus says.

"Yours?" John Mark asks, tired of their duplicity.

"Thomas dug it for my family when my father died," Lazarus says. "Nicodemus was my father's friend. Now you know all that you need to know."

"John Mark," Nicodemus whispers. "The less you know, the better."

I've never found that to be true, he thinks.

10

A MOTHERLESS CHILD

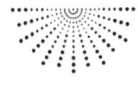

MARY

I am in the kitchen with Barabbas. I made him tea. It's a
miracle I found what I needed, but the right herbs were
there. Chamomile to comfort the soul. Honey to loosen the
tongue. Anise to stir the repentant soul to speak. I make hot
water and honey for myself, but I don't think it will do any
good.

He begins to tell me about his life. He says I will never
understand, but then remembers that Lazarus was once a
Zealot and acknowledges that I am one with a reputation for
knowing.

What kind of reputation do I have among the Zealots? I wish to
ask. It is more important, though, that I accept this beginning
and let the healing proceed.

Each time he tells of an ambush, a murder, or something
he was ashamed of, he pauses. I touch my heart then his chest
with the same two fingers. I mouth, *I forgive you.* He shakes his
head, as if not comprehending, takes a sip of tea, and begins
again.

Yes, Martha is awake. *Stay.* I can only do one thing at a
time. *Stay. I can't deal with you now.*

I am doing holy work, something that can only be done

today. Her voice is gravelly, like the pumice stone she uses for her laundry. Above me, a man's smooth voice casts words but reveals nothing of the speaker's motives. I am seeing now how having a voice can be a disadvantage. It keeps others from going where they need to go. I need now to concentrate on Barabbas. I need to further the work Jesus began in him. To listen. To pray for the tea. To be a guide.

I forgive you.

Jesus once said to me that what we bind on earth is bound in heaven. A listener, however, can loosen, by the same mysterious power, things on earth that are unspeakable.

"A day is coming," Jesus also said, "when hell itself will be broken into and its captives released."

"A day?" I asked.

"You must be silent, Mary. Make use of every hour of that day. As above, so below."

I forgive you, I mouth again. This has been Barabbas's third confession. *Thanks be to God.*

I hear whispering above me. Some men have come halfway down the stairs to the landing. One of the voices is John. He is talking with Peter. No. He and Peter are describing to a third person how they went to the Monkey's house and saw Jesus on trial. I sense they are talking to James. Today is a day for stories. Yesterday, they became scattered, but today they reconnect their brotherhood. Each disciple must tell the others what they saw and did while Jesus was dying. I imagine that soon James will tell how he and Simon the Zealot and Thomas the giant came to Bethany after Jesus was arrested. John and Peter returned to the city. The others went around the northern wall until they found a distant place to watch their rabbi's death. They whisper it. They seek forgiveness.

John is telling how his father—yes, in this company, he is now willing to call Caiaphas his father—rejected him. John is afraid. He thought he could come back to Jerusalem with Jesus and find some kind of common ground between the men. After the trial, he went to the high priest. Typical of the man we call the Monkey, he rebuffed John's peace offer. I did not see this, but I am not surprised to hear of it now.

"I have only one friend in Jerusalem now," John says. "Malchus, the high priest's servant."

"The one whose ear I cut off?" Peter confesses.

In Peter's voice is sorrow—sorrow that is shifting, moving toward healing. I am glad to hear it. It has taken a full twenty-four hours for him to go from the shame he felt at failing to defend Jesus to feeling guilt for having taken a sword and done violence. Jesus always walked in the way of peace and expected his disciples to follow this same gentle path.

"If we stay in Jerusalem, then Caiaphas will arrest us all," John says now.

James tells John that he has more bad news. John's mother wasn't well when John left three years ago for Galilee. In fact, it is common knowledge in Jerusalem that she suffered from madness. She committed suicide on the eve of the winter solstice. In my dreams, I saw her fall. It was in the middle of the night. The next day, I told Martha and Lazarus.

I have been a fool. John is my friend. When he and Jesus came to raise my brother from the dead, I did not tell him about his mother's fall. In the week that followed, I began to speak of it a dozen times. I lacked courage. Yesterday, Martha spent the day with James. As they traveled Jerusalem's streets, she must have told him about John's mother. James and John pretend to be brothers, yet one has to wonder who they are hoping to deceive. James, the rough and simple Galilean fisherman, could never have been raised in the same family as John, the slender, quiet young man who, in spite of his efforts, cannot hide his Jerusalem accent. Their brotherhood is one of friendship, not blood.

James is gentle. He finds the words I lacked. He begins to tell the story of what happened to John's mother. He tells it slowly.

Suddenly, they stop.

Martha is there, asking about me. James tells her I am alone in the kitchen with Barabbas. He and John have to work to keep her quiet. My priestly duties are over. I wish I had more time. There will be only so many hours in this day.

James and John come with her into the kitchen. Martha has questions, but I have no answers for her. In the silence that follows, it is obvious to everyone that we are sisters.

I serve tea to James. He still has an unenviable task ahead of him. He has not mentioned that John's mother committed suicide.

"How did I not know?" John asks.

James tells how the whole affair was kept secret.

"Why? She was a noblewoman. She was the daughter of a high priest. Her acts of charity—"

"She hanged herself in the Monkey's kitchen," Martha says bluntly. "Tied a rope to the hook for hanging meat and stepped off the table."

My face is red. I hate my sister. Why are words given to those who don't know when to be quiet? If I were able to speak, I'd tell John how the women of Jerusalem came from every quarter and demanded the body. They washed it, anointed it with oil, and buried her with respect. They wept for her, because the men would not. In fact, the only man who came to the internment was Annas, John's grandfather. The old man was the high priest before the Monkey. The man came, even though it caused him to lose all respect in the council. The man came, even though his son-in-law forbade it.

If I were able to speak, I would tell John how long and valiantly this woman fought against the noon-day demon. I know a bit of that dull grayness. The demon's wet blanket has fallen on my life for weeks and months. This beautiful soul had it for years. John, I wish I could tell you that it wasn't grief for you that made her tie that rope. You are not responsible for this. No man is. The noon-day demon comes without invitation.

"I'm with you," James says. The big man has John buried in his chest. They weep together.

Softly, in another part of the room, I hear the other Mary —the one from Galilee, the mother of Jesus—talking to Joanna and Salome. She says, "This is the reason. Don't you see it? My son is on the cross, and he gives me to this man named John. Of all the disciples, this is the one who has room for me."

If I could speak and had the courage, I would add one more thing. When Jesus was being condemned, I was in a trance. I hovered above the holy city, my mind separate from my body. In this dream state, I saw Jesus carry his cross, winding slowly through the labyrinthine streets and the crowds. He brought healing to everyone he passed. When they raised him up on the cross, he extended his ministry to all the lost souls of the world. It was then that I saw John's mother. She was there in the cathedral of Jesus's healing work. Jesus went to John's mother and embraced her.

James says, "Jesus loves your mother. She is free now from those who hated her."

11

TELLING THEM WHERE TO GO

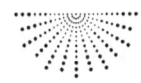

MARTHA

It is almost noon. I go downstairs to look for Lazarus and Mary. James, Peter, and John are in my way on the stairs. I find Mary and Barabbas seated at the table drinking tea. Incredible. Meanwhile, John is weeping.

"He's being too loud," I say.

Mary stands up and tries to bring me tea.

"No. You need to do something about John."

She brings the three men down to the kitchen. Why? Because it's the worst place to bring them. She sits them at the end of the table and offers John my tea. He takes it, but soon has his face buried in James's shoulder, muffling his moans. It is a small improvement.

"Where's Nicodemus?" I ask.

No one knows.

"Lazarus?"

Mary shrugs. She is still pretending to not speak. She points to the bump on her head. It looks better. I'm not buying her act.

Barabbas says, "They left out the front door. That's all I know."

"Together?"

"Yes."

"John has no reason to weep and many reasons to worry," I say. "We all do. Nicodemus is supposed to be teaching the men out in the courtyard. That's not his voice. He's left us. There are only few places for him within a Sabbath day's walk. One of them is the complex of the high priest."

They all nod.

Do something, I want to shout.

The kitchen around us is huge. Magnificent. It needs a good cleaning, though.

"Where would they be going?" I ask Mary again. "Any guesses?"

She pantomimes a large man.

"Thomas?"

She nods, and I am relieved. I want someone to find Thomas. Then the four of us can go home to Bethany and decide whatever is next for our lives.

"Let's hope they are discreet." I survey the kitchen. I am both envious and disgusted. All this room and yet nothing is laid out for the convenience of the cooks. They must cross here and there to make the meals. The simplest banquet would be chaos. If I had this much room, I know what I would do.

"There are things we could do while we wait for them," I say, looking at Barabbas. He turns his head away. *Yes. You remember me.* If I had been successful in the Fortress Antonia, he'd be dead on a cross by now. I failed. Jesus died, and Barabbas came here to begin his rehabilitation program. Work will be good for him.

"Can we trust him?" I say, pointing to Barabbas. Without meaning to, I feel my bag. *Yes, my money is still there.*

"Perhaps we should ask Simon to come down and watch him," James suggests.

"Have the fox guard the chicken coop?"

"Simon's not a Zealot anymore. Remember what he said last night?"

"No." I honestly don't.

"We were arguing about who was to blame."

"Blame?"

"For Jesus dying. You said Judas."

"Yes. Judas gave Mary that bump on her head too."

"But Simon said that the *am ha'aretz* were to blame. The Romans thought Jesus was another revolutionary. You villagers keep letting your sons go up into the hills to become Zealots. Simon said this was wrong. See. Simon's not a Zealot."

This is the longest string of words I've ever heard James put together.

"But Jesus is dead," I say. "I don't know why, but—"

"You do know." James smacks the table.

"No. I think it all got away from everyone. Mistakes were made . . ."

"You were there. Jesus died because the Romans mistook him for a Zealot. Martha, try to remember."

"I am trying. But one thing I've learned is that they can all be so . . . capricious—that's the word, isn't it?"

"No. It was almost noon—this time yesterday. We stood together outside the Fortress Antonia. And Pilate had been with Jesus a long time. Questioning him. What do you think the governor asked this Galilean that Herod had sent to him? Do you remember what Herod dressed Jesus up in? How he sent him to Pilate?"

"I saw he had something purple on. It was all tattered," I say this knowing it was a robe. Someone had whipped Jesus so that there were only shreds down his bloody back. "How should I know what was said behind closed doors?"

"Come on." James is in my face. This glutton was pathetic and weak yesterday. Now, he's changed. I wipe his spittle from my face. He goes on, "The governor had one question for

Jesus: 'Are you a king?' And Jesus—I'm sure about this—didn't defend himself. No, he probably said something about his spiritual kingdom. That was it."

"No, Jesus would know better than to use the word *kingdom* when he was being questioned. He'd be a fool."

"Jesus knew enough of our traditions and customs to ride a donkey through the Eastern Gate. He had us waving palms, like he was a Maccabean king."

"And he had a giant holding the donkey's reigns," Barabbas says. "You mustn't forget the effect a giant can have upon the crowds."

"Shut up," I say to Barabbas. The table goes quiet.

Then John speaks. "I know what Jesus said to Pilate. The same thing he kept saying to us. 'My kingdom is not of this world. If it were, I could call upon a thousand-thousand to defend me.'"

"Sounds like something a Zealot Messiah would say," Barabbas adds. "Boasting of troops in the hills while they make a cross for him and two friends out beside the old quarry."

"Okay, John," James says. "Tell Martha what Jesus said to us on that Sunday when he rode the donkey into Jerusalem. I volunteered to be his bodyguard, and you were beside me."

"He asked us if we could drink the cup of sorrows he was about to drink."

"I said we could," James says. "I spoke for you and Thomas and all of us. I knew he was talking about dying."

"Well, now that he's dead, we don't have to do that, do we?" I say.

Barabbas is the only one who nods his head in agreement with me. At least John has dried his eyes and stopped moaning.

"Are you still hiding from Caiaphas?" I ask him.

"Yes."

"Well, go somewhere else. I don't want you following

Mary to Bethany. We're only two miles from the Monkey. Go back to Galilee."

"Jesus told me to take his mother into my home," John says.

"Yes, I was there." That much I remember. "Did somebody give you a house?"

"No."

"Then you go live with that woman up north."

John looks like this hasn't occurred to him.

"Look," I say. "Nobody dying on a cross makes much sense. Maybe he got things confused. I don't think he intended for any of us to hang around here after he was gone."

"Caiaphas threatened me," John says to Mary.

"Ungrateful kids get that from time to time." I say this because John was an orphan. My father—may the Holy One smile gently on his soul—gave aide to Zealots fleeing the massacre at Sepphoris. They had an infant whose parents had been crucified. The child needed parents. And it was known that Caiaphas's wife was barren. Like Lazarus, our father had a sense of humor. He took the child from the Zealots and placed it in a basket upon that particular priest's doorstep. So like Moses in the bulrushes, John was found and raised by a leading family in the city. And yes, John might have found himself inheriting a home, if he hadn't left everything and followed Jesus.

"Well, you have a new mother now," I say, wishing the conversation to end.

Mary is leaning on John, mouthing to him that she will follow him.

"Stay with the bandit," I say to James and my sister. Then John comes upstairs with me.

12

CLOSING IN ON DEATH

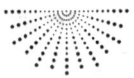

THOMAS

Thomas waits to die. More than most people in his situation, he has thought about death and even formed some cohesive ideas about life beyond death. Of course, having been a disciple of Jesus for three years and a friend of Lazarus for ten gives Thomas a leg up. Right now, he literally needs a leg up. The left leg, shattered and pinned under a boulder, no longer pains him. He takes this as a good sign. Death will come soon.

For the tenth time, he feels around the stone and estimates its dimensions—oddly shaped, though longer than his forearm in each dimension. Thomas guesses the stone weighs thirteen hundred pounds. Given the gentle grade beneath the stone and no obstructions, such as somebody's ankle, Thomas can picture himself putting his back into the stone and causing it to roll forward. That would require, however, approaching the project with two good legs firmly braced with rested muscles. He is a big man, scraping his head on the seven-foot-high doorways of Jerusalem's gates. Given this physical advantage, as well as a good eye for sizing an object's mass, density, and if it could become a usable chiseled block once squared, Thomas became a stonemason. This was a good choice

twenty years ago, for the lavish civic projects of the Herodians, especially the temple, meant job security for all engaged
in the building trades.

Now, he is going to die beneath a stone.

This stone is virgin limestone, untouched by hammer and
chisel, at least on the sides that Thomas can feel. A gift from
an angry god.

Thomas speaks into the eternal night. "Have you no
compassion?

Then he falls silent. He has lost too much blood. He is
cold, having spent thirty-eight hours below Jerusalem's
cobbled streets—far enough into the earth that the air is
always fifty-five degrees, the spring water flowing from Gihon,
much colder. Sensing the end to be near, he makes the appropriate chant:

Naked, I came into this earth.
I take nothing with me now.
Man's days are short
(even if he be a giant),
But you are eternal.
Have mercy.

Men are like grass,
Brittle and brown in the drought
Or fading before the winter wind.
I take now my last breath,
A shallow sigh.
Have mercy.

To THE UNINITIATED, DEATH AND SENSORY DEPRIVATION FEEL identical. Thomas's mind wanders back in time. His parents had wealth and servants. He hadn't spent his childhood learning a trade, but he wasn't lazy either. He had the gift of curiosity. He could spend an afternoon watching an anthill. He liked the order of the little insects. He observed how first several, then a platoon, then a full colony of workers would fall in and follow the trail laid down by a single scout. Working patiently, he led ants a half block from their home to reach a honey-coated stick.

At that age, there was no indication that Thomas was different. He fell in with the other boys of Sepphoris in the region of Galilee to study the Torah and prepare to accept the covenant of Abraham, Moses, and Elijah. It wasn't until he was almost a man that his deformity manifested itself. When the other boys stopped growing in their early teens, Thomas did not. People saw his size and expected him to be violent. His own father came to fear and distrust him. His own father made him an exile. From his sixteenth birthday, he was never seen in his birthplace again.

When we die, do we become children again? Thomas had reason to hope this was true. His friend Lazarus was more childlike after his short journey into the beyond. Not only was Lazarus quieter and less motivated, he seemed more willing to accept fantastic things. Something about this new Lazarus made Thomas want to follow him. So it was that he had entered this tunnel with Lazarus in the crazy hope that they might do something to save Jesus.

No man can save another man from his fate.

Shortly before his arrest, Jesus repeated his favorite nickname for Thomas. Jesus called Thomas his twin, even though Jesus was short and Thomas a giant. It was the kind of flip of expectations that was common for Jesus. Once, while the other disciples slept, Jesus had told Thomas that they would share the same death.

Crushed under stone, Thomas thinks. *Jesus, you will be tried by the Sanhedrin and found to be a blasphemer. They will take you out and throw stones at you until you die. Did you know that? Yes, so we both die the same way.*

Thomas lies with half of his body submerged in the cold water. If there were a gentle spring rain, the tunnel would fill and Thomas would drown. But he knows that isn't his fate. Like his Jesus, falling stones will do the deed.

Soon. It's incredible that I still breathe.

Knowing nothing else to do, Thomas names the people he loves in this world. His mother. Does she count? He doesn't know if she is still in this world.

"Lazarus. Martha."

He hesitates before saying, "Mary." He is still angry at her for suggesting they take this tunnel into the city.

He names his brother disciples.

"I should start with the least. Simon the Zealot. Levi the Tax Collector. Andrew. Nathaniel."

These last two haven't done anything to prove themselves worthy of being Jesus's disciples, other than living near Capernaum where Jesus began his ministry. Still, Thomas loves them. He wishes to say goodbye to them in person.

Ordering the list this way will, in time, lead to Judas Iscariot. What *does* he do with Judas? So he starts over. This time approaching it as he thinks his twin Jesus would do.

"First, there is John and James and Peter."

Here, he stops again, for the name Peter means *rock.* Jesus had given Simon bar Jonah that nickname to avoid confusion with the many other Simons they would encounter in their journeys. He already had a Simon who was once a Zealot, and in Bethany, they would eat at the home of a Simon who was once a leper. But *Petros*—rock—was a unique name, especially for a fisherman who didn't know how to swim.

"It seems we have too many rocks now," Thomas shouts in the tunnel.

The word *Peter* echoes back to him.

Thomas now remembers the day Peter got one of Jesus's questions right. It was a rarity. They were in Paneion, the farthest north Jesus ever took them. Everyone was nervous. This was a pagan shrine. It lay a full day north of the last Jewish town. Judas wasn't happy with the tolls they paid to be on the Roman road headed into the province of Syria. Jesus stopped to admire the temple to Caesar Augustus.

"Thomas, come here," Jesus said. "See this marvelous stonework."

They came to the sacred spring in a grotto. Every niche in the rock face held a statue to a false god. There was a throng of people there—pagan pilgrims who came to this spot from throughout the Roman world so they might drink the sacred waters that tumbled down around the green space. Jesus led them farther, ordering Judas to cast a coin into the palm of the gatekeeper. The walls of the grotto rose up, and it became a chasm. The voices of those worshipping in many languages became a loud roar as their chants echoed around the disciples. They went up all the way to where the water came out of the cleft in the rock.

"The water from here becomes the Jordan River. You all were baptized in that river by the Dipping Man." Jesus smiled and then asked his question: "Who do you say that I am?"

Watching the water flow out of the rock, Thomas said, "You are the new Moses."

"That answer is the safe one to give here," Jesus said. Then turning to the others, he said, "But if you were in Jerusalem, who would you say that I am?"

They each gave various answers.

But Peter said, "You are Messiah, the King of the Jews."

"Fool!" Thomas shouts before passing out.

13

MARTHA PLANS THE DAY

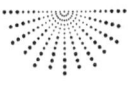

MARTHA

On the way up the stairs, I say to John, "If either you or Judas had an interest in Mary, you should have told her before this."

"It would have meant losing Jesus," John says.

I want to scream. Why are all men such idiots?

There are still people sleeping. It's noon. I wake them up. I get them packing their things. No one has much. The disciples have long strips of cloth they fold things into and use like belts. None of them have more than two copper coins, a seashell, a bit of Roman glass, a dried fig or stale cheese, trinkets. The women have cloth bags, except one girl. Hers is leather like mine. I'll have to ask her about it.

Mary, the Mother of Jesus, is awake. She greets John and tells him that she is reluctant to return to Galilee. From what I catch of the conversation, the little house in Nazareth is crowded. She has two other grown sons who haven't left home. They have made it clear that Jesus got what he deserved.

John asks Peter if Capernaum would be a better place to go.

I look at the two girls still lying on the floor. Their eyes are open—wary, like a deer that has been caught nibbling the herb garden in the center of the village at night. They look like twins. They shiver. Perhaps they are in shock. Someone has placed an expensive blanket over them.

"Who are they?"

"Don't you remember?" the lady in blue asks.

"I was busy with the meal," I say, even though I didn't cook and I didn't serve. Habit. But also a lie, because when I do cater a banquet or serve the Passover in Bethany, I listen to everything. Because I don't drink, I learn. But last night, I drank.

"Salome and Joanna."

I look around the room and notice how slowly everyone is moving. "You know, I've noticed something about Galileans. They drink."

"As if a man who's drowned needs to drink."

"We need to get our things together. We might have to leave before the Sabbath is over."

She nods and speaks to the girls. I return to the men.

"Look at the tables. Cups tipped over. Food going to waste." I point, and they shrug.

Jesus taught his men to be courteous to those who hosted them. I never had any complaints about them sleeping in my place. But now Jesus is gone. They also know that Nicodemus has servants.

"If you men wish to be helpful, then clean off the table. I'll take the serving bowls downstairs."

If only we could make this room look how it looked before the Passover. Remove all evidence that Jesus ever ate here with his men. Remove every trace of our sleeping here. Then maybe Nicodemus can clear his name and disavow any knowledge of the prophet from Nazareth. Maybe then the Monkey will go back to doing whatever it is that high priests do.

Maybe then Bethany will be forgotten, and we won't have to leave our home.

I CARRY THINGS DOWN AND UP. IT TAKES ME THREE TRIPS. Simon the Zealot explains how he found the body of Judas with a rope around his neck. Judas tried to hang himself from the window in the pinnacle tower and misjudged the strength of the rope belt James had loaned him. The rope broke, and he fell fifty feet into the Kidron Valley. His belly burst open. Simon had a hard time gathering the fallen man together. He had to drag Judas away before a patrolling guard found him. When suicides are discovered, even when they are not success-ful, the body is always hitched to an ass and dragged by one foot to Gehenna. Criminals also are thrown among the smol-dering fires of Jerusalem's dump.

"Jesus would have gone there, if not for Nicodemus," I hear myself saying. But I'm not grateful. I'm mad at Judas. "You should have left it to the authorities, Simon."

"So they could have ended up side by side," John muses.

"No!" Peter says. Too loud. We all hush him.

"Less talking, more packing," I whisper to the disciples.

Of all the disciples, only Simon the Zealot would have thought to save Judas from Gehenna. Simon has carried men off the field of battle. Combat and suicide are the same thing in my book. He took pity—misplaced pity, but pity.

"I took him by his long black hair. I dragged him into Absalom's Tomb," Simon says.

Peter groans at this. At some point this week, the disciples had been with Jesus near this tomb. It is famous. I don't know what Simon was thinking when he used it to hide a body.

"Remember what Jesus said about Absalom's Tomb," someone says.

They discuss it, recalling how it was Judas who had pointed it out to Jesus. The two of them had walked around it, admiring the perfect proportions and beautiful carved stone top that graces the tomb like one of the hats the Levites wear as they serve in the temple. When they rejoined the group, Thomas had to correct them.

"People have it wrong," Thomas said. "The tomb is empty, yes. But it wasn't made for Absalom. King David ruled a thousand years ago. This stone isn't that old. Its lettering is still crisp. It's Maccabean in style. Not from ancient times. Only a hundred and fifty years old, at most."

"Thomas knows stone," I say to them.

"But Jesus ignored his twin," John says. "Jesus was making a point. He wanted Judas to know that the pride he had in his long hair and his Jerusalem connections would lead to ruin. Absalom rebelled against his father. And Jesus said . . ."

John pauses, and they all stop their work. That John can remember things word for word is amazing, but it's not worth everyone stopping what they are doing.

"'Just as David had his beloved and trusted son rise up against him, so I will have one of my own rebel against me.'"

"Wasn't Absalom hanged by the neck in a tree?" Simon the Zealot asks.

"Maybe," I say. "But putting Judas's body in such a well-known place is still stupid."

14

MARK EXPLAINS WOMEN

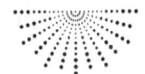

Even though things are not going as planned, John Mark expected to have a pleasant day. He has not gone far from the Jaffa Gate before encountering three of his uncles and two cousins. They are escaping the crowded tenement. Everyone living in the Ophel knows that going to the Jaffa Gate and back is the limit. It is as far as one is allowed to walk on a Sabbath day.

"John Mark, why are you not at the feet of your rabbi?"

"He sent me off to look for a giant."

"Maybe he's looking for a way to get rid of you."

"I don't think—"

"You should consider yourself lucky. Worse things have happened to our people. Did you hear what happened to Simon from Cyrene yesterday?"

There is a well nearby. They sit on its wall. It being the Sabbath, no women are in their way, so they have time to rest and talk. John Mark had not heard about his relative's misfortune.

"The Romans made your uncle Simon carry a cross."

Simon is a common name and the word *uncle* could be used to describe any relative, no matter how distant. In this case, the man wasn't even a resident of the Ophel or a member of the immigrant community there. Some Jews had remained in Libya and other regions of North Africa while Mark's family went east, first to Alexandria and then here to Jerusalem. This Simon was a pilgrim from Cyrene, here for this week to observe the festival.

"Three Zealots were crucified yesterday. You were ill or you would have encountered them. They marched the convicted men through all the streets of the city, and the first two made it out the Jaffa Gate to the old stone quarry without any problems."

John Mark nods. He's smart enough to guess what comes next.

"Those two were rugged bandits, you see. They had been living off the land for years. Hanging on the cross was like a Sabbath's day for them. But this third guy . . . I hear that he wasn't really a Zealot at all."

The other men debate this until the youngest of the cousins, a boy of ten, speaks up.

"Jesus the Nazarene was a rabbi from Galilee."

The older men brush this aside.

"Tell me about this," Mark whispers to the boy.

Jesus doesn't interest them. They were in the fields working when he entered the city riding a donkey. Their sympathies lie with the man from their homeland. They enter into a heated discussion about who this Simon was related to.

"Rufus," one says with authority.

The Romans can be capricious. Darker-skinned people like themselves always get picked for compulsive duties. Africans are often pulled aside at the gate in the morning as they are going out to the fields and made to carry stone all day. The Romans always have a road they are building or an aqueduct that needs repairing. Two weeks ago, they were all pulled from their beds to fight a fire in wealthy quarter of the city.

"I need to be going. Rest well," Mark says. With a nod, he invites his youngest cousin to join him. The streets are crowded because of the holiday, and he is able to ask again about Jesus.

"Your mother . . . Ask her." The boy sways back and forth. He is only eighteen months younger than Mark, but his family has more recently arrived in Jerusalem. They are staying at Miriam's until, perhaps years from now, they can find somewhere else.

Mark hurries him along. "If you tell me what you know, I'll show you a trick."

"Where?"

"Near the temple. Tell me, what does Jesus have to do with my mother?"

"Hasn't she told you?" The boy says this with a note of judgment. Mark is of age, and with his father gone, he should exercise some leadership in the household.

"Told me what?"

"You've seen the women that come Sunday afternoons?"

"I go to study every day. Why would I care about my mother's friends?" Mark says.

"Rabbi Jesus was at your house last Sunday."

"No, he was in the temple. Caused some trouble there. Are you sure?"

"I saw him."

"Was he with a giant?"

The boy shrugs.

"You'd know if you saw him. Besides, why would a man from Galilee come to the Ophel?"

"Invited? No. Maybe hiding." The boy is becoming cautious. "I think it has something to do with the witch. You know the woman from Magdala who used to . . ."

"A witch?"

"Oh, I just call her that because she has green eyes and red hair. There's a white streak that runs down one side." The boy points from the crown of his head, down past his left ear. "Her name is Mary."

"What do either of them have to do with my mother?"

"Your mother says that Mary of Magdala followed this Jesus for a year up north and he made her a rabbi."

"Women can't be rabbis."

"They can be teachers of other women."

"And if a blind man leads a blind man, they both will fall into the pit."

The boy looks at Mark blankly. Obviously, he has not had the benefit of being schooled by the great Nicodemus.

"Nicodemus says women cannot be trusted because it was a woman who was tempted by the serpent in the Garden of Eden." Mark puts up one finger, reciting a familiar lesson.

"But he was right there beside her."

"Who—Jesus beside this Mary?"

"No. Adam was right beside Eve when the serpent spoke to them in the garden."

Mark stops. He closes his eyes. People pass around them on the busy street. He has to remember the passage from Genesis word by word. He starts in the beginning. The lines of tight Hebrew text flow by in his mind. Yes, Adam was there and said nothing. Mark opens his eyes and puts up a second finger.

"And women cannot handle the holy scriptures because they bleed each month and are swayed toward madness by the changing face of moon."

"All of them? Even those who do not have children? Or the ones who are old, like your mother?"

"And that leads us to the third reason. The Holy One gave to women the ability to bear children. They alone can suckle an infant. They alone can teach us how to speak and walk in a natural way. If they also were given the gift of spiritual discernment, then what would be left for men to do? As it is, women can devote their entire attention to the house. Men can rest on the Sabbath and read the scriptures. While they work in the field, they can mull over the word of God. As an ox chews its cud, so a man discerns the hidden things of the spiritual world."

"Rabbi Mary says, 'As a woman kneads the leaven into the dough until it raises the whole loaf, so the spirit of God is hidden in the hearts of both men and women. This is the way that leads to peace.'"

"Instead of spying on the women, you should be out in the fields helping our uncles. You are old enough."

"Next year, I will go with you to learn from Nicodemus," the boy says defiantly. "That's if I don't find that Rabbi Mary is a better teacher."

"Fool."

"Hey, I thought you were going to teach me a trick."

"Have you told me everything you know about Jesus and the women?"

The boy acts as if torn. For many weeks, he has been keeping this secret. He has gone out and helped with the spring planting. But on Sundays, he has stayed home, claiming that his mother needs him. Actually, Mary has begun to teach him how to read.

They are nearing their destination. Ahead is a knot of pilgrims lining up to ascend the grand stairs to the temple courts. Even though it is Sabbath, the Levites are still singing. Pilgrims are still invited to file once more by the beautiful temple. It is as if an extra grace day has been added to the end of the festival. How fortunate they are. The smell of roasting lamb hangs in the air. Because of the record crowds, the final sacrifice was made after dark.

"No laws are being broken," Caiaphas had said to his aides who begged him to let the priests rest. "When there is a windfall at harvest time, the wise farmer works until it is in the barn and is thankful."

"It's just up there. Tell me what you know or I won't show you my trick."

"The women believe that this Jesus is Messiah."

"Was. A dead man can't be a king. So they won't be meeting tomorrow?"

The boy shrugs and then nods. Until this moment, he had not thought how the death of Jesus might affect Rabbi Mary and his opportunity to learn to read.

"This Mary will go back to Magdala."

"No. She doesn't live up north. She lives in Bethany with her brother, Lazarus the leather merchant."

Mark groans. "What else do you know?"

The boy shakes his head, as if there was nothing more to tell.

"Good. Watch. Tell me everything."

"Why?"

"Because our house is in danger. Your witch has been a thorn in the high priest's side for the past year. Then two weeks ago, Jesus and the people of Bethany conspired to play a trick on the pilgrims. Lazarus pretended to be dead and Jesus pretended to bring him back to life. And now you tell me that Jesus and the witch came to my house to hide out a few days before his arrest?"

"No. The witch . . . Rabbi Mary wasn't there. Only Jesus and his men. They were hungry. Our mothers gave them food."

Mark groans again.

"Why are you groaning? I was the one who had to fetch water for all of them. I had to clean up when they left so the men wouldn't suspect anything as they came in from the fields."

"So you've had some practice at keeping secrets? You don't mind deceiving our uncles?"

The boy's face turns red.

"No. This is a good thing. You are young and you haven't

learned this yet, but knowledge is everything. If I know a secret and you don't, I have something over you. Women are easily fooled. That's why we must watch them. Sometimes, men can be tricked, if they aren't aware of what is really going on. Observe everything. Reveal only what you need to."

The boy nods.

"You see those pilgrims over there?"

"The ones who are throwing coins down the shaft?"

"Yes. Do you think I can get them to do something different?"

"Like what?"

"How about if we pick a name and the pilgrims start shouting that name down the shaft instead of pitching coins? What name should we pick?"

"Simon? Or John?"

Mark nods as if those are good suggestions, then says, "We should pick something less common. That way we'll know it's the trick that's working. I know. How about Thomas?"

Mark is gifted at languages. Having already noted where each group of pilgrims are from, he greets them in their own language. He then explains that there is a benevolent spirit of the deep named Thomas. Good luck can be found by calling his name in this place. This makes more sense to the pilgrims than throwing money away.

15
A BOWL OF WATER

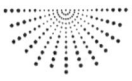

MARTHA

My father taught me many things. A saying for every situation. *"Sleep with your bag packed and near. You never know when you'll be sent into exile," "Rest when you're dead,"* and *"Rest when you shouldn't and you may end up dead."*

So it's afternoon, and I'm wondering what more can be done. Worrying about Lazarus and Thomas won't bring them back any sooner. Is there anything more we can do that will put us in a safer position? I've already explored the back door out into the alleyway. It is under the stairs and across from the kitchen. Easy to miss. Some of us could escape that way, if we saw them coming through the courtyard door.

From the balcony, I can look down into the courtyard. The men are listening to some teacher drone on. I can only see some of them, though. I hear, but don't see, the fountain in the courtyard. Its burbling is more enlightening than this man's wisdom.

I return to the table. There is a large bowl of water. I don't know why it is there. I don't remember . . . Who puts a bowl of water on the table like this? It could ruin the finish.

I touch the water, and a bit of last night returns to me. I remember where we each sat. I think Mary brought the bowl out at the end of the meal. Should I get rid of it? When Mary brought the bowl to the table, we all watched her. She couldn't speak, but Lazarus whispered to me, "Remember the Dipping Man."

He was talking about the wilderness prophet named John, who baptized people. I never went out to see him. Lazarus did. He said that the baptism affirmed God's love for the common people. Lazarus spoke of seeing the rich putting aside their fine clothes and entering the muddy Jordan River, tax collectors were told to make restitution to those they had cheated, and soldiers left their swords in order to be pushed under and reminded that they had no more power than any other mortal. Anyone who disrupts the authority of kings and priests the way the Dipping Man did is bound to lose their head. Now, like the Dipping Man, Jesus is dead.

When I found Lazarus yesterday, he was dripping wet.

"I've been swimming," he said.

No. He didn't say swimming. He said that strange word that they use for what the Dipping Man does. He said, "I've been *baptized*."

I asked where.

He said, "In the Pool of Siloam, where Hezekiah's tunnel empties."

I looked to Mary. I thought they were kidding me, like they always do. *Slow Martha. Tell her a joke on Friday, and she'll laugh on the Sabbath.*

I didn't laugh. The Pool of Siloam is for wealthy pilgrims who are preparing to enter the temple. If a leather merchant from Bethany dips there, they'll stone him for ruining their sacred ritual bath.

"Foolish Lazarus," I said. "You'll catch your death . . ."

As we dust, I say to Jesus's mother that the wine we

have in Bethany is weak and we mix it two to one with water from our well.

"Why not?" I say. "Our well is good. Sweet. Not bitter like Kerioth, to the south. Water costs us nothing. But grapes barely grow on the edge of the desert. Half of those that set on our precious vines get gleaned by the passing pilgrims on their way up to the temple."

"You'll have to come to Galilee sometime," Jesus's mother says. "The vines are abundant. Wine is plentiful."

I am amazed at this woman. She just lost her son, and yet she seems at peace.

"My aunt Rachel oversees Bethany's wine making. She should relinquish this task to someone younger. Then she could actually leave Bethany. She isn't happy . . ."

"Oh?"

"Aunt Rachel is as shrunken as a forgotten grape in the winter," I say, because I've heard Lazarus speak about her this way.

"She has reason to be bitter?"

"Don't all *am ha'aretz* who live this close to Jerusalem have reason to be bitter?" I ask this, even though Rachel doesn't resent the wealthy Hasmoneans the way I do. She rejoiced to see Simon the Leper move to our village. And yet she has more reason than any of us to hate them.

"Tell me why Rachel is bitter."

"Thirty-three years ago, when winter had turned to spring, the Herodian named Archelaus ascended to the throne, his father's reign finally ended—only forty years too long."

"I remember those kings well," she says. "I gave birth to Jesus that year." She nods her head to the south, and that surprises me. She is from Galilee, and she doesn't look that old.

"The people of Bethany did not greet the new Herodian king joyfully. My father was in Jerusalem with Lazarus. People were in the city streets, shouting their support of a contender for the throne. My father had loaded a donkey with palm branches—a sign that someone of Maccabean descent should become king of the Jews, instead of these Idumean foreigners —and Lazarus, only a toddler then, rode on it."

"So they were in the city."

"It saved Lazarus's life."

"How?"

"The road the new king took up from Jericho to Jerusalem passes by Bethany. Only a few elderly men lined the road to greet him. Archelaus stopped his royal procession. He asked where the men of the village were. Our uncles were silent. He asked where the women were. And the elderly men said that they were with a woman named Rachel, who had just given birth to a son."

Jesus's mother flushes, trembling. I'm not going to go on. What if she has a fit? This is the wrong story to tell her after she just lost her son. But she nods that I should go on. Her hand takes my hand.

I continue, "I, too, was with Rachel. Mary was only a few months old and in my arms. Our mother—did you know?— died in childbirth. I was twelve and glad to have learned our village's birthing songs. Archelaus's soldiers came into the house. They had no shame. They first took Mary and saw that she was a girl. Then they went to Rachel's bed and took the child from her."

Jesus's mother begins to sing, long and sweet.

Rachel, Rachel, weeping for her child.
Rachel, Rachel, never to be comforted.

Her song grows louder, with no care for the men worshipping in the courtyard.

For her only child, is no more.

Then she goes to the table and swirls her hand through the water in the bowl.

"Our tears," she says.

"Yes, it was this time of year," I say, because I don't know what else to say. "The soldiers went through all the houses of our village, taking whatever they wanted. Then they went on to raid the neighboring towns. They even went as far as Bethlehem, four miles away."

"I know," she says.

I feel ashamed. I always go to stay with Rachel on the Sabbath after Passover. We sit silently with her and remember. Yes, it is the one day of the year I do no work. Today, instead of being with her, I am stuck here.

"Go on."

"Rachel's husband left her soon after that. He went to join the resistance. Rebels, even back then. Maybe every land has them."

"Yes. Only a few miles from Nazareth, the Zealots made the city of Sepphoris their stronghold. They had enough men and weapons to defeat any local army. The Herodians did then what Herodians do to maintain their power. Young King Antipas, who took hold of the north, called upon the Romans. Nothing resists a Roman legion. And when the walls fell and the Zealots surrendered, the Roman General Varus had crosses planted on the road between Sepphoris and Magdala —every few yards, both sides, men and women. We passed by their bodies when we returned from Egypt."

John comes over to stand beside us. He holds this woman in his arms.

"That is why, when the Herodians rebuilt Sepphoris, my husband, Joseph, refused to work there. Other carpenters were being paid well. We remained poor. And Jesus followed in his father's footsteps."

I look over and see Simon the Zealot watching us.

"I try to stay out of it," I say. "Rachel and I do all that we can to keep Bethany free of politics. To me, Zealots are just bandits."

He nods. I feel, though, that I must say one more thing about the past. "Rachel's husband went to fight with them and never returned. Back then, the Zealots were only killing the elites. Jerusalem's nobility sticks together. Even those not related to the Herodian family acted like they were. This what we say in Bethany: 'Zealots are like the lions that harry the sheep.' The lions make the sheep stronger by eating their weak and slow. In Jerusalem, all noble families pretend to be Herodian so they don't look weak. They don't want to be the lone straggler the Zealots pick off."

"Well said," Simon agrees.

"And that is why I have a broken chain decorating my bag." I show this Zealot logo to him. "No, I don't support the Zealots, but I do understand why they fight."

"Your bag is beautiful," Jesus's mother says.

"It is who I am. I am this bag. I always have what I need to be self-sufficient. I'm never without handwork to do. I keep busy. I keep prepared. Coins for a meal or a bribe. And my story is told in its stitches."

16

A FREE MAN

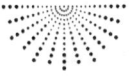

THOMAS

"Peter."

Thomas names a few more people and then falls asleep. In his dream, he is free. The darkness has given way to the midafternoon sun. Thomas looks around and realizes that he knows this place, even though he hasn't been here in years. It is a quarry he used to pick through looking for stone to make ossuaries—stone boxes in which the rich of Jerusalem place the bones of their ancestors. The quarry had long ago run out of its vein of building stone. What remained was of little use, except for small projects. Thomas sees himself rummaging through the scrap pile.

I look younger, he thinks.

Jesus appears. "What are you looking for?"

"Stone to make a box," Thomas hears himself reply. Then he holds up his arm, motioning from the tip of his left hand to his elbow. "About this long."

"A giant's cubit?" It's the kind of thing Jesus would say. This is where dream and reality collide, for before he left to go north, Thomas had a commission. The wealthy family of Joseph Caiaphas wanted an ossuary. Thomas never found the right stone. He left the job unfulfilled. Then he found Jesus.

"What about this one?" Jesus points to a rock that is about the same size as the one that now pins Thomas's leg.

"I don't know how to move it," Thomas says.

Jesus picks it up easily. Then he puts it down and says, "I'll teach you."

Jesus motions him to stand and follow. Going a little ways, Jesus points to the ground. Three holes have been dug into the stone. Thomas knows why. The Romans have begun to use the old quarry for crucifixions. Simon the Zealot once described it to him. They make a post hole, attach their victim to a wooden cross, and drop the cross into the hole.

"That's where I died," Jesus says. "Come."

They walk a dozen more yards until they come to where a new grave has been hollowed into the limestone. The great gravestone lies aside. Thomas follows Jesus inside.

They walk for a while into the cave. Jesus has found a torch and lit it. Thomas hears voices ahead. Muffled cries. Some are moaning. Others are repeating senseless phrases. *I know I am right. I told her a thousand times. When will it be lunch? One can't have enough . . .*

"There is no music in hell," Jesus says.

"The dead have no hope," Thomas says in agreement.

They come at last to a great locked gate. The ironwork reaches to the ceiling a hundred feet above them. Jesus produces a set of keys, inserts one into the lock, and swings the door open. At the sound of the door moving on its hinges, the voices below cease. Jesus hands his keys to Thomas.

"What are these?"

"The keys to heaven and hell. Whatever you bind on earth will be bound in heaven, and whatever you loose on earth will be loosed in heaven."

Thomas awakes. He is in great pain. His left leg erupts as if on fire.

He reaches down and finds that the stone is gone. His

hands can now reach down to feel the shattered bones that once were his kneecap. Freedom brings pain, but it also sparks hope.

Inch by inch, he scoots back up the tunnel.

For a brief hour, hope fights with pain and wins.

17

VISITING THE FUTURE

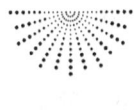

MARY

My sister is sweeping the kitchen. It is good to see her quiet. She has Barabbas with her, moving things. It is Sabbath for another hour. She is confined. She can't sing as she works, like she usually does. Barabbas repeatedly whispers that they must be quiet until Joseph has stopped teaching and the last man has left the courtyard. He is more patient than I would be. James and John have come to join me as I sit halfway down the stairs. From here, we can see into the courtyard, but not all of it.

I have chosen this step carefully. It is my job to keep a watch on all three parties—the friends of Jesus upstairs, Martha and Barabbas in the kitchen, and the men gathered for worship in the courtyard. A high window at the end of the hall brings light and air in from the courtyard into the main part of the mansion. From this step, I glimpse heads nodding as Joseph teaches. He drones like an old ox, ruminating the Torah. He is sitting so I can't see him. I have been counting his crowd, though. Every so often, one stands up and bows, makes some excuse and heads out the great door that leads to the street. Soon, Joseph will be down to ten, and he'll have to stop.

"Why would a Pharisee skip worship?" John asks. "I recognize the voice of the man who is teaching—not Nicodemus, but Joseph of Arimathea. A poor substitute. The men look bored."

I smile. Jesus has spoiled us. We can't imagine sitting still for another teacher. Until last night, John was pretending to be a Galilean fisherman. Now, he has dropped the fake accent. He speaks like a native of this city. I can see he's planning to stay in Jerusalem, even though it will be dangerous for him.

The work in the kitchen stops. I hear my sister interrogating Barabbas. There is a mutter—something indistinguishable. Only the tone reaches us. She speaks a long threatening sentence. He gives a one-word reply.

John goes down to where the stairway turns. He leans, listening.

"She doesn't believe him," John whispers. "'You watched them go. What were they saying?'"

Barabbas wasn't paying attention. He has no idea why a merchant and a Pharisee would roam the streets on the Sabbath. I know, but I can't say. It would be too complicated to pantomime that they have gone to see where Jesus is buried. A fool's errand. The guards won't let them even get close. Pontius Pilate gave an order. No amount of money can bribe a Roman soldier to disobey the governor. But they must try, for Jesus is lost without a friend to call him out from *Sheol*.

Martha is anxious. Poor Martha. She doesn't know how to rest and wait.

"She's telling him to move the woodpile. Sweep underneath it. Then restack the wood. Neatly."

John returns and sits with James on the step above me. James has been thinking.

"If Thomas survived the earthquake, I don't think he'd stay in Jerusalem."

I nod in agreement. It may be that the reason I have such

a hard time seeing him is because he has already left. James and John were with me when Martha asked about Thomas.

"Does he live?" she asked, knowing that I see things other people don't.

I made a balancing motion with my hands. I meant that things could go either way.

She read it as an encouraging sign. "If he isn't dead now, then he will live."

"And he wouldn't go to Bethany," James says now.

"Why not?" John asks.

"He knows that Judas betrayed all of us. He is a wanted man, just like Lazarus. The high priest remembers how Thomas helped Jesus scare the money changers out of the temple last Sunday. Going to Bethany would just make it easier for Caiaphas to kill two birds with one stone. Thomas will go north."

"But won't Thomas stay somewhere near to wait for the rest of us?" John asks.

"Yes, that is what I was thinking. He knows where to look for us."

"Not here?"

"No. Emmaus. The cave, just off the road north."

John and I nod. James is smarter than he looks. There is a cave Jesus used as a safe camping place seven miles from the city. It is far enough not to be watched by the temple guards. A year ago, Jesus sent me home to Bethany, having brought his disciples as far south as Emmaus. It is where Thomas would wait to reconnect with his friends.

I catch a little glimpse. As is often the case, visions don't give clear answers. I see James and Lazarus and someone else walking to Emmaus. I see them breaking bread and giving thanks. It is a hopeful vision. How do I share it?

They leave me. They want to go upstairs and consult with the others. Simon the Zealot thinks it is a ridiculous idea. As does Peter. John consults Jesus's mother and then returns to say that the women are not ready to leave the city yet. There is more. Then silence. Then James says that he will go alone to Emmaus.

I resume my lonely watch on the step. Joseph drones on. Martha sweeps as Barabbas moves the wood from corner to corner. I close my eyes and let my inner vision roam the streets. There's something interesting. A young man. He is the same one I saw spying on the disciples Thursday night as Jesus led the Passover meal. Now, too, he is up to no good. He has told the pilgrims near the temple stairway that if they yell Thomas's name into the shaft that joins the tunnels under the temple mount, it will bring them good luck. Now, he and the boy with him are laughing at the foreigners behind their backs.

A temple guard has hold of him. He thinks their behavior is suspicious.

"Who are you?" the temple guard asks.

"My name is Gershon," this boy lies. "We are strangers here. We don't mean any offense. We just find your customs odd. Who is this Thomas that is being called for?"

"He is a known troublemaker," the guard replies.

MARTHA EMERGES FROM THE KITCHEN. SHE GOES BY ME AND finds James and John in the room above.

"You must be hungry. If you come quietly, I will feed you."

I follow them to the table. I have no problem being quiet. Martha sets cheese and figs and grapes before them, then sits beside me. Obviously, something is on her mind.

"Do you still interpret dreams? I'm troubled by what the drink made me dream."

What can I say?

"Good." She takes my silence as agreement.

"I dreamed there was this dismal city—a city where it might be always winter. No sign of the spring day we have here today. Damp and gray. It had a wall around it. Then on top of the wall, where you expect there to be a flat space for the sentry to walk, they had made their wall narrow. And they had planted thornbushes, except the thornbushes were black and did not bend in the wind. The wind was cold, and I wanted to leave this place—for I knew they were killing people like us within that city."

Martha looks at me. There is more, but she wants to make sure that I understand this much and am taking her seriously. People who do not have frequent visions the way I do are frightened when it unexpectedly happens to them, but this sounds like a dream that would frighten even me.

"I say *they* because I didn't know these men. They were outside the wall and inside the wall, always looking mean. It was as if they meant to herd all of humanity within their city and then slaughter us like cattle."

I nod.

"Instead of spears, they had in their hands iron clubs. And when they wanted to hurt someone, they didn't have to come near them. No. They stood off and raised the club to their shoulder, made a noise, and the man or woman, or once I saw them doing it to a child, whoever they pointed their club at fell dead."

There are tears in Martha's eyes. John sits near us. He wants to comfort her, but she turns back to me.

"Mary, am I seeing something from the past? Something that happened before Noah? Back before God cleansed the earth through the great baptism of the flood? Back when men were truly evil? Or is this something that is yet to happen?"

John is about to speak. I wave him off.

"Then there was a line of people were being marched into the city," Martha continues. "They looked like refugees of some coming war. They were hungry and cold. Their odd clothes hung dirty and damp."

She stands to look out the window, confirming to herself that here, today, it is still spring.

"And in the pitiful crowd, I saw a familiar face. It was Jesus. He looked at me, then pointed to the gate he was about to go through and enter the city. 'You will die,' I said to him.

"'I have died,' he said to me. '*Shalom*. My peace I give to you. Not as the world gives it. *Shalom*. Peace.' And then he passed under the gate of this city. Soon, he was lost in the crowd, and I remembered once more that I just saw him on a cross."

I nod. I hold her hand and mouth that she isn't crazy. This dream feels very much like the vision I had when Jesus was being crucified. Wherever there is suffering, Jesus is there. Our people have suffered and will suffer again. The gray men Martha saw are no different from our current Romans or the Seleucids our ancestors suffered under.

"They went through the gate, and he pointed up, begging me to read what was written there. It was in a strange language, and I could not read . . . cannot read—" Martha stops.

I turn her head toward me. This is important. I know it. I look into her eyes. Deep in the darkness, I see letters.

Quickly, I run downstairs to the kitchen table where I take a handful of flour and let the powder fall. I transcribe the message letter by letter into the flour.

John shakes his head. "I don't know these letters."

I write below it, word by word, using the Greek that John knows.

"Do you want me to tell Martha that?" John asks.

I shake my head, but Martha says, "Tell me."

He reads, "Through work, freedom."

We see her taking in each word in her literal way. I pray for her to see it as a lie. The gray men had built this city of death. To make it a complete hell, they had to add this lie: *Through work, freedom.* It would be the last thing our people would read before entering the city. They would labor, but they would not be free. And now Jesus goes with them under that sign.

Martha laughs.

"That Jesus," she says. "He's still messing with my mind. Every time he was in Bethany, he told me not to work so hard. Now he's gone. And he comes in my dream and says, 'Through work, freedom.' No. That isn't him. That's me. Dreams, who can believe them? They're just foolishness."

After that, Martha wipes the table clean and leaves us. She has food to take to the others.

I spread the flour again and write the Greek words, *Through work, freedom.* I point to the word *work.* I then point my index finger into the palm of my right hand. I do the same with the other hand and spread my arms wide. I bow my head, my hands still wide, then I take his hand and guide it to make a stabbing motion on my side.

"Jesus?" John asks. "You mean his work was to die?"

I nod.

"So now Jesus is free?"

I shake my head. Jesus was always free. Doesn't John know that? I point to his chest. To my chest. To Barabbas. I point upstairs to the others. They hadn't been at the cross, so they watch my pantomime with curiosity.

"Oh. His work was to die and set all of us free," John says.

Yes. Yes. I see it in a flash. John will tumble this one thought like a stone made smooth in the sea. He will outlive us all. When he is old, he will write another account of Jesus. In it, Jesus won't look like a failed Messiah who made the mistake of getting himself crucified. John will take Jesus's painful pilgrimage through Jerusalem and polish it into a gemstone for the soul. He will tell how Jesus did his work on Friday with intention and grace. John will write, and the world will read. I can't imagine how the story of Jesus will be of any interest to a future generation. But I see my friend very old. I see him bent over the page. Writing in the smallest of Greek letters. Line upon line.

There are many books in the world. It does not need another one, John. But the world will want this one.

RECRUITING A SPY

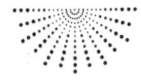

MARK

L ater, Mark tells his cousin what he really needs.

"We need someone to watch the women while the men are out in the fields and I am studying at the house of Nicodemus."

"Spy? I'm not a spy."

"You listened in on the women when you weren't supposed to. Don't be offended. I appreciate what you've done. When the men are away, someone has to keep an eye on things."

"But . . . it's wrong."

"It's wrong to get caught. I was like you when I first came to the city," Mark confides. "I observed things that I knew were not right. Secret things that, if told, would get good people in trouble. Some things are best left unsaid. Don't mention my mother's friend Mary. Don't ever speak of this Jesus the Nazarene again. He is dead, and our family doesn't know his people. You understand?"

The boy nods slowly.

"If this Mary comes back, you need to tell me."

"Why?"

"Because I think that Rabbi Nicodemus may have been

deceived by Lazarus the leather merchant. He continues to trust him, even though Jesus is dead. Caiaphas will find out soon. Not everyone in the city wants our people to be here. Listen to what is said on the streets. They do not want people from Africa becoming full residents of Jerusalem. If Lazarus gets arrested and Nicodemus is tied in with the same mess . . . It could be bad news for all of us."

"Why?"

"Because Nicodemus is our patron. He and Uncle Barnabas have made a way for our people here. And . . ."

"What?"

"Mary is a witch. Besides, many of the great heroes of our scriptures were spies."

"Who?"

"Joseph, the son of Israel, was sent by his father to spy on his brothers."

"Yes, but his brothers hated him for it."

"That's how he became a hero. His brothers would have killed him, but a caravan appeared and they decided to sell him into slavery instead. Joseph became a slave in Egypt."

"Mark, you always want us to go back to Egypt. Do you want to be a slave like Joseph?"

"No. I want to help my people like he helped his. I don't want us immigrants to be looked down on."

"And being a spy helps with this?"

"Being observant helps. Don't take anything at face value. Everyone has a secret. Until you discover it, you can't understand their motives. You are vulnerable. The people who rule this city all have secrets. Until we discover why they do what they do, we are always at their mercy."

"So you want me to spy for you?"

"I want you to grow up. Not embarrass our family. Blend in to this city. But most of all, be observant."

They have come now to the great western wall of the temple complex. Here is a trench, and his cousin leans over to see if he can spit and have it reach the bottom. The trench allows the pilgrims to see down to the foundations of the temple area. Far below the street, one can see the rough stones that Solomon laid to support the small flat courtyard around the temple he was building. Then as centuries passed, the rubble of city life raised the street level of Jerusalem. The second temple courtyard was laid by Zerubbabel. It can be seen as a layer of gray blocks rising a yard above Solomon's foundation. These stop a yard below where Mark and his cousin stand. Forty years ago, Herod the Great laid a new set of foundation stones, massive in size. From the quarry just west of the city, he hauled stone and squared the blocks until each one was the size of a room in Mark's house.

Mark says, "We are not here to look at the buildings but to watch the people. Thousands of people are going up to hear the Levites sing Sabbath prayers in the temple courts. But only a dozen men huddle in that house."

He points now to the simple home of Gamaliel. Already, men are leaving.

"Rabbi Nicodemus is often able to keep his minyan in place until the sun is ready to set. I don't think this teacher will fare as well."

"Why?"

"We should observe and find out."

Soon, a pattern emerges. A young man would ask a question of the rabbi, saying, "What do you think of . . ." And the old man would stroke his beard and say, "Your question is in . . ." Then a boy would be asked to fetch this scroll or that from the back room. Everyone waits. Often the wrong scroll is brought. An hour of this is all Mark or his cousin can stand.

"I thought you said Gamaliel is a great teacher."

"He is. He has accumulated more scrolls than anyone else in Jerusalem. He knows where the answers lie. However, no one has the patience to be taught by him."

"Except for you, John Mark," a voice says.

The boys are startled. The voice belongs to their relative Barnabas.

"Uncle," Mark says respectfully. "I thought you did Sabbath at Rabbi Nicodemus's house."

"I do. But today Joseph of Arimathea is leading the discussion. It's like watching a cow chew its cud."

"Gamaliel is not much better," the cousin says.

Barnabas shakes his head. "Do you suppose I would hear anything more interesting at your mother's house?"

Mark shrugs. "If you go there, tell my mother I have been given an errand to do and may not be home tonight."

"Work? On the Sabbath?"

"Oh. No, I'm looking for a man who was injured and seems to be lost."

"Was he hit on the head?"

"If he was, that would explain why he's so hard to find."

19

THE BIRTH CANAL

THOMAS

Thomas travels as far as he can up the tunnel. In the darkness, the only indication he is indeed moving in the right direction is that the water moves in the opposite way. He is weary. Each inch a struggle. Each movement freshens his pain. But he has never been one to quit. He has carried stones that others thought impossible to lift. He has tackled problems that more experienced builders gave up on. He knows how to tear down and reconstruct walls without damaging adjacent structures. The job of surviving an earthquake in Hezekiah's tunnel is no different. He must get to the secret entrance to the tunnel Lazarus had shown him beneath the pool where women did their laundry.

"Gihon," he says the name of the place into the darkness. "Gihon, Gihon." He repeats it three times, allowing himself to imagine it to be the magic word that opens an invisible door.

Thomas, Thomas, the echo comes back, warped beyond recognition.

The women are saying my name as they do their chores.

This is impossible, and he knows it. How could their voices dip beneath the water? Sound is not like clothing. It can't be pushed beneath the surface of the pool.

Thomas, Thomas, it comes again. A little louder this time. Not an echo.

This impossibility leads Thomas to confront another. Lazarus had taken him to the marble wall that surrounds the spring early on Friday morning. Together, they had felt for the space beneath that wall, where the cold spring water was flowing into the tunnel. Lazarus had plunged into the opening, and he had followed. Thomas had become stuck. He barely freed himself. He emerged into this subterranean life like a child born weeks after its time and with great difficulty.

"How can a man, once he is old, be born again?" He speaks to the tunnel ahead of him. Thomas loves irony, except when it gets personal. These words are the ones Nicodemus had spoken on the night Lazarus emerged from the tomb. They were sitting in the grotto outside of Bethany—what?— two weeks ago. Nicodemus was trying to get Jesus to explain how a man can be alive again after going into the grave.

"You must be born again," Jesus had said.

Right. And with a broken leg, I will swim again through a passage too small and be born again into the light? Impossible.

Thomas, Thomas, the voices come again.

"No. I cannot come."

"Thomas," this time distinctly, a voice like that of Jesus.

So Thomas decides that at the first opportunity he will turn and go a different way.

In time—or what passes for time in this place midway between earth and eternity—Thomas finds a place where the tunnel divides. To his left, a dry channel uphill. He can feel that this side passage is larger and smoother. It does not have the grit of the recent earthquake lining the tunnel floor. Some of the stones Thomas crawl over are sharp. Abrasions cover his body.

Thomas, Thomas, the voices come from the easier passage to his left. Thomas chooses to go the other way. He moves on this narrow, bitter path. The voices repeat behind him. They call him to turn around. But they also fade and become more fanciful.

> *Jesus, why have you come to us?*
> *You are not meant for hell.*
> *Your hand now is on our shackles.*
> *Jesus, why have you come to us?*

Thomas finds another branch in the tunnel. This one goes farther to the right. He takes it, even though it leads downhill.

"One way is as good as another," he says.

This time, there is no echo. The voices fade behind him. There is only a trickle of water flowing beneath his belly now. He elbows his way forward, dragging his legs behind him. The surface below him is smoother now, the limestone transitioning to sandstone. Soon, it will be clay. Thomas reasons that if it becomes clay, then this passage is heading south into the Tyropoeon Valley.

I'm in hell, but at least I know where I am headed, he thinks.

20

TAMAR DOES THE LAUNDRY

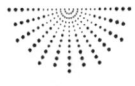

MARK

I t is now late, and Mark has wasted too much of the day. He uses the Water Gate to leave the city. As usual, the guards are sleeping. Climbing the hill, he approaches the Gihon Spring. It is empty, except for Tamar working in the corner of the pool that can't be observed from the wall. She lays her finished laundry on the nearby bushes to dry.

"I thought I might find you here."

"What do you, a Jew, have to do with me, an Idumean?" she replies. Her lips twist in a way to suggest insolence, but her eyes show interest.

"What does an Idumean have to do with the high priest's laundry?" Mark smiles. "Besides, the people beyond the Dead Sea are Jews now, thanks to Judas the Hammer."

"We are Jews when we choose to be Jews."

This is an old joke, but Mark pretends to enjoy it. Herod the Great came from Idumea but married a Hasmonean princess so he could be king of the Jews.

"So you are not pretending to be Jewish enough to obey the Sabbath?"

"Oh, these." She points to the clothing on the bushes. "I

found them in my way when I came to bathe, as is my custom on the Sabbath. I put them over there."

"So I came too late." Mark regrets saying this as soon as it leaves his mouth.

She turns from him, snarling, "I'm not that kind of girl."

"I'm sorry . . . I didn't . . ."

She is dark and thin. Her arms, though small, are muscular. She wades over to where she had other laundry soaking, weighed down by rocks, and moves it to the flat stone. "I have work to do. Why did you come?"

"To ask if you have seen a man my rabbi is looking for."

"Come back tomorrow. I have too much work to do today."

"Why?"

"Why tomorrow? Or why am I made to work on the day of rest?"

Mark hesitates. "Both."

"Okay. I'll give you these two answers for free. The Monkey makes me work, not because he needs these done right away . . ." She motions again to the drying laundry and then quickly adds an obscene gesture toward the city. "He works me because he can."

Mark nods. "My rabbi dislikes him too."

"I have agreed to do laundry on the Sabbath, with the understanding that I will also do it on the first day of the week, and the other women will do my chores on both days."

"Why?"

"Because I want to be taught. There is a man who is exiled from the city but still cares what goes on in there. He comes each Sunday and teaches me while I do the wash. I tell him what I know in exchange. You see why I am hesitant to answer your questions. I don't usually give information out for free."

"Is this man Simon the Leper?"

"So many questions." She laughs. "Yes. Is he the man you are looking for?"

"No. Early on Friday, two men came and swam into Hezekiah's tunnel."

"They entered under the stone at that end of the pool?"

"Yes. The smaller man emerged in the city."

"The giant did not," Tamar says. "This Thomas was a disciple of Jesus?"

"Yes."

"And you ask about it because Jesus was your rabbi?"

"No!"

"It doesn't matter to me, except that Jesus robbed me of a precious hour of sleep. They brought him into the Monkey house on Friday. He bled on the Sanhedrin chamber floor. I had to clean it up."

"So you don't know anything about Thomas?"

"I don't know if he lives. I do know that he was the first person to tell Simon the Leper the truth."

"That his leprosy has disappeared?"

"As if it never existed."

"I feel sorry for him being exiled."

"Why?" Tamar stops her washing. She puts her hands on her hips. "It happens."

"It shouldn't."

"Many things shouldn't happen. You and I are seeds cast upon the waters. We are refugees carried along by prejudice and war. We are not born slaves or displaced people. We are born free. But in every city around the world, we are put into bondage. It is what it is."

Mark has no answer for this, so he joins her in her work. They talk of many things. Soon, it is time for her to go back into the city.

"I need to go on to Bethany," he tells her.

"Is it far?" Tamar asks.

"Two miles. On the other side of the Mount of Olives."

"Bethany. Just the right distance away," Tamar says. "I would rather live there than here."

"Do you know what it means?" Mark asks.

"No."

"House of poverty. Bethany's on the edge of the desert, you see."

"A matter of perspective," she responds. "I think it's on the edge of freedom."

A WARNING FROM MALCHUS

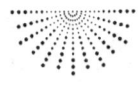

MARY

I find myself remembering what my demons said to Jesus
when he freed me from them. They had made me come
down to the dock because they wanted to mock Jesus. Demons
are like that. They always have something to say. They snarl
insults. But oftentimes, they don't realize that there is enough
truth in what they say to give you the strength to fight them.
They told me that my only hope was arriving with the day's
catch of fish. They laughed about how badly Jesus would
smell. They were right. Peter and James rowed a boat to
Magdala's dock on the calm Sea of Galilee. And Jesus was
with them. I stood on top of a pile of fish.

"Come out of her," Jesus said to my demons.

And what did they say to him? They cried, "Why? Have you
come for us before the time?"

"Now is my time," Jesus responded.

It still is your time, I think.

I stand and go silently to the servants' door. I have no plan
beyond it. I go through and down the alley to the corner
where the house meets the main street. I see a man. It is
Malchus. I pull back. I hear this servant of the high priest
knocking on Nicodemus's courtyard door. There are two or

three men who come out to speak with Malchus on the street. They explain that Nicodemus is not here and that they are leaving because they are weary of being treated to such a poor substitute as Joseph of Arimathea.

"Go in," one says. "You'll be needed to make a minyan soon."

"No, I'll wait for Nicodemus here," Malchus says.

The number remaining to listen to Joseph drone on is approaching the ten. Good. A prayer service begins and ends with ten good men, a minyan, because ten of that gender were needed to save ancient Sodom from destruction. We'll never know how many good women were in Sodom and Gomorrah when it received judgment from the Lord and was destroyed with fire and brimstone. Abraham only made a deal for there being enough men to save the city. There wasn't. I believe it takes a smaller number of good women to save a city. Jesus said we could begin our prayer services with just two or three—and gender didn't matter.

The men bid Malchus goodbye. I'm frustrated by Malchus being in my way. I'll have to go back inside to my spot on the stairs.

He sticks his head around the corner. Oops.

"You? Why haven't you gone back to Bethany?"

Malchus doesn't look happy to see me. When he helped me out of the pit below the high priest's courtyard yesterday afternoon, he told me to flee the city. I motion that he should be quiet and follow me. I can tell that he has news for John. He confirms this.

"I wasn't really looking for Nicodemus. I want to get a warning to the disciples of the Nazarene."

I nod. I guess I should trust that Malchus is now on our side, spying on the Monkey for us.

Malchus has learned to be quiet. The stairs don't creak beneath us. Martha is having Barabbas restack the woodpile in the kitchen. They are too busy to notice us. The men upstairs drop back into the shadows of the great room, except for John. He greets his friend.

"You must leave," Malchus says. "Caiaphas is plotting against Nicodemus. They have long been enemies. The high priest wants to keep the African refugees from joining any of the religious orders. Nicodemus is preparing John Mark to become a Pharisee. And . . ."

"And Jesus," John says. "I heard my father call upon Nicodemus to testify against him."

"Then why have you chosen to hide here?"

"Jesus said this would be our safe house in the city."

"Jesus is dead," Malchus hisses. "I know the others can't leave the city with the Sabbath, but you know ways to get past the locked gates."

"I won't abandon my friends," John says. "There's more. This woman has become my mother. I no longer have a home with the high priest. I am not the son of Caiaphas."

Jesus's mother comes to us. She stands in the square of late afternoon light cast by the high western window. Malchus is speechless before her beauty and stillness.

She says, "Jesus asked John to take me into his house. He has another house in the city, doesn't he?"

"Then you know," Malchus says to John.

"I just learned that my mother is dead. Are you telling me I inherited a house?"

"Your grandfather has never given up on you. Caiaphas stopped sending spies to look for you years ago. To him, you were dead when you followed John the Baptist. There is a house, though, set aside for you. Annas has rented it out to pilgrims and made me responsible for it. The tenants left before the Sabbath. But why stay in the city? None of you should be here."

"I have no other home," John says.

"Take us there," Jesus's mother said.

So one by one, Malchus and I take them down the stairs

and out the alley door. We teach them to be quiet. When all that remain are Joanna and Salome, Martha looks up from her cleaning and sees me in the hallway. She shakes her head, for the hundredth time accusing me of being idle. I pantomime that I am going up to sleep. She scowls.

I get to the landing and wave the girls off. No, they cannot come. They must stay. They nod as if they understand. I slip to the alley door and disappear.

NICODEMUS RETURNS

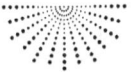

MARTHA

This will have to do. Years of grime have been washed from the walls. Barabbas is stacking the last of the wood. Suddenly, the door to the back alley swings open. Nicodemus.

I say, "Where is Lazarus?"

He moves aside, and my brother is there. His face is bruised. He's wearing rich man's clothes. There is a tear. No, two—one on the left sleeve and the other running from the garment's hem to his knees.

"What happened?"

"They didn't believe his story," Nicodemus answers.

I can see that the Pharisee, too, is battered. His clothing ripped worse than my brother's.

"The temple guards did this because you were walking around on the Sabbath?"

"No, because we—"

"Were looking for Thomas," my brother cuts him off. Lazarus's left eye twitches. It's his tell. He is lying.

"Fool!" I say, and they bid me to be quiet. It angers me that men always choose to lie. They are pulling a chair out for me, telling me to settle down and breathe. They treat me like I am a child about to have a temper tantrum.

Nicodemus whispers, "*Control her. The men are still meeting in the courtyard.*"

"I know that," I say. "Now tell me the truth."

Lazarus sits beside me. Nicodemus pours him a cup of water, then one for himself.

"We went out the Jaffa Gate. I pretended to be his rich friend Cleopas," Lazarus says.

"It got us through the gate."

"Why?" I ask.

"I think Thomas may have gone to Emmaus." Lazarus's eye is twitching again.

"Fools. The two of you can't go as far as that on the Sabbath."

"Martha, if you promise to be calm, I will tell you," Nicodemus says.

"*The truth?*"

"He wanted to see the tomb where you put Jesus."

I look to Barabbas. I love my brother, but he has never had half the sense I see right now in this bandit.

"It was all my idea. I've been to *Sheol* and I couldn't let Jesus go alone," Lazarus says.

"That explains everything. Were you going to stand at the mouth of his grave and shout directions? Turn left at the—"

"The tomb was sealed."

"And there were guards. Roman soldiers. One of them remembered that you and I were trying to get Jesus released instead of Barabbas," Nicodemus adds. "He called me a liar."

"We didn't expect them to be so difficult." Lazarus shrugs. "I wanted to stop at Jesus's tomb and then go on our way to look for Thomas."

"They held us. Roughed us up. Kept asking us if we were spies. Wanted to know if the disciples and their giant were planning to steal the body."

I laugh at that. It is hard to imagine the crew upstairs taking any initiative.

"Why?" I ask again.

"I needed to see the tomb where Jesus was laid," Lazarus says.

"I had a document that would grant us permission to take the body to Bethany," Nicodemus says.

I chuckle. The old man has become such a prolific forger —a talent his colleagues never knew he had.

"So on a Sabbath, the two of you went looking for a dead man? What? Were you going to carry the body off? Nicodemus has the head, Lazarus the feet? Or did you hope to find Jesus's donkey tied up near the grave? Did you have another document to go out the Eastern Gate? Or were you going to go the way of the Dung Gate and through Gehenna, like the other two who were crucified yesterday went?

"I know the underworld," my brother begins again.

Nicodemus sighs.

"And you fools thought that if you took Jesus's body to Bethany, his spirit would tag along like a lost lamb?"

"Jesus called me from the grave. I can only return the favor if he travels the same way I did," Lazarus says with a shrug.

"We *were* fools," Nicodemus admits. "We didn't know a Roman guard would still be posted there. I never expected they would take us to see Pontius Pilate."

"They took you to him?"

"The soldiers had spent the night out there, guarding the tomb. Their replacements came while they were still trying to decide what to do. Someone suggested that they take us back with them to the barracks and let their superior decide. That man took us to another man. Well, we got to see a lot of the fortress." Lazarus is trying to tell this like it's another of his stories.

"You could have gotten yourself crucified."

Nicodemus snorts. "They wouldn't do that. They're reasonable people."

"So those bruises are self-inflicted?"

"No. They are soldiers. They don't believe in making a decision without first seeing if there is someone higher up who can be responsible. We went up the chain. Every officer had to question us in his own way. Some thought a few bruises would change our story."

"I had to keep pretending to be Cleopas of Antioch. I said, 'I'm only looking for a grave.'"

"To be buried in Jerusalem?" I say this sarcastically, even though I know that rich foreigners consider the city to be sacred and want to be buried here.

"We got to Pilate, and he was drunk. Kept thinking that I was Joseph of Arimathea. Kept telling us that he had already decided the matter. If I didn't want Jesus in my tomb, I should have never volunteered it."

"So your brother went with the flow," Nicodemus says. "I was impressed. He shifted his accent, and suddenly I had to look over to make sure that my friend Joseph hadn't joined us."

"Pilate likes Joseph, whom he's met, better than a stranger from Antioch. When he thought I was Cleopas, he accused me of being a spy from his rival governor in Syria. It was easier . . ."

"But you look nothing like him," Barabbas says.

"Pilate needed someone to talk to. He told us how his wife had dreamed of Jesus. How he had made her angry by sending the man to die. Said something about our Mary deceiving his wife." Nicodemus spits my sister's name like it is a curse. "Caiaphas has wanted to arrest your sister for months. He couldn't, though. Pilate's wife was one of the women your sister has been teaching. Seems Mary has friends in high places—or had. Pilate is angry . . ."

My brother interrupts with a perfect imitation of Pilate's

voice, only obviously drunk, "You, Joseph of Ari-ma-thay-oh . . . , take this body from your beautiful tomb. I command it. Take it to the marketplace. Put it up in the marketplace, right here in the center of Jerusalem. For let me tell you the last thing my wife says to me . . . Let's see, what was that? Oh, yes. 'For Mary of Magdala has predicted it.' In one of her dreams, I suppose. 'That the days are coming when people will come from miles around to see this body of Jesus. A man who saved others, but couldn't save himself.'"

"Not in my market!" I say in horror.

"We reminded him that he posted guards and sealed the tomb," Nicodemus says. "He says, 'Oh. Then we'll have to wait a few days. Maybe three or four.'"

My brother returns with the imitation of Pilate, "Caiaphas is afraid that the man's disciples will steal the body. Why? I haven't a clue. So. We wait till they're gone—the disciples, that is. We'll build a proper gallows right there in the center of things. And we'll hang the body of Jesus on it."

"It took us a long time to get free from there," Nicodemus adds.

"And what about Thomas?" I ask.

"I sent one of my students, John Mark, to look for him."

"I know this boy," I say. "He steals fruit from the market."

My brother looks tired. Out in courtyard, the meeting is breaking up.

Before we go upstairs, I pull ointment out of my bag and tend Lazarus's wounds. I find myself wanting to weep. *For him or Jesus?*

AT THE LANDING, I GLANCE OVER MY SHOULDER TO THE WEST. The sun will soon set. Sabbath will be over. Below us, the servants arrive to cook the evening meal. I turn the corner and survey the emptiness.

"They're gone," Nicodemus says.

I hear a whimper in the darkness behind where the blankets have been stacked.

"Who's there?" I go toward it.

They pop up. Young women. Joanna and . . . It will come to me.

"It's us. We were afraid. A man came and told us to leave. That we were in danger."

"From what?" Nicodemus wants to know.

"The high priest?" the other girl— Sara? Salome? Some name with an S—says without confidence.

"Caiaphas? Why?"

"The man was the head servant of a major household, by the way he spoke," Joanna says. "If he had been in Herod's entourage, I would have known him."

I remember then that she is married to Herod's steward. Why can I remember that and not what else happened last night?

"Your sister took the disciples out in groups of two or three. She would be gone a long time and then come back for the next group. We waited."

"And the woman in blue?" I ask.

"She went with John and the stranger. They were first to go. But your sister never came back for us."

"This is a good thing," I say to Lazarus. "Mary will show the men how to get out of the city without being stopped at the gates. She's on her way to safety. We'll be going soon too."

"What about us?"

"You can't stay here," Nicodemus says.

RESCUING AN OX

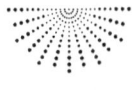

MARK

Mark is a mile on his way before it dawns on him that he is breaking the Sabbath. How can a man in training to be a Pharisee forget the Sabbath? It's the girl's fault. He had smelled her hair as she thrust wet clothing into his open arms. It hadn't felt like work. Now, he is walking two miles out of the city to visit another Pharisee. Surely, Simon will ask him where he came from. How will Mark explain himself? Everywhere is more than a Sabbath day's journey from Bethany.

What a terrible place to be exiled to. You can't go anywhere.

He could stop and wait, pretend he began his journey after sunset, but he is too hungry for that. He knows there will be a feast set before Simon. If he wants to be invited to that table, he has to find an exception to the Sabbath rule.

John Mark lifts his voice to empty path before him.

This day is a Sabbath.
Don't work.
For once you were slaves in Egypt.
The Lord your God brought you out of there
With a mighty hand and an outstretched arm.

The God of your freedom commands you
To observe a Sabbath day.

What was it Tamar said about Bethany being a place where one could find freedom? Thinking of this leads Mark to his excuse. He will quote something he heard Nicodemus say many months ago: "If a man's ox falls into a pit on the Sabbath, everyone expects him to rescue it. And if the opportunity comes to you to rescue a man from injury"—or Mark would add now, a woman from slavery—"on the Sabbath, will you not honor the God of Moses by working to rescue the person? Our God is the Lord of freedom."

Surely, Simon will accept this. Mark plans to explain that their mutual friend, Thomas the giant, may need to be rescued. "I have walked all this way to ask what you know of this fallen man's fate." Mark practices this little speech over and over as he walks to Bethany.

AN ODD SIGHT AWAITS HIM AS HE APPROACHES THE VILLAGE. An overweight man is running toward him, his arms outstretched, his long fine robe—not the thing those who run wear—flapping behind him. Mark stops.

"Have you any . . . news?" the running man asks.

Unless a village like Bethany could have two rich men, this must be Simon.

"News of my friends? Martha . . . Lazarus . . ."

"What?"

"You're coming from the city? My house is here . . ." It isn't necessary for the rich man to point. Bethany is a small village, a dozen homes. Only one of them is large. "My neighbors there . . . went into the city. I haven't heard from them for two days."

"Lazarus?"

"Yes."

"Your neighbor Lazarus did encounter a difficulty. It is why I have come to you."

"Lord have mercy." The man looks genuinely anguished.

"But he's okay. He escaped. You see, he fell into a pit."

"Oh, no. Why would he do that?"

"Actually, not a pit. A tunnel. He was with a stonemason . . ."

"Thomas, the disciple of Jesus?"

"Yes. They went into this tunnel so Thomas could show him the foundations of the city and—"

"The big guy?" Simon makes a motion with his hand high, indicating a giant. "Dear me. He seemed such a reasonable man. Why would he go into a tunnel? And with Passover and Jesus . . ."

Mark shrugs. "Lazarus has a thing for caves."

"And graves." Simon motions toward the grotto, just a short way off.

"He and Rabbi Nicodemus were going out to look at a newly dug grave when I saw them this morning."

"Nicodemus wasn't teaching?"

"No, he asked another man, Joseph of Arimathea, to take his place."

"The man with the newly dug grave?"

Obviously, this exile still keeps track of what goes on in the city.

"Nicodemus and Lazarus are anxious for their friend Thomas. In the pit . . . the tunnel, there had been an accident. A collapse of the roof. Lazarus made it safely to the city. Thomas, they hoped, had come back here."

"No. I haven't seen the giant since last Saturday night. Martha cooked a meal, and we honored Jesus at my house."

"Why?"

"He is the Messiah."

Mark nods, working hard not to let his face show his

incredulity. All day long, people have been telling him how Jesus was crucified, dead, and buried. Here, only two miles from the city where all of this took place, there is a man who still calls the criminal his Messiah.

"I have more bad news. Jesus is dead."

24

A GOLDEN LAMP

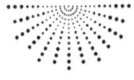

MARTHA

I am ready to leave as soon as the sun sets. My sandals are tightly laced. Lazarus, however, demands to be fed. As the servants bring the food, I remain standing. Joanna and the other girl are thankful for us. We are going to help them get out of town.

"We'll take you as far as Bethphage, the village that sits just beyond the ridge of the Mount of Olives."

They nod. I take it that they don't really know the city or the roadways.

I ask Joanna about her bag. She hands it to me. It is light. She doesn't carry much. The leather is expensive but not as well tooled as mine.

"You are *am ha'aretz*?" I ask.

She nods. "But my husband is Herod Antipas's chief steward."

"Why aren't you with him?" Nicodemus asks.

She chooses not to answer. Perhaps she wasn't offered a room with him. This seems unlikely. The pretend king from Galilee loves to show off. The bigger the retinue, the more claim he has to a title.

"My husband has too many things to care for. I would be

in the way," she says as the silence becomes uncomfortable. "Whenever Herod makes a journey, he has to go and . . ."

"So you have been to Jerusalem before?" I say, handing the bag back to her.

"Yes."

"You know the road back?"

She nods. It is obvious that her husband doesn't know she has followed Jesus to Jerusalem. More foolishness.

"Once at Bethphage, you'll see pilgrims, others from Galilee. If the weather is fair, they sleep in the open space near the well. If the weather isn't fair, there will still be some who can't afford a roof during the festival. You can sleep with them and then be on your way."

Nicodemus motions for me to sit. "Eat. You'll need your strength."

The other girl whispers something to Joanna. I remember them doing the same thing last night. *What was it?* It feels important, but my memory . . .

"You still have what I gave you?" Lazarus asks them.

Now, my mind lets me see it. While we were drinking last night, Lazarus asked them what they were going to do when the Sabbath was over. I expected them to say, "Go home." They didn't. They told him they were going to the tomb. They had spices; they wanted to care for the body.

I called them fools. I said, "Go home." I told them how Nicodemus had already wrapped the body in a long piece of linen and brought an exorbitant amount of spices. Between the rich man's tomb and those spices, nothing else needed to be done.

"Brother, what did you give these ladies?" I ask.

He motions for me to calm down.

Nicodemus says, "They have a little incense. He told me to give them some. What of it?"

The one girl points to her bag. I thought I smelled something when she placed it at her feet. I sit beside her now.

Joanna reaches into her own bag. She pulls out a small piece of cloth. Unwrapping it, she places on the table a piece of steel and a flint.

"Why did you give that to them?" I ask my brother.

"It is the one I carried when I went below."

"Yes. Mary and I sewed it into the fold of your robe. As is the custom of Bethany."

"I can't get near to the tomb, with the soldiers . . ."

"Who know you well," Nicodemus grunts.

"But the women can."

"And there's a stone, too heavy for us to move," Joanna says.

"The boundaries between this world and the next are permeable. Even that perfectly sealed stone lets in some air," Lazarus says with the wave of his hand. "Or smoke."

"You want them to burn incense at Jesus's tomb?" Then turning to the women, I say, "Unless you are fools, you'll stay east of the city. You'll go home the way sensible people from Galilee do, heading down to Jericho, and then north along the Jordan River. You avoid Samaria. You avoid Emmaus. You avoid the place where Jesus got himself killed. Understand?"

WE EAT IN SILENCE. THE SUN SETS. THE SABBATH ENDS.

I take my bag and stand. "We must return to Bethany." Then I notice how Lazarus is dressed—in the rich man's clothes. "Don't just sit there. Change back into your things."

"Take them," Nicodemus says to him.

"Why?" I ask.

"We must maintain the deception. Perhaps for a week."

My brother nods in agreement. "I've been pretending to be Cleopas of Antioch. It seems that Lazarus of Bethany is being accused of being too much alive."

"In a week, maybe less, Caiaphas will move on to something else," Nicodemus assures us. "He'll stop worrying about the disruption Jesus brought to this year's festival and start making plans for the Pentecost celebrations."

Finally, everyone gets up and gathers their things. Nicodemus, too, for it seems he wants to escort us to the gate.

"If we make it home tonight," I say to him, trying to sound sincere, "I'll return tomorrow with your robe. Thank you for your hospitality. We'll show ourselves out."

"No, I'll go with you as far as the Eastern Gate."

"I am not a frail maiden who needs your protection."

"But *I* am an old man who has had a confusing day," Nicodemus says. "The walk will help me settle my mind."

As if this is a common thing with him, a servant appears with a lit lamp. Nicodemus takes it without saying thank you, and we exit out the alleyway door. The clay lamp has been gilded so that it sparkles. We don't really need it. The men walk ahead, and I prod the girls to keep up. The road now is broad and smoothly cobbled, ramping slightly downward, each block flush and polished, so that even without a lamp, one could walk it barefoot.

There is a line at the Eastern Gate. It is slow to open, and the pilgrims are restless. When it does open, it will only be for an hour or two. The end of the Sabbath bumps up against the watch that begins for Zealots and other terrorists that would disturb Jerusalem's sleep.

"They are going as far as Bethphage, the village just over the ridge. Do you recognize anyone from your village?" I ask the girls.

There were other Galileans in the city. I vaguely remember Peter saying something about his wife being here. It was the reason he didn't leave town as soon as he heard Jesus was being executed. No, that isn't right. There was something about him finding Lazarus in the Pool of Siloam. Why is last night such a blur?

Nicodemus is making his goodbyes now. The line is moving. He hands me the lamp.

"Why?" I ask.

"You need it more than I do."

There is writing on the side of the lamp. I hold it up and point to it.

"It says, 'The Lord is my light and my salvation,'" he explains.

I remember this from the evening chants the men say in the grotto. I lower the lamp and notice finer writing scrolled around the hole at the top.

"And there?"

"Put oil here."

I hear Lazarus chuckle, so I hold it close to him. He reads Greek and some Hebrew. I have to move it back and forth, for his eyes are old. They do better with things in the distance. That is why it's no longer worth it for me to have him do the sewing for our leather goods. Even the stitching he is proud of is bad. There are clouds in his left eye.

When Jesus called Lazarus from the tomb, I asked him, "Why couldn't you have fixed that too?" I don't know why. I just say things. Now, Jesus is dead, and I regret it.

Nicodemus points to parapet that extends north and south from the Eastern Gate. "I was up there last Sunday."

Lazarus is surprised. "I thought you said you were teaching?"

"No, I left my students with another. I came in disguise to watch. I've told no one. I wore common clothes, but he still looked right up at me. His eyes seemed to pick me out . . ."

"Why?" I demand.

"I heard Jesus was coming into Jerusalem. I knew the temple guards would be ready to arrest him and I had to make a decision. I saw the crowds with palm branches. I saw you, Martha."

"Yes, we waited for him at the Kidron Brook, but Lazarus stayed home because you warned him . . ."

"I warned all of you. I saw that Mary was with you. You seemed happy. That bothered me because I knew what Caiaphas had the power to do. You all seemed so innocent, so trusting."

"And you had a decision to make about Jesus?" my brother asks.

"Yes. I decided to neither defend him or deny him. I decided to lie low this week."

My brother was lifting the lamp again, reading it, his lips moving. "It says, 'The Lord is my light and my salvation.'"

"And?"

"Around the hole, it reads, 'I have nothing to fear, for even the darkness of men's hearts serves God's glory.'"

We pass through the gate without incident. It's just my brother and me again. I doubt we'll see the women. A short distance beyond the gate, there is a valley that separates the walled city from its outlying villages.

I say, "If Jesus had not crossed this valley, he would have been free to keep teaching. The *am ha'aretz* would have kept him hidden. No authority would have bothered to look for him."

"Is that why you and Mary waited for him here?"

"He came down off that hill with the morning sun over him. It sparkled through his hair like a crown. After that, I couldn't say what I came to say. Mary had a prophesy. She didn't give it."

"It wouldn't have made any difference."

"But then we had the sense to go home."

"Nicodemus was good to us," he says.

"No! How can we trust him? Doesn't the Monkey control everyone in Jerusalem? Look. He even lied to me about the lamp."

"No. The Monkey doesn't control everyone." My brother

turns back to face the city. He lifts the lamp as if to give a blessing to the place. "Somewhere in there is a house. Mary is safe there. John and Jesus's mother remain in the city. The other disciples. Thomas—if he is alive . . . *shalom.*"

And with that, the women find us.

25

THE FELLOWSHIP THAT REMAINS

MARY

No one wants to sleep. The disciples do what they always did when on the road. They tell stories. Each one begins innocently, "Remember when . . ." They are back in Galilee fishing. They are carefree youth. The sea waters are calm. It is the blissful time before Jesus came into their lives. Then they lose control of the story, as often happens among amateurs. They could learn something from my brother. What started out as a way to forget shifts toward pain. They are led in each story to say something about Jesus. "I miss him," they each admit and then stop talking. Jesus's mother refuses to join in. They turn to me.

"What was it like growing up so close to Jerusalem?" James asks.

He has forgotten that I cannot speak. I run my hand through my close-cropped hair. I take his hand. I make him feel the bump, rising midway between the top of my crown and my left ear. It is where Judas struck me with a long stick. We were in the high priest's scriptorium and in the corner there were the rods the scrolls are wrapped upon.

"Ew," he says.

His touch awakens something. I smell Jesus. It is in Simon

the Leper's house. Today is gone. It is last week—last Saturday, at this very moment in the evening. The banquet is over. All of Bethany awaits a sweet dessert. The disciples are relaxed. Everyone is there, including Thomas and Judas. Jesus is beside my brother, and Simon stands up to play his role as host. He raises his cup. The room calms down. Martha appears at the kitchen door. Will it be a musical act or is Jesus to tell another story?

Quick, someone paint a picture. This is the last time we will all be together. Jesus stands and begins to teach. It doesn't matter, for I am there with my *alabastron* of precious perfumed oil. I interrupt the master. I make him sit while I pour oil over his head. It runs down into his beard. I do not remember what I said as I anointed him. I remember instead this last happy time when he was still with his disciples. If I could sing, I know what I would offer the group:

> *How good and pleasant is our unity,*
> *Aaron and Moses rejoicing as brothers,*
> *Leper and once-dead Lazarus sharing a common cup,*
> *Tax collector, Zealot, and am ha'aretz breaking bread.*
> *Shalom, and the scented oil flows into his beard.*
> *Shalom, and my tears kiss his feet.*

I should have known then that Judas would ruin it. That Judas would knock my song and voice right out of my head. But a week ago, Judas was the most beautiful of our group.

Now, we gather without Jesus. I cannot even sing a dirge. Silently, I weep.

"What's the matter?" they ask.

I am overwhelmed by another vision. I see the perfume—what was spilled when I anointed Jesus and broke the alabastron on the floor. The spirit of precious, lost things is haunting the house of Simon the Leper like a ghost. My actions of the past week embarrass me. Jesus was right in interpreting my anointing as a token preparation for his burial. Of course, on Friday eve, Nicodemus brought some spices from his household. There was anointing oil in a silver jar. Nicodemus brought a long piece of linen to wrap the body of Jesus for burial. It was all done in the rush before the Sabbath. If I had been better prepared, I would have brought Lazarus's burial cloth. Lazarus was Jesus's friend. And Joseph of Arimathea, a stranger crashing our funeral. He helped carry the body. He said, "Use that grave over there." So we did. If my brother hadn't been stuck in Hezekiah's tunnel, he would have insisted that we carry Jesus to Bethany. We would have found the strength.

Nicodemus and Joseph were blunt and efficient. The whole thing disturbed Martha. In Bethany, we take time with our dead. We lay them on the mourning stone—a flat hewn rock table in the middle of the grotto. We walk around the beloved traveler. We sing dirge songs so sweet the birds are hushed. The night is long, and we are faithful in prayer. Then, in my family's grave, Jesus's body would be safe. Who knows what will happen in Jerusalem? In Bethany, Jesus would rest. He always did.

The word *rest* doesn't sit easy with me now. *Rest.* Such a traitorous word. The watchman on the wall rests. He slumps a moment in sleep, and the Sabaeans attack out of the darkness. The city is lost. So also is the fortress we each guard around our sanity. Demons roam the wasteland like marauders on horseback. The word *rest* rings like a dinner bell for the demons. In Magdala, when I was mad, the demons had the key to my inner keep. No matter how diligently I stood watch for them, they entered and bred chaos. Jesus came and changed the locks.

I heard Jesus say, "Come to me and I will give you rest."

But Jesus is dead. I dare not rest. Foul spirits tap at my door, peeping in through the windows, looking for my soul. Madness hates the word *rest*. Without Jesus, no one really rests. I've tried to explain this to Martha, but she refuses to listen.

When I was a child, growing up—I wish I could tell this story to the disciples now—we had a small man in Bethany who was mad. I don't know what made him go mad. For all I know, he always was. Each day, he would go to the date palm tree that was there—this was before Simon the Leper built his house—and spend the morning searching the ground for a single date pit. At certain seasons, there would be many of these pits at the foot of the tree. Our village idiot would examine each one, rejecting one after another. Late in the afternoon, he would find the one seed he was looking for. Then he would take that precious seed to the village well and drop it in. Day after day. Lazarus said that there was a week when he could not find the particular pit he was looking for. Morning and night, he kneeled at that palm tree. He did not sleep. He searched.

Like many of my brother's stories, this one didn't have an ending. The man died eventually—sometime after I had left for Jerusalem and been married, but before Jesus found me in Magdala. Jesus once said that when a demon is cast out of a man, it goes traveling the wilderness for a long time. Eventually, it hears that the man it once inhabited is living a normal life. The house of his soul is clean. Unless the man has replaced the demon with something better—I once replaced my madness with Jesus—the demon will find seven other demons to join him. Together, they will reenter that man's mind. The final state of the man will be worse that the first.

Now, I smell the perfume that I used to anoint Jesus when he ate in the house that Simon the Leper built beside that same palm tree. I smell it in this house with its open windows overlooking the market. I know that with that smell, a demon has found me.

No! Jesus promised me you were banished for good. I try to speak. I must display my authority, not my doubts. *Stay away. I am keeping my part of the deal.*

This is why I must stay awake. The others may sleep, but I have made a bargain for my soul. When I lay in the pit below the Monkey's house, I promised to pray for Jesus while he made his three-day journey through the underworld. Now, I repeat my boast. I mouth to my demons that I will stay awake until Jesus is beyond their reach. I am nearly there. We count our days with the evening first. Jesus died on Friday—day one. Partial days are counted as full, I hope. Saturday began as we gathered with Nicodemus to drink for our sorrow—day two. In a little bit, the Sabbath will end. The lowest Saturday I have ever known will dip and fall beneath the western horizon. A third day will begin. This is how I count. The demons are free to disagree if they want.

With that settled, I try to focus again on what is being said around me. Another story, this one new to me.

"So there was a great catfish in Galilee. All the fishermen talked of it. My father says that it was there when his father began to fish." Peter goes on to tell how he spent so much of his youth searching for this one fish.

"What happened?" Simon the Zealot asks this because he isn't a fisherman.

"I found Jesus. I stopped fishing."

Everyone groans. I wonder if the way the village idiot of Bethany knew which palm seed to throw in the well wasn't by looking, but by smell. If the one he was searching for smelled different from the rest. Jesus smelled different after I anointed him. Lazarus smelled different after he journeyed through the underworld.

Since I cannot sing and it is time for prayer, Jesus's mother takes her turn. The lady in blue stands. She is empty, as we all are, but not defeated. With the open vowels that mark the way northerners speak, she begins to sing, soft and low:

Within the walls of Jerusalem, we sit and weep.
We remember Jesus.
We have hung our harps on the willows.
We have left our nets and boats for others.
Those who captured Jesus say,
"Go back to work."
Those who torment us say,
"Find another fish, follow another prophet."
How can we live again after what they have done?
If I do not remember Jesus,
If I do not put his kindness above all earthly joys,
Then let my muscles forget how to labor.
Let my tongue cling to the roof of my mouth.
Let me be mute.

I mouth my *amen,* and go to bed.

26

GOING HOME

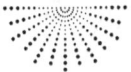

MARTHA

The road up the Mount of Olives is crowded with pilgrims. I take the lamp and lead Lazarus and the twins toward the side path. It is narrow and steep and winds among the tombs.

"This way is quicker."

"And has more Zealot bandits," Lazarus wheezes.

He is fading by the minute. I need to get him home. I don't want to end up carrying him. So we go among the tombs, allowing him to rest when he needs to.

"Where was Jesus arrested?" Joanna wants to know.

Lazarus points toward Gethsemane. It is nearby. There is a low wall between it and the tombs.

"We could sleep there," Lazarus says.

"No," I say.

In the next hour, we almost make it to the top. He rests again, and the twins seem interested in something back on the city walls. There are watch fires lit. They whisper to each other.

There is a rich man's tomb that has a bench for mourners. I sit beside Lazarus. We can see lamps dotting the court-yards around the temple for the pilgrims who sleep there under the stars. The dots of the city lights extend to the horizon, and the light from the stars comes down to meet it in the distance. I often stop here to rest. I rarely get out of the city before dark. My best sales take place after the market closes. If there is light, I recount my money here. Out of habit, I reach in my bag for what I brought for a bribe to save Jesus.

"Salome, look here." Joanna has her arm outstretched toward the city.

"What is it?" I ask.

"Herod's banner," Salome says with obvious relief.

"We can look for it each evening and we'll know," Joanna adds.

"What?" I ask again.

"How long we can stay and mourn Jesus."

Lazarus nods, and I am reminded that her husband is Herod's steward.

"He'll be looking for me back in Galilee," Joanna adds. "It takes the royal party four days to travel home, but we can make it in three."

"So you didn't tell him that you followed Jesus to Jerusalem. Why?"

"We had to come. Jesus's mother asked us to. She seemed to know . . ."

What is it about people named Mary? I repeat, "You should all be leaving town."

"Mary told us to stay," they say.

"His mother?"

"No. Your sister."

"Fools," I say. Then it strikes me odd. "My sister talked to you?"

"No. Your Mary's mute. She wrote it out for us."

Lazarus is amused. He knows I can't read. It's not considered important for a woman to know. I do my craft. I sell my leather goods. I keep the house. Apparently, the towns around the Sea of Galilee choose to teach even their girls. It doesn't make them better people.

"We'll watch for the banner each evening. We'll leave the day we see it gone."

One speaks. The other nods. They do everything together.

"Then you might as well come home with us," my brother offers.

"I'll be up before dawn tomorrow," I say. "You won't get much sleep, but you'll get more than I do. I have to gather my leather goods together and make it back to the market before someone steals my space. You'll have to fend for yourselves."

We don't go far before Lazarus stops. He is standing here among the graves telling a story. I don't know why my brother does this. When I'm in a hurry, he stops and talks. No, I do know. I've seen it more than once since his death. He is beaten. So he talks until he has the strength to take another step. Somehow, in talking, he finds his wind again.

I cut him off. I have something to say. I gather my thoughts.

Among the tombs, I hear the bleating of a lamb. It has escaped being butchered for the Passover meal. Now, in the darkness, it is afraid and alone. On any other night, I would have searched for it and put it out of its misery.

"I know that lamb's name," Lazarus says. "Barabbas."

"No. Not funny."

"Okay," he says with a shrug. "Say what you were going to say."

"I have sinned against Moses."

"How have you sinned?" my brother asks.

"When you do Sabbath in Bethany . . . I don't."

He nods. The women look confused.

"I always set aside work I can do without people knowing that I am working. When I was younger, I would hide a bundle out behind the grotto. When the rest of the village went there to worship, I would fall back and find a place where I wouldn't be seen but could still hear the service. I worked. Then when I was older and Father became too weak to stand in the grotto with the village, I would prop him by the door so he could greet the people coming and going from worship. I spread my leather out on the table and listened. Caught enough when the wind was right. I still prefer to do Sabbath that way."

"Why?" Joanna asks.

"Father died while Lazarus was off playing at being a Zealot. The business was in debt. I nearly lost the house."

Lazarus shakes his head. He isn't buying it. "You are the most successful merchant in the marketplace. You have money stashed away. You tried to use it to bribe the guards and get Jesus released. You don't need to work on Sabbath. Why do you keep working?"

"Everyone depends upon me."

"Perhaps yes. Perhaps no."

"If I stopped working . . . it would all be gone. You. Mary. Half of the village."

He keeps shaking his head.

I say, "None of you can work. You are sick. Mary is . . . undependable."

"And?"

"Jesus. More than once, Jesus depended upon me. He'd show up unannounced, his twelve men in tow. I'd feed them, do their laundry, mend their sandals."

Joanna laughs. "Salome and I helped Jesus when he traveled through Galilee. I had my husband bring food out of Herod's store room for me to take to Jesus. We always wondered who helped him when he traveled south."

"That isn't what I meant," I say.

"No, it isn't," Lazarus says.

"I could have saved Jesus . . . if only I wasn't one step behind. All day Friday, they kept moving him. I knew he would stand before Herod because Jesus is Galilean. I brought the money to bribe Herod's men. They are all greedy, easy to buy off. I had enough. But I didn't know Herod was at the other palace. If only I had worked harder."

"But that isn't what Jesus asked you to do."

"No."

"You are forgiven."

My brother's words are gentle, and I receive them. At last, we come to the crest, and I look back over the city. The moon rises behind us and lights the alabaster walls against the dark blue of the night. It is now three days past the full moon. It seems like forever. Thursday, we were glad. The people of Bethany gathered in my house for the Passover meal. I cooked in the open air and passed each dish through the window. Mary served, and Lazarus sang the prayers. All was perfect. Peaceful. Jesus wasn't there to complain about my working too hard. No, he was in Jerusalem preparing to be arrested.

"Fool," I say, not meaning to speak.

"Who?" Lazarus asks.

"Jesus."

The girls gasp, but I go on. I always speak the truth, even when it is inconvenient. "I shouldn't speak ill of the dead, but he should have left the day after he called you out of the grave. I told him—"

"I would have found my way back to Sheol without him," Lazarus says.

"What?"

"Jesus and Thomas stayed through Passover so they could help me adjust to being alive again. Why do you think I kept going out to the grotto and staring at the empty grave? I knew that beyond it lay *Sheol*. I thought, '*Sheol* is where I belong. Why should I be the only one to come back?' But they helped me readjust to life. And the night when Mary poured the oil over Jesus, I asked Thomas to roll the stone back so it wouldn't tempt me."

"Why didn't you tell me? I would have had the men of the village close it."

"Because *Sheol* still held me. It still spoke to me. I didn't have the courage. I would have found another way to die."

"Nonsense," I say.

"Martha, why don't you ever take me seriously?"

AS WE NEAR THE VILLAGE, THE GIRLS TALK ABOUT WATCHING Jesus die. Lazarus is interested in this, so we slow down— again. I am not interested.

"Your sister, Mary, didn't say a word at the cross or when Jesus was buried," Joanna says.

"She never talks," Salome agrees. "Was she born that way?"

"No," I say. "She started acting strange yesterday some-time. She'll get over it soon."

"Why did she make you touch Jesus's wounds?"

"Never happened."

"But we saw her do it to you. Is it a ritual you have here in Judaea?"

"No. We need to keep moving."

"Did she do the same thing when Lazarus died?"

"When our brother died, we worked together. We spent hours washing his body. If I was upset with Jesus, it was because we didn't have time to do things right for him."

Then Joanna asks my brother, "Was death gentle to you?"

"Until I came to *Sheol*. The pit on the other side of the grave is not a gentle place."

"When we laid him out on the mourning stone in the grotto, he looked peaceful," I say. "The work of dying with the fever had been hard on our little brother. He's not used to sweating."

"That's the way Jesus looked," Joanna says. "Like his work was done. They took him off the cross. They laid him on his mother's lap, and he looked . . ."

"Empty." Salome supplies this word. It's not right.

"Dead," I say. "They didn't empty him the way you do a water pitcher. They hung him on a cross. The Romans don't do things halfway. Jesus stopped breathing. He turned cold. They put a spear in his side to make sure. It took that fool Nicodemus hours to get him down. The grave wasn't right. It faced the wrong way. When you get to our grotto, you'll see that the opening is supposed to face west, not east." I give up trying to explain it to them. "Let's keep moving. I have work to do, and in the morning I'll be going back to Jerusalem to do a full day in the market."

"Martha, Martha," Lazarus says, imitating Jesus. *How annoying.* "Why not rest one day? Are you sure you want to go back into the city tomorrow?"

"I've missed Passover Friday—the best market day of the year. I can't afford to blow off another day. You still have your Cleopas clothes. You can come with me and continue to look for Thomas. And the two of you"—I point to the women —"need to get on your way to Galilee. Everyone has their work to do."

Lazarus nods, and we go on.

At the ridge above Bethany, with the grotto to our left and the moon a fist high above it, he says, "Jesus did his work on the cross. Then he died. Now, the night has come when no one can work."

"Okay," I say. "If you don't want to do the work of looking for your friend, then don't. Stay home. No. Show the women the shortcut to Jericho, then return home. And try to make yourself useful. Who knows—maybe Thomas is back in Bethany? If not, it will be up to that boy Mark. I will keep my ears open at the market. A broken plan is better than no plan."

"But a cracked pot keeps no water."

27

CHASING DEMONS

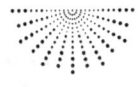

MARY

The first day of the week has come to us as we count
things. The Romans think us silly for lighting a candle
as the sun sets and calling it a new day. One of the duties of
Sabbath is to empty us of our self-importance and busyness. I
have been emptied. No—with Jesus dying, I am a cracked
pitcher that holds no water. Perhaps, I am empty enough to
sleep.

I race to my corner, away from the others. The woman in
blue, his mother, is watching me. I nod. I close my eyes . . . A
dream. A vision?

Watchmen on the wall? No, soldiers. Romans. The men I
saw on Friday. The seven sent to watch the tomb where we
laid Jesus.

"What are you guarding?" I ask, but they do not hear me.
No one does.

"Death," one says, not looking at me.

"Death," the others repeat, one after another, as if they
are calling roll.

With that, the scene changes. His tomb is open. The men
now are palm trees. In front of the tomb, I see the silent lake
of Galilee. I expect Jesus to step out of his grave and be again

near his home. Just beyond his tomb is the sea's stillness.
There is nothing so flat and filled with rest as Galilee when
there is no wind. Palm trees frame the lake, and the soldiers
have become sentinels for a gentler landscape.

Then I smell something evil. I turn and follow my nose.

Show yourself! I growl to *Death.*

I am not afraid but excited.

Magdala, Magdala,
Let me run your streets again.
Magdala, Magdala,
You city by the sea,
Let me be mad again with you,
As I was before Jesus came.

"Chase me to the well," the pig demon shouts.

I remember him well. His voice. His breath. His smell.
Our game is simple; he is not. He is fast and elusive. In
Magdala, before Jesus came, my goal had been to chase the
pig to the well. It is a well, much like the one in Bethany. A
hole in the earth with steps that go down a dozen feet to the
water. On one of the waning nights each month, when the full
moon had lost its charm and became a craggy face, he would
come to me as I slept and pull me from my bed to chase him
through the streets and down those stairs, round and round.

To the well! If only I could force him down that hole until,
like a leaf in a whirlpool, I drain him from this world.

"To hell, where you belong," I'd shout. I was good. He
was always better.

You can only chase a demon when you know its name, its
smell, its shape. The great demon's shape is that of a wild
boar, his smell halfway between lilies and honey. I asked my
brother about this smell. He agreed. It's not as nauseating as
you would expect, but rather seductive. And the demon's
name: *Death.*

I know this demon better than I know my own family. The Roman centurion who commanded the soldiers stationed in Magdala had an unquenchable curiousity about death. I pretended to be helpful. He invited me into his home, a luxurious villa overlooking the gentle sea. He became my benefactor. He took me to his bed. I told him story after story of how the pig demon came to this king or noble lady when they least expected it—how their faces looked surprised or sad or hideous. I imitated their voices as they pleaded with *Death*. Then my centurion would ask about his own fate or that of someone he loved or that of a man he hated intensely. I would demure, saying that he really didn't want to know. He would insist and promise this gift or that favor.

"If only you might go into another trance," he'd plead.

But *Death* was never at my beck and call. Think of how fierce animals often hide in sparse bush, silently, for hours, until lesser hunters go home. The best way to track Death is barefooted, unarmed except for a few smooth stones, and always mindful that you are but a lost stranger in a forest that he knows well.

So I'm in Magdala once more. Nothing good lasts forever. Not even sanity.

I know what to do. What I have to do. Chase it. Yet I can't seem to leave my bed. I see myself picking up pebbles. I find the perfect stones. My aim is true. The pig yelps each time I pummel him. I will him the way I want him to go. I run, and yet my bed is still below me each time I feel for it. Homes fly by as I run—not the jumbled streets of Jerusalem, but the ordered spokes of Magdala. My stones ricochet off the homes. No one wakes. We have the city to ourselves. This is how it feels. I am running. I am winning. But, no—my body isn't in Magdala. It's in Jerusalem. Another place to be crazy.

There are two Marys of Magdalen. One in pursuit of the demon Death. One safe in bed in the house that John now owns.

"To the well," the drooling damned thing repeats.

In Magdala, I only succeeded once. It was just after Passover. The city asleep, half empty because the faithful had traveled to Jerusalem and hadn't yet returned. The Roman soldiers who were stationed there had taken this opportunity to drink more than usual. They still were our betters, though, and as disciplined as steel. They still posted their watchman upon the wall and kept the city gate closed against the Zealots, the bandits of the night.

And like a thief, my demon came to me that night. *"Chase me to the well!"*

But I was not alone. That night, rebel Zealots came and killed the city's watchman. They took him from his post above the main gate. They opened the gate and came into the city. They wrote rebellious things upon our wall. They pitched the watchman's body into our well.

I did not know it, then. It had happened while I slept. So when my demon came just before the dawn, I happily chased him to the very same well.

It was a good run. I forced the pig to the edge. Here was where I usually lost him. Not this time. Perhaps my demon had an appointment with the poor watchman. Or, perhaps it was only a stone that dropped from the ledge and into the void—ringing and clattering against the rocks that row upon round row formed Magdala's well.

The one thing everyone in the city depended upon each day was that well. I am ashamed of it now. I risked poisoning the whole village. For what—my game? I am sorry.

Before daybreak, I returned to bed, my feet muddy, my body sweating, staining the Roman sheets of . . . what was his name? He didn't notice. The next morning, at a long table on the balcony overlooking the sea, we were at breakfast. There was goat cheese and figs. The centurion and I were happy as we discussed the day. Then suddenly, word came that the gate was open and the guard missing.

My benefactor rose. He was angry. He barked orders. He was almost out the door when I sang a prophecy:

The guard has not been bought,
Nor has he run from his post.
He is in Adam's well.
He has fallen, as we all fall.
And like a pilgrim
Baptized by the baptizer,
He shall travel through hell,
Before he is raised to join us again.

The villagers changed that day and began to hate the Zealots. They said, "These Zealots could have spoiled our well."

"Jesus has spoiled hell," I now hear the demon Death growl.

Then suddenly, I am back. This is the house that John now owns. Like everyone else, I have found a space on the floor to sleep. None of us have bedding. The disciples and I are used to it. But what about his mother? I look for the woman in blue but cannot see her. It is dark, very dark.

I have another vision. This time, I am awake. I see a vast desert full of bones—dry bones to the horizon, dry bones lying on the white sand. A windless place. It reeks of my demon boar, Death.

28

TWINS IN SHEOL

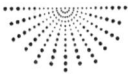

THOMAS

Thomas is surprised. The passage felt as if it would narrow and narrow until he'd be stuck. He debated if he would have the strength in that moment to push himself back, reversing his crawl, feet and broken leg first. It would be the courageous thing to do—to keep fighting as long as there is life.

Martha would expect me to keep crawling, he thinks. *But Jesus would smile and say, 'In my father's house, there is a place to rest. I go to prepare it.'*

And now, the passage opens. He emerges through a crack, just large enough to birth him, into an open space. The walls stretch off beyond his reach on each side, and the roof can no longer be felt. Even better, the walls have the gentle chipped surface of a man-made space.

An old cistern, he realizes. The passage he crawled through would fill it after a good rain.

Ahead of him, there is mud. No, clay. Wet clay. Slippery.

This makes him apprehensive, for he knows he is reaching the southern edge of the city. Rather than a cistern, this could be an abandoned clay pit. A dead end.

Before Jesus, Thomas had worked in the city. Beneath the

temple mount, there are vast stone-lined chambers for storing treasure. He spent years following behind the diggers. He had smoothed the walls where there was rock and added block where there was not. He constructed ceiling supports where needed. Then for each vault, he made a floor of smooth stone, butted together so that no precious offering to the Lord above would be lost to the ground below.

The first thing Thomas had heard Jesus teach was this: that each of us builds the house of our lives upon some type of foundation. The priesthood in Jerusalem has a foundation of gold and silver. They can wait out any economic crisis. They can buy off any challenger to their position. They are secure—that is, unless a Messiah comes and enlists the Zealots or the Romans to remove them from their lofty position.

Jesus taught the common people gathered on the hillside that most people build their lives on whatever they find at hand. They put together a foundation of shifting sand based upon what everyone says or the shared ignorance of their generation. Then Jesus came to Thomas and asked, "What do you do?"

"I'm a stonemason."

"Good. You shall be my twin. Together, we will teach people to build their house upon the rock of wisdom, truth, and love."

"Jesus, I will follow you into death," Thomas says it now to the empty pit. "Twins in *Sheol*."

"Listen," Jesus had said to the people of Galilee. "Build your house upon a rock. The storm will come. The waters will rise. But your house will remain forever."

Before he slips into sleep, Thomas prays for the storm—for the water to rise and fill this empty chamber—for surely it will be a better way to die than from starvation or the trauma of his injuries. It would be sweet to drown and have his last memory be that moment on the shores of the lake when Jesus smiled and called Thomas his twin.

29

INSOMNIA

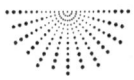

MARTHA

Having slept in this morning, I cannot sleep now. It is a curse—a familiar curse. My brother shares it. Thankfully, the two women from Galilee are asleep. They will have far to go tomorrow.

"The night knows all my secrets," Lazarus says.

"Get out of the doorway. The breeze is from the south." Everyone in Bethany understands that spring sickness comes from that direction. This is the most dangerous time for illnesses that come on the winds. My brother is careless.

"Having had it once and proved myself to be so inhospitable, I doubt the demon wants another go at my house."

He steps out and looks up. The moon is directly above us. "Full moon," he says.

Again, it's his eyes. The moon is days smaller than he thinks. It was full the night we celebrated Passover, though hidden by clouds in the dogwatch when Jesus was arrested. Now, the gibbous face is obviously ragged on the right. I was told as a girl that celestial mice gnaw the moon away each month only to have it be reshaped by the potter who makes all of creation. Everything is in transition; only God knows when our soul's bowl will be broken. Still, my brother shouldn't be so certain about things he barely sees.

"What were you three talking about?" I ask.

"When?"

"This morning, while I slept. Simon the Zealot says that you and Mary and Nicodemus had a conference about me in the kitchen."

"Mary can't talk."

"And?"

"Nicodemus thinks Mary is a witch."

"Half of Jerusalem is with him on that."

"No, he accused her of a specific act of sorcery."

"When? Last night in his fancy upper room? She does do well in such places." I'm leaving unsaid my fear that she might be mad again.

"No. At the tomb, in the afternoon when Jesus was about to be buried. You were there. I wasn't."

"All of us were upset."

"But he thinks Mary did something that pushed you over the edge."

"No, I'm used to her. I got angry at the Romans. And the Monkey. All of them. The soldiers took my club and used it to break the legs of the two thieves."

"The club Mary found?"

"Is that the way she tells it? We were together. She didn't want it. It doesn't matter. They didn't use it on Jesus, you'll remember."

"I wasn't there."

"I wasn't counting heads. None of the disciples were there. His men abandoned him. It was Mary. Nicodemus. Jesus's mother—"

"John was there. Peter was watching from the far side of the quarry."

"Okay. Them and the soldiers."

"Nicodemus says that he came with Joseph of Arimathea. He had a ladder."

"They speared him in the side."

"Nicodemus?"

"No. How can you be so dense? Jesus was already dead, his heart broken, his chest filled with water, like it does when men drown on the cross. The soldiers needed to do one more thing—always one more thing to wow the crowd. Drunk men were there, mocking our pain. Someone in the crowd shouted to the soldiers, 'Make sure of that one. He's a Messiah, you know.' They pushed me aside and thrust a spear up into him. The water and blood fell on me."

My hand brushes my hair. Suddenly, I realize I have a greasy mess in my hair. His blood.

"I must wash."

"You can't. The well is dark."

Yes. The jars are empty. Am I the only one who can do these things? I was gone two days. Why didn't Simon or someone else see them and fill them?

Lazarus reaches for my bag.

"What are you after?"

"The lamp Nicodemus gave you."

We go to the well. Lazarus holds the lamp. We go into the pit, round and round together.

As I wash, he says, "So Nicodemus brought a ladder. His friend Joseph of Arimathea was with him. The man had a tomb nearby. I went to see that tomb. The soldiers still guard it."

"Fool," I grunt. It feels so good to wash, though. I don't go on about his folly.

"They get Jesus down. His mother held him. She was quiet and still. She rocked his broken body like he was a child."

"Mary told you this?"

"No. Nicodemus said it. He wanted to draw a contrast."

"Between her and the soldiers. I get it."

"No. Between her and *you*. He used the word *hysteria*."

"I hate that word."

"There's more. Nicodemus described how each person was doing what needed to be done. Not you. Nicodemus went into the tomb with this same lamp. He checked it for snakes. None. He had spices and a long burial cloth. He looked at you and Mary, knowing it is the duty of women to wrap the body."

"For God's sake, go on," I say. *Can he tell this any slower?*

"Then Mary took your hand and forced you to touch each of Jesus's wounds. She made you thrust your hand into his side. Do you remember this?"

I wash my hair. I can't let him see me weep. "No."

"Nicodemus does. He accused Mary. He said one word. It was his explanation for your madness, your drinking, your sleeping in this morning."

"Hysteria?"

"No. Witchcraft!"

"And what did Mary say?"

"Mary can't speak."

I groan. "You two have your own language. Tell me everything or don't begin a story like this."

"Okay. Mary gestured that she had an explanation she wanted me to give Nicodemus. She went on and on, begging me to understand and interpret for her."

"And?"

"It wasn't witchcraft. Mary wanted you to feel the completeness of Jesus's injuries, the coldness of his body—to know that Jesus's death wasn't like mine. He was executed. I had the spring fever and passed naturally. I could be called back. Jesus's wounds are permanent."

"And this would make me mad? I'm used to Mary. I've seen crucifixions. I've handled wounded bodies and prepared them for burial. Me, get emotional?"

"I've seen you butcher a birth-sick goat in front of its bleating kid."

"So you told Nicodemus he was wrong about me being hysterical?"

"No, I told him you were worried, that Mary was going mad again and that I might catch a fever. Martha, I wasn't there when Jesus died. I didn't see him buried. What happened?"

I rinse the blood again. I know it's just the lamplight, but the water runs red.

"Nothing." *Everything!*

"You've rinsed your hair three times. Why?"

"Once for the Holy One, who made me a woman, such that I bleed and am humiliated every month at this time, but has never provided me with a child."

"There was Mary."

"She doesn't count."

The lamp goes out. We struggle up the steps, the gibbous moon our only light. Winded, we sit on the wall near the well's round pit.

"And?"

"Once for Jesus, who bled on me."

"Yes?"

"And once for the great mothering spirit, who led Sara out of Babylon long ago and will, in the end, close my eyes and tell me that my work is done."

PART II
THE HIGHEST SUNDAY

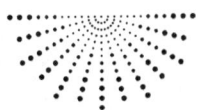

There are more things in heaven and earth, Horatio,
Than are dreamt of in your philosophy.
- Shakespeare *Hamlet* (1.5.167-8)

CAN THESE BONES LIVE?

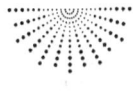

MARY

I can't sleep. I get up and go down the stairs. In the dimness, I can see someone standing near the door. It's Jesus's mother.

"I was expecting you," she says. "Let's go to the tomb."

We walk through the empty market square. I look back at John's house. A fire has just been lit in the market to provide illumination for merchants who are setting up their booths early. It illuminates the two-story house with stairs on the outside. These connect the alley with the single large room that John now owns. This space was probably intended as a warehouse, but with festival rentals being what they are, it has now been made over for sleeping. A whole village may come to Passover as a group. This past week, John's room may have slept a dozen times the mere handful of us that remain of Jesus's people.

I see the number in my mind, twelve times twelve. That would be a holy number. I imagine 144 sleeping bodies filling the great empty room. With that calculation, a vision is suddenly thrust upon me. I see the floor of John's house covered in bodies. They do not sleep. They are dead. I wonder at this. Is this what has become of all the joy and hope Jesus brought to the world? I hold up my hand to bid Jesus's mother to stop. I am so filled with dread that I can't go on. I can't dismiss the vision either. Then the voice of God rings out.

"Can these bodies live again?"

Now I know where the vision has taken me. I am in the days of the prophet Ezekiel. The dead bodies are the whole house of Israel. God repeats the question.

"Can these bodies live again?"

I want to say that they will live again at the end of time when the dead and the living are raised for the final judgment. I am mute. I am seeing what Ezekiel saw, but I am also drawn back to what Jesus said when my brother was in the grave. Martha and I were humble before him. We were like students who have emptied their minds of all they thought they knew and for a moment are simply ready to receive their lesson.

"Only the Lord-God knows," I say.

"Mary, you're speaking!" Jesus's mother says. She is startled.

"No," I say. This is all a vision. The bodies on the floor aren't real. It's not like it was when Jesus came to Bethany and said, "I am the resurrection."

"No!" I say again. My vision is not of Lazarus, who quietly passed on and then was sweetly laid in a grotto. It is not even of the crucified, who we lovingly buried in a rich man's grave. I am still dealing with my demon Death. I smell him. The bodies are those of fallen soldiers. Death has led me far from this city. I see a vast battlefield. Some kind of ultimate battle has been fought. All the armies of the world have met. All have died. There has been no winner, only losers. The courageous and the coward lie side by side. The righteous and the rebellious are lifeless together. Row upon row, as poppies grow, and yet all without color. All without the red bloom of hope. All without breath. And the birds have come and picked their bones dry.

Then the Lord-God speaks a third time, louder than before.

"Mary, Mary. Can these people live?"

I look around. My ears are ringing. Surely others have heard this. Jesus mother stares at me.

"What?" *I ask.*

"You're able to speak again. I can hear you. You said no."

I shake my head. That is not what I mean to say. Instead, the vision calls me to pray. I sing:

> *Breathe, O breathe,*
> *O Holy One.*
> *Come from the four corners,*
> *Come from north and south,*
> *Come from east and west.*
> *Breathe, O breathe,*
> *On all who are slain.*
> *Upon the bones,*
> *Make them rattle together,*
> *Upon the knees and joints*
> *Too dry to bend,*
> *Upon the chaos of battle*
> *And the stillness of the mourner's bench,*
> *Breathe upon ALL.*

I AM SHOUTING. MY FIRST SONG SINCE JESUS DIED. THE merchants and early travelers stop and stare.

"Yes. Yes," Jesus's mother says.

I look back to where we had slept the night. The place is still there. It has not been replaced by a valley of dry bones. There are the stairs that lead to the darkened room. The only other notable feature of the house that John has inherited is on the east corner—a balcony, large enough for two or three to step out and down into the market. I see it now. Two figures. John and Peter. They are talking. Peter waves his arms as he always does. The man would not be able to speak if his hands were tied. They turn now and notice us.

Then my vision returns. I am in the room again. There are exactly 144 bodies on the floor. Men and women. Old and young. Rich and poor. All races. They wear the clothing of every nation.

"They are not dead. They only sleep," I hear the voice of Jesus say. Thomas told me that Jesus said these exact words before they left the safety of the land beyond the Jordan and came to Bethany. He said my brother was sleeping.

"Can these bodies live?" I repeat.

"Yes," his mother answers, even though the question is not for her.

So I sing again what I am seeing:

> *Bone comes to bone,*
> *Ligament and muscle and flesh,*
> *And the spirit blows again.*
> *And they rise, a mighty army.*

AND SUDDENLY, I AM CONCERNED. I SEE THE BONFIRE THAT HAS been lit for the merchants leaping up, fueled by a mighty wind. It rises like a tornado into the sky. Doesn't anyone else see it? It swirls and bends and reaches out an orange and white-hot arm for the balcony where Peter and John stand. It roars into the room. I want to see what it is doing.

"The Holy Spirit will blow again," I say to the woman in blue.

"Yes."

"In the last day," I say, though I know this to be wrong. It is the kind of thing my sister Martha would say, and she is always wrong when she speaks of spiritual things. So I stop. I turn to face each of the four directions of our world. At each compass point, I breathe out the dryness of our mortal desert. Then, through my nose, I breathe in the gift of a new breath. When I have come once again around to face west, I lift my arms and sing:

"Come, Holy Spirit, Come,"
The people say.
144 in a room.
They stand, flames upon their heads.
"Come, Holy Spirit, Come,"
The nations say.
Seven billion on a planet,
They stand, their hunger fed, their wounds made whole.
"Come, Holy Spirit, Come,"
The cosmos says.
Worlds without end—
"I am the Alpha and the Omega,
The beginning and the End."

I HEAR AN ECHO IN THE DISTANCE, BUT NOT IN MY VOICE. I hear Jesus.

"Yes," his mother says. "Amen."

Suddenly, lightning falls out of a clear sky. A second later, thunder from the direction of his tomb.

"We must hurry," I say to her.

31

A RAPE AVERTED

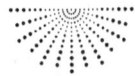

TAMAR

When Tamar, the high priest's slave, isn't doing laundry, she is sweeping the courtyard or cleaning the council chamber and its adjacent rooms. While only sixteen, she has become the most trusted of the serving girls.

Malchus noticed her intelligence the day she was purchased. Unlike the others on the block, her eyes followed the bidding. He alone speaks to her in her native dialect—the language of the Idumeans, Parthians, and Kindah people, who drop the *h* sound from each *th*, *sh*, and *wh* word. He alone of the servants remembers his childhood and uses idioms seldom heard in Jerusalem, but common for caravanners traveling the desert beyond the Dead Sea, men on camels commuting to Babylon, Al Warqa, and Ur.

Because Caiaphas trusts Malchus, he has put the young man in charge of his whole household. Because Malchus trusts Tamar, she is given more to do. Any task that requires attention to detail is given to her. The high priest's vestments and the Egyptian cotton bedding he lies on. The mosaics of his private chamber, as well as those beneath the high-backed red chair, where he leads the seventy elders of the Sanhedrin.

Tamar's only reward for all this is to sleep in past dawn on

Sundays. She has no personal possessions, no bag—she never travels; she shares a windowless six-by-six room with two other slave girls. Passover has been mad—the high priest in a rage, Malchus gone on errands. An unexpected special session of the council to deal with Jesus the Nazarene. His blood upon her floors.

She remains in bed. She hears the others beginning to clean the corridors. It is still dark. And yet her dream was vivid. A flash of lightning. A rumble, even though her room is windowless and there were no signs of an approaching storm last night. The air is dry. Her rough wool blanket gathers sparks upon her fingernails. No, it was something different.

She needs it to be dry today. She longs to go again beyond the city walls to the Gihon Spring. Yesterday had been her best day since coming to the city. John Mark became a companion beside her in the washing pool. Today, if it is fair, she will find other laundry to do and go looking for the strange Pharisee from Bethany. This Simon will teach her, honoring his deal for her services as a messenger. She now understands that the only reason he met her there on Sundays was because he missed teaching his classes now that he is in exile. Surely, he doesn't know this about himself, for men are so dim-witted when it comes to the heart.

Sleep. I want to be ready for his lessons.

But the events of Friday keep catching her mind, like the stray knot she found in the smooth linen fabric of Caiaphas's priestly tunic.

"This innermost layer was stitched wrong," she had complained to Malchus. "One stitch departs from the chain. See? It breaks here."

"That is the *spirit stitch*," Malchus said. "We can't always have the perfection we long for."

Now, as she begs her mind to rest—*Let me sleep one more hour*—she sees again the broken chain and knows that the high priest wore this undergarment when he called the Sanhedrin together and decided what to do with Jesus. *Perhaps it annoyed him. Like a gnat, it rode his back. It is my fault. I should have fixed it.*

Friday. Forget Friday. The seventy men of the council gathered at dawn. They came full of grumbles. They trashed the room. Some carried their breakfasts with them. They ground their date pits and fig stems into the floor. The senile ones left urine here and there. Jesus bled from being beaten. The raised dais where he stood trial before Caiaphas was constructed from fine white marble and illuminated by an oculus in the roof above. The Nazarene's blood oddly stained this floor—a pattern like three intersecting rings.

"Mind, soul, and body," Malchus had said when she showed it to him. "The unity we have in life, but we lose in death."

"I can't get it to come out."

"Try vinegar."

It took a great deal of effort. It had to be done because the high priest would be angered by any blemish to the room from which his power goes out, like ripples in a pond, to Jerusalem and beyond. He chants beneath his breath when the others pray.

Hear, O Israel,
The Lord your God is one,
Reigning in far-off glory.
But here on earth,
Caiaphas's will must be done.

To symbolize his power, the high priest had a mosaic labyrinth installed in the center of the marble dais. He thinks himself like the Minotaur of Crete, bull-like in his strength but as wise and crafty as Daedalus.

"Politics is a maze," he once said to Malchus. "Many paths to power, many dead ends—only room for one at the center."

Tamar alone is patient enough to wax and polish the red chair. Her rag polishes the dark flint glass that defines the mosaic labyrinth on this illuminated circle of power. She deserves her weekends away from these cares. Sleep comes, for a moment. She dreams of sheets billowing in the breeze. A body is leaning on top of her. A hand is pulling up her skirt.

"No."

She knows the smell of the man above her. It is the nameless guard who raped her three weeks ago. Malchus learned of it and had the man resigned to guarding the vaults below the temple.

"I'll tell the Monkey," she gasps.

"Maybe you won't live to do that."

Still, she struggles. He is drunk and having difficulty.

"Stop!" There is light. A torch. Malchus in the doorway.

Tamar shoves the man off.

"Who gave you the right?" the temple guard growls. "You protecting your Idumean whore again?"

"Go. The high priest is in his chambers. You were to be there with your unit."

"But it's not dawn yet."

"Aren't you hearing what I'm saying? He's on his red chair. He's counted the men. One missing, and I've been sent to look for you. Now, if you want to be alive tomorrow, go. Leave Jerusalem. Never come back."

"Where?"

"I don't care. Go. Or would you rather I tell Caiaphas where I found you?"

32

BETHANY IN THE DARK

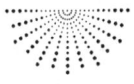

MARTHA

"Thomas can find himself," I say it low, hoping not to wake our guests. Lazarus knocks things around as if he wants to wake the dead. In the dimness and with his bad eyes, he has bumped my stool over twice and nearly cracked a jar.

"You don't need to go to Jerusalem," I add.

To make matters worse, he's jabbering at me, saying I should stay home, saying he knows where Thomas is now. That he's been thinking about it and the way the tunnels run. How can Joanna and Salome still be sleeping?

"No, I don't want to wake them," I whisper.

The women from Galilee have chosen to sleep along the west and east walls of my front room. My table is between them. The house's one small window—I can't imagine having all the windows Nicodemus has—is above Joanna. The moon was just setting when I looked out. I got three hours of sleep. Plenty. The door I am making my way toward, with every grunting inch, is north. I have my bag almost packed. I would be out it and on my way if it weren't for Lazarus.

He has the Pharisee's lamp on the table and tries to light it. He doesn't have his flint and steel; he has mine. He's not familiar with it, has the wrong edge of it.

"Don't do that," I say.

"You'll need the lamp to find the rest of your things."

"I've got them." *Almost.* "I don't want the lamp hot or filled with oil. I'm going to put it in my pack and take it back to Nicodemus."

"He gave it to you as a gift."

"Why?"

"Because you're in mourning."

"No."

"If not for Jesus, at least for Thomas."

"He's alive. At least Mary thought he was. You can ask Simon the Leper today to tell his spies to look for him. In a week, maybe two, we'll get word of a giant who made his way to Emmaus or back north or out into the territory that Phillip is king over."

"Don't call Simon a leper. Thomas told the man that he was clean."

My brother has the lamp lit. *Idiot!*

He continues, "And I'm going to Emmaus today to ask about Thomas."

"What time is it?"

Damn! The girls are awake. They stretch and come to admire the lamp.

"Go back and rest," I say. "You have a long journey. You'll want to make it through Jericho and far enough up the Jordan to camp without having to pay—"

"We are going to the tomb," Joanna says. "We'll go with you as far as the city."

"No. I'm ready to leave now."

"You can use the lamp to burn the incense," my brother says.

"No." I pull him to the door and hiss, "*You were all meant to sleep in. Then you said you'd get them on their way.* You'll slow me down."

"We'll be ready," Salome says, going past Lazarus, through

the door, and toward the well that her young eyes must be able to see. She has taken the water jug with her.

"You were going to fill that before you left. They won't be a problem. Neither will I," my brother says. Then with a shrug, he says to Joanna, "I'd go with you to the grave, but . . ."

"We know. Thank you."

"You're staying here. It's safer," I tell Lazarus.

"No. I'll go look for Thomas in Emmaus. There is a cave Mary told me about . . ."

"How? No. I won't . . ."

But he shakes his head and goes out the door. He is still dressed like Cleopas. I can't imagine that the deception will last the day. The Monkey will have men looking for him, for our sister, for any disciples that remain. Thomas is smart to avoid us.

The women and I catch up with Lazarus a short way out of Bethany. The sky is just turning pink. I listen for the owl that always hoots at me when I go into the city. If I am alone, I hoot back. It is the changing of the shifts. The creature of the night goes to rest, and I begin my day. When my work is done, we repeat the ritual as he goes the other way.

"IT IS FINISHED. GO HOME," THE LEVITE ANNOUNCES FROM the parapet near the Eastern Gate. He has a cone made from an ox horn that makes his voice carry. A man beside him blows a trumpet, and the Levite repeats his words.

"That's something new," I say.

"The Monkey was nervous that people would linger this year. Nicodemus told me," Lazarus says.

"Why? When pilgrims stay, they spend more money."

"The Monkey thinks this year is different. He doesn't want them stopping in Bethany and seeing me. He doesn't want the last thing they remember from their pilgrimage to be a fool claiming he was raised from the dead. He's also afraid of the Zealots."

We have made it to the top of the Mount of Olives. The sun is just above the horizon behind us. I usually have to wait here for the gates to open. Now, I can see pilgrims streaming out.

Stop. Stop. Why are you leaving?

It is so frustrating. I am tempted to pull out a blanket right here and sell my wares. But my father fought for us to have a space in the city market, to not be peasant merchants selling cheap trinkets by the road. And so we have come every Passover and had our best days of the year at the end of the festival.

This year, nothing worked. Jesus died and ruined Friday. I usually replenish my stores by working on Sabbath. This year, I was hungover—me, hungover!—and stuck in the city. Now, they are letting my customers go home empty-handed. What? Am I suddenly cursed? Will nothing ever work for me again?

"I will go around the city to the north, skirting the walls," Lazarus explains to the women. "Follow Martha to the market, then go out the Jaffa Gate."

"Emmaus is seven miles away," I say to him. "Do you think you have enough wind to make it there?"

He is wheezing already. There is nothing else to do. On the way down the hill, he explains to the women how anxious the Monkey is to see Pilate and his extra troops go back to Caesarea. See, I've said it many times before: the priesthood doesn't have the best interests of the merchants in mind as they make their schemes.

I love to see the Romans in the city. All that leather. Sandals, belts, thongs to hold their pieces of armor together. Things that scrape against our rough stone walls and pound against our pavement. Things that wear out and need replacing. The captains all know me by name. I pay them to make recommendations. It's a living.

"Every few years, the Zealots decide to do some mischief. A fire is set here and there. Dead fish are thrown into the purification pools. One year, the Roman standards were stolen off the parapet. These things cause the governor to remain longer than expected. Capturing criminals and doing crucifixions takes time."

"Herod stays longer too. He doesn't want to go back to Galilee until he knows the roads are safe," Joanna says.

"When they are here, the Monkey has to share power. When they go home, he alone runs the city from his red chair."

Why does Lazarus keep talking when he should be saving his breath?

"Maybe we should move to Caesarea," I say.

"Yes," Lazarus says in his most sarcastic voice. "Then Mary will be free to go mad again."

"I'm only trying to suggest places where you can be safe and we can practice our trade."

"There are soldiers stationed in Galilee," Joanna says, trying to be helpful. "Tiberius has a market just as active as Jerusalem's."

"But no Sabbath laws. It's open every day and late into the night," the other one adds.

"Sounds like paradise," my brother says.

What was that? There was a flash of lightning but no storm.

"One Messiah. Two Messiah. Three Messiah . . ." Lazarus counts. "Six Messiah. Seven——"

Boom!

Yes, there it is. The thunder. The lightning bolt hit on the far side of the city. We wait for more, but there isn't.

"Was there any of that when Jesus called me out?" Lazarus asks.

"No."

"I'm glad we stayed," Joanna says.

"Fools. You can't go to his tomb now. It's been . . ." I can't think. Whatever the flash was about isn't good. Maybe a new Zealot trick. "Go home. We all need things to get back to normal."

They act as if I have lost my mind again. So I pick up my bag, and we go on. At the Kidron, Lazarus turns and goes north. We have to push our way through the gate. Pilgrims in a hurry to go home. They know the importance of home. Why did they leave it in the first place?

On the other side of the gate, I turn, looking for our Galilean guests. They are nowhere to be seen. Good. They've come to their senses.

At the market, one-eyed Jacob is setting up his booth on my square.

"I didn't think you were coming," he says lamely.

"Why?"

"You weren't here Friday."

"I have a life, you know." I do have a life back in Bethany. He looks confused by this.

"Did you hear the thunder?" another asks.

"No," I say.

33

A GRAVE IS LIKE A WELL

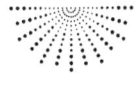

MARY

We walk by the well that serves the sprawling western quarter of the city. I want to tell Jesus's mother about my demon and the well in Magdala, but she puts her finger to my lips.

"You've said enough."

Already, even though there is so little light that every step is gray on gray and drawing water will require going down the great circle into the well at least ten steps below the street, a woman is here. I see the water jar in her hand. I see her stop and look into the pit. I see her turn and notice us. Her eyes are a quick blink of white in the gray, then she steps down. Soon, I see her a half woman. Then none.

She must be a whore. No other woman would come for water at this time. If she slips on the damp steps and falls in, no one will save her.

"Were you with Jesus when he spoke to the woman?"

His mother beside me is asking me about a different well. Another woman. It's one of the stories John told last night.

"My son would talk to anyone," she says, shaking her head.

I'm ready to move on, but she holds me back. She wants

to wait and see if this woman is safe, to see the magic undone and the half woman appear whole with her water jug filled.

"There will be another woman after her," I say. "It is their time for the well. Jerusalem is not that different from Samaria. The women who have . . ."

"Unusual occupations?"

"Yes. They come to draw water before the streets are full."

"And you weren't there when Jesus stopped by Jacob's well?"

"No. That's why it was unusual. At first, Jesus didn't allow women to follow him. He only chose twelve men. Then he took his men through Samaria and found this well. Jesus sent the men away, but John didn't go far. He stayed and watched, knowing that . . ."

I'm not sure how much detail I should provide. John was ashamed when he told me this story. He even left this part out when he retold it last night. He and the others speak of this as the time when Jesus decided that he needed the help women could provide. Soon after this, he went back to Galilee and recruited Joanna and Salome to provide food for the disciples as they went from place to place. He also went to Magdala and found me.

"John was worried about your son's reputation," I say bluntly.

Still, she laughs. "What did John actually hear my son say?"

"That Jesus knew where one could find a well giving living water. That those who drink that well's water can have eternal life."

"Oh?"

"The woman only wanted to know who she should believe. So many things we get told . . ."

She nods. She wants me to go on.

"You should ask John. He has training. He also remembers everything perfectly. One day, he'll write these things down, perhaps. Ask him. I only remember the things I understood, which wasn't that much."

"But I'm asking you."

"There are many religions. The Greeks do one thing, the Parthians another. Even in Israel, everyone interprets Moses differently." I know these aren't the exact words Jesus said. I search my memory for how John relayed it to me. We listen for the sound of a water jug being filled and the woman's safe return from the pit.

"'The day is coming,' Jesus said, 'when people won't have to risk their necks traveling to distant lands in order to worship in temples made by human hands. Everyone, everywhere, will be free to worship in spirit and truth.'"

"'And the Holy Spirit will fall on them all,'" Jesus's mother says, as if once again reading my mind.

The woman emerges safely from the well, and we travel on to the tomb. I am worried that the guards will detain us at the gate. It is early, and while pilgrims will be wanting to go home, the city is closed against Zealots at night.

The doors are open. The guards wave us on.

"You two leaving? Good. Have a nice trip home."

They push us through.

Why? I see the answer in their faces. The high priest is nervous. He wants to empty the city. I think of how Jesus carried his cross through all of her streets. Jesus blessed every block. He made this a healing place. Now, the healing work is done. The Monkey wants no more of it.

The tomb is not far from the gate. We walk there quickly.

I can see that something is wrong.

The gravestone has been rolled away. I run.

"Wait, there will be guards," Jesus's mother calls after me.

I don't wait. I plunge through the dark hole. I tumble into the grave.

I stand and see everything. There are the graveclothes that once wrapped his body. There is the napkin I laid upon his eyes. I had kissed him. He was cold and still when I covered his face. But now that napkin is folded—a neat square where his head once was.

I smell the stale darkness. I sense demon Death laughing, forcing me to look.

I see the shelf where a second body could be laid. It, too, is empty. There is nothing to do about it here. I turn and go to his mother. It is best to say bad news simply.

"The grave is empty. They've taken his body."

"Bandits?" she whispers.

I see the look of confusion on her face and nod, though it is more likely to have been the high priest.

"Then we must tell Peter and John."

"Yes." *And after we do, I will go and give the Monkey a piece of my mind. I don't care if it lands me in his pit again.*

34

SHARING A RICH MAN'S BREAKFAST

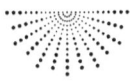

MARK

Mark is awake and watching when Martha, Lazarus, and two strangers leave. He stays in the shadows and confirms that they are headed toward Jerusalem. He silently returns to Simon's house and awaits the dawn and start of the new week.

Simon and his two women servants move slowly. They are missing the man who had recently been fired. Simon proposes to walk with Mark into town.

"I thought you were exiled?"

They have just begun a rich breakfast. There is bread and cheese. There is a fruit-and-nut mixture in a clay jar that was delivered this week from a friend Simon has near Jericho. There are olives. Hot water is brought, and Mark is shown how to mix this with honey in a cup for a sweet drink. They relax, and Simon tells how he was indeed exiled because three witnesses—men whom he had considered his friends— witnessed before the council and the high priest that there were leprous white lesions on Simon's back.

"It is contagious," Mark says. When in Egypt, he had seen the huts of the leper colony outside of Alexandria. His father had been both graphic and anxious as he described to Mark the dangers of the dreaded disease.

"Yes, so I left Jerusalem and came here. Then a week ago Saturday, I had the miracle worker from Nazareth—I still can't believe the man is dead. You say they crucified him? Dreadful. A mistake. The man had wisdom—sitting right where you sit. I was here. He told me to check and see if the spots were still there."

"What did you see?"

"I couldn't see anything. The spots were on my back. I had been trusting people to look for me. But Margaret said I should ask Thomas because he was trustworthy, so I did."

The man pauses as if the story is done.

"And?"

"I fired my head servant. The man worked for Caiaphas. I don't trust any of them now."

"But the priesthood has to certify you clean if you ever want to go back to Jerusalem."

"I don't want to. I want to live the rest of my days here in Bethany and be buried in a tomb beside the palm tree that was planted by my ancestor—if it doesn't die first."

"But you said you were going in today . . ."

"Yes, yes. Only as far as Gihon Spring."

"To see Tamar?"

Mark finds Simon easy to talk to. The Pharisee is a spymaster for Jerusalem's council while he is in exile. They need someone outside of the city to foster relationships with the various informants. Information can be bought. It is helpful if you want to know which Zealot groups are planning attacks. Simon had observed the development of the wilderness prophet named John who baptized people in the Jordan River. He reported the Dipping Man's death a day before the news arrived otherwise in Jerusalem. He followed the ministry of Jesus also.

"I'm done spying for those fools," Simon says.

Mark is incredulous. Simon goes a step further and refers to Caiaphas as the Monkey.

"Yes. You would call him that, too, if you saw the man moving along the hallways of power, like an ape brachiating from tree to tree. He'd grab a respected elder and call the man *friend*. With long arms, he'd pull the elder into an alcove and browbeat the man. The man is forced to give the Monkey what he wants. 'Yes, Caiaphas. Yes.' A promised vote. A compromising piece of information about an enemy. A favor never to be repaid. Or . . . a false report on the state of a trusted colleague's medical condition."

There is a long silence as Mark considers this. Simon is not one to rush silences. He allows his words to sink in.

Then the boy does something he had not planned to do. As one spy to another, he tells Simon what he learned from Tamar. While washing the high priest's clothes, the two teens had played a game. They challenged each other to tell something they had done in secret. The one with the most shocking story would win the game.

"Tamar told me that she is being abused by a man from the temple guard."

"And the Monkey?"

"He beats her whenever she makes the slightest mistake."

"Sounds like the Jerusalem I knew. Here's my advice to you, my friend: escape it while you can."

A FALLING STAR

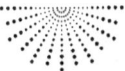

TAMAR

"**S**omething has happened," Malchus says as he leads Tamar from her room.

"I must wash." Those are her first words since the attack.

"Not now." He leads her past the other servants already on their knees in the corridor. They don't look up. It's obvious they knew the man was coming to her bedroom.

At the end of the corridor, Tamar turns back and shouts a long Arabic curse. It speaks of betrayal and the incapacity of humans to rise above their animal natures when others depend upon them. It curses the mothers of these women. It names Rahab the whore, Hagar the concubine, and Leviathan the chaotic she-cow of the deep. Malchus notices when she completes it that her head is once again held high. She has stopped trembling.

"I want to gather my things and go out to Gihon," she says.

"No. You will be cleaning the meeting room for the Sanhedrin—perhaps several times for Caiaphas . . ."

They have come to the door of the chamber. It is closed, and voices can be heard within. Malchus cracks it open an inch and listens.

"So you were awake. You were standing guard," says the voice of the high priest.

Closing the door, Malchus says to Tamar, "Today will be as bad as Friday was."

There is nothing she can do until the interrogation was over, so Malchus takes her out to the courtyard. There are water jars and a basin in the corner. He faces the other way as she washes.

"Why is today different?" she asks.

The day dawns, and Malchus answers her question softly. Already, people are gathering in the courtyard. Pilgrims that need assistance to make their journey home have been told to see the high priest. One family had an unexpected death and need to inquire about a tomb. Others come because they had been cheated in the city or had their sandals stolen at one of the ritual purification baths. Various rooms of the complex are set aside and low-ranking priests assigned to handle these issues. The first day of the week after Passover is always busy, and Malchus thought he would be spending it going between the various rooms, assisting the priests in their ministrations. Instead, he will be dealing with the fallout of an empty tomb.

"Something has happened," he repeats. "I was there and I can't explain it. Those men, as they come before the high priest, won't make sense of it either. That's the last man. He's having them brought in one at a time to see if their stories change—or if one will turn on another to save his own skin."

"Who? The temple guards?"

"No. Roman soldiers. Seven of them, detailed to guard a new grave outside the Jaffa Gate where they put the body of Jesus the Nazarene."

"Why are they here?"

"They were given to Caiaphas because after what happened last Sunday, neither Pilate nor he want the Galileans to disturb the end of the festival. I went out to check on them because I knew their watch would soon be over and a new one coming."

Malchus pauses a long time. Tamar tells him she is ready. She gathers her wash rags and broom, and they return to the narthex of the council chamber. They watch as the Roman is brought out between two temple guards. The man looks pale, the guards grim.

"What's happening now?" Malchus asks.

"We are beating each one and throwing them in the pit," the guard replies in the broken Hebrew the unit uses when they want to hide their speech from foreigners. "Now, he wants the first man back so he can hear it all again. Stories change, you know."

Malchus is about to go in, but Tamar holds him back.

"And what is your story?" she asked. "You don't leave your bed to watch Romans change their shifts."

"Remember how when they arrested Jesus, I lost my ear?"

"It was fine when I saw you."

"Now, I think I've lost my mind. Did you hear that boom?"

"The storm? Yes, I heard it. Then seeing the courtyard dry, I thought it was a dream."

"No. The night was clear. I was sleeping on the roof and then I got up. I had no reason. I looked west and saw the horizon glowing. Then a flash, darkness again, and, after a short time, the boom."

"You were mistaken. The sun rises . . ." She nods her head to the east.

"But the tomb where they put Jesus—the man who healed my ear after it had been cut off by a sword—was west, just outside the Jaffa Gate. I knew something had happened. I thought maybe a star had fallen."

"Stars fall?"

"There are stories of it. When they do, a hot, heavy rock can be found."

"No." Tamar is incredulous.

"I went down and out to search for it. The guards at the gate had heard it too. They were planning to open the gates early and let the pilgrims go home. They waved me through."

"You found your fallen star?"

"No. I found the Roman soldiers out cold on the ground."

"They fell asleep?"

"No. They were rigid, like they were in shock, like they had been thrown away from the grave with some force."

"A rich man's grave? Like my dream?"

"They had been guarding the new tomb of Joseph of Arimathea. It is on the side of the old quarry. I knew they would be there. Pilate allowed Jesus to be buried there, so the crosses would be empty for the Sabbath. Caiaphas wanted the tomb guarded, and he wanted the Romans to do it."

"Your temple guards are too busy with other things."

"Romans never sleep or drink on duty."

"Except this time."

"No, they had been knocked out."

"What? Did someone with a club sneak up on them?"

"No, I'm telling you. It was a fallen star."

"Or that one disciple—the giant."

"Thomas?"

"He kept your guard from arresting Jesus in the temple."

"My men are idiots. These are Romans. And it didn't look like a struggle. Even Thomas couldn't sneak up on all of them at once."

"A star? What about the Zealots? Poisoning? Sleeping potion?"

"No. When I shook them, they woke up—dazed, but still sober. They each said they had seen a light and heard a boom."

"So where's your heavy star-rock?"

"We couldn't find it. We looked for it. I told them they needed to find it."

"Why?"

"Because the grave was empty. Jesus's body was gone."

"Your star could do that?"

Malchus shrugs. "If it can't, then those soldiers are dead men. You see what I am saying? I came upon them and woke each of them. When they got their wits and saw that the stone they had been guarding was rolled back and the body gone, they got desperate. They decided to commit suicide rather than facing Pilate. They wanted me to help them."

"So you offered them a star, like hope to drowning men."

"Yes. And now they are here. One at a time, Caiaphas brings them into his chamber and asks them to say what has happened."

"Meanwhile, they keep tracking mud in and out."

As if proving her point, a man is dragged in, bruised and beaten.

"Why doesn't the Monkey just send them back to Pilate?"

"Because he knows their story rings true. He does this, you know. When what he hears isn't what he wants, he gets to work on the witnesses. Yes, I know where this is going. The Monkey isn't breaking them. He is remolding their story. He told me that we will keep the soldiers here until noon. He will bring them in and out. Time in the pit. Time before the red chair. Repeat. At noon, he will gather the full council and bring these men out in a line. By that time, they'll be ready to tell the council a different truth—the right truth—then they'll beg for the opportunity to be witnesses for Caiaphas throughout the city."

"And I'm supposed to stand here waiting to clean the place."

"Yes. The council chamber has to be ready for the show."

JACOB'S LADDER

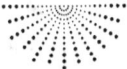

THOMAS

S uddenly, light.

Thomas blinks and tries to comprehend.

Light forces his eyes closed—red and bright, even through his eyelids.

Shechinah! Glory. Have mercy on me, a sinner!

But he cannot speak.

Slowly, he opens his eyes. Blinks. Opens barely again and sees angels. Refocusing, he decides that the nearest vision is a lit torch stuck in the mud a few feet from his face. This is not from direct looking, but the flickering nature of what dances on the walls.

Part of Thomas's way of being with Jesus was a cultivated reluctance to simply accept the religious explanation that others might give a phenomena. When Simon the Leper wanted to thank Jesus for healing him, Thomas offered an alternative explanation for the disappearing spots. Often, Thomas reminded the other disciples that some miracles could simply be a change of mind.

"Jesus is good at curing hysteria," he would say to Peter and John.

"No, the glory of God is pitching his tent among us," John would say in response.

"Lord, have mercy," Peter would chant like a mantra.

A hundred, maybe a thousand times, these words were exchanged over the three years they journeyed together.

So now, Thomas stills himself. His eyes resolve the torch flickering in the white clay mud. He takes a moment to think about where he has found himself—in the Essene quarter in the south of Jerusalem near the Tyropoeon Valley.

Years ago, he spent time with these men. They refused to work for the Herodians, so he had to seek them out. The work crews that put stone together to form new walls or dug the vaults beneath the temple never had Essenes among them. This made him curious about their beliefs. He knew they were serious, intentional about living a pure life, and ascetic, avoiding the materialism that afflicted the other religious people of the city. He sought them out.

There had been one potter named Jacob, who told Thomas about a boy of elderly parents who had been raised by the Essenes in Qumran when they died. This young man left to become a prophet, baptizing people in preparation for the coming kingdom of God.

"You're telling me that John the Baptizer is an Essene?" Thomas had asked.

"I'm telling you that he left us. He does the same rituals for purification that we do for our initiates. He took what we hold private and made it public," Jacob answered.

"When I am done with my work here, I will go up the Jordan River and look for this prophet."

"Why don't you stay here and become an Essene?"

"Because I like to work. The Herodians are the only ones who see my value."

Jacob laughed at this, but he told Thomas what he needed to know: how to find the wilderness prophet also known as the Dipping Man. After his purification, Thomas didn't feel like working again for the Herodians, so he went north and eventually found Jesus.

"Jesus?" Thomas mutters at the light.

Then other torches are thrown down. There is shouting and a great confusion. Beyond where he can see, there is a multitude, gasping as people come to see the giant found stuck in the clay.

Thomas tries to interpret what his light-deprived eyes are seeing. His mind wants to find a simple explanation, but his heart sees angels. He remembers the story he loved as a child —how the ancestor of the nation, a man named Jacob, was forced to leave his home. The boy went east toward the Jordan River and the safety of the land beyond it. And on the first night away from home, he chose a stone for his pillow. As he slept, he saw angels rising and falling on a stairway to heaven. Jacob knew then that there was a way to get from where he was to where God was.

"Jacob's ladder! Lord, have mercy!" Thomas shouts.

A scurry. Voices. Now, he makes out distinct words.

"Father, Father. A monster."

"Jacob, come quick."

"Look in your pit. A man birthed by the earth."

"It's in your pit."

"It calls for you. The monster knows your name."

"Run, Father. Run!" a boy shouts.

"Nonsense."

This last voice sounds familiar to Thomas.

PETER AND JOHN

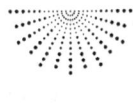

MARY

"We must hurry," I say. "The others need to know that Jesus's body has been taken."

Jesus's mother is hesitant. No. Fixed. Maybe it's the shock of it—that her son's corpse would be subject to more abuse. I can't explain this city to people who live near the quiet Sea of Galilee. I put my arm around her and turn her away.

"Where are the guards?" she asks.

"No one needs to guard an empty tomb," I say.

She stops. She looks back. "You said the graveclothes were neatly folded. Bandits wouldn't do that."

"I did? Why does that matter?"

I don't remember saying this. I do remember the inside of the grave being dark, like a well. I left it as soon as I could.

"There was a Roman guard. Seven big men. They were there to prevent my son's body from being taken. They arrived on Friday before we went to Nicodemus's house. They had orders from Pilate to secure the tomb."

"Zealots, then."

"Why? The Zealots don't have anything to do with my son."

"The order must have come from the high priest, then. We must go."

We push our way against the flow of pilgrims exiting the city. I am glad for this. Being busy, going against the tide, means I don't have time to tell her how devious the Monkey is. Passover is over. The Sabbath done. The Monkey is free to do something outrageous, just to flex his muscle. Herod and most of the Romans troops will go, but he still runs Jerusalem. And he'll prove it by putting Jesus's body on display. Perhaps, even now. We will get back to the marketplace and find some grim tower being constructed. The pilgrims get to go home, but we poor residents of this place are going to be reminded for weeks to come that we made the mistake of loving the wrong Messiah.

Past the gate, the crowds thin, but she stops again.

"We need to tell Peter and John," I repeat. "They may already be worried for us."

Let John explain it to her. Let him take care of moving this woman to safety. Peter will be packing the disciples up to leave. Martha was right. *We've stayed too long.*

"Caiaphas has no interest in moving my son's body," she says, resisting me. "And Pilate wouldn't allow his men to leave their post until the danger of a disruption was past. We must consider this matter carefully."

She goes over to the well and sits down. She pats the stone wall beside her as if I must join in this wool gathering.

"No." *I give up on her and walk away.*

"Consider how it would look if Thomas had gone into your brother's tomb," she shouts after me.

What an odd thing to say. I remember Thomas carefully unwrapping Lazarus when he had left *Sheol.* I took those grave cloths and neatly folded them. They still smelled sweet, even though my brother had been dead four days.

Up ahead is the market. Everything looks normal. My sister is setting up her stall, her back to me. Peter, James, and

John are still on the balcony. James points at Martha. I'm sure she has been too busy to notice them. I arrive at the stairs, and Peter and John come down halfway to meet me.

"They have taken Jesus's body," I say quickly. "The tomb is empty."

"You can talk," John says.

"Yes, but I'm telling you . . ."

"Did you go to the right grave?" Peter asks stupidly.

"Yes. Jesus's mother was with me. We are not fools."

John pushes past me, running. Peter follows him. I sit on the stairs.

Why am I out of breath? I must have been running. Running since I left the woman at the well. I watch Peter. He is heavy-set, short, muscular. He runs better than I would have expected. John has long strides and grace. He paces himself.

Will they stop at the well to chat with Jesus's mother? No. They are going to the tomb. What do they expect to see?

I'm weeping. I can't see anymore. Tears make everything blurry.

Why now? I didn't weep at his cross. Martha did. Now, she is making a sale. I hear her voice. The customer is reluctant, but she will win him over. I can't go to the Monkey in this state. He'll see my tears and laugh. What is happening to me?

3 8

A SEALED SCROLL

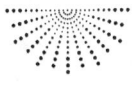

MARK

As they prepare to leave Bethany, Mark feels a curious discomfort. Something is about to change. The air smells different. He expects mature men to behave rationally. He didn't expect a rich man to show such concern for an *am ha'aretz* like his neighbor Lazarus. He didn't expect a Pharisee to trust the medical opinion of a craftsman like Thomas. And why would Simon take time each week to tutor a washwoman like Tamar?

"Wait. I need you to take something to Nicodemus," Simon says. He disappears into a back room and, after a long time, emerges with a parchment scroll sealed with red wax.

"A deed?" Mark asks.

"No, a redemption."

Mark receives it with a dubious look.

"Is Rabbi Nicodemus to open it?"

"Oh, no. He must take it and unseal it before the full council. It is my letter to the full Sanhedrin. I still have that right. The Monkey can't take that from me. Nicodemus knows how to do this."

Mark notes that the man has been careless. He holds the scroll around its middle, and the wax seal has not been allowed to harden completely. The signet ring's impression is blurred. Mark does the same, holding the scroll so the wax will soften further.

They walk the two miles to the Gihon Spring and say goodbye. Tamar isn't there. Near the bottom of the Mount of Olives, Mark leaves the crowded road and winds his way among the tombs. He soon finds one that provides him a private place to sit.

He carefully separates the wax seal. Reading what Simon had written, he whistles.

"You shouldn't cross the Monkey," he whispers. He stands, half tempted to destroy the scroll. Except it *is* a redemption. And it concerns Tamar.

He returns to the road in time to see a familiar figure. His cousin ducks in and out of the pilgrim crowd ascending the Mount of Olives, looking here and there on the ground.

"What? Have you lost something?" Mark shouts.

"I'm looking for whatever they may have dropped."

It is what boys do. The pilgrims often lose coins and other valuables as they climb the steep switchback road up the Mount of Olives.

"Have you found much?"

The boy shrugs and says, "The bandits did it again."

"What?"

"Killed somebody and stashed their body in a tomb. I smelled it."

"Where?"

The boy points to the south, where one tomb has a higher top, sticking up like the miter cap on a high priest.

"Absalom's Tomb?" Mark asks.

"Go smell it for yourself." The boy makes a face.

"I haven't time for that. I need you to do something for me."

The boy nods.

"Tell my mother that I'm okay and I'll be home tonight for dinner. Then hang around."

"You mean spy?"

"Yes. Let me know if the women who followed Rabbi Jesus are still meeting."

"Why can't you—"

"I need to get this to Nicodemus." Mark reveals the scroll. "His life might be in danger."

Then Mark puts a finger to his lips.

THE LETTER THAT JOHN MARK CARRIES READS:

HONORED COUNCIL MEMBERS AND OUR RESPECTED LORD Caiaphas,

IT HAS BEEN SEVEN YEARS SINCE I WAS PARTED FROM YOU. THIS Passover was, in fact, the anniversary of my exile, and its concluding Sabbath, my jubilee. For, as I wrote you before, my leprosy has disappeared. I have completed my time of purification. Do not fear; I remain uninterested in returning to the city.

There is, however, a certain matter of payment. In my confinement, I have tried to be useful. In fact, the honorable Caiaphas and I had an agreement. I provided a continuous stream of information during these years. I never asked for compensation, other than what I had been promised.

I did, however, receive the services of a man who had at one time worked for the high priest. Imagine my chagrin when I discovered that this man had been spying on me. I have released him—No, I actually wish to return him in exchange for another of your servants.

Seeing how I ask nothing else, you should honor me in this: I wish to redeem Tamar the Idumean. I am prepared to send my representative to the

Jaffa Gate to fulfill the needed terms for her release and pay any outstanding debt she might owe.

If, in your wisdom, you feel this uneducated washwoman is of greater worth than the skilled man I have released to you, then come announce that at the gate. The women of the city will receive that as good news.

You may send your response through the honorable Nicodemus or his student, John Mark the African, who has recently become my friend.

As Always,

Simon of Bethany,
   Formerly known as the Leper.

39

SEEING JESUS

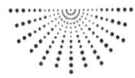

MARY

Joanna and Salome, too, have gone to the tomb and found it empty. They return to the city and stop to speak with Jesus's mother at the well before they come to me.

"She's still there?" I ask.

"Yes. Oh, she told us that you're able to talk again. Isn't it wonderful?"

I could throttle them. They babble on about seeing angels.

"No. If you were at the well, then you heard a demon. I know him."

They laugh. They say how Jesus's mother knew what it all meant before they told her.

"She didn't need to see the angels," Joanna says.

"Did you see Peter and John?" I ask.

"No."

I dry my eyes. There is work to do. I head to the tomb again. The streets are beginning to fill, and it seems as though the demons have possessed the crowd instead of me. I find myself pushed off course. I'm thrust into unfamiliar back-streets. I make several wrong turns. At last, I am through the gate and going to the tomb.

I notice now that the gravestone was not rolled away. It was flung out and now lies flat. It is like the resting stone in the grotto in Bethany—the place where we lay the bodies of our beloved before their burial. Jesus didn't have a resting stone. He came down from the cross and was laid upon his mother's lap. Graves like this have their stone doors placed in a channel so that the stones are rolled down the groove to seal the tomb. It would take many men to push it out and make the gravestone lay flat like this. Perhaps Thomas could, but I doubt it.

The disciples are nowhere to be found. I look into the empty tomb. It is strange to see his graveclothes still there, the napkin neatly folded. Jesus used to do that at the end of a meal. If he was dining at a rich man's house and we had napkins, he would fold it when he was done eating to let people know he was ready to teach. I always watched. His best stories came after a meal had been enjoyed and he folded a napkin.

Outside the tomb, I again fall into weeping—not for me, but for Jesus. I look down to see that my sandals have fallen off. I kneel as if upon holy ground. I prop my elbows on his gravestone. The dark mouth of the tomb is before me. I weep into that echoing emptiness. My voice grows louder and louder. I imagine angels and demons tumbling in Sheol under its attack.

"Woman!" A voice of authority behind me. "Why do you weep?"

I stop my lament. There is anger. I make my words cool. "You know very well. The body of Jesus the Nazarene is missing. If you tell me where it has been taken . . ."

"But who are *you* looking for?" The voice is gentler. He must not be a temple guard or one of the priests. Perhaps a lowly gardener confused by all the activity around Joseph of Arimathea's tomb.

"If you know anything . . ." I stand, preparing my face to reason with him.

"Mary."
It is Jesus.

40

CLEOPAS GOES TO EMMAUS

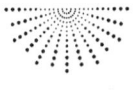

LAZARUS

It would take Lazarus an hour and add two miles to his seven-mile walk to Emmaus if he would go, as promised, around the northern flank of the city, past the Fuller's tower and the pens where sacrificial lambs are kept.

"It is an ugly wall," he complains to Martha.

"Go that way or don't go at all."

It is said that old married couples whittle away at the same argument for years. This brother and sister have spent most of lives in closer proximity than the married couples of Bethany. The tasks of village life often separate men from women. But being in the leather trade together caused them to work the conflict between beauty and function down to a sliver beneath their fingernails. Lazarus was tired of Martha telling him to leave off the final filigrees to the sacred lettering he embossed on the priesthood's belts.

"We have a business to run," Martha would tell him.

"But unvocalized text lacks beauty," he'd reply. "It is the difference between saying *well* and *wall*."

"Our contract is to write the letters, not the vowel marks. Beauty doesn't matter on the backside of a belt."

And so their last words together on this new day are both bitter and flat.

Lazarus thinks of it as he comes to the corner where the new wall joins the old. Ahead of him lies the newly constructed Damascus Gate. His task is to follow the outer wall, keeping it always to his left, and not enter any gate. The old gate that served northbound traffic still stands as a useless appendage within the city. As a pearl is built within an oyster, so layers of houses have been accreted onto Jerusalem.

The city has prospered under Roman rule. It has grown from something of little value to the jewel of Judaism that the whole world travels to see. New walls constantly need to be built, farther and farther out, just as a rock crab looks for larger and larger seashells to protect it. Like a glistening mantel that gets surpassed and built again, better and newer and with the luster of modern sensibility. The new northern wall has smoother blocks and a gilded gate. Those returning to Syria pass under cornices sculpted with fanciful animals before having to travel through godforsaken Samaria. Lazarus hates it.

The old gate has a scripture at eye height, saying:

You will go out in joy
and be led forth in peace;
the mountains and hills
will burst into song before you,
and all the trees of the field
will clap their hands.

Wanting to run his fingers along those words, as he had done when he was a child, he turns left and enters the city at the Sheep Gate. It is quiet. The sheep for Passover no longer need it. The time for sacrificing is over. *The new Damascus Gate would make a fitting entrance for Sheol,* he thinks. But when Jesus called him and Lazarus exited his grave in

Bethany, he was wondering if he remembered the old gate right. He hadn't seen it in years. Something about this fool's errand to Emmaus made him want to feel that hope again. But his sister made him promise not to cross through the city.

"Oh, believe me. I understand the danger," he had assured her. Understanding and fearing are two different things. He already died once. Keeping safe is less interesting to him now. Besides, his Cleopas clothing is grand. With nice clothes comes respect. Leather merchants rarely get that.

I won't come to any harm, he now says to himself. *I'll avoid any place where someone might recognize me. I'll practice being Cleopas while I can.*

This means steering clear of the market square, as well as the Fortress Antonia and the tomb of Jesus. The Jaffa Gate, which leads out to Emmaus, should also be off-limits because he and Nicodemus had only yesterday been marched through it like criminals. But if he doesn't linger, the morning shift who hadn't seen this display will be there. They know him as Cleopas of Antioch. They will be busy with the pilgrims leaving or hungover from the end of the Passover Sabbath, so he hurries at first.

He has always enjoyed free time in the city. It is rare that he has a chance to comb the back alleys unencumbered, as he usually is going to and from the market. This also gives him a chance to ask about Thomas. Perhaps his friend has surfaced in one of the honeycomb of caverns under Bethesda, the newer north quarter of the city. He comes now to a pool with a colonnade around it that perfectly reflects the deep blue morning sky. It is as still as a mirror.

"Watch for angels," the man beside him whispers. "They stir the waters and bring healing."

Jerusalem has grown. It is now double the size it was when Lazarus first met Jesus. Some streets are unfamiliar. Twice, he gets lost. Each time, déjà vu causes him to mouth the word

Sheol. His shortcut, now, is adding considerable time to his journey. He stops and chats with strangers.

"Have you seen a giant?"

"No."

He takes more risks as the morning goes on. Being greeted as a rich man is wonderful. Finally, he comes to the well near the center of Jerusalem, a half mile inside the Jaffa Gate. This will be a cool place to sit. He is thirsty. Then he sees a familiar face.

"What are you doing here?"

Mary the mother of Jesus blinks at him. To her, he appears as a rich man. Then recognition dawns.

"Why, look at you," she says. "A change of clothes? When we met, you were half drowned in muddy rags, Lazarus. I didn't expect this—"

"Shh, I'm pretending to be someone else."

"Being dead and then alive again isn't safe in this city?"

Then she laughs—a long laugh. Lazarus is startled and concerned. It seems so uncontrolled. Could she be—what had Nicodemus called it—hysterical? People are staring.

"I wasn't expecting you," she finally says, recovering herself. "I'm sitting here thinking, 'Who can I tell? Everyone will think me nuts.' Then you come—of all people. You will understand."

"What?"

"That Jesus has left his tomb. It is empty, Lazarus. Empty."

She looks sincere. All he can do is stare at her. Then he sees movement in the crowd—tops of spears bouncing above the heads. The shift change is happening. Lazarus has lost track of time.

"No time," he says and heads down an alley.

There's a tap on his shoulder. He moves faster. A beefy hand grabs his shoulder and turns him. It's James.

"Lazarus, I saw you run from Jesus's mother. Why?"

"I want to—"

"You're wearing rich clothes. A disguise?"

"Yes."

"Good. Come with me to Emmaus."

Lazarus blinks. How did James know? Together, they join a crowd of pilgrims and are hurried through the gates by guards still wanting to empty the city. James does a lot of shoving and keeps a good pace in the traffic.

"If we are going to get there and back before the gates close for the night, we should hurry," James grunts.

Lazarus struggles to stay up and, finally winded, stops. James concedes and sits beside him on a stone. Behind their backs is a large pit and the detritus of a defunct quarry. They look across the gap and see the knob where the Romans do their crucifixions. Even a quarter mile away, it feels too close.

They don't speak of it. Instead, they speak of their common task of finding Thomas.

"I think Jesus's mother is still in shock," Lazarus says.

"She seemed fine last night. But grief is like a stray cat. Man or woman, it doesn't matter. You send it away. You throw stones at it. But then it's mewing on your chest when morning comes."

Lazarus nods. Of all the disciples, he hadn't expected James to be philosophical.

The fisherman continues, "I thought the young women, Salome and Joanna, would be ready to go home and forget what's happened here. I ran into them just before I saw you. They were giggling. They were going to speak to your sister. I saw her wave them away, but they keep coming."

"Yes, Martha is tired of them."

"I thought Martha was going to hit them, so I came down off the balcony . . ."

"Where?"

"The place John inherited has a balcony overlooking the

market. We've been watching Martha. It amazes us that she's right back to work."

"Salome and Joanna stayed with us last night. I gave them incense to burn at the tomb."

"You thought they'd get around the guards?"

"I thought the smell would help Jesus find his way back to us."

"You're a drowning man grasping at straws."

"Yes."

"Joanna and Salome were telling Martha that the tomb is empty, the stone rolled back. No Jesus."

"That's what Jesus's mother was trying to tell me."

James shrugs and asks, "So what do we do now?"

The day is fresh. Around them, pilgrims sing:

> *When Israel came out of Egypt,*
> *The sea clapped twice and fled.*
> *When Elijah stood on Carmel,*
> *The sky broke in two*
> *and fire fell.*
> *And when our Messiah comes,*
> *the mountains will leap like lambs.*

"We go with them to Emmaus. Perhaps we'll find Thomas," Lazarus says.

"Yes. Maybe he broke into Jesus's tomb, though it doesn't sound like the kind of thing he'd do."

"I think Thomas is dead, but I would rather walk with you than dwell on our sadness."

AND THEN HE APPEARED TO PETER

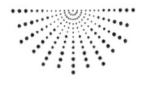

MARY

I am reluctant to leave him. I must have held him very tight. He is solid, the wounds in his hands and side obvious, yet he is not like my brother was when he came out of the tomb.

My brother's new life was maddeningly similar to his old. He had to be helped from his graveclothes, and he still takes a long time to do simple chores. He blinks in the twilight, but then again his eyes have always been bad. Why couldn't his arthritis and astigmatism have been fixed?

Jesus is different. I have the sense that his body is just here to give me something to hold and establish as real. He could be whatever he wanted. He doesn't need to blink. If he ran, he would not tire. If Jesus were attacked again, he would not be hurt. If he wanted to travel to the Pillars of Hercules or the Indus River, he would do so instantly. All the limits of mortality are gone.

In too, too short a time, he says bluntly, *"Do not hold on to me. Go instead and tell the others that I live."*

I know he means his disciples. This is his command, yet I choose instead to follow my own instincts. It doesn't take a third eye to see that the disciples will be skeptical. Joanna and

Salome are already in John's house, telling their good news. I doubt my joining them will help. It will take all day for them to wear down the guys. There are others I want to tell.

Besides, I am sure John saw what I saw—the graveclothes lying there as if the body had simply gone out of them, the napkin neatly folded. How like Jesus. John would have seen that and believed. He will support Joanna and Salome.

"Is it because they are women that you doubt?" I imagine John arguing. "Jesus would do things this way. Of course he reveals this miracle stage by stage. First, announcing his new life in the dim dawn to women who simply arrived at his tomb without preconceptions. In each town, did he not first ask the women—and then the aged, the outcast, the poor, and the children—to be his ambassadors of hope?"

Maybe Peter will be helpful and join with John. One can always hope. I can see him quoting for the skeptics all the times that Jesus talked of dying and being raised on the third day. He'll remind them that Jesus called him Satan when Peter suggested he didn't have to die. The men will argue about whether Jesus meant that he would literally die and be raised in three days or if it was all a figure of speech. It will be a long discussion, and nothing I might say will be given any credence. I won't be missed.

Instead, I will visit the women I have been teaching. I will go under the colonnade of the temple to the women's court. There, where Gentiles are allowed to have their worship, I will meet with Pilate's wife and the other women who have the misfortune of living with men in power. Then in the afternoon, I will go, as I often do on Sundays, to the home of Miriam the African, situated upon the Ophel. I haven't time for dim-witted disciples.

But first, I must go to the Pool of Siloam and wash my tears. For too long, I have been a prisoner of hope. I went from the pit beneath the Monkey's house to the cross where Jesus died to the table where his friends spent the long night blaming each other. I've been a prisoner in the houses of Nicodemus the Pharisee and John the Orphan. I have spent the long night with the demon Death and this unhappy morning with an empty grave.

There is, though, a baptizing place where Jesus took his men when they felt swallowed up by this city and its deceit—the Pool of Siloam, where Hezekiah's tunnel empties and my brother emerged blinking into the twilight for the second time this month. It was there that Jesus said that he would be like Jonah, three days in the belly of the whale. Would that Jerusalem will come to believe as easily as Nineveh did, for something greater has happened today than what happened to Jonah or my brother.

I wash, dipping myself three times. For the creator God, who made life. For Jesus the Messiah, or as the world will come to know him, the Christ. For the great, enfolding Holy Spirit, who hovered over the waters when the universe was birthed, who guided Noah's family on their journey, who made a way for Miriam and Moses and their multitude through the Red Sea, who came to Jesus when he stood in the Jordan before the Dipping Man. Come, Holy Spirit, come! For I am but a baby, newly birthed, and acquiring afresh my tongue. I do not know how to speak the great message I have been given.

I let the morning sun dry me as I walk barefoot up the broad Herodian road in the bustling Tyropoeon Valley. Craftsmen pass by, burdened with their half-finished wares. A potter carries jars to the kiln for firing. A woman squats by the road, weaving a basket. And there is Peter. His head is down; he doesn't see me. I step aside and let him pass. He mumbles to himself. I could have touched him. Now, he's a few yards down the way.

Jesus is with him. Jesus calls to him, "Simon bar Jonah, who are you looking for?"

Peter doesn't recognize him. His face shows confusion.

Simon, son of Jonah, is Peter's real name. They continue on together, heading toward the Pool of Siloam. I know that I am not to follow. I have others to tell.

MIDDAY MARTHA

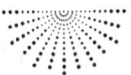

MARTHA

I'm having a good day. Three sales this morning. Considering how few pilgrims there are here, that isn't bad. Two were to men who made good money during the festival and now wanted a nice leather sack to hang on their belts.

"Don't you have something fancier?"

"No. Too much embroidery invites thieves. My money bags are functional and discreet," I say.

A well-dressed man is at the next stall, sniffing the purple linen sack that is supposed to contain myrrh from Arabia. I hope he asks to look into the sack before making a purchase. My neighbor's incense is diluted with sand. All of the Idumean merchants commit some form of adulteration, but his are egregious.

Good. The bag is being opened. No! Doesn't the rich man see that the merchant has palmed the bag in question and is now opening a substitute? The merchant's knife is making quick work of the stitches.

"Martha."

In the crowd to my left is Simon the Zealot. He is coming toward me. The glint of the dagger he keeps below his robe can be seen, now that I know where to look for it. Memory. Mad memory. It rushes in. Suddenly, I'm back, three days ago. He sat in my kitchen, and we calmly discussed how we were going to save Jesus. He had men. I had my club and a bribe.

Before my eyes, I see only the cross. Jesus being pinned to it. The one soldier kneeling on his arm. All of the soldiers taunting him. Men pushing to spit on him.

They did their work efficiently with the two thieves. They didn't have scribes urging them to be cruel. The soldiers tied the hands of the thieves. It was sufficient for the Zealots to have their crosses eased up against the sky. But you, they nailed. You, they dropped in a hole. They used my club to break the bones of the other two at the end of three hours—a quick end to an abbreviated crucifixion. But you, they thrust a spear into your side. I saw it. I can't unsee it.

"Martha." Simon has the twins from Galilee in tow. They've pushed out the rich man who was coming my way.

"I thought you'd be gone," I say.

He grins. "Things change."

"We found the tomb empty," Joanna says.

"Then why's he grinning like that?" I say.

There is swearing. The air is filled with the rankest language. Who is swearing?

I am!

I calm down and explain myself, "An empty grave means that the Romans are abusing Jesus's body."

"No," Joanna says.

"We saw angels," says Salome. "They asked us why we were seeking the living among the dead."

"And?" I look to Simon the Zealot for the punch line. I really don't have time for this.

"You should come with us to the tomb."

"I can't," I say.

"The guards are gone. It's just lying there, open . . ."

"And angels. They're sure to talk with you. So . . ."

"Majestic. Light and color." Joanna reaches up her hand, as if describing someone tall, like Thomas.

Simon motions for them to calm down. They are speaking over each other and repeating themselves. Strangers are staring at us.

"Let's go upstairs." He motions to a house facing the market square. "John inherited that loft. We are safe there."

"You've checked this out?" I ask Simon the Zealot. I know the answer before he shakes his head. It wouldn't be safe for him to go to the tomb.

"But I believe them. Let's go inside, and I'll explain."

"I haven't time for this."

I HAVE MAYBE A HALF HOUR'S PEACE, AND THEN JESUS'S mother comes. It's noon, and the only stalls with any business are the ones that sell food.

"Jesus is alive."

"You too," I say.

"Let me help you," the woman says. She gives me a cross made from a palm frond.

I see a potential customer move on.

"I understand it," she says. "I mean, his dying."

"I don't."

She was there. That's the only reason why I'm still holding this silly thing that she made for me. I have no idea how to take Jesus's death. I've seen men crucified before, but his was different. He kept Mary sane. He brought Lazarus out of the grave. I had a lot riding on him. His dying ripped me to shreds. Here is his mother making crosses out of palms. I saw them lower Jesus's dead body into her arms. His hand fell limp at her side. The wounds of the nails made me sick.

"I was sitting and thinking about it when I found this palm branch."

She points toward the well and the Jaffa Gate beyond. West. There are many palm trees in the city. There is nothing unusual about finding a frond. The poor gather them for kindling. I don't. They smoke and stink when they burn. Beyond the western wall is the quarry where Jesus died.

"No, it wasn't bent that way when I found it. It was straight the way it was in my hand when I saw my Jesus ride into Jerusalem on a donkey. I waved and waved. No, maybe it's not the same one. But I did stop last Sunday in the afternoon by that well. A woman offered me a drink, and I told her my story . . ."

"There's a point?" I prod her.

"Yes. We were in Bethlehem when Jesus was born. Did you know that? The woman I sat with was from somewhere in Judaea. She had an accent like yours."

"*Am ha'aretz?*" I ask. The customers have fled, looking for a place to eat their lunch, so I let the woman speak.

"Yes. She, you, and I. We are people of the land—*am ha'aretz*. Jesus came for us. But he also came for those who are captive under the earth, like your brother was. The woman was about my age, and I asked her if she had children. I don't remember now how she answered because soon I was telling her about Jesus and how he was born in Bethlehem."

"You needed to talk. Go back there. Maybe someone else has time for your story."

She laughs. *Hysteria?* I step back. I don't want to catch it.

"No, listen. God doesn't send us angels so that we have someone to talk to. He sends his messengers and prophets to us to tell us what we need to understand. Martha, I am as sane as you are. But when Jesus was eight days old, a prophet was sent to us. His name was Simeon, and he lived in the temple. He took the baby from my arms. Joseph and I let him because we knew he was about to say a word from God."

And now this woman is chanting. She has taken the cross

from my hand and spins around. Everyone has turned to us. She sings loudly:

This child is destined to rise.
This child is destined to sink to the depths of Sheol.
He will cause the falling and rising of many in Israel.
He will be lifted up on a cross
and become a sign of all that some hate;
Their cruelty to him will reveal what is in their hearts.
Then, too, a sword will pierce your heart,
A grief beyond words for those who love him.
But look at him.
This child will conquer death,
And become your salvation
And the hope of all nations—
a light revealing God's love for the Gentiles
and the glory of Israel.
Now dismiss your servant in peace,
For I have seen your salvation.

She's calm again. She fixes me in her gaze. She hands me back the palm cross.

"Those were his exact words. How can I take a palm and wave it in joy if Jesus isn't still this day the Messiah? How can I shape this palm into a cross if Jesus's death hasn't brought to us this day salvation? How can I be brave and say these things for all to hear if Jesus hasn't this day burst out from his grave and is now, once again, alive?"

"But you don't understand," I say.

She leaves me, going up the stairs and into the house John inherited.

"Show's over," I say to the crowd.

So, AS IF THE DAY COULD NOT GET ANY WORSE, HERE COMES Nicodemus.

"You lose your sidekick?" I ask.

"No. I haven't seen Cleopas since yesterday, but the ruse may have been discovered. Tell your brother that he is in real danger now."

"Why?"

"Because someone—maybe your Thomas got together with the man's disciples—has opened the grave and stolen the body."

"Thomas wouldn't do that. You've met the disciples. Do they strike you as risk-takers?"

"No. But the body was stolen."

"I heard the tomb is empty. I've also heard that your friend is behind it."

"Who—Caiaphas? Why would he do that?"

"Why would anyone? He must have something planned."

"There were Roman soldiers guarding the tomb. They were overcome by someone. The high priest is questioning those men now. He wants the Sanhedrin to meet at noon. I'm going there now. Don't you see? I'm in the middle of this."

"Pilate must still be drunk or too hungover to deal with his own men."

"He looked pretty into it yesterday."

I consider this a bit strange. Romans don't promote such men. They don't drink unless they have someone present whose health they want to drink to. Even their decadence is political.

"You've heard something about Thomas, then?"

"Mark came back, saying he knew where a giant might be hiding. He'll check it out this afternoon. In the meantime, I've got to find the disciples before the temple guards do."

"Why?"

"Because Caiaphas will get the truth out of them. They'll tell how I hosted you all on Friday night. It's called aiding and abetting criminals. I've been a fool. I was Jesus's refuge in the city."

I've never seen Nicodemus this way. Sweat runs down his great forehead, even though the day is pleasant. He shifts from foot to foot as he speaks. He is beyond upset. I fear he'll have a stroke.

"What does this have to do with me?" I ask.

"Because you are the cause of these troubles. You offended the soldiers at the cross, or don't you remember that? You and your sister are responsible for bringing Jesus back from across the Jordan. His death is on your head. He was safe before you called him back to do a miracle for your brother. Well, you got what you wanted and you're back to selling leather like nothing happened. You want the city to think that I'm behind this?"

"I don't care what the city thinks. It is time for me to be back to work."

He shakes his head like he doesn't understand that this is my only livelihood. I sell leather or I starve.

"Do you know where the disciples went?"

"No," I lie.

"Tell me . . . Swear to me on your father's grave. Did they tell you their plans? Do they hope to fool people into thinking Jesus is alive again?"

"No. I would never be a part of such a thing. I am the most honest merchant on this square. I don't cheat anyone. I don't lie about bodies that aren't where they were left. I swear that I know nothing. Now, leave me."

MIDDAY MARK

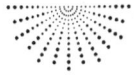

MARK

Mark again finds Nicodemus's door locked. As he pushes on it, the voice of the head servant comes from within.

"Who are you?"

"John Mark, a student."

"You're late."

"I have been running an errand for Master Nicodemus. I have an important message."

"Come around to the side door."

The head servant takes the scroll from him but says that he is too late to join his lessons.

"I need to explain something to the master." Until this moment, Mark thought he had a good relationship with the head servant. When he was passing through the market, he would grab things for the servants. He never ignored them the way the other students did. "What's going on?"

"He's been called to another council meeting. You weren't here yesterday, were you?"

"No. The errand the rabbi sent me on involved going to Bethany and spending the night."

"At the home of the one the master calls Cleopas?"

"No. Simon the Leper."

At this, the older man draws back, but Mark adds, "Simon was never a leper. It is something the Monkey made up to exile him. What's going on?"

Mark can hear the sound of lessons being taught deeper in the building. He longs to be back studying. This is now the third day, if you count the Sabbath.

"You should leave. Come back when things are less . . ."

"You think the house is in danger?"

"Yes."

Mark understands. The high priest wouldn't be calling another council meeting this soon unless he meant to act quickly on some issue. It occurs to him that the body in Absalom's Tomb may not be that of Thomas, but of Jesus. Why Nicodemus and Lazarus of Bethany—or Cleopas, if you preferred a disguise that was getting thinner by the hour—would aid the giant in stealing this body was beyond him. The land under his feet suddenly feels insubstantial. What if the women who met at his mother's house are also involved? What if there is another man who looked like Jesus? There are rumors of a twin. Does Nicodemus think he can unseat the Monkey from his red chair by saying that the man the high priest had crucified was innocent and God had shown this by making him alive again?

"Go," the head servant urges him out.

"Tell Master Nicodemus I have failed to locate the disciple named Thomas."

"The giant?"

"Yes. But when I do, I may have to—" Mark is about to say, *go to the authorities.* He knows, even as the thought is formed, that he cannot do that. "If this is goodbye, tell him I am grateful. He has been a godsend to me and my family. I wish I could pay him back, but it may be best for me to leave."

There are tears in Mark's eyes as he goes out into the alley. He dries them quickly. He is on his own now. First, he needs information. There are places in Jerusalem where news gets exchanged. One is the market, but he wants to steer clear of that for now. Being seen with Martha will not serve his purposes.

The other place for news is the porch where money changers sit in front of the temple. They shout out their exchange rates, first in one language and then in another. A constant babble. And even when they are waiting for one customer, they are shouting for the next. But there is a secret code running beneath it all, their own cross talk. They are not in competition with each other as it appears. They instead collude, evaluating each face in the crowd. Deciding together when to raise and when to lower their rates.

Mark has discovered that they also exchange news. It doesn't take long for him to hear that the man who helped Jesus disrupt their enterprise—yes, Thomas the giant—has returned to Jerusalem. Even though the gatekeepers have promised to keep him out, he has found another way in.

"He lies low, but we must watch for him," the money changers say in their secret tongue.

There is more. The high priest is questioning the soldiers who guarded Jesus's tomb. This matters to the money changers because any trouble in the city will cause the Roman troops to remain longer. The money changers have more freedom to gouge temple worshippers when only Caiaphas rules the city.

"The body of one of the crucified men is missing," the money changers say. *"Galilean women are saying that this man is alive. Pilate is drunk. He's demanding that Herod and the priesthood settle the matter quickly, find the body, and put it on display."*

No wonder the Sanhedrin is meeting again. A week ago, Mark would have laughed at this. Now, he listens closely. It is obvious that no one in the temple knows where Thomas or the other disciples are hiding.

Leaving the temple, though, Mark hears on the street the

voices of children. They are spreading the news that a monster has been found under the house of Jacob the potter. Mark hastens down the Herodian road and into the Tyropoeon Valley, which leads to the Essene Quarter of the city.

———

HE SEES HER FIRST.

"Mary of Bethany, I have something to ask of you."

She stops, recognizing him even though they have never been introduced. "John Mark of Africa, or should I say *Gershon*?" There is laughter in her voice.

"I'm never called that." Mark quickly feels off-balance in this encounter. The road falls steeply to the south at this point. His left foot, always the weaker one, is below and sideways against a stone. The city people wanted steps to be put in, but the Romans insisted that a road be built that was suitable for carts. Garbage and crucified men are carried on sledges and carts this way and then out the Dung Gate. Efficiency for the city's protectors always goes ahead of the needs of the many pedestrians who travel this way.

Mary crosses her arms.

Mark speaks quickly. "I know what you have done."

"I am a seer, not a doer."

"I mean what the disciples have done. The body of Jesus the Nazarene has been taken."

"You mean he is gone. No one took him from the tomb."

"Nonsense."

"Believe what you want to believe. What you see will depend upon what you believe. Right now, he is walking to Emmaus between my brother and the disciple called James. They don't see him because they don't believe."

"No. You have a man that looks like Jesus that you are hoping to use to . . ."

"To what? We have no interest in the high priest's red chair or a kingdom on this earth or an empire like the Romans rule. We only have Jesus. His life. His peace. His kingdom beyond the grave."

"Tell me, where can I find the one they call Thomas?"

"Yes. The giant is the only twin that Jesus has. I don't know if he's even alive."

"You don't know that he has been seen with the Essenes?"

"No. I see in my mind that God is like a potter who crushes his creation and then reforms it into another shape when it suits him. I see that God has done this to Thomas. I don't know if my friend has survived."

"Jerusalem's children speak of a monster found in the clay."

"Since you have been truthful to me, I will let you know where to find the other disciples."

"Why?" Mark wasn't aware that a deal was being made.

"Because they can answer your questions. Would you believe me if I told you something incredible?"

"No."

"I didn't think so. Go to the marketplace. The house on the north face of the square with a fig tree beside it. Do you know it?"

Mark nodded.

"There is a large second-floor room. Talk to John, who owns it now, or to Peter."

"No, I think I'll first go to Absalom's Tomb and see the body."

Mary laughs and goes by him.

HOSPICE CARE

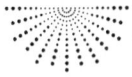

THOMAS

So Thomas is not dead. Yet.

Would I be in any more pain than this if the Lord-God had decided to torment my soul for all eternity in payment for my sins? No. Is it possible for me to be in this much pain and not be dead? Thomas doubts this.

Fortunately, there are long periods of unconsciousness.

In one waking period, he hears children whispering to each other. One asks if Thomas is the whale that swallowed Jonah. Everything about his rescue makes him wish to have died. He remembers how they tied a rope around his waist and dragged him, as if he were the opposing team of a tug-of-war match, across the clay, which held his broken leg back, as if demanding one last token for the hound, Cerberus. Obtaining a ladder did not end the struggle, for Thomas outweighs three grown men and the pit is twelve feet below street level.

His brow is fevered. Infected. He lies on a straw mat within the dark house. The potter's wife works to keep spectators away. Thomas drifts in and out. She brings him hot broth, demanding that he drink it all. There are drugs in the mix. She has made shrewd bargains to obtain these herbs. Tomorrow, she will need to trade more of her meager savings to keep him quiet.

Before he drifts back to sleep, he asks her about his knee.

"It is bad."

"Is the leg black? Warm to the touch?"

"Yes. But I've seen worse. One of them lived."

Then he asks her what day and time it is.

"Sunday afternoon."

Thomas groans. He thought it sometime in the middle of the week.

"How long were you below the city?" she asks.

"Since Friday morning."

"Why?"

"Because I am a fool. I thought I could save Jesus the Nazarene."

She laughs. "I thought it was you with the donkey."

"Yes. One week ago today."

"Then we should keep you hidden."

"Why? Does Caiaphas still have Jesus under arrest?"

"No. The Monkey turned your rabbi over to the Romans."

"Good."

Pausing to look Thomas in the eye, she tells him the bad news clearly and fully. The Romans crucified Jesus along with two thieves. Her nephew watched as a centurion thrust a spear into his side. He was dead. Water and blood flowed from the wound. The Romans considered the matter closed and had even allowed Jesus to be buried in a tomb near the old quarry. But then, the Monkey insisted that soldiers watch the grave. Word on the street was that turning in one of Jesus's disciples could earn you a silver coin as a bounty.

"For you, they should pay double. Don't worry. We Essenes will keep you safe until you recover."

"Then I'll be gone."

THOMAS IS ASLEEP WHEN THE BOY COMES.

It is not hard for John Mark to discover which house the giant is being hidden in. Listening to children is an art. Approaching the adults who guard the door is another matter. He takes his time, acting like a bored teen skipping his classes. He pauses, as if not expecting to be amused by this, but then showing curiosity about the spinning of pots. After a while, he asks if the clay comes that way from the earth or requires some preparation.

Jacob explains the strenuous work he made his own teenager do. "You must lift the mass above your head and slam it down on the flat stone over there. Then cut the clay in half and merge one half into the other. Then slam it again. Repeat ten or fifteen times."

"Why?"

"To remove the air—little bubbles that will explode in the kiln. You also must feel through it for stones and twigs."

Mark asks the man how he learned his trade and how the Essenes came to settle in this part of Jerusalem.

"Haven't you ever seen this being done before?" Jacob asks.

"No," Mark lies. The conversation is circuitous but eventually yields several hard facts. The giant had been discovered embedded in the clay shortly after dawn that morning. And yes, this same giant was a follower of Jesus. But neither the potter nor his wife seems to doubt Thomas when he said he had been injured on Friday and lost in the labyrinth of tunnels under the city since then.

"See, I show you," the woman says. She is in the process of changing Thomas's bandages. The giant doesn't seem to notice their presence. "The skin of his whole left leg is blotchy. His calves are cool. Compare the one to the other. See?"

Mark does not hesitate. He gradually shifts his role, no

longer an idle boy. He is there to learn, and the Essenes are willing to teach. In fact, he is a physician in training.

"And this. Note that the left foot stinks, but the right one does not."

"Yes," Mark says. "This is what the Greeks call gangrene. Very serious."

"One more thing. The skin. Here and here, it crackles as you push on it. And the man has no feeling."

"The disease is progressing?"

"Yes. If he were injured this morning, it wouldn't be like this. The man is strong. He could suffer through the shattered knee. Not this. It is darkness in the deep body fluids that allow us to live. It takes days to show itself this clearly."

"So he won't walk again."

"I'm not sure that he will wake again."

As Mark prepares to leave, Jacob asks him again who he is.

"I am Gershon. I study medicine and old texts."

"You are indeed a stranger," the potter says. This surprises Mark, who hadn't expected a common craftsman to know the meaning of the name. "We Essenes are not a people who wish to cause trouble for Jerusalem's priesthood. But we will fight for our right to care for those who come to us in need."

"I do not work for the Monkey."

"Then who?"

"My rabbi and this broken man have a mutual friend. I was sent to look for Thomas. We were concerned when his companion came out of the tunnel, but he did not."

"You tell your rabbi that the giant is being well cared for, but do not tell him where."

Mark swears that he will keep Thomas's location a secret, then adds, "If he wakes, you should try to move him or help him leave the city. He has more enemies than friends in Jerusalem. The word of a giant being found in a clay pit is already on the street. It won't take long for the Monkey's spies to find him here."

"Why does a high priest care what we Essenes do?"

"Because this Thomas was a disciple of Jesus."

"The man they crucified?"

"Yes. And his body was stolen either last night or early this morning. It would have taken someone with Thomas's strength to pull it off."

"Perhaps our giant has a twin."

45

CONVERSION

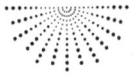

MARTHA

Now, Mary. Could things get any worse?

"Martha, Martha. I have good news . . ."

"This is new," I say, pointing to her mouth.

Mary waves me to the low wall that divides the market from the Jaffa way. She motions for me to sit. There aren't any customers. A scribe comes through, promising a silver coin to pilgrims who leave before sunset. They must be desperate to empty the city. Why?

I go with her. She is always so hard to read. What if she still has bad news about Thomas or Lazarus? What Mary considers good news is always subject to her own interpretation. She is calm, relaxed. She pats the stone beside her. She doesn't want me to stand. She wants me to sit beside her. It's like she is offering me her peace. As if peace can be given like a cup of cold water on a hot day. Like being at rest is something that can be shared from person to person. This calm is what I have seen in her when she makes a prophesy that everyone doubts for a week. Then the thing comes true, and she turns very quiet. She grieves like we all do for Jesus—not speaking, not singing—but today, she speaks. I can't keep up.

"Jesus's tomb is empty."

"You're the third person to tell me that. It's no longer news. Tell me something I don't know. Our brother?"

"He's on his way to Emmaus. He's with James."

"Good. Maybe the two of them can keep each other out of trouble."

"I see them walking with him . . ."

"Thomas?"

"No." She laughs. "Jesus."

This troubles me more than anything. My sister loves Jesus. She also loved Judas—before, that is. The Monkey has triumphed. How can she pretend to be at peace with it all?

"And Thomas?"

"Haven't you heard what they are saying on the streets? How a monster has come out of the mud like Behemoth, below the potter's house?" She tilts her head to the south, and I know she means the Essene quarter.

"I have been too busy."

"Who else but Thomas? Thomas lives, though he is badly injured. I see you helping him heal."

"You mean I should leave my stand and go for the herbs our mother taught me to gather?"

"No. The potter's wife is giving that kind of medicine. You need to lift his soul."

"How can I? You may not think it, but I am in mourning, too."

"Do you charge more for your leatherwork because you are in mourning?"

"No. I remember Jesus and treat each customer fairly." I say this because it is true. Knowing him has changed the way I do business.

"Good. If—"

I stop her. I turn her chin so she will take my question seriously. "Why did you make me do it?"

"What?"

"Stick my hand into his side. Feel with you the nail holes. Why did you make me handle Jesus's dead body?"

"This is difficult. I need you to follow each word. Stop worrying that a customer might come. Stop glancing over to your bag as if someone might sneak past us and steal it. Pay attention to what I am saying because I will only say it once and I will only say it to you."

I nod. I turn my back on my stall.

She breathes a deep breath and begins: "Just before Jesus died, Judas came and knocked me unconscious, and in that state I saw things as they really are. I saw Jesus carry his cross throughout the crowded streets of Jerusalem. He walked the whole city. The city is a labyrinth of the whole world, and as he made every turn, he went deeper and deeper into the sorrow of every soul. He came at last to the center of it all. There, he gave up his life."

"I saw him give up," I interrupt. "I saw him relinquish the spirit."

"Yes. But in that moment, I saw something in my vision. I saw that people would doubt this too. I saw that many in the world would not accept that Jesus really died, and if they didn't believe that he loved them enough to die for them, then his healing wouldn't come to them. They would continue to travel their own labyrinth of sorrow, even though Jesus has by his death provided the way out."

"How can they doubt that Jesus died?"

"Haven't you been listening? Half the wise men in Jerusalem don't believe our brother died. The Monkey tells his minions that our brother was pretending. That he got inside the tomb and there was food and drink for him to have until Jesus came and did a sham miracle."

"They wouldn't dare say that to me."

"Yes. Because you saw our brother die."

"Lazarus wasn't like Jesus. He didn't suffer. He went softly, like a flower that simply wilts. The spirit left him easy. That's why I didn't mourn like you did . . ."

"But you did," Mary insists. "You may not have wept. No, you went out and wondered through the wilderness in the night, barefoot. I saw you cursing God. You came home with a thornbush stuck to the side of your robe . . ."

"I did not."

"When I pointed to it, you grabbed it with both hands and threw it away. You were too angry to notice the pain. Grief strikes different people different ways."

"When Jesus died, I didn't get angry."

She laughs again.

"Hey, I thought you had something serious to tell me."

Again, she takes a deep breath. I've never seen my sister taking time to choose her words.

"When our emotions pass, it is often easy to doubt that we saw what we saw. I didn't want you to doubt that Jesus died. You had to put your hand in his side. You had to feel the holes made by the nails. You had to know he was cold. Put your cheek on his chest. Know that he was gone."

"Why?"

"It is a blessing. There will come many to you who have not seen what you have been able to see. They will doubt that he died. But you are blessed because you know he died to heal the whole world."

"Okay." I have to say it. Mary is pausing, like I'm a child that needs time to grasp each point.

"There is more," she says and pauses again. I close my eyes. I breathe.

I try to guess what she is going to say next. Instead, I remember Jesus laughing as Thomas unwrapped Lazarus. He thought it funny that our brother came out of our family grave with his face covered, his hands out. Confused. Even hours later, puzzled by this new life.

"You mean Jesus is alive?"

"Yes."

We sit. I have nothing to say. I have nothing to do. Bandits can have my bag, I don't care.

Finally, I say, "I wish I could see him."

"You will," she assures me. "But if you don't, you will still be blessed."

I laugh at this because it seems the most improbable thing I have ever heard. If James and Lazarus are walking with Jesus right now and Mary saw him this morning, but he doesn't come to me . . .

"Trust me, you'll be okay."

I'll murder him, I think. *Always teaching Mary, never teaching me.*

Instead, I say, "You've got other people to tell?"

She gets up. "Yes."

"I'll be okay." And I am.

AFTER TALKING WITH MARY, I DON'T FEEL MUCH LIKE SELLING. I have a few things and a few customers. They expect me to haggle.

"You want to know about a real bargain?"

"Yes?" they say cautiously.

"Have you heard about Jesus of Nazareth?"

"The man they crucified?"

"Yes."

"He died to heal the world and now he lives."

Then they stare at me like they are expecting me to give a punch line for my joke.

"I'm serious," I say.

They shake their heads and leave me. I have just decided to pack up when Simon the Zealot comes.

"I've been up there, watching you talk with Mary." He

points to a balcony on one of the houses that line the square. There is a disciple on it.

"Yes, we had a good talk," I say. This time, I notice the glint, not of his dagger but in his eye.

"I've come to apologize. They sent me to lock the door, but I had to come out and speak with you first."

"Do you want to know what Mary told me?"

"No, I know what she is saying. All of the women have been saying the same thing. We men haven't been listening. Jesus is alive."

"It's the only explanation for how my Mary looked."

"Yes. I believe them now. Even though Jesus hasn't shown himself to me."

"Perhaps in time. He's walking with James and my brother now. Maybe he's leaving Jerusalem, and you'll have to go find him."

"No. John and Peter want us to stay here. They look worried, though. They think the women will lead the Monkey's men back to where we are staying. They asked me to lock the door and to stand guard at the balcony with my dagger. I told them I had to talk with you first."

"Why?"

"Because you haven't seen him either. If you believe, then I believe."

I laugh. "I've never known anyone to care what I thought."

"And I want to give you this." He hands me his dagger and says, "I think I know what Jesus wants. He wants us not to fear death. He wants us to be peaceful. He has taught us the same lesson over and over."

"What is that?"

"Compassion." And he turns to go.

"*Shalom*," I say. "Peace."

"Yes, *shalom*."

I lift my hands to the market and all the people of Jerusalem. Like Mary, I sing for them a blessing:

For all that is,
Shalom.
For all that will be,
Yes!

SPYING ON JESUS

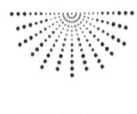

MARK

By the time Mark leaves the home of Jacob the potter, it is late. He looks at the shadows and calculates whether he will need to find a torch to search the inner chamber of Absalom's Tomb. Even if the west-facing door is easily opened, there won't be much light. With pilgrims camping in the Kidron and beginning their evening meal, he will have difficulty being discreet. A better plan would be to go to the new homeowner, John, and see if the man's sudden prosperity has made him willing to share a meal with a poor immigrant from Africa.

He crosses the marketplace. The fig tree is familiar to him. When he first came to Jerusalem two years ago, he would often spend hours in its shadows, listening to the words foreigners used. From his studies in Alexandria, he was already fluent in both the pidgin Greek of trading and the more nuanced, archaic Greek of poets like Homer. His love of words, though, kept him entertained as he watched Macedonians, Parthians, and Arabs from the empty quarter struggling to negotiate with merchants who had home-field advantage. It was under the fig tree that Nicodemus found him and told him that he had a scholarship if Mark was willing to abandon the mundane business of the street and pursue the word of God.

Martha is already packing away her wares. The square is nearly empty. The door at the top of the stairs is locked. Mark decides not to knock. Instead, he returns to the fig tree and climbs. A limb provides both shade and a way for Mark to look in through the balcony door.

On Thursday, he had been in a similar position, observing the final meal the rabbi from Nazareth had with his disciples. Mark counts heads and names those he can. There are ten men, where once there were twelve. Thomas is not with them, for obvious reasons. After Jesus's arrest and the events of Friday, that there are still so many seems miraculous in itself.

There is a meal laid out on the table, and the men take their places. Passover is over, so there isn't lamb. Instead, the small dried fish that arrives each day from Galilee has been heaped in the center. There is also fresh bread. Even from the tree, Mark can tell it has just been made, for the loaves are rounded and puffy. With the end of the festival, yeast has quickly returned to the dough troughs of the women. The bread of life has risen.

John, now, stands alone at the end of the table. He raises a loaf of bread and pauses. Mark knows what should come next. There is a prayer where the host of a meal gives thanks for the bread and the wine. Bread is made only by the labor of our brows, the toiling of farmers in the fields, the work of women kneading the dough, the watchfulness of servants tending the fires that bake it. But wine is a gift. A blessing that the Lord-God did not have to bestow upon this planet. Grace provides new wine for the afflicted. Grace provides old wine for those whose tastes for other foods have been dimmed by the passing of time.

In place of the expected prayer, John speaks another. The men seated at the table join in.

Our Father
Who abides in heaven,
Holy and worshipped is your name,
Thy kingdom come.
Thy will be done
Here in Jerusalem now,
With you in glory, forever.
Give us day by day
The bread that sustains our body,
And forgive us our failure to be compassionate,
As we forgive those who mistreat us.
Don't forsake us in situations that are beyond our capabilities,
And give us the courage to respond appropriately to evil.
Amen. Amen.

John breaks the bread.

Instantly, Jesus is beside him.

Mark holds the branch tightly. He calms his mind. He notes how each person in the room receives the sudden appearance. Most are startled. Several have fallen back in fear. The bench that three had been sitting on tips over. In the confusion, though, the heavy man called James expresses delight, his beefy hands clapping. Simon the Zealot has a knowing smile. Peter is subdued. John embraces Jesus, the bread having fallen from his hands.

Mark has time to observe the scene. It looks authentic. If Jesus had been hidden in the back of the room, this would not be the response. Mark can also see the door from his post. It remained closed.

Jesus motions for them to be calm and resume their seats. His hands have two dark marks where the nails would have been. He says, "*Shalom.* Peace."

He takes a dried fish from the table, breaks a piece from it, and eats it. "I am not a ghost. This is the body you are familiar with. But I have been made new."

"How?" Peter asks.

"Think of the farmers, sowing their seed. What they plant is not this bread. Resurrection is but one step in a much longer process. It is like baking. When the time is right, the dough is hidden for a while and then brought forth changed."

"And death is as painful as fire?" Peter speaks again.

The others, like Mark, seem content to watch this thing unfold.

"It is when you do it the way I did."

"I am sorry. I failed you."

"Don't be sorry. It was meant to be."

Then Jesus raises his hands and sings in a sweet voice:

> *A seed is sown, small and fragile.*
> *It rises up, imperishable.*
> *In this soil, we are often ashamed,*
> *But now, Glory!*
> *Life is lived in weakness.*
> *We are raised in power.*
> *The body is a natural thing.*
> *Being human is a spiritual thing.*

Then Jesus's expression turns serious. "I don't have long to be with you. Listen. You have completed the first phase of your process of discipleship. You have watched what I have done. You have practiced it in my presence. My peace I give to you as your most cherished possession. My spirit I give to you as your guide. As you have been forgiven, go forth and bring healing and forgiveness to others. You and the women shall be my witnesses."

Into the silence of the room, he speaks a final word: "*Shalom.*"

With this, Jesus disappears.

THE END OF THE DAY

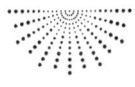

MARTHA

When my brother arrives, I say to him, "Did you enjoy your companions on your walk?"

He says nothing. He hugs me. My brother has never hugged me. Even when he lay dying, he was fevered but coldly objective. He doesn't show emotion. He is like our father. Since he's come back from *Sheol*, he's been worse. Now, he embraces me. There are tears in his eyes but laughter on his face. In time, he looks down and sees that I have everything packed away.

"You are ready to go home?"

"Yes. Maybe Jesus will join us."

Lazarus is still dressed as Cleopas, so we discuss going out of the city separately.

"If we are seen together, they'll know I am Lazarus."

"If they see me leaving the market before the last customer has gone, they'll doubt I am Martha."

"How concerned should we be about the Monkey?"

"I think we should stay in Bethany for a while. I may have to come back because Mary says that Thomas needs me."

"Thomas is alive?"

"Yes. Two miracles on the same day."

LAZARUS GOES OUT BY WAY OF THE EASTERN GATE, AND I take the longer route through the Sheep Gate. It has been a long time since I have gone that way, and I am surprised to see the new baths in Bethsaida. We meet at the top of the Mount of Olives.

Before going home, I turn and pray to the west:

> *Blessed are You, Lord our God,*
> *Ruler of the world, who rewards the undeserving with goodness,*
> *And who has rewarded me with goodness.*

It is one of the prayers my mother taught me. I think of her and, for the first time, have hope that I will see her again. We will go with Jesus into the new rest he has created. There, she will say, "Martha, Martha, come to bed," and I will be able to obey her. Then suddenly, I have another prayer to offer:

> *Blessed are You, Lord our God,*
> *Keeper of keys, who rewards the hopeless with renewal,*
> *And who has given me the gift to see it three times.*
> *Blessed are You, Lord my God,*
> *For raising Lazarus, Jesus, and Thomas.*

MIRIAM'S SONG

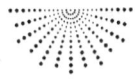

MARK

When Mark climbs down from the fig tree, he encounters his cousin.

"You know it's easier to do this spying thing when your accomplice isn't underfoot, staring at you and drawing attention."

"Who were you watching?"

"No one."

"Your mother has two new houseguests."

"Who?"

"A woman from Galilee, the mother of that man they crucified."

"And?"

"You'll never guess."

"Mary from Magdala?"

"Yes. How did you know?"

"Never mind. I need you to do something for me. Stay here as long as you can. Watch that door." He points to John's upper room at the top of the stairs. "If anyone leaves, take note of his appearance, then come tell me."

"Where are you going?"

"Home."

MARK ARRIVES ON THE OPHEL AS THE SUN IS ABOUT TO SET.
He takes his time. His mother will have questions. He will too.
Answers might be harder to come by. There is something else.
She deserves an apology. This is a new concept to Mark.

A meal has been set before his uncles and other relatives.
He is relieved to see that the pilgrims who have been camping
on their roof are gone. The home's children and women have
been fed and are resting. He can eat with the men. A strange
woman is serving. She banters with them, keeping them entertained. She tells her stories with a quaint Galilean accent.

"Where's my mother?"

"On the roof, I think." Like all Galileans, she doesn't nod
with her head toward the upstairs, but lifts her left shoulder.

"You were Jesus's mother?"

"Still am."

Several of the men smile with her.

"Where is the other Mary?"

"She's sleeping in the next room. Poor dear. She kept vigil.
Awake more than any of us until my son came back."

"Why is my mother on the roof?"

"To sing. Think. Aren't you studying to be a Pharisee?
What is your mother's name?"

"Miriam."

The strange woman nods and lifts the empty bread plate
as if it is a tambourine and taps it.

Mark's uncle laughs at this. "I think the woman means to
remind you that when Moses parted the Red Sea, his sister
Miriam sang a song of thanksgiving. Something about today is
making these women thankful. Even the dead man's mother
tells us jokes."

Passing Mary the Magdalene, Mark notes the gentle way
she sleeps. Then standing on the top step, he hears his mother
sing:

I will sing to the Lord,
For he is highly exalted.
Both death and our fears
He has hurled into the sea.
Jesus is my strength,
My defense against all evil;
Jesus has become my salvation.
Jesus is a warrior;
Pontius Pilate and his army
He has hurled into the sea.
The best of the Monkey's men
Are drowned in a sea of confusion.

The devil, too,
Has been fooled.
Sheol robbed of its treasures.
The devil roars.
He goes from empty room
To empty room.
"Where are my prisoners?
What has happened to hell?"

The enemy had boasted,
"I will hold each soul in endless sorrow.
I will gorge myself on them.
I will devour all meaning from their days."
Who among men is like Jesus?
Majestic in holiness,
Awesome in glory,
Working wonders,
Rising from the dead?

You stretch out your right hand,
And the earth swallows your enemies.
In your unfailing love, you will lead

The people you have redeemed.
In your strength, you will guide them
To your holy dwelling.
The Lord reigns
For ever and ever.

Sing to the Lord,
For he is highly exalted.
Both death and our fears
He has hurled into the sea.

Then she turns and faces Mark. The west is only an orange glow now. Lamps are being lit here and there throughout the city. They seem like fallen stars.

"I've seen him," Mark says.

PART III
THE WEEKS AHEAD

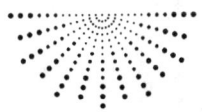

Change is not what we expect from religious people.
They tend to love the past more than the present or the future.
- Fr. Richard Rohr

N

Capernaum

SEA
OF
GALILEE

• Nazareth

GALILEE
REGION

Caesarea

MEDITERRANEAN
SEA

SAMARITAN REGION

JORDAN RIVER

Joppa

JUDEA
REGION

Jericho

Emmaus

Jerusalem

Bethany

A Day's Walk

Machaerus

DEAD
SEA

TO
EGYPT

WHAT WILL RACHEL SAY?

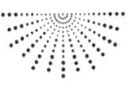

MARTHA

I don't know what's wrong with me. The sun is up, and I lie here.

"Why didn't you wake me?" I say. No one answers.

I go into the front room and discover my water jars are missing. Who? Did Mary sneak back while I slept? No.

Lazarus is at the well, his back toward me. He has a jar in each hand. I go out. He is talking and now puts the jars down. The man cannot talk without waving his hands. I've come far enough to see that he is talking to someone sitting on the stone wall that surrounds the well. Aunt Rachel. I hurry.

"Martha, what is this? You sleep late and send a man to the well."

Her voice is loud enough for all to hear.

Rachel's jars are beside her. They are empty because she is old and filling them involves climbing down the slippery steps into the well's pit. Men are too valuable to the village for us to allow them to do this task. She is right. Other places may have other customs, but in Bethany, girls learn to navigate these slippery steps as soon as they can walk. My aunt is the oldest woman in our village. Like all old people, she awakes before dawn, looking for something to do. She brings her empty jars to the well. Often, she leaves them there and goes out to bother the people in the fields as they seek to work before the sun gets too hot. Other times, she sits here and waits to chat with those of us who anxiously care for the needs of our household. She hasn't filled her own jars for years. Now, I am reminded that she wasn't with us for Passover.

"It is good to see you, Aunt. How was your time to Kerioth?"

"How was your time in the city? I told you that Jesus would come to a bad end. That he would ruin your family. And see? You must be sick or something. Do you have your brother's spring fever? Sleeping in like this. Next, you'll be singing like Mary—that poor demonic child. Your brother's been telling me that she's gotten so bad that she's staying in the city and telling people that Jesus never died."

"That isn't what I said," Lazarus manages to insert.

"Poor dear. Your brother says that you and Mary followed Jesus to the cross and watched him being put up. Why? You watch a man die the first time the Romans do it. Gawking at them is for city folk to do; we have more sense in Bethany—at least we used to. I know you wanted to protect Mary; you always do. But a sickness like hers only spreads. Anything good come from you standing with her? Obviously not. Your duties are here. Let someone else take care of Mary, if they can."

"She doesn't need to be taken care of," I say.

"But she's running around telling people that the Romans can't manage to kill Jesus. It's the kind of madness that gets women stoned to death these days. Sometimes it takes time. The Romans may want the man to be up there as a warning for a few days. They do things to extend his suffering and keep him begging for death. They tie his shoulders so that he doesn't suffocate in the first few hours. They'll do this if they think he has a strong heart. A man can last four or five days. But they always kill them in the end."

"Jesus's heart broke. He drowned in his own fluids. They put a spear in his side. Blood and water flowed like a river. I was below. My hair . . ." I don't know why I am telling her this. I want her to know that it wasn't Mary that brought me to the cross. I went there on my own. I stood closer than anyone. Mary didn't come until it was too late. I'm brushing tears from my eyes.

"Martha, Martha. Be strong. You must be. Your family needs you to—"

"Jesus died on Friday, a few hours before sunset. He was carried to a nearby grave," my brother interrupts. "Martha and Mary worked together to wrap him in spices. They accepted that he was dead and prayed the appropriate prayers. Just as they had prayed for me. Just as they put me in a grave, so Jesus was placed in the grave of Joseph of Arimathea, just outside the city. Then all of us rested for the Sabbath."

"Yes. I heard you came back after the Sabbath. But you didn't speak to anyone. You arrived in the darkness and then left the village before anyone awoke the next day. What kind of nonsense is that?"

"I had work to do. I wanted to sell my goods to the pilgrims before they left."

"Then why didn't you come back before the Sabbath? You should have been here on Sunday afternoon when I returned. Others came out to greet me. I had to walk all the way from Hebron, but again, you didn't return until dark. Coming and going, but leaving your elders to fetch their own water. I could have died." She nods toward the well's steps.

"Jesus died," Lazarus continues. "Mary isn't in the city telling people that he didn't die. She saying that on Sunday, Jesus came back to life, rolled away his own stone, and was seen by many in Jerusalem. Mary and I saw him."

"Did you see him?" She turns to me.

"No, but—"

"Of course you didn't. You're the only one in the family who understands."

"What?"

"We are born with nothing. We live. We learn to work. We suffer. Nothing is permanent. Then we die. Nothing changes that. The only humanity we have. The only thing that separates us from the animals, is that we know enough to care for those who are kinfolk and respect those who are our elders."

"You are a bitter old woman," Lazarus says. "A woman who can walk forty-five miles to Kerioth just to insult us at Passover time doesn't need anyone to fetch her water."

Rachel's face turns red, then she turns and stumbles toward her house. There are women already at the bread oven. They see her. She goes limp near them, and two of them come on each side of her. They help her home. Rachel's jars remain by the well. I go to them.

"You need to rest."

"No. I'm fine. But you . . . what are you doing?"

"I'm getting ready to go into the city again."

"Don't."

"I want to see Jesus again."

"You're being greedy. Let him show himself here. There are others who need to see him."

He looks at me with a raised eyebrow. Then he shrugs and takes one of Rachel's jars. He goes down the steps into the well. His hands feel the stone walls. He whistles, and it echoes. There is a smile on his face. I imagine him in Hezekiah's tunnel telling the giant how as a child he loved to explore the subterranean world. I take the other jar and follow. He fills the jar and hands it up to me.

For the first time in my life, I notice the dampness and smell of this place. The air of Bethany is dry from the surrounding dessert. The air here is what I imagine Jericho must be like.

"Does the Jordan River smell like this?"

He smiles. "No, near the Jordan something is always in bloom. Oranges. You would smell the oranges."

"Like Beersheba?" The oasis has citrus trees. Oranges free for the picking in the fall. Father and I went there to sell our leather goods once. The villagers offered us fruit in exchange. They didn't have money, only oranges.

"Jericho on the Jordan is deep. No seasons. Fruit all year round. And the people are prosperous. Trade flows through the city. Tax collectors at every gate. Spices and camels. You smell the caravans in Jericho."

"I want to go there. I envy the traveling you've been able to do, brother."

"I've been neglecting Bethany," he says.

I nod, accepting it as an apology. He hands me another jar. We trade full for empty, and the work goes quickly.

"What was Rachel saying to you before I came?"

"The usual. That nothing good will come of anything we do. That I am too much like my father and Mary is too much like her mother."

"A woman Mary never knew is responsible for her madness?"

"Our mother wasn't mad. Neither is Mary."

"Yes. Spiritual, but not mad." It is my apology for all the things I have said against them. "Rachel never liked Jesus. Said that nothing good would come of following him. I had that argument with her every day. At the well, we would talk about the Dipping Man, and she'd say nothing good would come of people going out into the wilderness to listen to him. Then when Jesus began to teach, she said nothing good would come of it either."

He hands me the last jar, but I sit on the top step. I want to stay in this paradise a bit longer. I say, "It's not safe for us in Jerusalem. I'm not going into the market until I have to. I don't trust the Monkey. Mary has her ways of staying out of his grasp. Before Friday, I could pass for normal. No one thought of me as a friend of Jesus. It's like we've become revolutionaries by choosing to believe that Jesus lives. We are members of a new secret order and we must be careful—you especially. The Monkey wants to grab you and toss you into his pit or worse. I'm thinking that Jesus's miracles are only one to a customer."

"Okay."

He takes our water jars back to my house. I take the two that belong to Rachel. The villagers who aren't in the fields are in their doorways. They've heard Rachel's anger. The women of Bethany stand with children on their hips. They watch to see what we will do next. They stare in wonder. It is as if a new day is dawning.

I bring Rachel's water jars to her empty doorway. I set them just within the darkness. I can smell incense. The people of Kerioth burn it at Passover time. It scents their clothing. I know Rachel is near. Neither of us speak. The bitter myrrh is something borrowed from the Moabite people who live in tents to the east. It isn't found in Moses's instructions for the meal.

"Pagan rituals. They creep in at the borders," is what our father would say.

"Jesus lives. There are no borders," I say to the darkness that holds my aunt.

NOT ENOUGH ANGELS

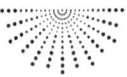

THOMAS

O n Monday, the potter's wife is concerned that Thomas is sleeping too much. She has heard of people with blows to the head simply sleeping away. So she cuts back on the poppy milk and tries milder herbs into his tea. She calls in the men to help her roll him over. He wakes, and she peppers him with questions. When he drifts midsentence, she nudges him hard with the club she keeps by the door.

"For your own good," she says.

"The rock was on my knee, not my head."

"I keep you from dying. Don't complain. What would you know of healing?"

"Men fall in the quarries. We aren't allowed to work slowly and safely. I've seen women seeking to save their men. Women in the north, around Galilee, do one thing. Women of Judaea do the opposite. When either of them gets lucky, they consider themselves great healers."

"Was your Jesus always lucky?"

"Yes. Until this week."

"He taught his disciples his secrets, no?"

"He taught us how to pray. He sent us out in groups of two. There wasn't anything secret about it. When we thought of Jesus, even though he was far away, good things happened. People found *shalom*. Yes, sometimes that meant recovering their physical health."

"How? Did you cause the blind to see?"

"I saw a man needing to be led. Those helping him said he was blind. I had no reason to doubt them. Jesus spit in some dirt and made mud. Then he put it on the man's eyes. There was never anything secret about what Jesus did. He made mud, and the man said that he could see."

"Some herbs hidden in his palm?"

"If so, that is unfortunate. Those secrets died with Jesus. He never told anyone how he did his miracles. He expected us to do things the same way, though. When people came to us and we failed to help them, he'd say, 'Where is your faith?' He said it to us, his disciples. He didn't say it to the sick person. He never blamed the sick for their difficulties, only us when we failed to help."

"Let's hope I'm as lucky as Jesus was at this." The water is hot, and she makes a thinner mixture of her healing tea.

Thomas receives it with gratitude, then is disappointed when it doesn't hit him as yesterday's had. She still looks at him with an eyebrow raised. Obviously, she wants him to say more about his life with Jesus. He tries to turn away.

"Stay on this side until I tell you to roll over."

"Why?"

"It is how we heal. You know something better?"

"We healed those who appeared to be lame."

"Any of them faking lameness as well as you are?"

"We went out by twos. Jesus wasn't with us. The healings still happened. You happy now?"

"Who did you go out with?'

"John."

"Oh, the Monkey's son."

Thomas groans. "Even you know this?"

"We hate the man, but we still pray for his family. We're not animals, you know."

"So I traveled with John. Sometimes a woman came with us."

"Mary of Magdala?"

"Yes. How did you—"

"Everyone knows Mary the Sorcerer. Continue."

"We made a good team. I was sorry when Jesus sent her back to Bethany."

"But that was good for us. She has done many healings here in Jerusalem."

"I'm not safe here." Thomas groans again.

"Yes, you are. The Monkey can do nothing in our neighborhood. The Essenes are not his people."

"Jesus didn't belong to Caiaphas either. That didn't save him."

"Have you always been this dense? Or is it just the herbs I give you? Miracles are still happening. Jesus is still lucky for you. See, you are alive. Earthquake and cave in, yet here you are. Yesterday, a boy came who is studying medicine. He looked at you and said you would be dead by nightfall. But today is a new day, and you are still here."

"I had a visitor?"

"Yes. Not someone you'd know. An African immigrant. Said his name was Gershon. Don't worry. We made him promise to tell no one."

"And you trust strangers who come pretending to be physicians?"

"We are Essenes; we aren't stupid. We live in this city, even though the priesthood doesn't like us and the Sanhedrin never gives us justice. We recognize others who face discrimination. There is a trust among us. We keep each other informed."

"Why do the Essenes stay in Jerusalem? You have a community down by the Dead Sea. No one bothers you in Qumran. Why here?"

"You've spent a summer in the Great Valley? No. On days like today, Jerusalem is a paradise. Smell the bougainvillea and the other highland vegetation. Down near the Dead Sea, it is already hot and humid. Even in the spring, the damp, salt-laden air smells like a dead thing. Besides, Jacob and I have our own family."

"Celibacy is not for you?"

"It is not required. Those in Qumran live by a higher code of purity."

"They copy the scriptures, I am told."

"Yes. They live separately so they can focus on the work of copying each letter of holy text without error. They dwell in singleness of mind, singleness of heart, singleness of relationship—married to the word. Only a few of the Essenes have that calling. The rest must live in other communal gatherings. Each community has different rules according to the work they do."

"And what is your work?"

"To wait near the temple but never enter it until the Messiah arrives with his armies of angels."

"The Messiah has come. He just forgot the angels. Big mistake."

"We saw you and Jesus come into the city a week ago Sunday. The crowds called him Messiah, and we watched. We listened for the battle trumpet from heaven. We were ready. We wanted him to be the one. Instead, in Jesus's train, we saw one giant and a lot of women and children. Then you and he went into the temple with a whip."

"It wasn't what you were expecting?"

"No. Should we have changed our expectations?"

Thomas shakes his head.

"Did you know that his cousin, John the Baptist, was an orphan?" Jacob continues. "He was the only child of elderly parents and, like many unfortunates, he was raised by the Essenes in Qumran."

"Yes, the *am ha'aretz* call him the Dipping Man."

"He went up the Jordan River and out into the wilderness. We watched him. He drew crowds of people and helped them to know God. The man dipped them in muddy water but made their souls clean. He spoke of a new kingdom. So, of course, we had expectations for him. Then Herod had him beheaded."

"Not enough angels."

"No. Not the right Messiah."

"You know the hardest thing about following Jesus? The way he constantly made us give up on what we thought we knew. He challenged our expectations every day. Everyone struggled with it. I did. He once told me that I was his twin. It surprised me. I asked why. He said, 'Because you have become, over these three years, the most flexible of my disciples. Your mind is quick to drop old prejudices and grasp new truths.'"

"Is flexibility what got you into that cave? You, a giant crawling into a wee little tunnel?"

"No, it was Mary, the one you call a sorceress. She told her brother, Lazarus, and I that we would get safely into the city the day Jesus was arrested if we followed her instructions. I had come to depend upon her gift. She told us to use Hezekiah's tunnel."

"The same Mary that helped you and John do healings?"

"Yes. Jesus sent her with us . . ."

"Now, you listen to me. We should find this woman."

"No."

"Then perhaps John, the one you traveled with. He must have had enough faith for you both. Maybe he'll pray for you. You will walk again."

"No."

"You are stubborn."

"I'm just being reasonable. If the Monkey finds me, he

might also find the others through watching me. Best if we all stay separate."

"You think the Monkey would harm his own son?"

"Yes. John rejected his family when he came north. He got baptized by the Dipping Man and began following Jesus. His father was cruel to him before all that. No reason to expect the two to make up now."

The woman nods and is silent for a while.

"Men can be stubborn."

"Okay."

"No, it isn't. It costs us everything."

Thomas doesn't reply. He closes his eyes and waits for her to leave.

"No. Stay with me now. I'm saying that men never count the cost of things."

"I know—"

"Stop. Listen for once. All boys want to please their fathers; John never could. You'd think they would just accept it for what it is. You don't get to pick your kids."

"John was adopted."

"Yes. He was put on their doorstep, and his mother, God rest her soul, loved him as soon as she saw him—her little Johnny. He was the only thing keeping her alive. Then he left. Said he wanted to find truth."

"You said, 'her soul.' Is she dead?"

"Hanged herself, poor dear. She waited three years for John to come home. The Monkey went out to the city gate and did what men do when they don't want their sons to get their money after they die. He broke a clay water jar before the other elders and said, 'I have no son.' Had it recorded and the scroll stored where the city keeps all of its records. Men! Like the boy he raised was a piece of land. He came back to find her body."

"You can't blame John or the Monkey for it. Some things are overdetermined."

"What?"

"We don't know what was going through her mind. Could have been . . ."

"Just her time?"

"No. I'm saying her suicide might have happened at some other time. There may have been a dozen reasons for it."

"When you see John, tell him that. I'm sure he'll find it comforting."

"I don't plan to see John. If do, and he hasn't learned of his mother's death, he won't hear it from me. If he has, I doubt he'll be asking my opinion on it. If he doesn't ask, I won't offer. Unlike you, I know when to stay quiet."

"Still, I think we should look for this John. Ask him to pray, you being lame and all."

"I doubt he's still in Jerusalem. Why would he stay?"

"But if he has . . ."

"No."

"Have it your way, then."

"Do you know if the other man in the cave with me survived?"

"We only found you. Who was he?"

"Lazarus of Bethany."

"Wait. Is this the same Lazarus that Jesus brought back from the dead?"

"No, when Jesus had me roll back the stone from Lazarus's grave, the cool air came in and revived the man. He was lucky —at least, then he was. I'm asking about Friday."

"Is that what you believe?"

"I didn't see Lazarus die. When you hear of a miracle, you should always ask yourself, 'What is more likely?' Do I think it is likely that of all the people who have come and gone on the planet, the humble leather merchant from Bethany gets to be the first person to come back from the dead? Or is it more likely that his sisters made a mistake and he was in a deep swoon?"

"Nonsense," the woman huffs and leaves him.

Good. Let me rest.

The potter's wife, however, is determined to prevent Thomas from sleeping away.

"It's your turn to keep him talking," she says to her husband.

Jacob stirs Thomas gently and gets no response. He tells his wife that he was too late.

"The man is only faking death. Take my club."

"I hear you are asking about Lazarus," he says when he had poked Thomas a few times.

"Put me back in the hole."

"Okay, but first I want to tell you that your friends are still in town. Lazarus has been seen wearing rich man's clothes and pretending to be someone named Cleopas."

"Why? Don't they know that the high priest and his thugs are looking for us?"

"Yes. Everyone knows that. But we don't like the high priest. I know this man, Lazarus. If he has a chance to play a trick on the priesthood, he will. I bet Jesus's other disciples feel the same. Things don't go back to normal just because the Monkey wants it so. An injustice has been done. A good man silenced. We little people will find a way to disrupt the system. Jesus belonged to us."

AN ALLIANCE IS FORMED

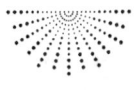

MARK

O n Monday, Mark goes to his class. He follows the same routine as he did on Friday. The previous week feels very distant to him. It is as if he has become a different person. He pauses to whisper a thank-you to his mother's sleeping form before leaving the house. He notices that Martha isn't setting up her stall as he cuts through the market. It rained during the night, and the streets glisten. A bird sings a bright song, and he hears it as:

> *Morning has broken,*
> *like the first morning*

The door at Nicodemus's house is once again locked. The head servant stands in front, directing students to go around to the kitchen alley door.

"You shouldn't have come," he says to Mark.

"I am still a student. That hasn't changed, has it?"

But it has. Mark finds it hard to concentrate. Midmorning, when there is a break between a scroll from Philo, whom Mark has always felt a kinship with, and Gamaliel, whom he does not, he slips out. Searching various rooms, he is surprised to find the master up in the empty banquet room. An early lunch has been spread before the Pharisee.

"I have good news—" Mark begins. He is ready to speak of Thomas, but Nicodemus cuts him off.

"What does this say?" He lifts the still-sealed scroll.

"How would I know?"

"But you do."

Obviously, being the only one in the large space doesn't bother the man. Long pauses don't bother him either. Mark waits him out. The man begins his lunch.

Below, the rooms are crowded with students being taught by other rabbis. In the scriptorium, a dozen scribes copy scrolls. The house is a beehive. People are pretending that life goes on. At the end of the day, however, after the students and lesser scribes have left, Nicodemus will break bread in this place with those men he considers to be his equals. Being a Pharisee is as much a life of fellowship as it is a set of beliefs.

There isn't room in a true Pharisee's life, he often says, *for a woman.*

"But some Pharisee orders require marriage?" Mark once asked.

"I said, 'a true Pharisee.'"

Until Mark met Tamar, he had accepted this wisdom. Now, the fate of Tamar is in his master's hand. Mark finally breaks the silence.

"There is a reason that you must break the seals in front of the whole council. Simon doesn't want you to be blamed for what it says."

"He is still my friend, even if we haven't seen each other since the day he was exiled."

Nicodemus motions for Mark to sit and eat.

"I don't care if you broke the scroll's seal or if you read it over Simon's shoulder as he wrote. I know it is not in your nature to allow something hidden to remain so. So tell me, what does the scroll say?"

"Simon knows that he was unjustly exiled. His skin condition was a falsehood perpetrated by the high priest. He wants to make a trade. His silence and willingness to remain out of the city for the servant girl Tamar. To be effective, Caiaphas must be surprised by it. You should present it as an ordinary matter of business, then be as surprised as anyone when it is read before the whole council."

Nicodemus makes a face as if the apple slices on his plate have gone wormy. "I don't like this role. In order to free the girl, I have to stand by and let my friend give up any claim for justice or compensation. And Caiaphas will be able to continue terrorizing the city."

"You aren't planning on challenging the high priest, are you?"

"No. Not me. I don't have the stomach for politics. I need you around just to keep me from unintentionally making things worse. Do you want to know why we are having our lunch an hour early? Caiaphas has requested that we spend the afternoon with him. I don't think he means to entertain us. The whole council is gathering. We will be traveling in a formal procession out of the city to Absalom's Tomb in the Kidron. Now, impress me. Tell me why I have received this unusual summons?"

"Because a body has been found in Absalom's Tomb."

"Yes." Nicodemus pours Mark a cup of wine. "Once again, you are a step ahead of everyone. Caiaphas only learned of the body this morning."

"It was there when I came back from Bethany yesterday morning."

"That makes sense. Caiaphas thinks it is Jesus. This is why we are going on this grand expedition together. He wants the whole Sanhedrin to be his witnesses as he produces the body of the man the people of Jerusalem think has beaten death. It will be a grand show. Then we will all go to the market where

Caiaphas is building a stage to put the poor man's body on display."

"He will be disappointed."

"Yes?"

"The body in the tomb isn't that of Jesus."

"Who, then? Thomas?"

"No. Thomas was alive yesterday afternoon. He was in the Essene quarter, as you and Cleopas predicted."

"Lazarus. That's the last time I'll try to deceive you. I was friends with his father, you know. Both father and son share a gift for deception. He wasn't able to fool you, though."

"I don't believe it's true."

"What?"

"What you said to me—that the less I know about this thing the better. I think in every aspect of life, awareness beats ignorance."

"You may be on to something there." Nicodemus pauses, as if turning this idea over in his mind and forming an aphorism out of it. "Yes, awareness does serve the soul, even when the heart and mind would rather remain ignorant. Well said. What have you learned about Thomas?"

"He was badly injured on Friday and spent the Sabbath crawling beneath the city. He emerged in a clay pit and is being cared for by good people. If he is lucky, he will pass away in his sleep before the priesthood discovers where he is being hidden."

"So you don't think he stole the body of Jesus?"

"No, I felt Thomas's leg. It's been broken for days."

"The other disciples, then? Have you found the body of Jesus?"

"I don't think Jesus is lost."

"The tomb is empty. Jesus has disappeared."

"Yes. That may be a better word for it."

Nicodemus smiles. "I, too, think something as subtle as the difference between disappeared and lost is going on here.

That's why I hope you will be with me when I go out with the other elders of Jerusalem and discover who really *is* buried in Absalom's Tomb."

"Me?"

"You have a gift for understanding people. I have been as gullible as my friend Simon of Bethany. It makes me vulnerable. Some of the other members of the Sanhedrin have servants who come to help them. I don't need help finding my seat or someone to cut my meat, but I do need help with discernment. You can read the crowd. Tell me when it's the right time to present our little scroll."

52

GO AWAY

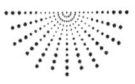

MARY

I awake in a strange house. The African immigrants around me speak common Greek because most of them were born in Alexandria, where the Ptolemies have ruled for a dozen generations. They speak it badly, though. Every third word is something borrowed—some Coptic expressions mixed willy-nilly with a little Latin. The Romans came to rule their part of the world a hundred years ago, just as it was with us. Instead of constantly fighting them, though, the Ptolemaic rulers chose to trade and make themselves valuable to the Romans. In hindsight, their choice makes more sense.

When I come into the kitchen, I see the men grabbing their lunches and leaving. They have fields to care for.

"Where's John Mark?" I ask.

"He's always gone before we are. Eager to study," is the consensus.

Miriam greets me with an embrace, then Jesus's mother appears in the door with a full water jar.

"Did you go early to talk with the whores?" I ask.

"Yes, someone has to tell them about Jesus."

I am beginning to really appreciate this woman. She goes to reach for the other jar, but I take it instead.

"I'll go," I say. "These are my people."

"Yes, they seem prepared for my good news."

"We'll have the table to ourselves when you get back," Miriam says. I can see she is getting ready to make bread. It will be a working conversation. It will probably move back and forth to the roof where she has an oven. Around us in the house there is the sound of children and other women, some of whom I have not met. I don't really like going for water, but I need information.

I pass a temple guard near the court where this quarter of the city has its well. He is looking for pilgrims, seeking to bribe them into leaving the city early.

"Is the man they crucified still missing?" I ask.

He scowls. "What do you think?"

I shouldn't have asked. He pulls my scarf back and sees my one week of stubbly shaven hair.

"Are you with them? Yes, I know you are." Recognition dawns. "You are mad Mary—the one who cast a spell on the Romans and made them sleep."

He grabs my arm. I'm quicker, though. I slip away.

"Stop her."

The jar shatters. I know where I must go next. Down alleyways and crossing the Tyropoeon Valley, I am a shadow in the morning light. The strange spices the immigrants use in their cooking gives way to the austerity of the Essene Quarter.

Near the potter's house, I inquire about Thomas, but I am told nothing until Jacob's wife comes out of a dark doorway.

"Did your brother live?"

"Yes. Lazarus escaped through the Pool of Siloam. Thomas was cut off from him. He searched and called. They are friends, and I can think of nothing . . ."

"We'll see if the man will speak to you."

"Have others visited?" I ask.

"The boy—an African. He pretended to know medicine."

"Yes, I know him. I passed him yesterday. He was

searching on behalf of Nicodemus the Pharisee. My brother, Nicodemus, Thomas—all friends."

"And you?"

"I sing only for Jesus who lives."

"Well, you are more likely to be crazy than dangerous. I'll trust you. I don't know if you will be received by the broken man, though. He knows now that Jesus was crucified and buried, then stolen and taken to Absalom's Tomb. He is disgusted by this deceit."

"Absalom's Tomb?"

"Yes. The Monkey knows. It was a stupid stunt. Children playing among the graves could smell him. They looked in, saw your Jesus, and told the temple guard. If I were you, I'd go far away. The joke has soured."

"It wasn't Jesus."

The woman shrugs. "We've stood here too long."

She takes me into the house. The room is empty, except of a wide variety of pots.

"Tell me again why I should take you to a man who doesn't want to see you?"

"If I restore him to hope, then he will heal."

She considers this. "If you upset him, he will die. You are too well known in this city. You have already drawn attention to us that we don't need. We can't move him now, or he will die. Come back in a few days."

"Let me buy that pot," I say. "If someone asks why I am here, you can say that."

So with a new water jar in hand, I go into an alley and through two more houses until I am lost and finally around the bend to another darkened room. As soon as I enter, I can smell death.

"Thomas. It's me, Mary."

"Go away."

"Jesus lives."

"No, his body has been moved. Go look for it in the

Kidron Valley."

"That isn't Jesus. Remember what happened to my brother? This is the time for resurrections, a time of miracles."

"Your brother I saw. Jesus I haven't seen. But I have seen men crucified. There is nothing left to call back to life. Every joint is pulled out of socket. The lungs fill with fluid. There is no hope. It will take more than calling his name to bring back Jesus from *Sheol*. It will take more than hiding a body on the other side of town to fool me. Go back to Magdala if you want to tell tall tales. The people in this city are wise to you."

"Why would I lie about this?"

"You are better at lying than I am. You know how to sell a few general predictions and make it sound like you have already returned to how you were when we found you in Magdala."

"No." I am in tears.

"Go away," he repeats.

"I am still Mary. But you!" I sing for him. With all my heart, I pour out an appeal in a language that is not of the earth.

> *Jesus, Jesus,*
> *Love this man.*
> *Show yourself to him,*
> *Jesus, Jesus.*

I hear my prayer return empty.

"Stop," he says. "Even if I see Jesus, I will not believe. Not until I put my finger in his wounds. This finger must feel the hole in hands and feet. My hand must go into his side, for there the soldiers prove a man is dead before allowing his friends to have the body. Let me smell the spices you wrapped him in and let me hear him call my name. I need to feel that broken body breathing, his chest against my cheek, before I will believe."

53

RELATIONSHIPS

MARTHA

I try to work on my leatherwork, but nothing feels right. The stitches can't be made evenly. Each scrap has some blemish. I keep rotating things, trying to work out a reasonable use of my material. Finally, Lazarus returns. He has spent the day on the highway talking to pilgrims as they pass by. I know this is dangerous, but we both want to know how wide the news of Jesus's new life has spread.

"I didn't have to ask," he says. "People were talking about Jesus as they passed me."

"Jesus told Joanna and Salome that he would see everyone in Galilee," I say.

"When?"

"He didn't say when. Actually, it wasn't him at first. The angels on Sunday morning said that Jesus was going before them to Galilee. Then when Jesus met the women on the road, he spoke again of going north."

"When?"

"Before must mean before."

Lazarus looks at me like I'm speaking nonsense.

"I want to see Jesus," I say. "Everyone else has. I think he meant that before the women return to Galilee, he would go there before them."

"Instantly?"

"Why not?"

"Because the men are staying here. The disciples don't plan to leave Jerusalem without Thomas."

"They are being foolish, as usual." *Why can't he get this?* "Look, Simon the Zealot gave me his dagger. He seems to think he won't have to protect himself. But I don't see Jesus kicking the Monkey off his red chair. The city is still dangerous. Besides, Joanna and Salome have to go home when Herod leaves. That could be any day now. The men should go to Galilee and support the women's story."

"John and Jesus's mother might never leave at all."

"Why?"

"Because John has a house in the city. Didn't you hear Jesus tell his mother to go and stay in John's house?"

"Yes. At the cross. He wasn't thinking straight. He was thirsty and dying of suffocation. Why should what he said then keep them here? Jerusalem is a lost cause. Jesus wants us in Galilee."

"And yet while he was on the cross," Lazarus says, even though he wasn't there, "he used one of his last words to give his mother into John's care. He knew John would be staying in Jerusalem. The city's not a lost cause. Our Mary had a number of people here believing in Jesus even before this week."

"The African immigrants and some other women, I know. They aren't his people. They know of Jesus through Mary. Jesus showed himself to you, Mary, and the disciples because you are longtime friends. Now, he's going to Galilee to be with his own people."

"With Jesus, every relationship matters. John had just lost his mother . . ."

"But John didn't know he had a house in the city. And Jesus couldn't have known it."

Lazarus raises an eyebrow. I read his expression. *Who am I to say what Jesus knows or doesn't know?*

"So you think Jesus gave John care of his mother because he wants some of his people here and some scattered around elsewhere? Then he's free to go back to heaven. That's what you're saying?"

"Yes. Does that bother you?"

"He hasn't seen everybody yet." It sounds petty. I add, "No, I'm not bothered by it. He can do what he wants to. He's Messiah now. I'm okay . . ."

Lazarus shrugs. "We'll have to wait and see."

"He should show himself to Thomas. Help Thomas to heal and then . . ." I shake my head. "He has to get everyone together again and let me cook, like . . ."

"What about Judas?" Lazarus asks.

"Jesus should never have chosen him."

"Martha, have you given any thought as to what Jesus was doing on Saturday while we were resting with Nicodemus?"

"Being dead. Just like you. Lost and wandering around *Sheol*."

"I don't think Jesus was lost," my brother counters.

"What are you saying?"

"I believe Jesus came into *Sheol* after his burial, not broken and meek, but radiant and strong. I think he conquered the devil. He destroyed the powers that have held human beings captive since Adam and Eve first disobeyed God. Everything is different now."

"What does this have to do with Judas?"

"It has to do with both Judas and Thomas. Since Jesus conquered hell, people are only bound by what they allow to bind them. Jesus will heal Thomas and unite him with the group when your friend is ready to be healed. Judas, even though he took his own life, will find that the gates of *Sheol* are wide open. He doesn't have to stay there unless he chooses to."

"Is that what you believe?" I ask.

"I don't know what to believe. I only know that Jesus loves. Jesus values relationships. He does whatever he does to bring healing to where we are broken."

I find myself nodding as he says this. I keep thinking about Jesus giving his mother into John's care. If there is anyone in danger of being captured by the Monkey, it is John. Jesus should know better. He should be sending everyone back to Galilee where it's safer.

"If Jesus cares so much about family ties, why did he break our family apart?" I ask.

"Did he?" Again, the raised eyebrow. Lazarus has been friends with Jesus a long time. I am barely sure that I can call myself a friend of Jesus.

"Even now, Mary isn't with us."

"Remember the day Mary left us? You were trying to bring her back to Bethany after her divorce. Our father didn't want you to."

"It would mean returning the dowry. He couldn't see past the money."

"So she went north. How was that Jesus's fault?"

"When he found her in Magdala, he didn't send her home." I don't mean for my voice to sound so accusing, but it does.

"Perhaps it took a year for Jesus to heal her."

"If he can travel from place to place instantly, why can't he heal instantly?"

"Because healing is a lifelong process. Look at me. It's been two weeks since Jesus brought me back to life, and I still feel like I have one foot in the grave."

"You do. As long as the Monkey rules Jerusalem, we all have one foot in the grave."

"Galilee isn't any safer."

"So what are we meant to do?" I ask.

"Rest and be thankful."

"Easy for you to say." I already have my table full of half-completed leatherwork. I want to have a serious talk with him about taking our trade somewhere else. Perhaps we could sell our leather goods in another city. The conversation seems to be taking me further and further away from where I want it to go.

"No. It's not easier for me. I've seen Jesus. But I don't know anything more than I did before. Death and life are still mysteries to me. I want to know more. I can't rest until I get my questions answered."

There is still a sadness to him. I don't understand it. I don't understand myself. He is right; everything has changed.

OPENING ABSALOM'S TOMB

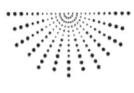

MARK

They have gone out the city gate and Absalom's Tomb is in sight when Nicodemus pulls Mark to the front of the line.

"Lord Caiaphas, I want you to meet my assistant."

"Why?"

"Of all the students I have had at my school," Nicodemus persists, "this one has the sharpest intuition. He discerns things the others hardly notice."

"He's an African." This statement is said flatly, as if Nicodemus needs to be shown the obvious. "Besides. You are too young to need an aide."

The procession is led by the temple guard. Their leather breastplates have been dyed dark. Underneath, they wear light blue tunics. Mark counts them and realizes that only a few dozen of the 144 that serve the high priest have been left back in the city. Behind them walk the seventy elders. At the end of the line are the seven Roman soldiers who guarded the tomb of Jesus the previous day when the body went missing. They are without armor, heads down, ashamed.

Caiaphas urges his people to be dignified but leads them at a pace too rapid for that, especially on the rough ground near the tombs. From time to time, he lifts his staff with its golden nob high and waves.

When he is out of their hearing, Mark whispers, "Why did you do that?"

"To establish you as an impartial witness. If there is another body—one similar, but not the same as Jesus—you will have opportunity to tell others what you saw. He can't deny that you are here."

At the tomb, Caiaphas calls a stop. Standing near its door, he directs the various groups where to stand. He calls the Roman soldiers forward. They flank him, bruises marking their faces.

"Why are they here?" someone asks.

"These soldiers were guarding Jesus's tomb when the body was stolen," Caiaphas shouts. "I want all of you to look at them."

"Must have been some fight," a voice shouts from the back of the crowd. There are those on the council who enjoy making fun of the Romans.

"Yes. The disciples of Jesus are dangerous. They have a giant among them. That giant is at large, terrorizing our community."

Malchus, standing behind his master, can be seen shaking his head. This causes the temple guards to mutter among themselves. The ones who had been on duty in the courtyard repeat how they had been ordered to cast the Romans into the pit, how they were told to abuse the Romans when they were brought out. Caiaphas lets this chatter go on, assuming it is the sound of appreciation for his handling of the situation. He is wrong.

"Someone, or something, knocked them out cold." A single voice rises up over the murmuring. "A demon. Not the Galileans."

There are nods of appreciation among the temple guards. They feel sorry for the Romans. Soldiers, even when on different teams, find themselves defending each other when their commanders are being unreasonable. The sounds grow, men repeating things, a supportive applause for the Romans who had drawn an unfortunate assignment.

Caiaphas's face turns red. He tells Malchus to deal with the men. When quiet returns to the hillside, an elderly member of the Sanhedrin can be heard saying, "I'd have thought Pilate would put these men to death. They fell asleep, didn't they?"

"Brother Simeon, you have become so forgetful lately. You were there. The meeting just yesterday . . ." Caiaphas bobs like a snake when he speaks this way. "Pontius Pilate gave the men over to us. He put the matter into our hands. We met, don't you remember? It is our policy to be merciful. Besides, people are superstitious. They would rather believe that a falling star or some other supernatural force freed Jesus the Nazarene from his grave, that there is a magical force that can give a crucified man a second chance at life. We must constantly deal with superstition. The Lord our God is one God. He doesn't allow demons to free dead men. He doesn't allow peasants from Nazareth to claim to be his son."

"So bring the body of Jesus out," a member of the Sadducee party says, tired of the delay.

"*I want you to be with the men going into that tomb, Mark,*" Nicodemus whispers. "*We need a second opinion.*"

The tomb door is finally pushed aside. The smell causes the soldiers to gag. An elder faints. Others stumble down the hillside.

"*This is worse than Thomas's gangrened leg,*" Mark whispers as Nicodemus pushes forward.

"*I smelled worse when I traveled in Egypt,*" Nicodemus whispers. "*Go!*"

The soldiers are ordered in. Mark goes with them, an eighth man. He moves too quickly for the high priest to object. There is a mumble of voices within. Then silence.

"We're waiting," Caiaphas shouts.

At last, Mark appears in the dark opening. He announces to the crowd, "It's Judas, the man from Kerioth."

"You are mistaken," the high priest responds.

"Do you want this body brought out into the light?" Mark asks.

"No, the Roman soldiers are to bring Jesus out."

Then Caiaphas turns to the captain of his own temple guard. "Quick. You bring out the right body."

The man goes in reluctantly, taking Mark's place inside the crowded tomb. A mumbled discussion ensues.

"Idiots! If there are two bodies, bring them both out," Caiaphas says impatiently.

Judas is alone. They drag him out by his coal dark hair because none of the soldiers are willing to touch the bloated body. His bloody tunic shifts, exposing his nakedness, and Mark reaches over to pull it back into place. The largest of the soldiers stumbles to the side of the tomb and retches loudly. Even the children in the crowd can tell that this is not a crucified man, but a fallen one.

"Is there not another body?"

"Look for yourself."

As Judas lies in the noonday sun, the Pharisees, who believe in the future resurrection and the redemption of all, express their pity for him. Nicodemus lifts up his voice in a prayer for the dead. The high priest glares at him, but the other members of his order join with him.

"This man was a suicide. Stop praying for his soul," Caiaphas commands.

Nicodemus only increases his volume. It is a long prayer.

"Let Israel now say . . ." He lines out the responses.

The raspy voices of the deaf elders join him with enthusiasm, for they were taught this prayer long ago and find hope in it. They don't care for Judas or Jesus, but affirm that any man who has owned the covenant of faith deserves respect. Their voices echo off the walls of Jerusalem.

Caiaphas, however, maintains control over the younger Sadducees, for they do not believe in life beyond death. They look down at their feet and wait. Their rabbis teach a different prayer for those who die. It speaks of friends living on in the memory of those they leave behind, but nothing more.

". . . bless the sacred Lord-God forever and ever. Amen. Amen."

"Amen. Amen."

"Finally! We have more important things to do today," Caiaphas says.

Having heard the *amen* of the prayer, many in the crowd take the high priest's words as a dismissal. The Sadducee council members feel their leader's embarrassment and shuffle away. Nicodemus holds up his hand, however, and keeps those of his order near.

"I have a request to make," he says. "Since Judas of Kerioth was seeking entrance into my order, we request his body."

"You can't have it. It was obviously a suicide." Caiaphas points to the broken piece of rope still attached to Judas's neck. "It is our custom to have such sinners dragged to Gehenna."

"When you received the bribe money back from this man," Nicodemus says, "you complained that it was blood money and could not be mixed in with the temple's funds. The council considered the matter and decided to purchase a field to bury those who die unexpectedly while visiting the city. I have located a suitable field between here and Bethany. A potter's field. The clay has run out. I will provide whatever additional funds are needed to purchase it."

"You would redeem the body of a man who hanged himself?"

"Who knows?" Nicodemus says. "It looks to me like he

fell. Were you there? Perhaps he changed his mind at the last moment. We . . . I believe in offering grace. Nevertheless, we still have a quorum, and I ask you to bring it to a vote."

"Take it," Caiaphas spits and barks orders to the soldiers, both the ones under his authority and those who are not. Everyone will need to redouble their efforts in searching for Jesus and his mischievous disciples. This has been a waste of time. The city will remain in a state of chaos until the empty tomb is explained. It is doubtful that Herod or Pilate will leave without some closure to the incident.

"Oh, one more thing," Nicodemus adds. "Give me a few of the temple guards to carry the body."

"No, I have work for them. You can take those Roman men there. They need practice in keeping dead bodies from escaping their grip."

Nicodemus explains to Mark where the potter's field is. The Romans fashion a rude stretcher from two flagpoles nearby. The banner is meant to welcome pilgrims coming to the holy city for the festival, but Caiaphas is too busy to note the theft.

"Where are you going?" Mark asks.

"To the Jaffa Gate. I must purchase the property."

"And after I see the body laid to rest?"

"Go to Simon's house and tell him about Thomas. Perhaps, you can also see Lazarus."

"And ask him to return Cleopas's clothes?"

"No. Ask them what they think of Jesus's disappearance."

55

THE SCAPEGOAT

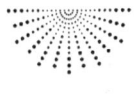

MARY

It happens from time to time. I return from seeing Thomas, and I am so filled with sorrow that I do not think I will ever sing again. How can I go from the joy of knowing that Jesus lives to the darkness of this despair? I am a leaf, blown in the wind. The spirit does with me what it wills. But then the spirit decides to make itself into something solid—an object I can handle and, by handling it, send my grief away. This is why artists make their art. Why a block of marble is purchased and chiseled by a man until it takes the shape of his dead wife. Why there is a mosaic of the city of Troy in Magdala or a poem sung in Greek theaters around the world about brave Achilles? Because we need art to make our humanity real.

Today, I go into the market. I find several small scraps of leather, bits of wool, and other rejected items behind the stall of a man whom my sister used to compete with for customers. I find two small scraps of hide taken from the same goat and cut each so they are the matching halves of my design. They are goats in miniature, a right and left side. I stitch them together. It is the spirit, because my work is finer than Martha's. I have all but the belly sewed when I flip it inside out like a pocket. I fill it plump with sawdust and stitch the belly so my binding forms an udder.

"There," I say to my craft. "You are the scapegoat. Come to life, and I will offer you up in place of the fallen man."

Now I know. My grief is not for Thomas. Jesus has other plans for him. He will not die, at least not with the Essenes in Jerusalem. I grieve for Judas. Will the grace of the Lord-God stretch this wide? What is the spirit teaching me through the work of my fingers?

I breathe into the nostrils of my goat. It does not stir. I think of how the spirit came in Ezekiel's vision and how that same call was mine when I went out to look for Jesus in his tomb and found it empty.

> *Breathe, oh breath of God,*
> *Into this slain one and make him live.*

Three times I say this and breathe into my goat's nostrils. Nothing happens, and I realize that it is impossible for us to go backward. Time's arrow only flies in one direction. You cannot make the hide back into the animal. You cannot go back to the altar and offer a goat in place of a lamb once the gift has been given. You cannot unbetray Jesus.

The disciples around me watch what I am doing.

Finally, I explain, "This is for Judas. Jesus lives, and Judas does not. This is not the way his story should end. You all loved Judas. When we walked the dusty roads and spoke the kingdom of God, he was one of us. Then when he betrayed Jesus, you each decided to hate him."

"I didn't," Simon the Zealot says. "I buried him in Absalom's Tomb. He was, of all of you, the one whom I found easiest to call my brother."

"Judas lacked flexibility," John adds. "I don't blame him for betraying Jesus. We all had our doubts."

I make each disciple lay their hands upon the scapegoat. I make them each say, "I forgive you, Judas."

It is our custom, each fall, for the priests of the city to choose one goat to symbolize all of the people of Israel. In a ceremony, they lay the sins of the people on the head of that goat. It becomes our scapegoat. The goat is then taken out the Dung Gate, past the city's dump, and driven into the wilderness.

I know our sins were laid upon the head of Jesus as he died on the cross. But what about Judas?

It is three in the afternoon—the hour Jesus died. I take my scapegoat and leave the puzzled disciples. I go south through the city and out the Dung Gate. I skirt the burning piles of rags in Gehenna. Dogs snarl and bay around me. I keep walking. The wind blows smoke after me. I smell the animal dung as it smolders. My skirt is torn by thornbushes, but I don't care. I am barefoot, and the earth becomes white sand swirling around my toes.

In time, I come to a place without a name. I turn a complete circle and cannot see any sign of human existence. I face south.

"Hoot, hoot," I sing.

I turn to the west and hoot again. Then to the north.

As I turn toward the northeast and Bethany, which I know lies some three miles in that direction over the broken hill, my call is answered.

"Hoot, hoot, hoot." My owl—distant at first, but approaching.

I lift the scapegoat. It comes over my head. The owl takes Judas in a smooth swoop. It does not pause but flies on to the west.

"Judas, Judas, your sins will be cast into the sea and remembered no more."

56

SOMEONE TO BELIEVE

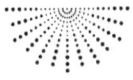

MARTHA

The light turns golden. Soon, the sun will set. I take the lamp Nicodemus gave us and check to see if it has oil. The oil of the rich man smells like the wind. His oil is light and from the first squeezing of the olives. By the time spring has come, most of what is here in Bethany has a rancid scent to it. I go to the window and prepare to say the evening prayer. I see Lazarus heading out the door.

"Where are you going?"

He doesn't answer. He stands in the middle of the square that is the center of our village life. He raises his hands in a gesture that moves from horizon to horizon. As the sun dips in the west, he shouts one word in that direction: "Good!"

He then turns and does the same thing to the north and the south and the east. This is something I remember Jesus doing a week ago Monday. He had spent the last night he was going to spend in Bethany. He said goodbye to me. He said goodbye to the village.

No, I don't expect Jesus to appear again in my house. Bethany is no longer his village. He doesn't need us as a place to lay his head when he visits the city. I don't think he needs me to cook for him or his men.

Mary told me that Jesus prayed to the four corners of our village in order to set a boundary. The evil of the city cannot touch us here. He wanted our house to always be a place of refuge. I think Jesus's prayer still stands. Bethany is a sanctuary. So instead of praying the way Jesus did, my brother is simply repeating the word *good*.

He pauses and raises his hand to his eyes, as if looking for something on the western horizon. I see it too. The line of pilgrims is down to a scattered few. Those still on the road have been foolish. They should have stayed in Bethphage where they would be welcomed. Here, they will be allowed to sleep in the grotto but not light a fire. They can drink from our well but not carry water away. We have always told pilgrims that these are the rules.

One small, dark figure, however, has separated from the rest. He is not going toward the grotto. He goes to the great house of the man who was once a leper.

Here I am, standing with an unlit lamp. The time for singing the evening prayer is upon us. I sing:

> *I lift up my eyes to the hills.*
> *From where does my help come?*
> *Not from the sweat of my own brow.*
> *Not from the keenness of my eyes*
> *Or the wisdom of my mind.*
> *Help comes*
> *From the Lord-God,*
> *Maker of heaven and earth.*
> *And from Jesus,*
> *Whom he raised from the dead.*
> *Amen.*

When Lazarus comes back into the house, he looks surprised that I haven't lit the lamp.

I say, "We need to go out again."

"Why?"

"To see Simon and the African boy. We may have to correct what the boy tells our neighbor."

"That is the first time I've heard you call him that."

"What?"

"Neighbor." Lazarus sits down. He wants to talk. He motions for me to take a seat beside him. "Remember the last night Jesus was here?"

"Yes. I cooked a meal for you all. Jesus and the twelve, you and Mary. James helped me bring food over from Simon's house."

"Neighborly of him."

"Yes. I didn't ask him, though. I told his servant that it was owed to us."

"Still, it was Jesus who helped us all to see Simon as our neighbor."

"Your point?"

"That the last story Jesus told was that night—at least, the last one I remember hearing. It was about a Samaritan who stops to help a fallen man . . ."

"The man beat up by robbers on the road that goes to Jericho from Jerusalem. So?"

"A Samaritan who is like our little African boy, just doing the humane thing. And when Jesus tells the story, he is speaking about what it means to be a neighbor. He is saying that the circle of the people we call our neighbors needs to be stretched out. The circle includes, not just Rachel and the women you see every day at the well, but also Simon and this African boy and the women from Galilee and the soldiers from Rome."

"I remember cooking all that food. I begged for Mary to come in and help me. Instead, I got James. Useless, because he kept wanting to taste everything instead of serving it."

"But Jesus wasn't hungry."

"Yes, James finally told me that they had eaten in

Jerusalem. The mother of that African boy has a home on the Ophel."

"And then?"

"I complained."

He raises his eyebrows and says, "And?"

I feel tears in my eyes. *Why?*

"I complained because Mary was just sitting there. She knew it was the last time for him to be in our home. She knew. I didn't. I'm slow. I get angry. Is that why Jesus appeared to her? Is that why you two have seen him and I haven't? Am I being punished?"

"No. No." He embraces me. My brother. This feels so good. *Why am I weeping?*

Lazarus has always been able to imitate voices. Now, in a perfect imitation of Jesus, he says, *"Martha, Martha. You are worried and upset about many things. Few things are needed, perhaps only one."*

Suddenly, we are laughing together. In the darkness, it is like Jesus is here.

I really hear Jesus. I hear him better than I did a week ago. I hear his gentleness. I hear him forgiving me. I hear him saying *shalom*—his favorite word. So much more than just peace. Wholeness, wellness, having life be a blessing. *Shalom* means we don't have to work to be loved.

"Why were you shouting *good* to our village?" I ask in time.

"When I left my grave, I couldn't shake this sense of foreboding, like everything would fall apart because I had broken the laws of nature. I didn't mean to. Jesus called me out, and I came. I thought nothing good would come of wanting to live again in this village. Now, I see that it is all good."

"You know what Rachel said?"

He shakes his head.

"The day after you came back to life, she went to each house in the village and said that you weren't as sick as we thought you were. 'Nothing odd about it.' Those were her words. I complained, and she said, 'Don't be so dramatic. You three are just like your mother.' Now, it's the day after Jesus defeats death, and she is saying the same things."

"Some things don't change."

"Why?"

"Have you ever known Rachel to change her mind?"

"She's dependable. I've needed that. I just don't like her being unhappy."

"That's what it costs."

"What?"

"I don't think we are punished for our doubts. I think, though, unhappiness comes to us when we hold on to the wrong way of thinking too long."

"I haven't been unhappy, you know. I've just been busy."

"Okay. I'm just talking about myself. I know where I have been. I was depressed when Jesus made me alive again. I couldn't imagine that I would be the only one ever to come back from death. I didn't deserve it. I didn't want it. I felt like I was a mistake. Every man lives once and then dies. End of story. Yesterday, I saw Jesus. James and I were on the way to Emmaus. Suddenly, I knew. I am alive, for now, as a gift—a free gift. As I have been given life, so I should help others find life. Unlike death, life requires rest. Sometimes we just have to sit."

"Okay."

"Not now," my brother says. "Now, we must go and beg another meal from Simon."

"I have things I can cook."

"Yes. But tonight, you have the one voice I think Simon will listen to."

"Why?"

"Because you believe without having seen."

INFORMING SIMON

MARK

When Mark arrives at Simon of Bethany's house, he is tired and hungry. The day has taxed him in ways he didn't expect. He resents Nicodemus for pushing him to the front, having him be the one who announced that the tomb contained Judas, and then putting him in charge of the seven Romans.

"It's only a little way," Mark had urged them. He knew where the potter's field was.

They thought there were plenty of more convenient places to stash the body among the rocks beside the road. Then when they found the potter's field, they complained about the clay being hard to dig.

"Look around you. You already have the holes dug by the potters. All you need to do is find the deepest one and then gather stones to cover the man."

"Why?"

"Because the wild animals will come and take the body. Judas was a friend of the council. If you don't do this right, I will suffer along with you. We eight could be mates together in the high priest's pit—or worse."

"So you are a servant of them, like Malchus?"

"I assist Nicodemus. I was drafted into this like you were. I didn't choose this."

"You went into the tomb with us. Why?"

"Because I knew both Jesus and this Judas. I'm a witness. Nothing more."

"Where were you when we needed you? Malchus found us knocked out and Jesus's tomb empty. That's when we needed someone who could identify people. How are we going to find his body without someone to tell us who stole it?"

"You won't find the body of Jesus," Mark said.

"Why?"

"Because he's still using it."

MARK KNOWS HE IS GOING TO HAVE TO EARN HIS MEAL AND lodging. Simon of Bethany will provide these in trade for information. Food is already on the table. Another place is quickly set.

"Did I show you my back when you were here before?" Simon asks.

Mark nods.

"Good. It's not that I need witnesses, but I enjoy it."

"Do you remember the disciple of Jesus named Judas?"

"Yes. The man from Kerioth? He had long, black hair like Absalom of old."

"The man had an accident."

"Judas? Terrible. Jesus made fun of Judas the night of the banquet—let's see, a week ago Saturday. After dinner, the rabbi told a story, and he had Judas and I pretend to be characters in it. It was all so much fun, and people laughed, but Judas didn't take it well."

"That would explain things."

"What? You mean Judas had something to do with Jesus dying?"

"He betrayed Jesus."

"Oh, my."

"Then he fell off the temple pinnacle, and whoever found his body decided to bury him in Absalom's Tomb."

His host leans back to reflect upon this irony, and Mark gives him a moment's silence.

"And the council didn't approve this?"

"No. In fact, they thought the body in that tomb belonged to Jesus."

"Why would they think that? You said that Nicodemus and Joseph arranged for Jesus to be laid in a tomb on the western side of the city."

"Because the body of Jesus has disappeared."

"They lost it?"

"No. That's another story. I'll tell you that later." Mark had decided to dole out his information in stages, moving from the easy to understand to the hard. "Is it okay if I start eating?"

"Yes, yes. More wine?"

"Thanks. I may be stopping by more often, if it's okay. Seems I've been put in charge of the potter's field."

"Good. I can always use another spy . . . No. You are an ambassador from the city. Always welcome in fair Bethany. How are you in charge of a vacant piece of land?"

"Nicodemus has purchased it as a burial plot for those who die unexpectedly while visiting the city."

"Thomas?"

"No. Thomas the giant survived the earthquake and is recuperating in the city."

"That is good news. Tell me where——"

There is pounding at the door. It's Lazarus and Martha. There is an uncomfortable moment as they are introduced to Mark.

"I think we have friends in common," Lazarus says to ease the tension. "Our sister, Mary, is friends with your mother. We also have a mutual acquaintance named Thomas."

"To our lost friends," Simon says, standing as if this is a toast. "Mark, here, was just telling us that Thomas has been found alive."

"He is being hidden in the city, but he is alive," Mark begins.

"How bad are his injuries?" Martha asks.

"Wait, how do you know he was injured?"

"Because if he could walk, he would leave Jerusalem."

Mark nods. "I am not a doctor. He is receiving good care. That is all I can say."

"To Thomas, our largest of friends." Lazarus raises his cup and all join.

"Mark, here, was just saying before you came that the body of Jesus has disappeared. Isn't that right?"

Mark already has his mouth full and waves the conversation on.

"Disappeared is not the right word," Lazarus picks up.

"Jesus is alive," Martha says bluntly. "He has been seen by many people."

"Here's to Jesus," Simon says lightly.

"You don't understand what I am saying. Jesus has rolled back the stone from his own grave and is now visiting people all around the city."

"Yes, I hear you. I think this calls for a celebration. Do you agree, Mark?"

Mark, with hesitation, says yes. "I, too, have seen Jesus."

"That settles it," Simon says. "Don't look at me so surprised. Old dogs can be taught new tricks; it just takes more patience. Since meeting Jesus, I've had to practice this. Things are never what you think. I was sick for seven years with a disease I didn't have. Why is everything we believe about death also above questioning? When you sit where I do, it doesn't seem so difficult to believe."

"Nicodemus sent me here to ask you what you thought about Jesus," Mark says.

"I think Jesus is marvelous. Oh, at first I didn't. I struggled to believe that Jesus could call Lazarus, here, out of the grave over there in the grotto. I was one of those who went over there to check to see if there was water or a breeze in the tomb that could have revived him. Then I had a meal here. I invited Jesus, thinking I could trick him into explaining how it was done. But you, Martha, were clever. You invited the people of Bethany into my house. It forced me to watch Jesus in his own element. I began to realize that the real difficult thing to believe was not that Lazarus could come back from the dead, but that Jesus could do something just as dramatic for me. Thomas told me not to consider the disappearance of the spots from my back to be a miracle. But I am free. Jesus made that happen. So I am learning to be both more ready to believe and more reluctant to be gullible like I was when I worked for the man in the red chair."

"Thomas would say that being both ready to believe and reluctant to be proved too gullible requires a certain mental flexibility," Lazarus says.

"But," Martha says emphatically, "you didn't see him die. None of you men did. It was Mary and me at the cross. It was Nicodemus and Joseph who came to help bury him. Why is it always women's work to be the ones who have to watch it happen? It was hard for me to believe. You men make it look so easy."

"You were the right one to tell me. I believed quickly because I trust you, Martha."

Mark leans back, looking relieved.

"I was worrying about how to tell you," he says to Simon. "I have seen Jesus. I climbed the fig tree that grows on the north of the Market Square, and I looked into the place where the disciples are staying. Jesus appeared to them. He spoke for a few minutes, then he disappeared. Yes, that *is* the right word. Not lost, but also not fully here."

MARK ARISES EARLY, ANXIOUS TO GET BACK TO JERUSALEM. Even though the discussion went late into the night, he has not been able to tell Simon about the scroll.

"Did you deliver it?"

"Yes. Nicodemus knows it has to do with obtaining Tamar's release. He thinks the opportunity may come on Thursday."

"I'm in no hurry. You are aware that Pontius Pilate and the Herodians will be leaving tomorrow."

Again, Simon's awareness of what was going on in Jerusalem surprises Mark.

"The men who helped me bury Judas weren't aware of that. They thought they would be stuck here until they found Jesus's body."

"You did a good thing, helping to make sure Judas was buried decently. I'm concerned, though."

"About what?"

Mark looks around the luxurious house and sees nothing that should trouble this man. He doesn't have a fountain bubbling in the courtyard the way Nicodemus has, but Simon's collection of artwork is astounding. The entryway has a mosaic depicting the Aeneas in Carthage being entertained by Queen Dido. Whereas nothing in Nicodemus's house shows the touch of a woman's hand, the breakfast table here is graced by a shallow bowl in which cut flowers float.

"I think the Monkey means to do Nicodemus harm."

"How can the Monkey harm him? He's the leader of the Pharisee order."

"That's what makes things dangerous. Oh, you and I know that he doesn't have any interest in politics. That doesn't keep the Monkey from being jealous. Fear is what keeps that man on his red chair. If he doesn't exile the occasional rival, then things slip away."

"He would exile Nicodemus?"

"Oh, he won't follow the same scheme he did with me. That would raise suspicion. No, he'll give him an important mission to do—something far, far away—then arrange for Nicodemus not to return. Something like that."

"Why are you telling me this? I'm just a messenger."

Simon laughs. "Some people are less than they seem. Some people are much, much more. You will go places you can't even imagine now. Seriously, I want you to consider something. You can come into my service anytime you wish. I would enjoy teaching you. When it's time, I'll help you go to Alexandria and study in the great library."

RACHEL AND THE TEMPLE GUARD

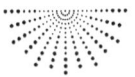

Martha

On Thursday, we learn that Jesus is still making appearances in Jerusalem. A visitor from the priesthood announces that those who are hiding the body of Jesus will be punished. He stands by the well and reads from a scroll. Everyone in the village comes to the center to listen—everyone except Simon. He smiles and waves at me from his doorway.

"And what if Jesus comes forward himself and turns himself in?" I ask our visitor.

He looks embarrassed. He has no response. He takes up his scroll and reads his message again.

"Tell Lord Caiaphas," Aunt Rachel says, "that we in Bethany are obedient and humble people. We will turn over to the council any information we receive about these traitors."

Rachel doesn't look good. She leans against one of the village's young women. Her face is ashen, her breath punctuated by rasps and coughs.

"I should draw that woman a map of Sheol," Lazarus whispers to me.

Our visitor leaves without stopping at Simon's house.

"I'm getting bread," Lazarus says openly.

"Why?"

"Because I want to go into the city."

"Don't . . ."

"I knew you wouldn't like it," he says.

"Let your brother take the leather goods into the market," Rachel says.

"Yes. I also have a rich man's clothes to return. Perhaps the time has come for those of us who believe Jesus lives to be as bold as those who are still looking for a misplaced body."

This causes the people to laugh and applaud until Rachel has another of her spells, slumping into the arms of the young women she is cultivating as her aides.

I see it in an instant. She is replacing me with them.

SWEEPING TO JESUS

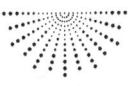

TAMAR

Tamar is of two minds about cleaning the Sanhedrin's council chamber this morning. A regular meeting is scheduled. The reports will be read, and the men will make their usual mess of the place. The meeting will last from nine o'clock in the morning until just before the evening meal. The elderly elders who have difficulty keeping their water will change their seats several times during the day. Many men will bring nuts with them and leave shells on the floor. An awning will be set in the courtyard for a noon meal. The men will stand to eat and, in their haste, cover the square with crumbs.

Not that many of them care to know just how many pilgrims visited the city during Passover week or how many days the average one stayed or exactly what they bought or how much of this revenue was retained for the temple. Except for a few younger ones, their eyes have that glazed look of oxen plowing the same furrow over and over.

This foolish waste of time isn't what bothers Tamar; it is that her fate lies in the balance. A scroll from Simon, the strange Pharisee from Bethany, will be presented in the midst of the routine business, requesting that Tamar be bartered like merchandise to pay for services rendered or, depending upon one's perspective, removed from this abusive servitude and given freely by grace to a new life that promises some measure of personal dignity.

Tamar doesn't know if she should clean the room with her usual care for detail and the high priest's unreasonable expectations or if her case would be furthered by her deliberately choosing to do something wrong. What would make the Monkey more willing to be rid of her? If she overplays her rebellious instincts, he will surely keep her. He enjoys being cruel. He enjoys crushing hope. But only a fool would clean the room so well that she would seem indispensable.

To make matters worse, the day dawns unseasonably hot and muggy. Sleepy elders are more incontinent. Everyone's tempers are raw. Those with carefully written reports to give are angered by the inattention of their colleagues. Those newly elected to council are disappointed to learn of the wearisome agenda that has been set for the day.

Everyone complains about the three additional meetings on the matter of Jesus the Nazarene—his trial, disappearance, and mistaken reburial—have provided the busiest week of the council. As Mark passes her in the hallway, he shows her the scroll Simon gave him. He begins to whisper to her what it says but is pushed along.

Noon comes, and she quickly goes back to the chamber and cleans until the men return from their meal in the courtyard. Her muscles ache.

As the Monkey passes her, he jabs her hard in the belly with the rod he carries. "You. Go out and sweep the courtyard."

She doubles over in pain. The bucket and rags she carries fall to the floor and are kicked aside by the shuffling, distracted members of the Sanhedrin. Malchus takes a step to help but is yanked along by the Monkey.

"Son, you have more important things to do. Are you prepared? Can you get us back onto the agenda we planned?

Or will you accept responsibility if I have to keep these gentlemen past their dinners?"

Bucket in hand, Tamar forces her way against the tide of sweaty men's bodies. Halfway to the courtyard door, she is overwhelmed and pushed down and back into a dark niche— a cupboard that is normally closed off and locked, but has been left open by a careless cook. Shelves and small pots surround her. This is where they store honey and fruit preserves. Her hand brushes sticky things, and without meaning to, she brings it to her mouth. Her mother used to say, "Hope is like honey."

"She's dead and I'm a slave," Tamar says to the sweet walls.

She doesn't give herself time to recover. Crawling on her knees, she returns to the corridor. But now her head is buzzing. She no longer understands what the men are saying. Light, sound, smells are like whirling wings above her. She imagines that she is in a hive of bees. The passing men are a blur of wings. She is small, like an insect. Time does not matter.

Rough hands pull her to her feet, but the dream only intensifies. Another man shoves her hard against the door that leads from the chamber's hallway to the courtyard. She hits it with her forehead but doesn't feel the blow. So hard was the throw that the heavy door opens and she falls out into the sunshine. She rolls down the stairs to the cobblestone pavement. She strikes her head—hard.

The courtyard is busy. Nearby, workers struggling to remove an awning from its supporting posts in the blinding sunlight. Having served the Sanhedrin's lunch, the caterers gather up their tables and put away their leftovers. Tamar doesn't notice them. She is surrounded by the dimness of another time. The day's warmth gives way to a damp chill. Instead of workers and cooks, there are soldiers standing around a charcoal fire. She smells the bite of the burning wood. She drifts above the courtyard. *Am I dead?*

But death is supposed to take her down to *Sheol*, where her past would parade before her eyes in disordered images. Instead, she is lifted up and allowed to view time as if it were a diorama, a specific moment that seemed ordinary before now.

She knows this to be the previous Friday. A man has been arrested in the night and a special meeting of the council called. She sees herself, a miniature frozen in time, sweeping the steps. Other soldiers, under the direction of Malchus, pull the arrested man from the pit that the Monkey uses as a jail.

This is not Sheol. It is a dream. In her childhood, Tamar learned that dreams are all about the details. We see with a new perspective the relationships and objects we had ignored before. She notices now how some of the men look anxious and Malchus keeps fiddling with his ear as he directs them. There is blood on the shoulder of his tunic. She remembers being told how a disciple of Jesus attacked Malchus with a sword.

"The ear flew clean off," a soldier said to her.

"Fool," she responded. "I can see he has both of his ears."

Now, she believes that Jesus healed her friend. The scene shifts slowly forward. They rough the man up. Malchus later told her he hoped to make Jesus look weak so the council would pity him and sentence the wayward prophet to time served. They parade the unfortunate man up the steps and into the chamber. She hears herself questioning the two disciples who had the courage to follow Jesus even here. She calls them liars, and the scene ends.

"Are you all right?"

A voice. With it, she returns to this day. This reality. This blinding sunshine.

They bring her water and want her to sit on the shady side of the courtyard, but she waves them off. She struggles to her feet and goes back to work. In time, the courtyard empties and she can work in peace. The tree to the south of the courtyard gives stingy shade and a multitude of useless little seed pods. She sweeps in rows—east to west, south to north.

Finally, she comes to the northeast corner of the courtyard where an old cistern lies below the pavement. In ancient cities like Jerusalem, Jericho, and Damascus, the subterranean landscape is littered with cavities, crawl spaces, and broken pottery. This cistern was carved out of the rock during the reign of Uzziah so that water could be stored for this quarter of the city. It served for two hundred years until the Babylonians laid siege and the need for water became desperate. The night before the city walls fell, a crack developed. The era of kings ended suddenly for the land of Judah, and the women who came to draw water that morning noted that the two events happened together.

Now, a stone is placed over this pit. It is moved aside whenever Caiaphas wants to hold a prisoner in the cistern. The afternoon sun illuminates this stone, and a man sits on it. She thinks this strange. There are cooler seats under the tree. As she sweeps nearer, she knows who this is. Jesus.

"Rabbi," she says softly. She feels the need to make an apology but can't frame the words.

There is bread in his hands.

Is he eating? Isn't he a ghost or a dream?

Jesus breaks off a piece and hands it to her. "Take. This will be bread for your journey."

Tamar takes it and eats. It is fine bread—sweet, sticky in her fingers, glistening as it passes through the sunlight.

"I have come to tell you to be brave. They will not give you your freedom. I will help. But you must summon more courage than you ever have before. I know you are able."

"How?"

"Some, God trusts with the means to decide their own fate." Jesus smiles. As he bids her *shalom*, he fades and disappears. Before going back to her sweeping, she licks the honey off her fingers.

With that, the door opens. The members of the Sanhedrin file out, heading across the courtyard to the gate and the city beyond. She moves closer, not bowing before them as she was taught, but watching each face. Midway through the seventy, she spots Nicodemus and Mark. They each see her but avert their eyes. Nicodemus speaks, drawing Mark away.

As they pass near her, Mark whispers, "Gihon. Midnight."

She nods, knowing she can leave the city by the Water Gate. But first, she must escape the compound.

She pushes past a doddering old man and his servant. Broom and rags in hand, she enters the chamber. Malchus is at his table, gathering documents. He shakes his head slightly and looks away. The Monkey is telling him what to do with a certain scrap of parchment. Noticing her, he smiles briefly.

Seeing that, she can imagine what happened. Nicodemus gave the scroll from Simon to his friend Joseph of Arimathea. Unlike the chief of the Pharisees, Joseph was never taken seriously. They would wait until adjournment was near. Joseph would begin in his usual rambling way, assuring the body that the matter he was presenting was trivial and could be dealt with rapidly.

The Monkey, however, is never distracted. Even though the council oversees the high priest's servants and household expenses, he must have stopped the motion and argued against her transfer to the house of Simon the Leper in Bethany. He wouldn't have to state his reasons, only imply that he would note how each member voted on this matter. The Monkey has his friends; he would reward them.

She is still his slave.

As the men prepare to leave the room, Malchus hangs back as if to give her specific instructions regarding her duties.

"Who is guarding the servants' door tonight?" Tamar asks.

"I'll take care of it."

LEAVING JERUSALEM

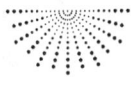

MARY

I have traveled to the Ophel each day so that I may teach the women gathering at Miriam's. In the evening, I retreat to the safety of John's house. I know that Jesus has prayed his blessing on that large room that overlooks the market. This space that might hold a fellowship of 144 people is surrounded by angels. It is invisible to the thugs that patrol the streets for the Monkey. It seems odd to sleep here with only a dozen other believers. More than once, since that morning when Jesus rose from his tomb, I have had a vision of this place filled with men and women. I have seen the Holy Spirit fall down on them. I have smelled its fragrance, like pine sap and frankincense. I know this room is destined for something more. The story goes on.

Miriam's house was crowded yesterday—mothers with their infants and children roaming throughout the house. We moved up to the rooftop. Every evening, the women tell their husbands and relatives. Already, people beg me to stay so I can witness to the men as they come back from their work. I have moved on from just talking about the events of Friday and Sunday. I teach them the stories Jesus told as we traveled from village to village around the Sea of Galilee. Jesus's mother no longer helps me here. It has become too dangerous for her to step outside of John's house. The Monkey heard that she was sitting near the well, persuading people that her son was alive.

"It is only someone who looks like Jesus," the Sadducees and their thugs say every time someone speaks of seeing him. "Don't you know all Galileans look alike?"

The disciples have also limited their travels for fear of being discovered. Each morning as I leave, I say to them, "May the Lord-God bless you with a spirit of courage."

Today, Simon the Zealot comes with me through the door. I am surprised.

"I see you've brought your bag. Aren't you returning tonight?"

"One never knows," Simon answers. "Jerusalem is okay for the rest. I feel a bit . . ."

"Claustrophobic?"

"Yes."

As we walk across the city, we speak of Judas. I noticed that Simon was somber when the news came about the Monkey's parade and how Absalom's Tomb yielded up the body of Judas instead of Jesus. The other disciples laughed. It released the last vestige of tension the disciples felt about having one of their own betray Jesus.

"Judas has been buried properly now," I say.

"I planned to go back for his body," Simon says. "Absalom's Tomb was safe enough for the Sabbath. Then I planned to take him to Kerioth early on Sunday. But Sunday came, and nothing happened according to our expectations."

"You don't need to do that now."

"I'll still stop by the potter's field and say a prayer."

"What made the two of you close?"

"We are both from the south. I grew up in Beersheba, five miles from Kerioth."

"You were introduced to me as a Galilean from Capernaum."

"Yes. I left a Zealot band operating near Jerusalem. All of my comrades were captured and crucified. Your sister knows this. She thought I could call together my troops to save Jesus. That morning, when Jesus was captured, I just needed a place to stay. I told Martha I would gather an army and help her. I lied. All my men are dead."

"Do the others know this?"

"Only Jesus. Judas knew it too. He kept my secret, though. He never betrayed me. He never let on that he knew me from before. You see, as a Zealot, I would often come into Kerioth to beg supplies for my men. Yes, and sometimes we stole their farm implements when we needed something to fashion into a weapon. The Romans knew who we were. They knew who I was. We were the toughest little band. We loved violence."

"But then Jesus called you to peace."

"It's never that simple. We sprang an ambush. Four Roman soldiers on horseback. Five of us, hidden in the night near the narrowest spot on a desolate road. In the darkness, they killed four of us, and we killed four of them. I escaped and traveled up the Jordan River. Each night, I camped just out of sight of the pilgrims traveling north. I listened to their speech. I thought about their manners. I became, in time, another man. Then I came to the Dipping Man. I stayed with him many months. I saw violence for what it was. And I asked to be baptized. I didn't take a new name, because Simon is so common. I did take a new birthplace. I let the north adopt me. In time, the Dipping Man sent me to Jesus."

"So are you going north?"

"No, I'm going to Beersheba and the surrounding hillsides. I may even cross over the Dead Sea and travel among the people of Moab."

"Why?"

"Long ago, Jesus told me that I would be his witness in the

south. He said that I would teach them, like myself, to adopt the ways of peace."

"You used to be sent out with Judas?"

"Yes. When the disciples were sent to different villages to practice healing and teaching, he sent me with Judas. We both complained. Judas said, 'You need me to stay with you and care for the finances.' I said, 'You need me to stay with you and protect you.' I was the only one who knew how to fight. But Jesus made me leave behind my sword and Judas leave his money bag whenever he sent us out, two by two."

"Who will you go with now?" I ask.

"Jesus said I would have a stranger go with me."

"Yes. I'm the strangest person you can find."

Simon shrugs. He doesn't look any happier about traveling with me than I am at the thought of going with him.

IT IS NIGHT. THE MOON IS BRIGHT. WE ARE IN THE POTTER'S field saying prayers for Judas. Suddenly, we see two figures on the road. They are dark against dark. Our eyes are keen. None of the disciples have night vision like Simon. For him, the two figures are strangers. I recognize them and laugh. I shout for them, and they are startled. We must seem to be evil spirits, calling out from the clay pits of this graveyard.

GIHON, MIDNIGHT

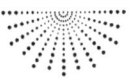

TAMAR

S hortly before midnight, Tamar waits in the bushes behind the Gihon Spring. Above her, the moon is bright. She has chosen her hiding place carefully, calming her breath, sorting the background insect noise from the faint scuffle of footsteps and approaching danger. She has also considered the odds of having two men deal honestly with her in the same night. She has seen soldiers playing dice squander good money on thin chances, but she is not about to be that foolish with her life. Against the likelihood that Malchus would fail to remove the guard at the compound's gate, she had stashed rope and plotted a way over the high priest's wall.

Now she hears one set of footsteps and allows herself to hope that it is Mark alone. She rises on her haunches, like a sprinter waiting for her race. If Mark has betrayed her, the only remedy will be to outrun her pursuer.

At last, when she is almost certain it is only him, he stops. The moonlight shines on his face. What's in his hands? He pulls a lit lamp out from under a clay pot.

"Tamar," he says.

"Idiot," she hisses.

"I wanted you to know it was me. Look." He holds out a small bag. "It's not much. In Bethany, Simon will help you."

"Put the lamp out." When he does, she stands and motions him to a more secluded spot.

"I can only go with you as far as Simon the Leper's house," he says.

"I can find it on my own. If you don't plan on escaping with me, then leave me now."

"I must go back. If we are both missing tomorrow, they will search my mother's house. They will question everyone and discover that many there believe that Jesus is alive."

"Will I be safe, even in Bethany? No. Don't answer that question. Instead, tell me if Simon and his people believe that Jesus is alive?"

"They do."

"Then we are in as much danger there as we are in Jerusalem. Tell me, do *you* think Jesus is alive?"

"That answer may take time. Let's begin . . ."

"You don't have to follow me." Tamar grabs the bag and starts up the Mount of Olives.

In spite of this, Mark follows in silence. When they have crested the hill, skirted around the village of Bethphage, and the moon has gone behind a cloud, Tamar speaks.

"You deserve to know what I think. I didn't expect to make it this far, yet here I am with Jerusalem behind me. If tomorrow morning I'm free from the Monkey, then I will believe."

"Believe what—that Jesus is alive?"

"One thing at a time. First, I will come to believe that some men can be trusted."

"Would it change your opinion of me if I told you that I saw Jesus alive and eating a piece of fish on Sunday evening? There are others, too, who—"

"Shh. That's not it. Stop talking like a Pharisee—a man being alive, another man pretending to be him and taking his place. This is the kind of talk other people can spend their days debating. Me? I'm trying to decide if I'm being stupid running away like this. Jesus said I should do it. If I'm okay tomorrow, then good—Jesus is God, or whatever. If I'm dead or in the Monkey's pit, then it doesn't matter what I think about Jesus. Ask me now, John Mark, and I will tell you that he is a malicious spirit. He gets people to have false hopes."

A mile later, the land declines gently toward a dry creek bed.

"The potter's field," Mark says.

"Do you have friends meeting you here?"

A man and a woman appear out of the darkness. Tamar prepares to run.

"Mark," the woman says, laughter in her voice. "We meet again."

Tamar takes off. She slips on the wet clay, loses her footing, and goes down.

"Are you all right?" The man leans over her, his speech gentle and Judaean. Tamar notes his belt with an empty leather loop where a dagger can be hung.

"Are you a Zealot?" she asks.

"Yes."

"Good. Not with the Monkey, then?"

"Let me help you. My name is Simon. We, too, are going quietly to the east. We didn't mean to startle you. My companion is Mary . . ."

"The witch?" Tamar asks.

This brings more laughter and introductions. No one explains why they are traveling at night. Their mutual need for secrecy is accepted. Tamar claims to be a free woman. Mark adds that he hopes Simon of Bethany will have a position for her.

"My sister is his neighbor. Tell Simon that he'll be in trouble with Martha if he doesn't treat you well," Mary says.

"I can't stay there," Tamar says.

Mary stops. She leaves the path and looks to the south. She lifts her hands in prayer. When she returns, her expression is sober. "Bethany is not far enough. You and the Zealot will need to travel on. But tomorrow, Mark and I will go back into the lion's den."

"You can trust me," Simon the Zealot says to Tamar. "I know what it means to be in exile."

62

SIMON'S BAPTISM

MARY

We wake Martha. It seems safer. She feeds us. Mark is anxious to walk back to Jerusalem. He stands for a long time in the doorway, making promises to Tamar.

"When it is safe, I will come and look for you."

"Don't. Let me search for you if I desire it. Right now, I don't know if I am free. I like these people. I like you. If I am free, then there is one thing I will know."

"Jesus?"

"No. Who is Jesus to me? It's not tomorrow yet. We'll see if he is a demon or a legitimate provider of hope. But if I am free, then I will choose if I even need a man. Mark, you are sweet. I need to find my own way first."

"Mark, go home," I say.

Martha has repacked the bags of both Simon and Tamar. Now, they have food for the journey. She hands these to them.

Simon thinks they can make Beersheba by dawn. "I have friends there who will take me in."

"Good. We have a busybody aunt who will turn you in if you even say the name Jesus," Martha says. When she has sent them on their way, she tells me I should rest because my services have been requested.

"Me?"

"Yes. Simon the Leper wants to be baptized. He wants Lazarus to do for him what the Dipping Man did for Jesus and his disciples. He wants you to sing."

"Where?"

"Bethany's well."

DURING THE NIGHT, I DREAM THE SONG I WILL SING.

In the beginning, there was only chaos.
The spirit of God hovered over the deep.
The waters ran in confusion.
God spoke his word and made the cosmos.
God spoke his word and made light.
God spoke his word and living souls teemed on the earth.
God's word became flesh.
Jesus!
The ark for Noah was Jesus;
The way through the Red Sea was Jesus;
The great whale that saved Jonah—
Jesus, always Jesus.
And when the Dipping Man came,
He prepared us for Jesus.
And the word came from God,
And we beheld his glory—
Glory that can only be from God.
Jesus, full of grace,
Jesus, full of truth,
Jesus, the healer of the world.

We go to Simon's house at noon, and there is a meal spread before us. Simon is dressed in a loincloth and a brilliantly white linen robe. He dances around us as we eat. He cannot contain himself.

We discuss how we each have been baptized. Lazarus had gone across the Jordan and found the Dipping Man at work near Aenon. I tell of meeting Jesus in Magdala and being baptized by the fishermen Peter and John.

Simon asks Martha if she wants to be baptized at the same time.

"I've already been baptized—twice. I do not need a third."

"When?"

"When Jesus died on the cross, they put a spear in his side. Water and blood flowed down on me. Wasn't that a baptism? Isn't it really about being baptized into the Messiah's death?"

"Yes," I say. "Every baptism is a dying. We are taken into the water having lived one life. We emerge to live another."

"My second baptism was the next night. Jesus was in the grave. Lazarus and I came back to Bethany. I still had Jesus's blood in my hair. We went into the well."

"I watched you," Simon says. "I could not sleep that night."

"Lazarus poured the water over me three times. Once for Jesus. Once for the great mothering spirit who brooded over the unformed world and still nurtures our hearts until we become fully who we are meant to be. And a third time for the great Creator, who has a perfect and eternal plan for all that is."

63

MARTHA BRINGS HER BAG

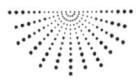

MARTHA

After the baptism, I ask Mary what she knows of Thomas.

She shakes her head. "Just that he lives. When I'm here, I only seem to see Bethany. But even in Jerusalem, he was distant."

"Mark says that he will die," I say. It isn't really what the boy said. He gave me a careful answer emphasizing the care he was receiving and the fact that the giant wasn't complaining of pain.

"Does his wound smell?" I had asked Mark.

"Yes."

It is Friday afternoon. Only a week ago, Jesus was dying before my eyes. Now, Thomas is in the same situation. Again, I feel helpless.

"I will go to him," I say. "And if he dies, I will wait near his grave until the third day."

"Send Mark as a messenger," Mary says. "Let us know when you are returning."

I pause. This feels odd, Mary being concerned about my returning to Bethany.

"Sister, sister, I am forty-two years old. We each have

become someone different over the past week. I set you free. This house, I set free. If I return, I return. Jesus has set me free. Tell Lazarus I am going off to look for *shalom*."

I carefully pack my bag, pausing to feel the embroidery and wondering what images I will add when I have the time. There are healing herbs—the bitter milk of the poppy, chamomile to comfort his soul, and anise to stir him to confession. As I arrange my bag, I find something that I had forgotten—a small bag of silver coins.

Mary is so startled that I am preparing to leave, especially this late in the day; she is speechless. I smile at this and give her a hug. Putting my finger to my lips, I press half of the coins into her palm.

"What is this?"

"It is for whatever you need. If it is too dangerous for Lazarus to sell leatherwork, use it for household expenses."

She nods and gives me one more piece of advice: "It's not the injury that is Thomas's problem."

"I know."

AFTER DEALING WITH THE GUARDS AT THE EASTERN GATE, I don't feel up for seeing Thomas. It is late. They questioned me because the Sabbath will soon be here.

"We are sending merchants out of the city, not letting them in."

"I am not here to sell. I have a sick friend I must sit with."

They are skeptical. They make me pour out my bag to show them that I have no finished work to sell. People behind me are grumbling.

"Guard the city. Let the scribes guard the Sabbath," a man's voice shouts.

From there, I knock on Nicodemus's door. It takes a great

deal of explanation to gain entry from the man behind the locked door. Finally, I recognize the voice.

"Barabbas. It's me, Martha. Let me in."

"You're back?"

He opens the door, and I embrace him. He looks at me, puzzled.

"The kitchen is still clean," he says.

"Martha! You have come." Finally, Nicodemus enters. "Welcome, welcome. Is everything all right?"

"Yes. We are all fine. I seem to be stuck again in Jerusalem for the Sabbath. Will you put me up?"

"We'll have dinner in the banquet room, then. Now that we have a guest," he says to Barabbas.

As we pass through the courtyard with its fountain, I whisper, *"Jesus lives."*

"And I've become a nobleman's head servant," Barabbas responds. *"Miracles are getting common."*

It turns out that Nicodemus always sends his people home for Sabbath eve. He enjoys the solitude as he prepares his lessons for the next day's worship. The only exception to this habit came last week when the disciples and I were tossed into his care, like castaways on a storm-swept beach. Barabbas has no home to spend the Sabbath, and now I am here again.

"The man has become my favorite cook," Nicodemus says.

I accept the wine that is poured out before me. The room looks entirely different to me now. Where before I looked at each furnishing and tried to gauge its cost, tonight I pause to consider the whole house. Lazarus says that Nicodemus is single-minded about the study of the scriptures. He never married and is childless, but he maintains this vast house entirely for the purpose of educating the next generation.

"I've come into town to see Thomas."

"I hope you're not too late."

"Mary saw him on Monday, and he sent her away. I'm not sure if he wants to see me."

Nicodemus raises an eyebrow, then says, "There is no shame in remaining single."

"Oh, I'm not wanting to see him because . . ."

"You hope to help him heal?"

"Yes."

"You brought him healing herbs in your bag?"

"Yes. The herbs provide me with a familiar place to start. An opening. Mary came empty-handed and was rejected. If he accepts my good intentions . . ."

"Then you will talk to him about Jesus." Nicodemus nods. Then he goes to a side table where he has a number of scrolls. He finds one and brings it back. "I've been working on the teaching that I will share tomorrow at worship. Actually, I have a number of readings, but this one might interest you. It is taken from the book of Job."

"Don't most rabbis stay within the writings of Moses on the Sabbath?"

"Yes, but Pharisees are also allowed to share from the wisdom writings. Have you ever wondered why good people suffer?"

"Yes. Does Job provide an answer?"

"No, but he asks the right questions."

"I think the men who come to listen to you tomorrow will want answers, not questions."

Nicodemus laughs. "I know now why Jesus liked being with your family. You have hit the nail on the head. We all have questions. Job had a terrible tragedy befall him. He was suffering. He tried to work his way through it. He tried to think his way through it. He found that all he could do is rest with his suffering."

"Thomas is resting with his suffering now."

"Yes. Out of his suffering, Job did find an answer." Nicodemus reads from the scroll:

Oh, that my words were engraved in stone forever.
For this I know, that my redeemer lives.
He stands again on this earth.
And even if I suffer and die,
I will live to see God.

"Do you think my Thomas knows this verse?"

"Perhaps."

"Do you believe that Jesus lives?"

"Yes. Oh, I didn't at first. I spoke with Malchus, and he gave me some absurd story about falling stars and Roman soldiers being struck into a coma."

"You don't find that plausible?"

"Well, I didn't see much choice. It was either that or believe that Roman soldiers were defeated by the men I had sleeping in this room. Can you picture any of them stealing a body? Then Malchus told me that Caiaphas plans to exile any member of the Sanhedrin that says Jesus lives. I decided to pack my bag."

"Any story the Monkey wants to repress that badly has to be true."

"Yes."

64

VISITING THE HOUSE OF CAIAPHAS

JOHN

In the morning, while the men of the city are going to their different meeting places for worship, John leaves the safety of his house by the market and walks to the high priest's complex. He keeps his hood up and greets no one. Going to the servants' entrance, he gains admission to the kitchen where the cook, Patches, is at work alone.

"You don't have the Sabbath off?"

"What, have you snuck in here to teach your father about Moses?"

John sits to wait while the news of a prodigal's return spreads among the servants. Malchus arrives shortly and hisses, "Are you insane?"

"In a good way."

Patches stirs the lentils. He is like a father to both of these young men. He mentored Malchus, recognizing early the sober lad's potential. He quietly prodded him to work harder than the other servants and, more importantly, learn the diplomacy skills that would prepare him to run an important house.

In contrast, Patches advised John to leave Jerusalem when he came of age. The boy never was good at lying. It was obvious, even to the cook, that John was too serious about his studies to become a Sadducee. If John wanted to become a Pharisee, he should do it far away.

"The Dipping Man may be a better father to you. You need something you aren't getting here," Patches had told him.

"My mother loves me," John said. "I don't want to break her heart."

"Let Malchus take your place."

"No."

But later, Malchus talked to John and said, "You are like the egg the blue jay lays in another bird's nest. You must either become a killer or find your fortune elsewhere."

It was the best decision John ever made. Malchus doesn't know this.

Now, John says, "I've come to thank you."

Malchus searches his friend's face for sarcasm, but John embraces him.

"I did all I could for her," Malchus says. "On bad days, I took her to the house above the market, so she wouldn't have to hear the Monkey rant."

"Is that where she learned about Jesus?"

"Yes."

John accepts this. "I want to know something else. With what everyone is saying on the streets and the embarrassment of not finding Jesus in Absalom's Tomb, is my father any closer to accepting that Jesus lives?"

Malchus is startled. "You are insane. Have you ever known the man to doubt himself?"

"Isn't there enough evidence for him to reconsider?"

"No."

"I heard that when the Dipping Man was beheaded, my father went out and wept in the public square. I heard that he had the council send an angry letter to Herod Antipas."

"All show. I was the one who told him it would help."

"Help?"

"That it would help make him popular with the people. They loved the wilderness prophet."

"And my father never did?"

"Everything the Baptizer did made your father angry. He called the Dipping Man a rogue Essene. When Jesus began to preach the same message and gather similar crowds, he hated him too. Neither of them ever encouraged people to go to the temple. When Herod chased Jesus across the Jordan, your father said good riddance."

"It didn't matter that I had chosen to follow first the Dipping Man, and then Jesus?"

"He had already given up on you. This was just after your mother died. Even if Jesus had raised *her* from the dead, I don't think your father would believe. No. Like salt in a wound, you all come back among us."

"Jesus came to help his friend, Lazarus."

"You don't see it? If Jesus were a real prophet, he wouldn't bring a peasant leatherworker from Bethany out of the grave."

"You believe it, though?"

"It doesn't matter what I believe."

"But it does."

"I believe that Jesus was capable of great good and that your father has the capacity to be insanely evil. I believe that an extraordinary event happened on Sunday. A power flashed down on us—a holocaust, such as the one Elijah called down on Mount Carmel. I believe Jesus walks between death and life and makes appearances at will. I don't believe he is the Messiah, though."

"Why?"

"Life goes on. Today is the Sabbath. All the servants of the high priest still have to do their duties. Joseph Caiaphas, with all his machinations, still sits on the red throne. The Romans still march through our streets. The men under my command still abuse the servant girls. If there is a new kingdom, then show it to me."

"Jesus's kingdom is of the heart."

"What good is a Messiah who conquers the grave but doesn't change anything?"

A FINAL APPEAL

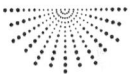

MARTHA

I sleep in the empty upper room, even though Nicodemus offers me better lodging in one of his many spare rooms below. I rest well, and when the men start arriving, Nicodemus shows me the spot on the stairway that will enable me to listen to his teaching.

About an hour later, after scripture readings, prayers, and comments by others, Nicodemus speaks. "I am about to share with you an important scripture text, but first, I need to request your indulgence as I complete a bit of business. I have been invited to go on a long and dangerous journey. I don't know if I shall return. Many who travel this way don't."

There is a great deal of confusion following this announcement.

"Please. Please. My affairs here in Jerusalem will be well cared for. To ensure this, I have asked two of my associates to care for my school and my house. Joseph of Arimathea, please come forward. I want to hand over my students to you. I know you will oversee the other rabbis and maintain the school. The scribes who copy the scriptures will also be under your direction. Are you willing to lead the weekly worship in this place as well?"

There is an audible groan from the men.

"Yes, I am humbled. I will maintain your standards."

"And now I want to introduce you to the young man who will inherit my house if some misfortune occurs and I am unable to return. John Mark, please step forward."

There is a gasp.

I creep to the open door and watch as a scroll is brought out and various signatures affixed. Wax is poured on the scroll, and Nicodemus presses his ring into the seal.

"Don't open this until you have to," he says to Mark with a wink.

It takes a while for the crowd to settle. I go back into the kitchen, pull my bag up on the large empty table, and empty its contents. Carefully, I rearrange things, putting them back so that what is most needed is at the top. I add some dried fruit and cheese. I know my host won't mind. The only question is how much I am willing to carry. I expect to walk a long ways.

"Jesus lives," I say.

"What, you too?"

Thomas is lying in a dark corner. I have tanned hides and dealt with death, potash, and the urine mixture we use to cure them. None of that compares to this.

"Did you see him with your own eyes?" Thomas asks.

"No."

"Why join in their madness, Martha?"

"Why not? You were the first one to receive Lazarus when he returned from the dead. My sister was the first one to embrace Jesus last Sunday. Why should I believe you when you unwrapped my brother's graveclothes and said, 'Look, he lives,' and not believe my Mary when she tells me now that Jesus lives and she has held him in her own arms?"

"Yes, but I wasn't saying that Lazarus had died. I was only saying that I had found him at the mouth of his grave alive. People sometimes get buried alive. You could have been mistaken. He could have been merely sick."

"Are you calling us liars? You talked with Lazarus. He told you about his journey through *Sheol.*"

"I know the dreams that men dream when they are gravely ill. They dream of traveling a dark tunnel. They dream of talking to lost loved ones. And when they recover, they speak of going through a tunnel into a light. I know, for I once thought myself to be dead too."

"My brother *was* dead. I have slaughtered animals. I know dead."

"But Lazarus slept away. When he came back, I sat with him in the grotto. What he says about the beyond is exactly what I saw. It is what everyone who comes near to death sees."

It is time to take a more deliberate tack.

"Yes. I see what you are saying," I concede. "When Jesus died, it wasn't at all like my brother's sleeping away from the fever."

"No. The Romans know how to execute a man."

"I was there. Did you know that?"

"No, I didn't. I'm sorry. It must have been hard."

"Mary was, too."

"Okay."

"I'm only saying this so you know something. Nobody on Friday had any expectations that Jesus would live again."

"So you say."

"I mean it. Do you think anyone who has witnessed an execution would, three days later, forget it? Do you think Mary or I would just wishfully think Jesus back to life?"

"No."

"And the crowds. Everyone in Jerusalem saw Jesus being marched to his death. How many of them are going to believe that Jesus is alive now?"

"I wouldn't expect any."

"Yet people we don't know are coming up to us on the street and saying they've seen Jesus. Half of Jerusalem is ready to accept it."

"I guess I'm the last holdout."

"It's nothing to be proud of, Thomas."

"It is who I am. You used to be like me. You were willing to wait and see. You'd weigh all the evidence before you made any decisions. This bit of Jesus being alive, it's too early to know how it will all pan out."

"You'll be dead before you have enough evidence to believe."

"Okay."

"It's not okay. Your life depends upon faith. I can smell your leg from here."

"I can't make myself believe."

I have nothing more to say. He rolls toward the wall. I look into my bag and wonder what there is in it that I should leave with the potter's wife to give him. No. I stand by his bed.

"Thomas, do you want to know?"

"What?"

"The thing Mary said that made me know."

"Tell me."

"That he smelled like lilies."

"They won't bloom for another month."

"Yes. It's the kind of thing Jesus would do for Mary. It's not something she would make up. If Jesus were to do something for you, what would it be?"

"Let me walk out of here."

"One more thing. Do you love me?"

"Yes, you know it. You've always known."

"Then why haven't you asked Lazarus to allow me to marry you?"

"Jesus. I was his twin on the road. Celibate like him."

"Before Jesus?"

"When I dug your father's grave, I had nothing. You owned a house. I couldn't afford you. Besides, Lazarus was away, and I would have had to speak to your village elder."

"Abraham?"

"No. You. Bethany always considered you to be the one in charge."

"Excuses."

"I see that now, but it's too late. As you said, I will die."

"And if you walk out of here?"

"If I live, Jesus still comes between us."

"Why?"

"You've changed."

"No."

"Yes. Believing what you do changes you. I can't respect you. It's gone."

"What?"

"My love. No, the feeling is there—though the rock flattened it a bit—but I cannot love someone who believes her fantasies. There, I said it. Good day. Thank you for your well wishes. I plan to never see you again. I wish you *shalom*. Goodbye."

66

A BLESSING FOR MIRIAM

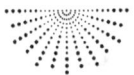

THOMAS

After Martha leaves, Thomas sleeps. They let him be. Day turns to night, and still he sleeps.

The next day, the potter's wife is surprised to discover that the room no longer smells bad. The giant is sitting up on his bed.

"Shalom," he says.

"Shalom. A new week has begun."

"I've been here seven days?"

"Yes."

"You haven't given me anything to eat?"

She shakes her head.

"That's why I'm so hungry."

After breakfast, the potter comes, and they help him to his feet. He takes a few steps. Leaning against the doorpost, he breathes deep, smelling the spring air.

"I live," he says.

"Yes, but it may not be wise to . . ."

"Let me stand here."

So they do. He notes that several young men enter the house across the way.

"Is that a school?"

"Yes," the potter answers. "The teacher is an Essene."

"When you've spent a week just this side of Sheol, it doesn't matter. Do you suppose that if you helped me get to that wall there, I could listen through the open door?"

He is moved to that spot. The sun bathes his face and legs. His color returns, and a look of sheer contentment spreads on his face as he listens to the students practice their lessons.

Later in the day, Mark stops by. Thomas asks him if the disciples are still in Jerusalem.

"Yes, but they may not be for long. The high priest is searching for them."

"Still?"

"Yes. All of Jerusalem is talking about Jesus."

"People keep seeing him?"

"New sightings every day. The disciples have taken risks too. They go out by twos and speak to people on the corners. The group Mary leads at my mother's house on the Ophel now includes as many men as women."

"I was under the Ophel. I was lost. That was only last Sabbath day. Now look at me."

"Are you ready to rejoin the disciples?"

"Do you think they want me?"

Mark shrugs. "How would I know?"

"You know where they are staying?"

"Yes."

"I can walk if I have someone to lean on."

"It's a second-floor house."

"I'll face that problem when I get there."

IT IS LATE WHEN MARK ENTERS HIS MOTHER'S HOUSE. SHE had saved him a meal, but he isn't hungry.

"I ate with Jesus and his disciples."

"Jesus?"

"Yes. He did the strangest thing. He appeared within the locked room as if he were a ghost and able to pass through walls. But he was solid to the touch. He asked the giant to come and put his hand in his side. Jesus's wounds were visible. He lives. He doesn't bleed."

"I wish I had been there."

"No. Jesus gave you a blessing the disciples and I don't have."

"What?"

"'Blessed are those who do not see and yet believe.'"

67

WALKING NORTH

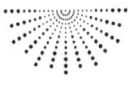

MARTHA

I travel alone but in a crowd. The pilgrims around me are speaking about Jesus. They ask if I have seen him.

"Not yet, but I shall," I say. "Maybe in this life. For sure in the next."

Most are skeptical, especially the men. They question the few who admit to having seen something. When details don't match, they are quick to say, "Aha."

"But Jesus made several appearances," I say. "Different places at different times to different people."

The people around me are mostly Galileans. They have known Jesus for years. Those who saw him alive are certain about who they saw. I see a pattern. His appearances seem tailored for the people present. He calls them by name. He may be holding an object from their village. To a group from Capernaum, Jesus appeared by a millstone, because that city is famous for the basalt that is useful for grinding grain.

They know I am Judaean. They ask me why I am traveling north. I tell them I have run out of work to do. They laugh. It is a silly answer.

"Oh, I know," one says. "You have left your man."

"I don't need a man."

"Yes, none of us do."

There is laughter. *I only need Jesus.*

Each day, the land is greener than the day before. On the evening of the second day, we come to a rise where we can see the Sea of Galilee before us. I have never seen anything like this. The water of the lake is flat and still. I am not leaving Thomas or seeking to see Jesus. I am simply being a pilgrim in love with the beauty of this world.

We come to the lake shore. I hear it singing as it laps against the round stones at its edge. It sings. Yes, I hear it.

It can be done tomorrow.
Rest for now.

Different groups break off. Some travel up the west side of the lake. Others turn east.

"Which way is Capernaum?"

I join the group headed west and come with them to Magdala. I see the heaps of fish on the dock. I remember how Mary was baptized. She tells of standing on a pile of fish in a crazed state when Jesus came to shore. He said her name, and she fell into the lake. When Peter and John fished her out of the lake, Jesus said that they had done for her what the Dipping Man did for his people. Some baptism. Not threefold and mysterious the way mine was.

I tell those from Capernaum that I am going to the house of Simon bar Jonah, the man I know as Peter. They know it.

"His wife was with us when we came down. There were others from there. They didn't wait for us."

I come upon a group from Nazareth and ask about Jesus's mother.

"Yes. She came south with us, but she is staying in the city. She says that Jerusalem is her new home."

"What about Joanna and Salome?"

"The twins?"

"Yes."

"They left Jerusalem on Sunday. They were in a hurry."

"Why?"

"They said, 'Jesus is going before us to Galilee.'"

"But they were wrong," a young boy says. "I saw Jesus in Jerusalem on the Sabbath."

"Where?"

"In the Essene Quarter. He was teaching the men there. Perhaps he's their Messiah too."

When I arrive in Capernaum, I anxiously ask around.

"Were we foolish to leave Jerusalem?" I ask Joanna when I find her.

"No one has seen him here," she says.

"But it was so clear," Salome chimes in. "The angels said, 'Go home.' Besides, Jesus knew Joanna had to return to Galilee to be with her husband."

68

DOING MARTHA'S PART FOR RACHEL

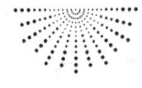

MARY

It's been days, and I've heard nothing. Nothing from Martha. No visits from Mark. Bethany has become boring. I help Lazarus as he works on the leather goods. The table now looks as it does when Martha is home, except she isn't. We keep having questions for her. Should there be four holes or five on a Roman soldier's girdle? How many of each length should we keep in stock? I begin each day by going to the well and staying while the other women fill their jars. I talk to them about Jesus. Most are receptive but reluctant to pray with me. They say they will wait for Martha.

Suddenly, a cry. It is the woman who looks in on Rachel each morning. I see what she sees. Rachel has died in the night.

"Quick, get Martha!" she screams.

Someone runs past me. "Don't you know where she is?"

SIMON PROVIDES THE SPICES AND A LONG PIECE OF FINE WHITE linen. Rachel had not prepared for her departure. The women prepare the body on Martha's table. Then the men come and carry her to the resting stone in the middle of the grotto.

"Where is Martha's bag? We need the scroll."

"She took it with her," I say.

"Where?"

"To Galilee." In speaking these words, I see a vision of a peaceful lake and my sister at rest. I know where she is. I have been searching the horizon, expecting her to come just in time, to be the one to speak. She alone has kind words to say for Aunt Rachel.

"Wait. I have a spare."

Quickly, I run back to the house. I find a scrap of parchment and pull my writing tools from my bag. I write:

> *Hear, O Israel: The Lord our God is one.*
> *And Jesus is our eternal hope.*

I do Martha's part for Rachel. Lazarus, as her only nephew, calls the people to remember her ancestry. Beginning with how Sara and Abram left Ur in Chaldea, he speaks of the faithful ones who left behind comforts and riches because they trusted God and looked forward to a reward beyond this life.

"They were each pilgrims in this world, living by faith," he says. "And faith is the assurance we each can have in God for the things we hope for. I remember when Rachel . . ."

Then my brother tells three personal stories about her. Each is like a pearl strung on the string of our memories. I see my aunt differently now. *Thank you.*

It is time for everyone, young and old, in the village to walk around and around the resting stone. Forty times, we circle Rachel's body. We chant:

> *Hear our prayer.*
> *We are the grass of the field.*

We were new this morning.
Now, we fade.
Now, it is evening.
Our days come to seventy years—
Eighty, for women with strong hearts.
Even our good days are filled with toil,
And no one lives without sorrow.
Soon, life ends.
Soon, we fly away.
The owl calls our name,
And our children forget our face.
May God show favor on this one tonight.
And may we remember her well,
For the days given this soul
Were only a loan.
May the holy one teach us
To number our days
Aware of this,
That we might be wise in heart
And hear in the chanting of this people
A farewell blessing:
And establish the work of our hands.
Yes, establish the work of our hands.
Amen.

The men struggle to roll the stone back so the body can be placed in the grave. I look for someone else to help them. My brother is exhausted from his work.

"Thomas!"

He has come. The giant easily helps the men roll back the stone. He lifts Rachel's body and carries her inside.

"*I hate caves,*" I hear him mutter within.

After returning the stone to its place, he asks me about Martha.

I shake my head. "Friend, you always seem to be in the wrong place at the wrong time. She's gone to Galilee."

"I guess I'll have to turn around."

"Turning around is good for the soul," I say.

"It's tiring. The disciples went north today. When Jesus came to us last night, he asked us why we didn't believe the women. Why they were still in Jerusalem when the women told them that he was going before us to Galilee."

"And?"

"They said they stayed because they were looking for me."

RESTING WITH JESUS

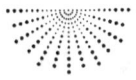

MARTHA

I awake early today. The house is silent around me. I listen for the snores of the men. Jesus's disciples arrived in the north on Thursday. They were traveling slowly because Thomas is not fully recovered.

"I'm surprised to see you," I said.

He grinned but said nothing.

"Where's Jesus?" Peter's wife asked.

"We thought he'd be here already."

Then Peter did something unexpected. He apologized for the men not listening to the women.

"We should have believed you, Joanna. We should have come back with you, Salome. We are sorry."

We clapped in amazement.

Now, it is the morning of the Sabbath. Still no Jesus. Thomas has also not apologized to me. I go out to where I can see a boat beating its way out. So little wind, the sails are limp. I hear Peter. His voice carries across the still water. I also hear James. I think Thomas is with them, for the boat sits low. The words come in pieces.

". . . down."

"We'll have to row . . ."

"I know."

They must be putting the sail down. It serves them right. They won't be able to fish. They'll have to rest with us.

The warm wind is at my back. They stop and put the sail up. It pushes them into the gray mist. In an hour, maybe two, they'll be back. They'll be hungry, so I make bread. It's a strange kitchen, but I find what I need. The other women awake.

"Go tend to your children. I'll deal with the men."

The shore is empty and silent. It is stony—little round rocks the size of my fist. I wasn't expecting this. There is a place where the stones become smaller, not quite sand, but pebbles. There are two other boats sitting here. No one else is fishing on the Sabbath. There is a streak in the shore where the men dragged their boat out, so that is where I wait for them.

I should gather sticks for a fire. They might have fish to cook.

I go back and get embers from Peter's home and dry moss for kindling.

Who is that?

Someone has started my fire. He sits with his back to me. The wind is stronger now, the smoke trailing south across the water. Do I smell fish?

The shore is empty except for him. I know who it is.

"Martha," he says softly without turning. "I have breakfast for you. Come sit."

So I do. The fish is good. He breaks my bread, and we share it.

There is a clay jar.

"Wine?" I ask.

"Like you've never tasted."

It is true. We sit and say little. In time, a silhouette can be seen in the mist—the darker gray of the men and their boat. They sound discouraged.

"They'll be okay," Jesus says.

"You could have picked better," I say, and he laughs.

"I'm not just trusting my legacy to the men. I will pour out my spirit on all."

"Women like Mary?"

"Yes. And others. You have to just let it be. You can't force it."

"You mean I shouldn't work so hard?"

He laughs again. I am reminded of how my father would laugh. When I was a girl, before Mary came and our mother died and . . .

"Your family will be okay also," Jesus says, as if he knows what I am thinking.

"They won't die?"

"Oh, everyone dies at least once. Your brother will have another go at it sometime. That doesn't mean that Mary and Lazarus won't continue to be okay. I've done my work. *Sheol* isn't what it used to be. Trust me."

I nod. We don't say anything for a while. We enjoy the morning and the wine.

The mist begins to lift. He says to me, "And Martha . . ."

"What?"

"Before you die, you should rest."

"You mean enjoy more times like this?"

He nods.

The men are coming. Soon, they will see us. We stand.

I hug Jesus. He is solid, just as Mary said.

"See you later," I say as I go. I leave my bag beside him.

I feel lighter without it.

= The End =

THE BETHANY'S PEOPLE SERIES

You may read **Bethany's People** in any order. Each novel dives deeply into a traumatic moment in the life of an intimate friend of Jesus. The first, *Mary Sees All,* tells how Bethany's Mary experienced Good Friday and the crucifixion of Jesus. *Martha Finds Rest* follows her sister's difficulties on the first Easter. In 2020 the prequel, *Lazarus Dies First,* will travel back to Jesus's teen years and chronicle the arguments he had with a friend who wanted to become a terrorist.

But there's more. The miracle of the living Christ, or Messiah, doesn't stay bottled up in little Bethany. Lazarus, Mary, and Martha join with others to carry the good news of God's love over the horizon; to Africa in *Mark Goes Everywhere,* to Europe in *West Across the Wine Dark Sea,* and to the Far East in *Martha's Apocalypse.* Please help this series go on by writing a review on Amazon.

The Series in Chronological Order

4 BCE to 30 AD - Lazarus Dies First: *A Few Too Many Messiahs.* The story of Jesus's unique friendship with Lazarus of Bethany. Against Jesus's advice, Lazarus joins the Zealot rebel movement. They stay in touch, though, as Jesus calls others to be his disciples. Then Lazarus dies and Jesus must put himself and his disciples in danger to save his friend. (Due fall, 2020)

Passover Week, 30 AD - Mary Sees All: *The Race to Save Jesus from the Cross.* Raising Lazarus a short time before the Passover festival puts Jesus in danger. Word comes to Bethany of his arrest. Martha, Mary, and Lazarus go different ways into Jerusalem with varied plans to save Jesus from the cross. There are as many explanations for Christ's death as there are witnesses. (Published June 2018)

Easter Weekend, 30 AD - Martha Finds Rest: *An Easter Story.* Martha knows that they are in danger. Jesus's enemies want to see Bethany's People silenced. Out of this well of trouble and sorrow, a new hope emerges. The miracle of the empty tomb confuses both Jesus's disciples and his enemies. Martha, though, has returned to her daily grind by then and is reluctant to miss any more work because of Jesus. Will she ever learn to rest in him? (October 2019)

33 to 63 AD - Mark Goes Everywhere. Mark is barely a man when he meets Jesus. The leadership role he assumes in the early church nearly overwhelms him. Nearby Bethany becomes his sanctuary, a safe retreat from the dangers of Jerusalem. Too soon, events force him to leave Palestine. First to travel through the Sinai Desert, then to share hardships in Asia Minor with the Apostle Paul, and then alone to Africa. (2021)

44 - 65 AD - West Across the Wine Dark Sea. Bethany's Mary goes to France, John to Turkey, and Luke is shipwrecked on his way to Rome. No longer a small local matter, the fate of Christianity goes on trial before the rulers of this world. Where will they find the courage to speak truth to power? (2022)

66 to 70 AD - Martha's Apocalypse A violent revolution threatened to destroy the land of the bible. Roman troops march on Galilee. Jerusalem will soon be under siege. The aged Martha of Bethany must act. Like a new Moses, she leads Bethany's People to safety beyond the Jordan River. Meanwhile, Thomas walks five thousand miles to India. (2023)

More...

These books take us to the end of the first century. On Patmos Island, John has another vision of Jesus. This may be the jump off for another series, one that follows the next generation. Mary, Martha, and even Lazarus have died (this being his second death). A second generation came on the scene and believed the stories told by these apostles. Spiritual passion, however, rarely gets transmitted to the grandchildren. How will those born into a new century come to faith? The Seven Angels of Asia Minor (Revelations 1:20) will tell this relevant story.

ABOUT THE AUTHOR

Bill Kemp is a United Methodist pastor, web-content provider, and an unofficial instigator for change. He divides his creative writing between historical fiction (Bethany's People), biblical drama, poetry, and nonfiction books, including ones that guide individuals and congregations through difficult transitions.

Some of his books for Church Leaders include: Fixing Church, Help My Church is Leaving Me, and Reality Check 101.

He cowrote "Going Home: Facing Life's Final Moments Without Fear" with Diane Kerner Arnett.

A full listing of works can be found at www.notperfectyet.com or on his Amazon Author's Page.

He also blogs at www.billkemp.info, podcasts at "A Gentle Soul," and provides workshops on creative writing and organizational transition. He is an avid photographer and adventurous traveler, along with his wife, Karen, and dog, Haley.